MICHAEL ROBERT

Everyday is Like Sunday

This book was professionally typeset on Reedsy.
Find out more at reedsy.com

Contents

Acknowledgement

Thank you to my husband, author Garry Michael. I love you in a forever sorta way! I couldn't do this without your love. Thank you for always being the number one fan of all things I attempt in life.

To the friends that have joined me on the journey of writing my eleventh novel. I thank you for your love and support. I came to writing later in life and appreciate the encouragement and support as I make my way.

To Tina A, Dawn B, Stefka, Melony, Laura, Lucy T, Nedra, Ebony, Renate, Zane, Emma, Emma-lou, Anja, Missy K, and Pat J, thank you for being such tremendous supporters in my writing career. I'm sure I've missed several people who support my work but thank you for your continued support.

To my favorite couple on our planet, Sam/Dar, thank you for always supporting my endeavors and truly wanting the best for my career. I know you're both reading way out of your normal genres, but you do it for love and I appreciate you.

To the best ARC Team. Thank you for taking your valuable time to read my latest book. Your words of encouragement and willingness to help are always appreciated.

To Garry, thank you for the amazing cover design and promotional edits you created for this book. Once again supporting your husband like only you can.

To all the Indy authors out there, thank you for sharing and posting. You have been the best hype team for my novel.

To all the bloggers, bookstagrammers, and book fanatics, I thank you for everything you've done to help promote my new novel. Without your support, success is difficult to achieve.

Last but certainly not least, the readers. I want to thank you for embracing my eleventh novel. I hope each and every one of you connect with this new story. Be sure to look for my next novel, coming spring of 2024.

PROLOGUE: Mike

Ten Years Ago

Cars continued pulling up in front of the Mathews' house, lining both sides of the tree-lined street. Mom was standing in their front yard, strength in her posture while greeting the arrivals as if she were hosting a special event. Mom took charge because Roger and Charla were grieving with the mourners inside the crowded house. That was my mother. Ridiculously positive and serene, she was an adversity warrior who was always up for these moments where she could share her resilience with others. She glanced across the street toward our house, sensing that I was watching from my upstairs bedroom window. I was.

"I can't show up there, Mom," I'd protested after she'd parked in our driveway after Cooper's funeral. *"There's no way I can face his folks or all of those crying people."*

Mom's smile was gentle before she let out a sigh. *"Go inside, honey. Take your suit off. Change into something more comfortable and relax a while, then I'll expect you to join me once you've had time to reset,"* she'd gently advised. *"Roger and Charla are like parents to you. They need you right now."*

"But, Mom," I'd begun, my voice too high for my liking and sounding like a six year old. *"Who holds a funeral on a Sunday?"* I gazed through the windshield at our garage door that was eight feet away. *"Sundays were Coop's favorite day,"* I sobbed.

Mom had reached for my hand and let me weep. I hadn't cried at the church and I'm sure she knew it would only be a matter of time. *"It's okay to hurt, honey. I know how much he meant to you."* Her head tilted to the side like she was prone to do when she expected me to behave better or to make wiser choices. *"Cooper would have been there for me,"* she'd added, using her mom powers to remind me of how to be a good person.

Mom was right. She was always right about the things that truly mattered and this was no exception. If I had been the one who died, Cooper wouldn't have left my mother's side until she'd have to force him out.

Cooper was dead.

Mom re-focused her attention on our house from the Matthews' yard as she tilted her head with a hand on her hip, her rare impatience with me glaringly on display. Even from that distance I received the message: *Get over here now.* I was stuck to the floor like someone had nailed my shiny church shoes to the hardwood. The shock of what happened was still fresh and my mind wandered to the what-ifs constantly. *What if I'd been there? What if I'd saved him? What if? What if? What if?* Cooper's lifeless body, unmoving beautiful face, and shaggy but stylish blond hair haunted my mind. He'd looked exactly the same in the casket as he would have at a formal dance at school.

We wore the same suit at his funeral. But I was still standing, while he was flat on his back in a bronze-colored eternity bed. We'd been born on the same day, lived on the same street in the same town, so of course we had the exact same suits. We'd purchased them on the same day at the same time, but the only difference was that I was three inches taller than Cooper. The height was the only thing we didn't have in common. Well, that and he was gay.

Cammie Swenson stepped from her dad's car that she'd driven from the church. I wondered how she could show her face at the funeral and now at Cooper's house after all the rumors about what she'd done. She stopped on her way into the house and hugged my mother, a betrayal of my heart when Mom held her closely. That was pure Mom on display though. *Love them all, all of the time,* was her mantra.

"She killed him," I muttered. "She fucking egged him on and he drowned while attempting to swim across the lake," I added, a bit louder this time, pissed that Mom hadn't slapped the shit outta Cammie for me.

I hadn't been at the lake that day because I had to work at the grocery store. Cooper, my girlfriend, Jennifer, and a group of our friends had gone to Campbell Lake. Cooper wasn't a strong swimmer even though I'd given him tips on relaxing if he ever found himself in distress. I'd even warned him about undertow dangers when our families went to Hawaii together three years ago before Dad died.

I'm a strong swimmer and could have rescued Cooper had I been there. *If I'd only been there.* Cooper needed me and I hadn't been there that day. I knew I'd let him down and I was convinced everyone else felt the same way. I could see the disappointment on their faces. *"Where were you, Mike? Your job was to protect Cooper. You let us all down, Mike."*

I backed away from the window after another stern look from Mom and sat on the edge of the bed staring into space. *What should I do now?* How could I go on without my best friend, my other half, my sidekick? Everyone knew who Cooper and Mike were to each other. We'd been connected at the hip from when we were born on the exact day, me one hour before him. Our newborn cribs were side by side as our Dads looked through the nursery window at the hospital. Our moms even shared a maternity ward room. Weren't we supposed to share death too?

My hand came between my knees and slid under the mattress, searching for the piece of paper. Panic set in when I couldn't feel the letter I'd hidden there six days ago. Quickly jumping off the bed, I lifted the mattress and found the folded paper shoved further back than I'd expected. Cooper had left the note on my desk the day he died, sticking out from under my laptop so I wouldn't miss it. Like most of the days of the week, he'd slept over last Sunday night but left to get ready for the lake trip Monday morning before I woke up. I opened the note and felt a stab to my heart when I recognized his neat handwriting with every letter of each word printed as a capital letter.

MIKE,

  I KNOW YOU PROBABLY DIDN'T MEAN IT LAST NIGHT, BUT I

WISHED YOU DID FEEL THE SAME WAY ABOUT ME. FINALLY KISSING YOU AND BEING HELD BY YOU WAS EVERYTHING TO ME.

DO YOU REALLY THINK YOU COULD LOVE ME LIKE I LOVE YOU? I WON'T LET OUR FRIENDSHIP SUFFER IF YOU DIDN'T MEAN WHAT YOU SAID. I KNOW YOU LOVE JENNIFER SO DON'T STRESS ABOUT STUFF IF YOU CAN'T LOVE ME LIKE I WANT YOU TO. I'LL TOTALLY UNDERSTAND.

AND OF COURSE MY DREAM CAME TRUE ON A SUNDAY. YOU KNOW HOW I AM ABOUT MY SUNDAYS, AND NOW EVERYDAY IS LIKE SUNDAY.

C.

He'd underlined his favorite mantra. Cooper was endlessly optimistic and I was sure that was why he and Mom clicked. I had kissed him but never got the chance to give Cooper an answer. His note held his final words for me. Every Sunday from that day on was awful with one heartbreak after another. Fifty two times a year. What I wouldn't give for just one more Sunday with him.

CHAPTER ONE: Mike

Present Day

"What now?" Jennifer asked, placing a hand on her hip and fixing her glare on me.

"Nothing," I whispered, disconnecting the call with my mother and stepping around her when I headed for the fridge.

She grabbed my arm before I could reach the place that offered the only comfort I could find these days. "Quit drowning your shit with beer," she stated, trying to yank me away from the fridge. "You're numb, Mike, and I'm tired of it."

"Yep, you're right. I am numb. Thanks for noticing, Jen." I shook her off and opened the door for another bottle. She was right, I was practically catatonic. I untwisted the cap and tossed the small disc toward the trash can in the kitchen corner, but I missed so I shrugged it off. Sitting at the kitchen island I placed my hands over my face and exhaled slowly. I couldn't catch my breath or a break these days.

"She's trying to get you to move home. Can't you understand that?" she asked.

I removed my hands from my face and gawked at her. "She's dying, Jennifer. Can you *understand* that?" I argued, shocked at how insensitive my wife could be. Jennifer and Mom had never truly bonded. Mom was otherworldly and a dreamer. Jennifer was a realist, a true stickler for the rules. She didn't have time for incense and magic, but she *was* focused on getting ahead in life, damn the costs.

"Has she run out of crystals and potions?" she snarked.

I stared blankly at my high school sweetheart. Not so sweet after ten years. "You're gross," I hissed. "Do you hear yourself? My mother has stage four breast cancer and you're joking about it?"

Jennifer looked nonplussed by her behavior and rolled her eyes. "Yeah, and she's ignored western medicine for most of her illness. I'm not a doctor, but anyone could have told her that herbs, coffee enemas, and her ridiculous crystals aren't a cure."

"Lay off of her," I warned. "My mother has been nothing but your biggest cheerleader from day one."

Jennifer laughed out loud at my statement. "Please," she began. "Your mom has never liked me. She can't stand that I'm an independent woman."

I downed the beer and went for another. "What she can't stand is how arrogant you've become since you started making the big bucks."

She cut me off by stepping in front of the fridge, holding her hand against my chest. "Are those *her* impressions of me or yours?" she asked.

I should have known better but I walked directly into her favorite topic: my disdain for her career. "Never mind," I responded, looking away and hoping she'd get the fuck out of my way. I needed another beer.

"I think it galls you both that I make half a million a year," she said. "And that I'm not a stay-at-home housewife doting on her husband."

I felt the familiar anger rising in my chest. Jennifer and I used to be nice to one another. In the beginning I think we actually liked each other. Time and dull routines had slowly eroded any warmth we used to share. I didn't blame Jennifer. I hadn't been the best or most engaging husband myself.

"My father is dead, Jennifer. We've covered that fact already," I reminded her. "And now Mom is headed in the same direction."

"So I'm going to go out on a limb here and guess that you want to take our house off the market now?" she asked.

"Probably not a smart idea for us to be mid-move if Mom becomes bedridden and her health continues declining."

"We *are* selling, and I *am* taking that promotion, Michael," she declared. "And, I *am* moving to San Francisco." She glared at me. "With *or* without you."

I fucking hated when she enunciated certain words in a sentence to get her point across. She sounded like the sorority girl she used to be. Also, when she called me by my proper name, I knew she was about to lecture me or argue her way to an eventual win. Somewhere along the way I stopped participating in our marriage and we all know where not being a team player gets you.

Jennifer was strong willed which was an attraction for me back in high school and college, but the past four years had been hell as she moved up the corporate ladder, pushing aside anyone in her path. I'd begun to think that included me. Maybe not today or tomorrow, but I felt like our time was running out.

Working from home during COVID gave me time to assess my life and I wasn't impressed with the direction it was headed. I wanted a good marriage but as the months and years ticked by, I realized that Jennifer and I wanted different lives. My dad's death, and now Mom's illness only magnified my desire for a life that was more fulfilling and less focused on wealth accumulation.

"I *am* caring for my mother, Jennifer," I responded, employing her grinding enunciation tactic.

She gave me her iciest stare. "Good for you, but I am not going back to Idaho Falls. I hated that shit hole in high school and I'm sure as fuck not returning," she announced. So much for the homecoming queen returning for a class reunion anytime soon.

"Even for the funeral?" I dared.

She removed her earrings and placed them in her palm. "We'll see where I'm at when the time comes."

"Thanks for the loving support, Jen." I watched as she walked down the hall, her high heels clicking on the engineered bamboo flooring. "You used to be nice," I mumbled.

She stopped outside the bedroom door. "Did you say something, Michael?"

"I said enjoy your shower."

I gazed outside on a wet spring day. Seattle was notoriously damp this time of year, even though the past few years had been drier and hotter than normal. Maybe the whole climate change thing was real. I immediately thought about Mom and whether she could last through the summer. I couldn't handle another death during the summer season. Dad had died close to the Fourth of July and then Cooper just before Labor Day a year later. I used to love the summers in Idaho with my best buddy and a father who spent time with me. Not so much anymore.

I felt alone in my own house these days. I had a wife according to a piece of paper, but the emotional side of that arrangement wasn't printed on my heart anymore. Tears streamed down my face as the reality that my mother would likely die soon flooded my thoughts. I'd be alone. Totally and completely alone and I was only twenty-seven. I had Jennifer though, didn't I?

No, I was definitely alone.

CHAPTER TWO: Mike

One Month Later

Jennifer and I went to the escrow office separately that morning to sign closing papers on the sale of our home in Seattle. After accepting an offer, we had thirty days to either buy a house in San Francisco or rent here in Seattle while she commuted for a few months before I joined her full time. She refused to buy a house in the Bay Area until she knew she'd like her new role at the tech company she worked for. Her decision would have nothing to do with how I felt about San Francisco. I'd been surprised at her suggestion for me to stay behind by myself and rent in Seattle because Jennifer hated renting. She said it was wasting valuable money and that you never got ahead doing that.

I'd worked from home ever since COVID restrictions began and there'd be no issue with my job if I moved with her to California. Like Jennifer I was also in tech, however, I spent my time writing code behind the scenes whereas my wife was front and center at her company. I didn't exactly want to move to San Francisco, but if I had to pick a location in California the Bay area sounded nice.

* * *

I was surprised to see her Tesla in the driveway of our nearly packed up Queen Anne neighborhood home when I turned the corner. I glanced at the digital clock on my dashboard and saw that it was only two. Jennifer never left work early. Never. Ever.

I tossed my keys on the hall table that was wrapped in protective bubble wrap, waiting for the movers to arrive, and made my way to the kitchen. The house was quiet. As I walked to the fridge I caught sight of her in my peripheral vision and nearly jumped out of my skin even though I'd assumed she was home. "Jesus, Jen," I muttered, stopping in my tracks. "Why are you home so early?"

Her expression said that she was pissed off about something but I wasn't alarmed. Pissed was her usual look these days as she plotted every move we made. Perhaps having no need to expend extra effort in selling a home in a hot Seattle housing market had made her angry. Jennifer preferred drama and upheaval. That way she could be the hero and fix something after complaining nonstop. *Why exactly had I married her?*

"What is this?" she asked, holding up a sheet of notebook paper, showing little emotion so I couldn't tell if I was in trouble or if she was just curious about a bill or something. I knew I couldn't be in hot water over a money issue because I wasn't the half of the partnership that liked spending copious amounts of cash. She made a lot. She spent a lot.

I grabbed a beer and sat at the island and waited for her to bitch about my beverage choice or something I'd done. I placed a hand under my shirt and rubbed over my abs, checking to see if my beer intake was starting to affect my body and wondering if maybe she'd finally gotten fed up with me. Thankfully we had a home gym and I was as fit as the day I graduated from high school. My wife was smoking hot so I considered staying in shape as part of my job requirement as her husband.

She waved the paper at me again and I spotted something familiar on the page from across the room. "What is that?" I asked, standing and moving toward the sofa where she sat.

"I just asked you the same thing." Jennifer unfolded the paper then turned the writing toward me. "Recognize this?" she asked.

Yeah, I recognized it alright. How the hell had she found that was a better question. The sudden urge to snatch it from her and run raced through my mind. The piece of paper had creases that crisscrossed every inch of its surface from me reading and rereading the note more than a thousand times over the past decade. "Where? How?" I stuttered, getting closer and confirming Cooper's handwriting. The note was the last message I'd received from him despite Mom telling me he visited her all the time during her microdosing voyages of discovery. She'd wanted to share his messages with me but I'd found it all a bit macabre.

"I found this in the bottom drawer of your desk in that locked box you keep," she stated, turning the words back to herself and scanning them carefully. "I'll assume the initial C on this paper stands for Cooper?" she interrogated. "And that you two were lovers in high school?"

"You went through my desk?" I accused, ignoring her accusation. "That metal box was locked."

"Yes, it was locked, but you keep the key in the top drawer, so how secure can that be?"

"What were you looking for?" I asked, grabbing the letter from her hand and sitting across from her on the matching love seat. I looked up in distress from the decade old note. "This is a violation of my personal space, Jen. You had no right," I protested.

"I am your wife, Michael. That gives me every right." She adjusted her pencil skirt, a skirt that hugged her curves to perfection and proved she was all woman and knew it. "I was looking for your passport to check the expiration date. You know how you forget things like that." A lame excuse if I'd ever heard one.

"You still had no right to go through my things," I argued, embarrassed at what she'd discovered. "This was a decade ago and was just a joke," I defended. "Why does it matter now?"

"You kissed him," she stated. "And apparently held him closely," she added with just a hint of repulsion in her voice.

"The note was one of his jokes. You know how Coop was."

She scooted forward on the sofa and reached for a glass of red wine I hadn't noticed sitting there. *How long has she been home?* She must have gone home immediately after escrow while I was running errands. She took a long drink, finishing the wine, then pointed toward the island at

11

the open bottle. I obediently stood and retrieved her bottle of wine while neither of us spoke a word. After refilling her glass, I sat back down across from her.

"He was in love with you, Michael."

I laughed and moved uncomfortably in my seat. "We were buddies, Jen. Best friends to be exact," I responded. "Sure, he loved me. I loved him. We grew up together for God's sake," I added, trying hard to keep the fire from my face.

Jennifer narrowed her eyes and stared at me. "What would Cooper be in your life if he was alive today, Michael?"

"What the fuck, Jen? Whattaya mean what would he be?" I asked, my voice rising as she challenged my story about my relationship with my now-dead friend. "He'd probably be in Idaho and he'd still be my best friend."

Jennifer took another drink of her wine and then ran her thumb and middle finger down the corners of her mouth, checking them to see if her lipstick rubbed off. "I don't believe you, Michael," she stated. "There's definitely something else implied in that letter."

I opened my palms toward her and looked at her in confusion. "You don't believe me?" I asked. "Like what part don't you believe?" I asked.

She ignored the question and continued glaring at me.

"Cooper is dead, Jennifer. He's been dead for nearly ten years and he isn't coming back so I don't care whether you believe me or not because none of this shit matters."

She leaned back and sank into the oversized pillows she'd insisted on buying for the couch. Like everything else, she'd wanted them and I didn't have a say, so I didn't argue about the ugly pillows. "Why did you marry me?" she asked, keeping her eyes on mine.

I knew what she was doing. She swore I had a dead giveaway when I lied to her. I refused to look away this time. Looking away was the tell as far as I knew and she was going to lose this time. There wasn't a chance in hell I'd be admitting my feelings for Cooper today. I'd held that secret for ten years. I could go another ten.

"Why did I marry you?" I repeated.

She held my gaze and nodded her head slowly, waiting for an answer, waiting to pounce.

"Well . . . well . . . lemme see, you know, because . . . uh . . . well, you know," I stumbled, trying to act cool while choosing the correct words and holding her angry gaze.

"I'm asking you an easy question, Michael. Why did *you* finally ask *me* to marry after I waited six years for you to ask?"

"We've been together for twelve if you count high school," I rushed to point out, buying time by remarking about a fact that didn't matter in regards to her question.

"Twelve, six, whatever, but why did you finally marry me?" she pushed.

I was out of answers. I didn't know why the fuck I'd asked her to marry me if the truth be told. "Because you told me to?" I asked, knowing immediately that I just failed the test.

She rolled her eyes at my answer. "I think it was because you finally realized he wasn't coming back," she revealed, catching me way off guard.

"Jesus," I responded. "That's ridiculous. What are you inferring here?"

"I'm inferring that if Cooper had lived, you and I would not be together, Michael. I'm not angry with you actually. To be truthful, the letter answered many questions I've had about us."

"You're my wife," I stated. "You've lost your mind over a joke."

"We haven't made love in six months, Michael."

Michael, Michael, Michael. I hated the way she spoke my name. My blood pressure was elevated and my face was on fire. Like a live lobster in a pot, I was cooked and she knew it.

"You're mean sometimes and I don't feel close to you," I sputtered, grasping for straws. "I don't think I live up to your high standards."

"I don't push you and you know it. I reserve my criticism for me and my goals, not yours, so how about we start telling the truth?"

"I don't want to move to California," I admitted. "I like it here in Seattle."

"The house has sold. You signed off this morning, so you're a tad late on that announcement, Einstein."

I stood and pointed at her. "See? You're mean. You belittle me and my mom and you act like I'm the enemy these days." I stomped toward the fridge for a beer.

"Get an extra bottle this time and save yourself another trip," she taunted.

Her tone of resentment had been evident for months, but today's taunts tipped the scale of how to be bitchy to your husband. I popped the cap off my beer and leaned against the kitchen island. "You want some truth?" I asked, taking a long cool drink of my favorite hydration these days. "I don't like you anymore. I love you but I don't think I like you."

I thought my remark would at least get a *fuck you* out of her. But no, she was silent as she returned my stare. After an uncomfortable moment of silence she asked again. "So tell me please, why exactly did you marry me?"

"Because I was alone," I blurted. "Cooper was dead and he wasn't coming back," I confessed. My jaw started trembling and my eyes began to fill as I fought the war I'd been fighting for a decade. Somehow I knew that today's battle would be the last one with my wife. "I miss him, Jen." The tears fell and I gripped the edge of the island. "I'm not happy with us, and honestly, I don't know why I married you. Were you ever happy?" I asked. "Was this what you wanted to hear?"

"Actually, no, it's not what I wanted to hear, but you needed to voice it, Michael," she began, standing and heading straight for me. I wondered for just an instant if she'd slap me or stab me with a kitchen knife, but of course, that wasn't who she was. Classy chicks like her don't end up in prison because of love. She was much too evolved to be that woman.

"I'm sorry," I whispered, tears cascading down my face, splattering on her expensive floors.

She wrapped her arms around me and let me weep, not once ridiculing my manhood or minimizing my feelings. After two or so minutes she pulled back, still holding my arms and gently smiling through her own tears. "And I'm truly sorry for your loss, Mike. We all loved Cooper, but I understood you loved him more. If I could give you anything, I would bring him back."

Her kind words caught me off guard. "So what now?" I asked.

"I'm going to California and you're staying he. . ." She paused before completing the word *here* and looked into my eyes. "Well, I don't actually know where you're staying, but we'll divorce, split the money, and move on with our lives," she answered in typical Jennifer takes control fashion. "I suggest you dig deep and figure out what Cooper meant to you. He isn't coming back but that doesn't mean you can't find a person you truly love."

"So that's it?" I asked. "Just like that?"

"You're not in love with me, Mike, and both of us are far too attractive to miss out on real love, so yeah, we're done."

CHAPTER THREE: Mike

"Ice cold bitch if you ask me, dude," Brandt said, flagging down the server with a wave of his hand. He turned back to me and narrowed his eyes. "Like, for real, she accomplished all that within three days?" he asked.

I nodded in agreement.

"A fucking lawyer and the completed divorce papers were ready to be signed and couriered to you?"

I nodded again and stared into my glass of beer. I was sure the foam spelled out loser as I drowned in my shitty life.

"Fuck her," he added.

"Apparently not anymore," I said, shrugging my shoulders.

He chuckled at my quip. "I'll admit Jennifer was smoking hot even if I am gay." The server brought another round and smiled at me for a bit longer than normal. Brandt caught it. "I fucking hate bringing you to my bars. No one is looking at me," he bitched. "You'd kill in this town if you were actually gay, Mike. Your full head of blond hair, the blue eyes, your ripped body, and that fucking face of yours. God! I'm so fucking jealous," he stated. He looked around to see who was checking us out and then turned back to me with a mischievous look on his face. "What about me and you?" he teased. "I'm a good teacher."

I should have been bothered by his offer. "About that," I began.

Brandt leaned forward, all of his attention on me possibly disclosing something juicy to him. "Yes? Do go on," he trilled.

"Stop it, you goofball." I felt my face warming. Brandt was my best buddy in Seattle. We worked out together after meeting at the gym two years prior when he was shamelessly flirting with me. And by shameless, I mean he came up to me in the shower and complimented the size of my dick. "How did you know you were gay?" I asked. Lowering my voice and nervously looking toward the two men next to us who were holding hands at their table. "Like was it obvious?" I added.

"Let's just say I wanted Dorothy's ruby slippers the very day I watched The Wizard of Oz, girl."

I hated when he called me girl but that was Brandt. Big, muscular, and manly, yet gay as fuck Brandt. "Come on," I urged. "How'd you know?"

He looked at me suspiciously. "Why are you asking, pretty boy?"

"I'm not exactly sure," I admitted.

"You need someone to lighten a burden?" he asked. "Because I *am* your guy when it comes to this topic. But remember, if you're thinking of becoming a big ol' cock sucker, I get first dibs."

I rolled my eyes. "Forget it," I complained, looking away in embarrassment.

I felt his hand on my knee under the table. "Go on, buddy. I'm just having fun with ya. I'll shut up now," he said. "Is this about your divorce?"

"Maybe," I acknowledged. "I'm not sure exactly if it is, but Jen found something and then said a bunch of stuff about me. My brain has been working through it and I'm getting nowhere so far."

"What'd she find?"

I wrung my hands nervously in my lap. "A letter."

"From?" he pushed, his eyes widening with every answered inquiry.

"I've never told anyone, Brandt. So I'm trusting you," I said.

"Hold on a second." He got our server's attention and held up four fingers. "We need to double the reinforcements. You can crash at my place since it's only a block away." He leaned back in his chair and crossed his arms. "Go."

I spent the next hour and a half telling Brandt everything about my childhood. From birth, to Cooper, Cooper's last days, the letter and what was in it, Jennifer and our marriage, and her discovery of the letter. Finishing up with me suddenly questioning my sexuality.

"Jen told me I needed to focus on what Cooper meant to me," I said, completing my story.

"Fuck, man," he said, exhaling slowly and shaking his head. "Shit, dude, I'm sorry too. You know, about this Cooper dude and everything."

I frowned at him. "Do you ever hear yourself speak?" I asked. He raised an eyebrow in question. "Are you sure you're actually gay? You drop the words *dude* and *man* more than any straight guy I've ever met."

"Part of my charm, dude," he acknowledged. "But fuck that. Back to this Cooper fella with that letter and shit. Did you do those things he wrote about in the letter?"

I nodded.

"Damn, dude. That's fucking hot, man."

"I'm trying to be serious," I stated. "I'm completely confused."

Brandt nodded up and down and kept his eyes trained on me while he gave thought to my admissions. "Wow," he began before he paused.

I didn't feel hopeful I'd get shit out of him that helped in any way if all he had was *wow*.

He stared past me for a moment before returning his gaze. "Let me ask you something," he said. He paused again and narrowed his eyes as he studied me some more. "Okay, listen up, dude. What were your plans that day after you read the letter? What were you going to say to Cooper?" he asked. I was about to reply when his eyes suddenly saucered. "Wait! Wait! Don't answer yet. Hang on to that question, man. Answer this one instead. What would you guys be doing today if Cooper had not died that day?"

We studied each other as the question hung like a dark cloud in the bar. Annie Lennox was singing and asking the question *why* in the background as the eighties-filled jukebox blared.

"I think I'd be with him," I confessed. "I wanted to tell him I loved him the same way he loved me."

Tears sprung from Brandt's eyes as I revealed a truth I'd kept hidden inside for ten years. "Oh fuck, Mike. God, that's heartbreaking, dude, and I'm so sorry," he gasped. "And now he's dead." He reached for a napkin and wiped his eyes. "What now?"

I didn't know the answer to that question. All I could do was shake my head. "I just don't know. Besides, what *can* I do now?"

CHAPTER FOUR: Mike

Ten Years ago

Having a summer job killed my social life. I wanted to hang out with my girlfriend and Cooper, but earning money to help pay for college was a necessity. Because my father died a year ago, mom and I were careful with the life insurance settlement because I didn't want Mom to struggle putting me through college and then end up broke when I finished, so most of the summer after high school graduation was spent bagging groceries and stocking shelves.

I turned the corner of aisle four near the checkout stands when I spotted my mother talking with Lee, my manager, near the front office. She hadn't told me she'd be shopping so I was surprised to see her. Stress contorted her face and I could tell from thirty feet away she'd been crying. Lee looked my way and motioned his eyes toward me, alerting Mom that I was incoming.

"Mom?" I questioned after hurrying over.

Her eyes glistened with tears immediately.

A kick to my gut made me pause. This wasn't a visit for groceries. I thought of my grandfather, my only other living relative. "Is everything okay, Mom? Is Grandpa okay?"

Lee ushered us toward the office door and out of the pathway of departing customers. "You need to go with your mother, Mike. We'll get coverage for you," he said, his sad eyes returning to Mom.

"M-mom?" I stuttered. "What's happening? Why are you here?"

My mother couldn't focus on my face or my questions.

"Okay, you're sorta freaking me out here," I stated, glancing around to see if any other employees had noticed my mom crying near the office.

"Let's go out to the car, honey," she said hoarsely, clearing her throat of whatever had her so upset.

"Just tell me here," I argued.

Lee placed his hand on my shoulder. "Go with your mother, son," he insisted.

"Please?" Mom asked.

I took off my apron and laid it on the counter of an unoccupied lane. Mom began walking toward the exit. "Take all the time you need, Mike," my boss added as I turned to follow my mother to the parking lot. Her car was right in front of the store, parked in a fire zone. This couldn't be good.

Mom was already in the car when I opened the door and found her sobbing. She reached for my hand and held it while she tried to calm herself. My mother was not a dramatic sort of woman by any means so I knew the news was bad. "What is it?" I whispered.

"Honey," she began. Her tone sent an instant warning to my heart. I remembered this voice from thirteen months earlier when my dad was killed in a car accident. "I need to share some awful news," she began. She stifled a sob, hiccupping and squeezing my hand.

Seconds felt like hours, days even, as I sat there begging the universe to reverse whatever she was about to tell me. "You're scaring me."

"I know, honey, and I'm sorry. Maybe we should drive home first, huh?" she offered.

"No!" I spoke too loudly. "Just tell me."

Mom turned away and stared through the front windshield as Mrs. Gomez wheeled her groceries out the front door near the Subway sandwich joint. Her dog, Mr. Ruffles, was sitting in the cart as usual. Mrs. Gomez went nowhere without her yappy Pomeranian sidekick.

"Cooper," she gasped, I heard her throat clench and prevent the rest of her words from following the one name I didn't want included in this conversation.

I quickly grabbed her arm to turn her toward me. "Cooper, what?" I asked in a quiet voice.

She sobbed silently.

21

"Cooper, what, Mom?" I asked more urgently. I grabbed my cell phone from my front pocket and turned it on. Lee didn't allow employees to look at their cells during work hours. In fact, he had closed captioned video feeds that assisted him in policing us. Dozens of texts from Jennifer and my friends made my phone ping continuously.

"Don't read those, honey," Mom insisted, reaching for my phone.

I instinctively pulled it out of her reach.

"Hand me your phone now, son," she added firmly.

I complied with her request. Whatever nightmare scenario I'd been imagining the last four minutes leapt to a dreadful feeling beyond my ability to stay calm. "What about Cooper?"

Mom's eyes leveled with mine. I recognized the emotion behind them. I didn't currently like her eyes very much even though my mother had a stunning green pair. Dad always told her how beautiful they were. I'd agreed with him until she delivered the news that he was dead. Something told me she was about to build a case for me to never want to look into her eyes again for as long as I lived.

In hindsight, I would've preferred a few more delays or hems and haws from her.

"Cooper drowned today, honey."

I heard her words but didn't allow them to sink in. I looked to my right at the store, watching life go on as customers paid for their groceries and pushed their half-full carts. If I didn't accept her statement then it couldn't be real, right?

"No he didn't," I said. I glanced at my cell phone in her hand. I saw the alerts from my friends but pretended I hadn't. "He texted me just a bit ago," I stated. "He's fine, Mom." I swallowed hard as the pain of her words tried to escape my lungs. "He's fine, Mom. I know Coop, and he's totally fine."

I couldn't look at my mother out of fear she was telling me the truth so I stared at my phone, willing for Cooper's name to pop up on the screen.

She grabbed my hand, her thumb rubbing gently over my knuckles as she wept softly. "I was just over at Roger and Charla's house, honey."

I loved Cooper's parents as if they were my own. I bet my mom loved Cooper as if he was her own too.

"They're going to need you, Michael."

22

I turned and faced her, carefully studying the emotions contorting her beautiful features. I'd seen this face once before. She was telling me the truth. I didn't want to believe her, mind you, but part of me said she wouldn't say such a thing were it not true. Another part of me insisted I keep denying her news. "I'm going back to work, Mom."

She stared at me like I was insane.

"Yeah, it's been busy today," I added. I opened the door but remained seated, staring out the front windshield. "Was Cooper home when you were there?" I whispered.

"Honey, listen to me," she began.

"NO!" I screamed. "I will not fucking listen to you, Mom. You always do this shit and I'm tired of it," I hissed. Tears erupted from my eyes as I stared at her. "You . . . you . . ." My throat closed. "You're lying to me," I muttered.

"I'll drive us home, honey. Close the door."

I jumped out of the car. "I'm going back to work," I said again before slamming the door shut. I stood gazing over the roof of the car at the parking lot as Mom sat patiently, making no attempt to force me to get back inside. Traffic drove by on Main Street like they hadn't heard the news. People in their cars acting like it was just another normal day in Idaho Falls. "Assholes," I mumbled.

Mr. Peterson who lived two houses down from Coop spotted me as he headed into the market. "You okay, Mike?" he asked from twenty feet away.

I stared at him through tear-flooded eyes. "Did you see Cooper today?" I asked. "Like right before you came here?" I added. I needed reinforcements against Mom's lies.

"Well no, son, I didn't. But there was a lot of activity at his house," he said. Then he narrowed his eyes because he was probably curious about the commotion at the Matthews' house. "Is Cooper okay?" he asked.

And then I ran. I ran as fast and as hard as I could. I had six blocks to cover. I'd walked them dozens of times to and from work, only running when I had to avoid being late. Today's trip would be the fastest sprint of my life. Mr. Peterson wouldn't lie.

CHAPTER FIVE: Mike

The phone rang seven times before Mom answered. Of course, I immediately thought that she wasn't okay, letting out a long-held breath when she finally picked up. "Hello?"

"Hey, Mom. It's Mike," I said.

She giggled like a school girl even though she was fifty years old. "Who else would it be, kiddo? I know my own son's voice, silly."

Kathleen Hill was an unusual woman. True, she was my mother, but she was admittedly an odd duck. "How are you feeling today, Mom?" I asked before getting into the reason I called. "Are you feeling strong?" I added.

"I have the Goddess Mother Earth on my side, honey. Of course, I feel strong," she stated. "And, I may have cancer, but I am a *Cancer* so I am aware of my astrological needs in this battle."

"That's all good, Mom, but Marie called me about your reluctance to continue the treatment plan we agreed on." Dr. Marie Hollister was the mother of one of my friends I'd known my entire life and Mom's oncologist. Mom had agreed that Marie could involve me with her care and contact me anytime she had concerns.

"She ratted me out again, huh?" she asked. "You can't trust Libras," she added. "All of 'em are a bunch of level headed narcs."

I ignored Mom referring to her doctor as a narc. "Why, Mom?" I asked, getting right to the purpose of my call. "I thought we agreed that you'd do one more cycle of chemo so we could see if another round helped."

"I don't trust that poison, son. I gave it three tries and nothing's working."

I moved my breakfast around my plate with a fork. Idaho was an hour ahead of Seattle and I'd phoned my mother before I started my day. "Which means what, Mom?" I asked.

"I have other things to try and I'm going back to *my* plan," she answered.

I didn't like her answer but her response wasn't unexpected. I'd been raised by her, witnessed all of her eccentricities, and knew quite well about her beliefs in treatments beyond western medicine and her general acceptance of what was considered outside of normal practices.

"I'd also like you to consider Marie's expertise. Can you do that for me, Mom?"

I heard a teapot whistling in the background. "Ahh," she said. "Green tea time. Have you read about the cancer fighting properties of green tea, honey?" she inquired.

"Mom, you're stage four. I love your willingness to try alternative methods but we're kinda beyond green tea," I said.

The clinking of a spoon in her mug, followed by a slurp, told me the tea was being consumed. "Oh, honey. I forgot to mention that Sarah from the crystal shop hooked me up with a local beekeeper. I've been adding organic honey to my tea for a week now."

"That's nice, Mom. Back to the chemo," I urged.

She blew right past me as usual. "How are *you*, Michael?" she asked. "Have you heard from Jennifer?"

I knew better than answering her which avoided the purpose of the call, but she was my mother and she cared.

"Only the divorce papers," I stated. "She's in a hurry to be single, I guess."

"I love Jennifer, honey," she began, about to enlighten me to where Jennifer's deficiencies lay. "But, like I said last week, her charts are not compatible with yours. Capricorns do not make good spouses, honey. It's really not her fault," she added.

"And Cancers, Mom?" I asked, trying to take some blame. I was a Cancer just like my mother. She was overjoyed at our astrological unity. "How are we at love matches? I was part of that marriage as you know."

"Yes, honey, but you can't be with a Capricorn," she reminded me, even though she'd said nothing about our stars aligning before I married my high

25

school sweetheart. "Like you, Cancer is your destiny, dear."

I wondered if she remembered that Cooper was a Cancer. Of course, she did. Not only were Coop and I born on the same day, my mother knew everything about the people in her life, especially the ones she loved. She'd loved Cooper like a son.

"Thanks, Mom. I'll keep that in mind next time."

"Cooper is a Cancer, Michael. Did you know that?" she asked.

I was about to confirm that she had already told me like a thousand times but I didn't think she was actually asking. "*Was* a Cancer, Mom. *Was*," I corrected.

"You'd be wrong about that, dear. Cooper is somewhere in another universe and will always be a Cancer," she declared. I heard another slurp of tea and the sound of pleasure after she swallowed. "And thank the higher power that he is," she added. "Did you know that he still comes to me in my visions, Michael?"

This wasn't the first time I'd heard her wild musings about Cooper. "Mom?" I asked. "Are you truly okay?"

She giggled that girly laugh. When I spoke with her on the phone I could convince myself that Mom was still the young, vibrant, otherworldly delight that she was just a couple of years ago before the breast cancer diagnosis. If you only spoke to her via phone you'd never know how seriously ill she was.

"I'm fine, dear," she answered, exhaling slowly like she was tired of the concern from her only child. "He knows, Michael," she stated.

"Who? Who knows what?" I asked.

"You never told him but he knows."

My blood ran cold at her words. My mother had been a believer in many unusual things when I was growing up. Dad always humored her and accepted whatever the latest embrace of the alternative was. He loved her unconditionally and I believe toward the end of his premature life, he'd seen enough of the unexplainable that he began to wonder about the connection Mom had with the spiritual world.

"Mom, who are we talking about?"

"Cooper, of course. I speak with him and your father regularly," she stated, as if she'd just hung up from a call with both of them. "Dad says hi, honey. And Cooper is waiting."

"Mom, are you taking too many pain pills?" I asked. "You sound a bit . . . uhm . . . are you okay?"

"I'm perfectly fine, honey. I don't take their poison pills. I've had my edible today though," she confessed. "You remember the blueberries I was telling you about?"

Her blueberries were flavored THC laden candies in a blueberry shape. "How many have you had?" I blurted with a chuckle.

"One," she said. "Maybe a couple."

"And you're not taking the pain meds Marie prescribed?"

"I can't be present for my visions and the celebration of my earthly life if I'm all doped up on that venom. Besides, what do opioids do for you? Bunch of overprescribed, mind numbing, concoctions if you ask me."

I kept my annoyance to myself. We both knew the prognosis. We were very aware that she had one, maybe two months tops. "The pain okay?" I asked. "You're not hurting?"

"You don't believe me about Dad and Cooper, do you?" she asked, blowing past my questions once again. "You know, the fact that we talk and stuff."

"Mom, it's weird, okay?" I argued. "They're both dead."

"Maybe here they are," she said. "In this spectrum perhaps, but not in the next."

I knew better but opened the door anyway. "The next?"

"The next location, honey," she explained, as if she were teaching me about gravity. "Where we go next in these limitless parallel universes around us."

"Okay, Mom. I hope you're right and I truly respect your opinions but back to the medicine. I want you to take your pills and agree to one more round of chemo. For me?" I asked, pulling out the last weapon I had to weaken her defenses. Mom hated disappointing her only child.

"I'm done with all that, Michael. I have a lot to do to prepare for my next journey. I love you, but I'm not interested in feeling horrible for the last few weeks of life in this realm if that's okay with you?"

Her acceptance of her predicament frightened me. I couldn't be without her. "I can't lose you, Mom," I whispered. "I'll be all alone if you don't fight harder." I broke into sobs, my tears dripping onto my cold eggs. I knew the end was near and that I selfishly wanted my mother to take whatever gave her the slightest chance of a miracle. Dad was dead. Cooper was dead. Jennifer was gone. I couldn't lose my mother.

"I'll find you, honey. Just like Dad and Cooper found me," she soothed. "Trust me, honey, you'll know it's me."

"I don't want you to find me, Mom," I cried. "I don't want you to leave me alone in this world."

And then out of the blue. "But what if you could see Cooper again?" she asked.

I loved my mother but I needed a blueberry.

CHAPTER SIX: Mike

Fifteen Years Ago

"See, I told you," I stated, staring down at Cooper who was on his knees and inches from my dick. He wasn't convinced as he shook his head. "Look really close," I urged.

He did as I asked and then looked up, still on his knees. "Wow," he said. "You do. And your dick is bigger too," he added, getting to his feet. "Check mine."

Cooper pulled his shorts and underwear down while I crouched down in front of him. We were doing our weekly pubic hair check, like we'd done since our thirteenth birthdays last month. My pubes were finally growing but I had bad news for him. "Nothing," I reported.

He appeared bummed. "You sure? Could ya look again, Mikey?"

I grabbed his hips and pulled him closer. Cooper's dick fattened up from my touch. "Keep your boner under control," I ordered. I tugged at his balls, lifting them, looking at all possible places he might have a hair growing.

He couldn't control his erection.

"Stop it, Coop."

"I can't help it, Mikey. It feels good when you're touching it," he sighed.

Cooper and I had no secrets when it came to our bodies or the types of things we thought about, but lately he'd been holding back. "You actually liked that?" I questioned, standing up and waiting for an answer. I was naked and he had his shorts and underwear down to his ankles. To me we were just bros hanging out but lately he'd become sensitive to conversations about girls and sex.

"What if I did?" he asked, looking away. He eventually turned back to me. "I *feel weird and shit, Mikey. Like when, well . . . you know . . . like when we're naked and stuff."*

"It's just us, buddy. We see each other naked all the time, so what's new?"

Cooper pulled his pants up and sat back on the bed staring at my body. His eyes took all of me in and he flushed red. "I . . . well, I kinda like looking at you and it makes me feel bad," he began. "Like I'm evil or something with my thoughts."

"What are you talking about?" I asked, suddenly wondering where my boxers were. I spotted them near the bathroom door where I'd dropped them. "I don't mind anyway, so don't sweat it, okay?" We were about to shower together like we often did, but now I wondered if he still wanted to. "We still showerin'?"

"You cool with what I just said?" he asked.

"Why wouldn't I be, Coop? I love you like a brother," I responded. "Right? We're brothers for life." I added.

"For life, Mikey," he answered.

Something about Cooper changed that day. I hadn't recognized it back then but wished I had.

CHAPTER SEVEN: Mike

I closed my laptop after a long day and looked around the room for my running shorts. I hadn't rented an apartment yet and was staying at a hotel across the street from Lake Union in downtown Seattle. I could've gone into our offices located nearby but I'd become protective of my work-from-home lifestyle. Since Jennifer moved to San Francisco, I'd stopped seeing people. An occasional beer with Brandt, frequent jogs around the lake, and worrying about Mom, occupied my time now.

I'd hesitated renting my own place since Mom's health was deteriorating. No need to lock myself into anything until I handled Mom's affairs which could end up forcing me to stay in Idaho Falls for months. Her impending death wasn't a secret to anyone who knew her, but I hoped she'd hang on. Mom embraced her mortality and somehow managed to present a cheerful and optimistic air to her friends. She spent more time keeping me and her friends spirit's uplifted than we deserved, but that was how my mother lived.

I called her three times a day and had hired a nurse to check in on her once a day at our family home in Idaho Falls, a home I'd be selling one of these days after she passed. *"I'd love for you to keep the house,"* she'd said. *"It'd be easier to pop in on you after I transition when I know where you'll be,"* she'd added, not joking in the least.

"I think I'll pass on the hauntings, Mom," I'd replied.

Mom wasn't well and I was heading home at the end of the week. I planned to work remotely from there and spend her final days by her side. I'd hoped my mother would make it through the summer but her health was declining rapidly. After speaking with her doctor, Marie, I knew it was time to return to the town and the house I grew up in.

* * *

"I'm not ready," I admitted, looking around the small room. The therapist's office was exactly as I imagined one would be. She sat in a chair in the center of the room with her diplomas on the wall behind her, and I was on a smallish sofa directly in front of her. "There are days when I think I am and then *BAM*, I freak out like a four year old at the thought of my mother being gone." My hands were in a battle in my lap as I poured out my heart to a shrink Brandt had recommended and hounded me to see for days.

"Imagining a world without our parents is difficult, Mike," she said. "We wonder if we have everything we need from them."

"My dad is dead too," I stated, making sure she knew I was almost completely parentless.

Beverly Clinton scribbled on her notepad and hummed.

"I'm an only child and not even thirty yet," I added for impact.

She glanced up at me. "Grandparents?" she inquired.

"One. A grandfather that no longer recognizes me. He doesn't know that his daughter, my mother, is dying. It's all a bit overwhelming," I admitted.

"Yes," she agreed. "You have many reasons to be overwhelmed. Do you feel strong enough to get through this on your own?"

Her question went right to the heart of why I'd called her in the first place. I'd had pain like none other eleven years ago when Dad died, followed by unimaginable agony after Cooper drowned a year later. Now I was recently divorced, my grandfather had Alzheimer's, and my mother was on death's door thanks to a brutal form of cancer.

"I'm not sure," I whispered.

She raised an eyebrow in concern.

I lifted a hand and waved her off. "Oh, no. Nothing like that. I'm not suicidal if you're wondering. I just feel bogged down right now."

"How about close friends?" she asked.

"One. A buddy of mine. Here in Seattle. Plus a coupla friends from work that I rarely see because I've worked remotely the past three years," I stated. "My best friend Cooper died ten years ago."

Psychologist Beverly Clinton placed her pen and notepad on a side table and stared at me intently. She studied me while I returned her stare and wondered what I'd said. "That is an unusual amount of death, Mike," she declared, stating the obvious.

I nodded.

She was right. At three hundred bucks an hour she should be. "Cooper? A male friend, correct?" she inquired.

I nodded again.

"Tell me about him."

I stared at my hands still clashing in my lap and wondered what one said about their best friend who'd been dead for ten years without sounding pathetic. I mean, it had been a decade and we were just teenagers back then. "I still miss him. I miss him very much," I whispered. "I need him right now to tell you the truth."

"You need him? Why do you say that, Mike?" she asked, leaning forward and touching my leg gently. I noticed she had tears forming in her eyes. Therapists aren't supposed to cry while their patients are struggling to keep it together, right?

"He would've helped me get through Mom's illness like he helped me when my father died. He'd know what to say and he'd make me feel safe."

My answer prompted more questions. Typical for therapy, I imagined. "Cooper would make you feel safe?" she asked. She had green eyes just like my mothers. In fact, I just noticed my therapist looked a lot like Mom.

"Yes. He had this way of sorta knowing what I needed. I was the bigger one physically but he made me feel safe. I never told him that," I stated casually. "I should have told him."

"You don't think Cooper knew this?" she asked.

"I'm sure he didn't. He always depended on me, so I guess he wouldn't have known how much I needed him."

EVERYDAY IS LIKE SUNDAY

"You needed him? Tell me what you mean by that, Mike."

"He was just that person. My person," I mumbled, staring into space as I reminisced about him. I refocused on her and smiled weakly. "He just got me, I guess."

"There are no other people you can turn to?" she asked.

"No one like him," I admitted. "We understood each other. You know what I mean?"

She nodded and sat back in her chair.

"We completed each other's sentences, counted on one another; stuff like that."

"You loved him?"

Warm tears filled my eyes so I looked out the window of her small office and into a courtyard of small shrubs with an old concrete bird feeder that had seen better days. A robin landed on the worn edge, probably searching for fresh water.

"I still do," I admitted in a soft voice. "I always have."

"As a friend?" she questioned. I slowly nodded up and down as tears etched down my face. And then she surprised me by scooting forward again, but this time reaching for my hand. No wonder Brandt liked her. She was caring and real. I hadn't expected that. "And perhaps as more than a friend?"

The robin gave us one more disgruntled look then flew off. My tears spoke the words I couldn't voice. I turned back to her and nodded two more times before I bent over and began to weep.

Ms. Clinton allowed me to cry and then compose myself. When I sat back, she had Kleenex waiting for me and gently smiled at me. "Why are you here, Mike?"

I inhaled deeply and decided that I needed to unburden myself once and for all. "I had the chance to tell him but I didn't," I began. "He told me he loved me in the . . . you know . . . the forever sorta way. He left me a note after he told me and I never got the chance to tell him that I felt exactly the same way about him."

"What did the note say?" she asked.

34

"It said he'd understand if I couldn't love him that way. He'd be okay with my decision. We kissed the night before. I held him as he confessed how he'd felt for me. He admitted he was in love with me."

"And, you?"

"I couldn't admit it. I wanted to but I couldn't," I said. "His note was to protect me, to protect our friendship. He wanted to make sure that I knew he would be fine with whatever I wanted."

"Why didn't you admit your feelings when he did?" she asked.

"Fear," I quickly responded. "I had a girlfriend then, and I was confused about my feelings for him."

"That's natural. You both were what, seventeen? Eighteen?"

"We'd just turned eighteen. We shared the same birthday," I said.

"But you already knew that Cooper was gay, correct?"

I nodded.

"He understood that you were not?"

"Yes, but we were close. We hugged and stuff like that."

She gazed at me thoughtfully before proceeding. "But something happened that night? The two of you took things to a different level?"

I picked at the bottom edge of my T-shirt, hesitating to explain what had happened. "He asked if I would kiss him. You know, guy stuff, teasing and shit like that. I think he wanted to see if I would be grossed out if we kissed."

"And were you?"

"Actually, no. I let him slide under my arm afterward and we fell asleep holding each other. That was the last time I saw him alive."

"What do you wish you could have done differently, Mike?" she asked. She held her hand up in pause. "Hang on a second. Let me rephrase that question." She pursed her lips and looked past me, deep in thought. "Here's a better question for you instead," she began. "Let's imagine that Cooper hadn't died and you were able to see him later that day. What would you have told him then?"

She knew what she was asking and I had to finally admit the truth to someone. "I probably wouldn't have told him. At least not right away," I confessed.

"He died and you never had the chance, so now you've spent ten years wondering why that matters? Does that sound correct?"

"Sort of," I admitted. "I've wondered my entire life what would've happened had I admitted I felt the same way about him."

"Have you ever been with a man, Mike?" The question came out of left field.

"I have not."

"Why is that?"

I knew what the answer to that question was. Hell, I'd married a woman because of the answer to her question. "Because he'd never be Cooper."

CHAPTER EIGHT: Mike

I pulled the rental car into the driveway of my childhood home. Not much had changed. Mom's flowers weren't nearly as abundant as usual due to her declining health. The lawn needed mowing because I'd arrived home on a Saturday and the lawn service came on Mondays. All the blinds were down and hid the interior of the house from where I sat. Mom loved to have the windows open so a summer breeze could fill the house, so I was surprised.

Stepping out of the rental I turned to look at Cooper's house. His folks had sold three years ago and moved to South Carolina for a job opportunity that Charla had. After going away to college, I didn't stop by their house anymore because the heartbreaking memories were too much for me.

My eyes went to the second story where Cooper's old bedroom window faced mine. If we weren't crashing at each other's houses, we always waved goodnight after turning out the lights. I laughed at the memory of him baring his ass to me from his bedroom one night about a month before he died. I think that was the first time that I had seen Cooper as someone sexual, someone that was appealing to me. The feeling scared me and I tapped it down as quickly as it had arrived in my mind. A cat stared at me from the windowsill of his old bedroom. Maybe I'd tell Mom in case she thought it could be a sign from the beyond. Maybe that was who was visiting her lately.

The front door was unlocked when I tried the handle. You could leave doors unlocked in a town like ours. Even though Idaho Falls was the second largest town in Idaho after Boise, there were only about sixty-five-thousand inhabitants. The town was big enough to have strip malls full of dining options and a decent theater for viewing the latest Hollywood blockbusters, but as a kid growing up, it was too small and too boring for us desperate-to-get-away teenagers.

Cooper and I wanted out when we turned eighteen. We'd both applied to Washington State University across the border and both of us were accepted. The university had over thirty thousand students in attendance every year, and was located in Pullman, Washington, a town with just over thirty-two thousand residents. The ironic thing about it was that the combo of the college and the town had less folks than the town we were eager to leave. Pullman's population doubled every September when college began, swelling the local business and available rentals.

After Cooper died I accepted another offer to attend The University of Washington in Seattle instead. He hadn't wanted to attend Seattle's home university so I decided to choose WSU as well so we could remain together. But after his death, I joined Jennifer at her first choice.

"Mom, I'm here," I yelled once I stepped inside. I immediately smelled incense burning, something I had endured my entire childhood. It was Saturday and I wondered what today's scent was and what it meant in Mom's belief in the otherworldly. "Mom?" I yelled again.

I rounded the corner to the kitchen and found her curled up on the sofa in the adjoining rec-room, wrapped in a heavy blanket even though August was hot with temperatures in the nineties.

"Hey, honey," she croaked weakly. She tried to sit up but I got to her before she could muster the strength. "You caught me in a weak moment," she began. "I'm resting up for my next adventure. The marigolds on the patio need to be dead-headed before the blooms get too ugly."

She loved marigolds and planted them every single year. She'd told me that in many cultures the marigold symbolizes purity, divinity, and the connection between life and death. She regaled me with a story once about how the potent fragrance of them was thought to attract the souls of the departed. *When I die and return, you'll know it's me when I mention marigolds,* she'd commented on the phone just last week.

"Still inviting the dead in, are ya?" I asked, sitting on the edge of the sofa and moving her bangs out of her eyes. Her once beautiful blonde hair was stringy and gray in color as if the hair itself had died before her final breath. "Still got your hair I see," I teased.

"Is that what this hay is?" she responded, tugging on a few strands and checking her fingers. She motioned to a glass of water with a straw in it. "Can you?" she asked.

I lifted the glass and adjusted the straw to her mouth and waited for her to slowly take a drink.

"Now don't be thinking your momma is done here on this plane, because I'm not."

"I didn't say a thing," I argued.

"Your face says it all, son. I might be a whisper of my old self in this strange shell, but I am still as bold and wise as ever."

"I think you're beautiful and wonderful, Mom," I stated. "A tad koo-koo I might add, but still my mom."

I reached for a book on her coffee table. The title was 'Parallel Universes And Your Place In Them', a typical Mom read for sure.

She thumped the book with a finger. "That book has all the answers, Mikey," she said. "Now of course, I've only known about parallel universes for a couple of years. Most people, you see, well . . . they think they're having déjà vu when they feel like they're reliving a familiar moment or a particular scene from their lives, when actually they're witnessing a tear between the two worlds *of* their lives," she began.

I pretended I was interested even though I'd dismissed my mother's ideas about these things years before.

She continued, "What they were blessed to have seen was their other life in one of many universes where they also dwell."

I turned the book over and saw an image of a woman who looked startlingly similar to Mom. The second time in less than a week that I'd noticed her doppelganger. Perhaps I was already looking for her and she was still here on earth with me. They both shared a kind of ethereal glow about them. Sure, Mom had lost a bit of her luster but her eyes mirrored her deep convictions.

"What do you suppose we're doing in our other worlds?" I asked. While on the flight from Seattle, I decided that I would be open to listening and sharing my mother's passion with her while I still had the chance. I knew these ideas were important to her, and since she was important to me, I wanted to participate.

Her eyes lit up as I imagined she was mentally exploring the vast options she'd considered before I'd asked. Her green eyes sparkled and she released a small giggle, reaching for my hand. "That world is incredible, son. Marigolds in every direction. A bright sun is out and I feel warm as I garden outside this very house. Dad is there of course. You and Cooper are shooting basketballs in the driveway. Not much has changed, but I am healthy and Dad is with us."

"That seems pretty specific, Mom," I said. "How old are we?"

"That was yesterday," she said delightfully. "Dad is sixty-one so you and Cooper must be what, going on twenty-eight?"

"And we're together? Me and Coop?"

"Just like always. Two peas in a pod."

"I like that world, Mom," I whispered, squeezing her hand. "Now tell me about today's incense."

Mom gave me the complete rundown on her latest Japanese incense for divine healing and what the properties of the scent did for one's mental state as they battled illness. I placed the book about parallel universes back on the table.

"I'd like you to read that when you can, son."

"I'll try," I agreed, starting to stand but she tugged at my arm knowing I was dismissing her request. "I will," I protested. "I promise even."

"We have homework to do, so having you read the book is important to me."

"Okay, I will, but first let's get you upright and find something to eat." I leaned over and placed her arms around my neck. "Hold on to me," I said. Mom scooted closer when I held her closer to me. She weighed nothing and the blanket fell away from her upper body. I was shocked by the reality of the situation. Our eyes met and mine filled with tears immediately. "Mom?"

"I know, honey, but let's not focus on what I look like, okay? Trust me, I am a whole being inside here," she offered before wiping my eyes.

My mother was wasting away. I'd visited for a weekend three months prior but she'd probably lost another twenty pounds since then. She was a tiny woman even when healthy, but this was too much for me.

"Are you able to eat?" I asked. "Can you keep anything down?"

"Popsicles," she blurted. "But you know what would be a real treat?" she asked.

"Tell me," I insisted.

"How about one of your famous tuna melts?"

"Heavy on the cheddar?" I asked. "Pickle juice in the tuna?"

She held up her emaciated hand and pointed her index finger at me. "Exactly like that."

"Coming up, Mom," I agreed. "How about we sit out on the patio too. Can you do that?"

"Can you lift a hundred pounds?" she asked.

I leaned over and kissed her on the cheek. "You ain't no hundred pounds, missy," I teased. I stood again and flexed my arms. "And besides, I'm stronger than the last time you saw me."

"I can see that and I'm happy you're here, son."

"Me too, Mom. You and I are gonna have some fun. How about that?" I asked.

"I can't wait," she said, giggling like a schoolgirl. Yes, my darling mother was still in that battered body. We had some time left and I planned on spending as much of it with her and absorbing her passion. I could use an infusion of passion and love. That was who my mother was. Whether in this universe or any other she may eventually dwell in.

CHAPTER NINE: Mike

The days passed slowly as Mom and I rediscovered our bond. I was an only child and a bit of a momma's boy growing up. Mom doted on her boys, as she called Dad and me, and we shared a close relationship even after I grew into a man. When my father died our relationship shifted slightly. I was almost seventeen when dad passed, basically a man, and I chose to pick up most of Dad's household responsibilities.

Mom and I were a team as we navigated life without him. She still led the way and I supported her however I could. I felt protective of and worried about her loss and what that meant for her future. In typical fashion, she was a rock and guided us through the first year of grief. She wasn't the kind to hide feelings and sometimes I didn't like sharing mine, but she always pulled me out of my funk. I not only loved my mother, but I respected her as well. Deeply.

"These smell stronger this year," I complained, holding a shriveled marigold bud in my hand and sniffing it. "Twice as bad as I remember."

Mom was in a padded wheelchair wrapped up in a cocoon of blankets. The date was August 10th and the weather was stifling. She claimed to enjoy watching me as I puttered around the backyard and the patio, picking up duties she would normally have been doing this time of the year.

"Extra powerful on purpose," she corrected. "When you're inviting spirits in you need the strongest essence you can get."

"And what about those," I asked, pointing at her rose bushes to encourage her to keep up the banter.

42

She squinted her eyes, struggling to cover them with a hand as she surveyed where I was pointing. "Those are for me. I still like beautiful smelling things even if we're summoning the dead over here."

I decided to humor her. The fact was, I was reading her parallel universes book and some of the content was causing me to reconsider what she's been saying for years. "Who are we summoning exactly? You know, just in case I want a vote on who we invite over."

"I'm not joking," she stated. "We can truly affect changes in our destiny," she added.

I sat my clippers down and walked across the patio to position her out of the sun. "Okay, give me an example," I said. "But hang on while I get us a popsicle."

"Grape," she ordered, choosing her favorite. I'd purchased the Pedialyte brand that included electrolytes and B vitamins. She hadn't mentioned the change to the healthier brand so I figured they tasted good, plus I could make sure she stayed hydrated.

I came back from the kitchen with two opened popsicles, and handed her one. "Perfect with the sun," she said. "I'll call this lunch."

"The hell you will," I instantly responded. "We're having a cucumber salad in a bit."

"Wow," she teased. "Busting out all my faves these days."

"Hush and give me an example of changing destiny before I lose interest."

"Okay, but don't act all surprised and weirded out when I tell you what I'm up to."

I pulled a patio chair closer to her, laughing at her use of the words *weirded out*. "So, you think I'm too *weirded out* by your ideas, do ya?"

"Your father began to accept my ideology," she reminded me. "Thank goodness because finding him will be much easier now."

"I'll tell you where he is, Mom," I quipped, having visited his grave the day before. "I don't think he's been hiding."

"Don't be a smart ass, son," she corrected. "And that was not your father, by the way."

I laughed out loud. "Then who did we bury?" I joked.

She tsked and looked away. We sat in silence and enjoyed our popsicles. She wasn't angry because she didn't get angry. Another amazing trait she possessed. We observed three hummingbirds as they flitted around her backyard feeder. I read her mind before she could speak. "They say humming birds are spiritual creatures," I offered. "Some even believe they're visitors of lost loved ones' souls."

"Would you be open to that idea?" Mom asked, looking beyond me and toward the manic birds.

"I would. Now tell me who we're summoning before I forget to ask again."

"Cooper," she answered, as easily as if I'd asked her a yes or no question. "Timing is everything in this particular event," she added.

I'm not sure how I knew her answer before she voiced it, but I wasn't surprised she said Cooper. "And why him?"

"I will be dying on August 30th, honey," she announced. "That date is important for you to remember."

"I know what the date is, Mom, and I'm not really excited about you sharing that news with me. Nobody is dying anytime soon and certainly not on that day."

"The date is the most important part," she declared. "And I'm making sure we are prepared."

I stood and walked to the edge of the patio, gazing across the lawn toward a giant maple tree in the yard. There were still a few loose boards from where a treehouse used to be attached to two of the largest branches, eight feet off the ground. A private fort for me and Cooper when we were kids.

"I'd prefer you didn't do that to me, Mom," I said, turning around and staring at her in disbelief. "That is unfair. Do you seriously want me to have to add your death to that date?" I was angry now and returned to staring at the yard so she couldn't see my face.

"Hear me out, son," she argued. "Please?"

I had given one hundred percent of my effort to be patient with her beliefs since I'd been home, but this news was a setback in my willingness to accept what I didn't understand. I wanted her to be happy and to feel heard but this was crossing a line.

"Not the thirtieth, Mom. You cannot die on that date," I declared. "I won't accept that date and I'm asking you not to talk about this to me again."

"It has to be that date, Michael," she insisted, her weak voice rising. "I'm doing it for you," she defended.

"NO!" I yelled. I turned back to her, sorry that I'd yelled. I leveled my voice and my emotions. "No, Mom. I mean it. Both *Cooper* and *you*? On the same day and just a month after Dad died? You cannot expect me to live with that reminder for the rest of my goddamned life."

And with that I stormed off the patio and around the house, ending up in the front yard. I glanced toward Cooper's bedroom window, expecting to see a cat. The cat wasn't there. Instead, I located it sitting on the front stoop. The black feline had yellow eyes that pierced mine from across the quiet street.

"What?" I whispered. "What the fuck do you want?"

I watched as the cat twirled its tail, slowly curling and uncurling the snake-like appendage; the yellow eyes boring through my soul.

CHAPTER TEN: Mike

Twelve Years Ago

Cooper began to fill out and catch up to me in the size department the year we turned sixteen. It was that summer on our birthdays that I began to notice how beautiful he'd become as he physically matured. Every time I felt a surge of emotion for him that I didn't understand, I'd tamp it down deep out of confusion.

We both took the driver's test for our licenses on July 12th, our actual birthday. "Street legal, buddy," he said, waving his temporary paper license in my face.

I grabbed it from him and stared at his handsome face in the black and white picture on the thin paper. "Yikes," I said. "Sorry the pic turned out so bad, dude."

Cooper snatched it back and stared at his image before looking at me. "The pic's not good, is it, Mikey?" he asked, looking sad. "Now I gotta show this for six more years and be embarrassed."

"Five," I reminded him. "We get new ones at twenty-one, bro."

"Shoot," he responded. Typical Coop. Too sweet to swear much. "Lemme see yours," he said.

I handed it to him and watched as he studied my image.

He looked at me and smiled. "Handsome as usual, Mikey. I wish mine looked this good."

In my eyes Cooper was good looking for a guy. In fact, I'd begun to see him as a beautiful boy. Different than I was in that regard. I had a squarer jaw with more masculine features. I also had that dimple in my chin that Coop said was like a small ass crack even though he also said it made me look super sexy.

46

"I think yours is good actually," I stated. Which I honestly did but had hesitated to admit to him that he always looked so damn sweet and innocent in pictures.

Cooper was blond and blue eyed like me with a smaller frame. Even though he was about three inches shorter, he was muscular because we were both active in sports and exercise. His face was where we differed. He had high cheekbones and delicate features that caused him to appear less manly. His soft features defied the naturally athletic boy he really was. Shaggy, blond, beach-bum hair framed a face with soft flawless skin that continued over his entire body. Coop had a muscular build but nature had given him a pretty face. A face that caused a heat to stir inside, a face I wanted to touch, a boy I wanted to protect out of fear he was too gentle to protect his own self.

"You sure the picture is okay?" he asked, startling me out of my daydream because he was simply too beautiful to look at.

"Yeah, I do," I said. "I was just pickin' on ya. You know you always look terrific in pictures," I reminded him because he did.

Both of our folks sat across the room in the DMV where they waited for us. I noticed that they smiled and whispered to each other.

"Let's go show the folks," Coop said, laughing and pointing out the foursome that were as tight as Coop and I were.

"Look at my dad," I whispered, cupping my mouth and leaning into Coop. I could see Dad was a minute from tears. He was a sensitive soul like Mom, but less weird about the world. "He's gonna hug the shit outta both of us, Coop," I added. "Consider yourself warned."

The moms hugged each other as we approached and commented on how their boys were growing up too fast. The dads stood side by side, bobbing their heads in unison like those goofy dogs you sit on a dashboard

"Get it over with, people," I urged, opening my arms. "Your boys are men now," I added, tugging Cooper toward me as we got crushed in a group hug.

"We'll get you a used car," Dad said, pulling me aside and resting his hands on my shoulders after the hugs ended. "Possibly when you're seventeen after you show Mom and me you can be responsible enough to have your own." He beamed at me and pulled me in for another hug. "I'll teach you how to tune it up and change your own oil too," he spoke into my ear, squeezing me one more time before

he pulled back, a tear in his eyes as usual.

Dad died the following summer, just before my seventeenth birthday.

CHAPTER ELEVEN: Mike

C hapter seven of the book Mom wanted me to read about parallel universes ended with a thought provoking idea:
Many people believe that when a person dies in one universe, they can still exist in another. In fact, others have daringly hypothesized that when one person dies in one dimension, a space can open for a departed to return to another in an exchange of universes.

I closed the book and set it beside me, watching as Mom fought sleep with labored breathing. She'd mentioned that she didn't want to waste a single living moment on sleep when she had so much to share with me, but the frailty of her body was catching up to her. We'd recovered from our disagreement about her desire to expire on the anniversary of Cooper's death; neither of us conceding our wishes.

I'd read the last paragraph of the chapter several times and wondered if Mom had been thinking about the specific passage as well. I had to admit the book had some interesting concepts. The proposed science stated that we had an infinite number of universes, with an infinite amount of possibilities.

The author counted the fact that there were billions of stars supporting billions of planets just inside our Milky Way galaxy. With billions, even trillions of galaxies going on to infinity, he opined that there could be countless other beings with countless other parallels to our own. In fact, we could surmise that just maybe, there were millions of parallels to our own lives currently living at the same time.

The book theorized that our lives in each universe were like a book. We had the basic storyline but that chapters could be different in each universe as we made casual choices that altered our journeys during our day-to-day lives. I thought about Mom's theory concerning déjà vu. I had experienced the phenomena before and I had to admit that it felt like I'd been there and seen that, even though there was no rationale for having actually done it before. Was that a rip in the parallels? A brief recognition of our other selves?

Out of curiosity, I picked the book up and began to read another theory about parallel universes:

Religion has held sway over humans for thousands of years. Is there a God? Does he/she/it really exist and do we pay a price for our misdeeds while on earth? Do we make decisions based out of the fear of retribution? Then there are those that suggest that perhaps there was a creator or creators that formed the world as we see it. The difference being that this entity is running simulations on a grand scale and that we all could be in an endless loop of simulated possibilities, therefore, an infinite number of possible realities and or universes.

"What a crock of shit," I muttered, placing the book in my lap and gazing at my mother. "What the hell are you up to?" I whispered. Her chest moved shallowly as she took short and weak breaths.

Marie had told me that Mom was in the final stages of life and that things would end soon. I hoped the hospice nurse was armed with morphine in the event that Mom wanted to ease her suffering. I doubted Mom would take the drug because she wanted to feel *all* of life, even the rough stuff. However, even with her idea of experiencing everything she had zero problems taking a couple of edibles or microdosing mushrooms, but she didn't count that as poisonous western medicine so it was acceptable.

Her eyes popped open and she turned toward me. "What day is it, honey?" she whispered, smiling at me like all was good in her world despite her body betraying her spirit.

"Tuesday, Mom," I responded.

"Did I ever tell you what the last words that Cooper spoke to me were?" she asked, motioning toward the cup for a drink.

I held the straw to her mouth as she took small sips. "No," I answered.

"Were they good words?" I asked, needing a bit of pleasant news for a change.

She told me how on that fateful Monday morning after Coop had slept over that he was in an exceptionally cheery mood and bounded into the kitchen to convince her to make him a big breakfast like she usually did on Sundays despite knowing it was Monday.

"Of course I could never say no to that boy," she pointed out. "He even told me not to wake you because you had a hard day of work ahead of you. Cooper was always looking out for you," she added, no doubt understanding his caring nature.

She continued the story by saying that she made his breakfast even though it wasn't Sunday because his happiness that morning was contagious and she was curious as to why he was so excited. "I couldn't stifle the boy's glee. Certainly not the first thing in the morning," she interjected.

I wondered if Cooper had revealed something to her that morning after the kiss we'd shared the night before. "Did he tell you why he was so happy?" I asked, nervously setting her plastic cup of water on the side table and diverting my eyes. "You know, Coop," I added, filling the pause with a nervous observation. "Always a ray of sunshine and happy to share his business."

"All he said was that he felt a big dream of his was coming true."

"He actually said that?" I asked.

She nodded.

"Did he say what this big dream of his was?"

"He did not. He licked his plate clean of crumbs and rinsed it off in the sink before giving me a hug."

"That was it?" I asked. "Nothing else?" I pushed. "No clue regarding this goal or dream of his?"

Mom didn't answer so I let it go. She tugged at her gown and stared out the window. "What is the date honey? Not the day but the actual date?" she asked without turning back toward me.

"The twenty-fifth, Mom."

"Hmm," she mused after taking note of the date. She turned back to me and tapped the side of her head. "I just remembered that he said something beautiful to me before he left," she began, getting back to the story.

I perked up immediately.

"When he got to the backdoor, he hesitated for a moment before turning back and thanking me for the terrific *Sunday* breakfast. I reminded him that it was Monday."

"Lemme guess," I interrupted. "He told you that *'every day is like Sunday',* right?"

Her eyes widened in surprise. "Yes, he did. How'd you know that?"

I smiled at her and the memory of his favorite saying.

"And then he left," she finished, giving me a suspicious look, her eyes narrowing before she smiled in a way that told me she'd been right about something. "So, you've heard that line before?" Mom asked.

"Yes, I have," I admitted. "It was his way of saying everything was perfect in the world."

"It's a wonderful expression, don't you think?" she asked. "So very much like Cooper to express his cheerfulness that way."

"He adored you, Mom. Did you know that?"

"Of course, I knew that, son. He came into existence on the exact day that my own son did. Not a coincidence in my opinion," she stated. "You two are star twins, but that story is for another day," she added.

I reached for and held her hand. "His last words to me were written in a letter, Mom," I whispered hoarsely, struggling with my emotions. "The last words he'd written were identical to the last words he spoke to you."

"That explains why you were so angry that his funeral was on a Sunday, wasn't it?" she inquired.

"Cooper loved Sundays, Mom, and holding his funeral that day ruined everything in my mind."

"I never saw the connection until now, honey. Every one of your Sundays since came with an entirely different meaning, didn't they?" she asked.

I looked away and fought the tears threatening my vision. "I hate them," I confessed.

"This coming Sunday is the 30th," she reminded me.

I returned my gaze to her and focused on her face, willing her to drop the absurd idea of hers. "Yes," I whispered. "Ten years to the day."

"I have to leave on that day, son."

I quickly looked away, knowing anger flashed on my face. I gathered my thoughts before turning back to her because I wanted to blow up at her about that fucking date she was so hung up on, but then I saw her face. There was a serenity etched across her features that scared the fuck out of me. She was ready to leave.

I slowly shook my head from side to side. "Please don't," I pleaded.

"We're doing it for you, Michael."

"Who is this *we* you're talking about?" I asked. "Do you hear how ridiculous that sounds, Mom?"

"Open your mind, honey. Do it for me, please?"

I walked across the room and stared out the bedroom window, wishing I was anywhere but there. The pain of my reality was too much to bear. My mother was going to die soon. I was going to be completely alone and no matter how much I wished the pain away, nothing was going to change.

Something caught the periphery of my vision and I focused on the sidewalk on our side of the street. The cat from Cooper's old house was sitting there watching me from my position in the bedroom window, his black tail swishing across the concrete. Sweeping left. Sweeping right.

CHAPTER TWELVE: Mike

Before closing the book, I reread the final paragraph for at least the tenth time. The outrageous theories began speaking to me. Perhaps Mom had known they would.

Are we, as humans, so arrogant to believe that we are alone in the vast universe? That only we have been given the opportunity for life. Does humanity selfishly believe that everything is and ends with us? Those are dangerously naïve assertions for mankind to make considering we can barely see past our own galaxy and have very little true understanding of how time or the universe works. Perhaps we aren't surrounded by what our eyes see. What if everything is an illusion and we're playing a part for a very clever magician? Shouldn't you dare to look behind the curtain?

The guest bedroom was at the back of the house and down the hall from my parent's room. I'd moved from my upstairs childhood bedroom after being home for a few days so I could be closer to Mom in case she needed my help during the night. On Saturday, I peeked into her room thinking she'd be asleep at two in the morning, but she wasn't.

"Mom?"

She turned to me and it took her a moment to associate my voice with my presence outside her door.

"It's Mike. Are you okay?" I asked, moving through the open door.

"Your father told me you're reading that book," she stated. "He says you think it's weird."

My father definitely would have used the word *weird* when describing how I would've felt about the book and its contents, but I don't know how he would have told her considering he died eleven years ago. He and I shared a loving understanding of the most important woman in our lives, and we did use words like weird to describe a potion or an idea of hers behind her back. Not to hurt her or make fun, but to share an understanding we had about our wonderful life with an intriguing woman living under the same roof with us.

"Sounds like Dad," I answered. "Where is he?"

She touched her head and smiled. "In here," she said. "I bet you thought I'd say in the garden or under the bed, didn't you?"

"The thought had crossed my mind," I admitted. "Tell him I miss him, and the next time he's spying on me, tell him to say hi," I joked, almost believing his and Mom's latest communication.

I grabbed her water cup and went to the master bathroom to refill it. I stared at myself in the mirror as the cool water filled the cup, wondering how close she was to dying. A strange thought for sure, but one that had been occupying my mind ever since Tuesday. Mom was coherent and still as nimble in her mind and clarity as she ever was. It was only her body that revealed she was losing the physical war she was waging. "Would you like a sip?" I asked, returning to her bedside.

"Get us a popsicle instead, would you?"

"You sure?" I asked. "It's two in the morning, Mom."

"When is it not popsicle time?" she answered. "Orange this time if we have one."

I came back to her room and opened the wrapper before placing a paper towel around the frozen concoction. "Can you hold it?" I asked, placing the wrapped wooden stick in her frail hand.

She grabbed it, ignoring my question and pointed at the chair beside her bed.

"Are you sure you're not tired?" I asked, sliding into the comfortable chair I'd dragged from the living room.

"I'll sleep when I'm dead," she quipped. "Or I won't, you never know."

"Gross," I replied, curling my lip and frowning. "I'd appreciate a more positive outlook if you don't mind, missy."

We were silent as we each enjoyed our frozen treat, Mom vacantly staring into space while occasionally making sounds of delight at her orange dessert. Her conversational transition was abrupt. "Would you be willing to share the letter that Cooper wrote to you?" she asked out of the blue. "I mean, if you feel okay about me knowing."

"Where did that come from and what makes you think I'd even have the letter with me?" I asked, still stunned she'd brought the note up, let alone be curious about the contents.

"You wouldn't come home without it, Michael. That letter is too important to you."

"I just told you the letter existed the other day," I defended. "Why do you want to see it?"

"For the sake of honesty, dear, I've seen the letter. Of course, I never read it because that would have violated your right to privacy, but you kept that piece of notebook paper near you for several months after Cooper died. I've seen you read it many times when you thought no one was around, so I guess I'm curious."

I was embarrassed by her disclosure and felt the heat rising up on my face. The room was dim and only lit by a nightlight so I knew I was safe from her seeing my deep blush. "The letter was personal, Mom. I feel like I'd be violating his trust."

"Can I ask something, honey?" she began, dragging the cold dessert across her lips. She licked the syrup and grinned at me. "Yummy," she giggled, reminding me of the girl who was still inside the worn out physical being. She waited as I hesitated to respond. Maybe the wait was too much for a person that was counting down the minutes of their life. "Cooper was in love with you, wasn't he?" she asked, practically telling me he'd been.

I could have denied her question, maybe told her she was losing it. But at that point, reality was what it was and I was done hiding from the fact that I had also been in love with him. "He told me the night before he died," I confessed. "The letter was just letting me know that if I couldn't love him that way, that he'd be okay with my decision," I added for clarification.

"You didn't know how he felt before?" she asked.

I shook my head.

"And you didn't feel the same?"

"I kissed him the night before he died, Mom," I confessed, choking up. "But I was too afraid to admit to myself what I was feeling for him. My feelings for him developed during our junior year but I hid it from him and from Jennifer."

"Was it because of Dad and me, honey?" she asked. "We wouldn't have been upset with your choices. I probably shouldn't share this, but I secretly wished you two were a couple."

"To be honest, I was afraid. I never recognized that the love I felt for him was more than my best friend. I didn't understand how things would've worked for that kind of thing."

"So, you never told him how you felt?"

I bit the inside of my cheek and thought of an answer that would make sense and explain my confusion. "Stupidly, I told him that night that I *might* feel the same way," I began. "I actually said *might*, Mom. I couldn't commit to the fact that I already knew how I felt about him."

"Oh, honey," she said, reaching for my hand. "I'm sorry."

I released a stifled sob before continuing. "He never knew, Mom. I didn't have the strength to tell him I loved him too. I can't tell you how long I've suffered over that night. I miss him and . . . and . . . I sometimes wished I'd died too."

I was shocked I'd admitted the truth to her. Three weeks of counseling had finally gotten me to share the fact with my therapist, but this was my mother. I'd never revealed that I felt like every choice I'd made after Cooper's death meant nothing to me. I was simply biding time and numbly living my life.

"Do you feel that way now?" she asked. "Because I'd worry for your safety if you did, Michael."

"I'm not gonna lie, Mom. My life sucks right now, but I'm working hard on my feelings and I want you to know that you and Dad were the best parents to me. I never doubted you both loved me, but I'm battling a huge fear of being alone," I admitted. "But no, I wouldn't harm myself if that's your worry. And I'm in therapy too."

"Thank you, honey," she whispered, focusing on me. "What if I had a solution?" she asked.

I laughed even though it may have seemed morbid considering her current state of health. "Does your solution include you sticking around? Because I could go for that big time, Mom," I quipped.

"I'm going to swap," she announced. "Dad and me for Cooper. How about that?"

I leaned closer and waved in her face. "Mom, are you in there?" I whispered.

"Stop it," she shushed, batting at my hand. "I'm lucid. This is not the ranting of a dying woman," she declared.

"You do realize that you sound like you've lost a marble or two?"

"What if I haven't? What if I could make something fantastic happen? Would you listen?"

My shoulders sagged and I exhaled slowly. She'd lost it and didn't know she'd lost it.

She sensed my resistance to her madness. "I'm not crazy, Michael. This is your mother and I am well aware of what I am talking about. End of discussion about my sanity," she stated. "I need to know if you're willing to listen to my plan?"

"What if I am?" I asked. "Would it make you happy?"

"Only if you can look me straight in the eye and tell me that you'll listen with an open heart and mind."

"Okay," I yielded, widening my eyes, so she could see my intent, staring back at her. "I'm willing to listen, Mom."

She studied my face in the dim room, making sure I wasn't just pacifying a dying woman's wish. Once convinced, she began. "It all started when I met Druzella."

"And who is Druzella?" I asked, trying my darndest not to give into my pre-programmed cynical self.

"*Madame* Druzella is a medium I met at a spiritual retreat last year," she announced.

58

"You're joking," I half gasped.

"Not in the least," she confirmed.

Of course she wasn't.

CHAPTER THIRTEEN: Mike

I listened to every word breathlessly uttered by Mom's dry lips, and then I listened some more. In fact, I paid attention until six in the morning as my mother enlightened me with a tale so outrageous, an idea so flawed in its reasoning, that I was convinced she had once and for all slipped out of reality. The woman before me in the rented hospital bed was an imposter, a stand-in for the mother who used to be of sound mind. She admittedly had been a tad on the fringe of normalcy my entire life, but this story took the cake by a longshot.

"An exchange?" I asked myself, taking a moment to suspend my common sense. "You and Dad for Cooper? And lemme guess, Dad's waiting for an answer?"

"Not waiting per se, but he'll be open to the idea," she explained.

"So we won't know for sure until you evolve, is that the term you prefer?" I asked incredulously. "And then once you get there he has to agree with the plan?"

"Michael," she admonished. "You said you'd listen."

"I am," I stated. "But this is some *out-there* shit, Mom. Even you have to admit that what you're saying has zero basis in science."

"And neither do miracles, virgin births, spontaneous combustion, alien visitation, or a whole host of supernatural occurrences," she defended as she fortified her stance. "What do you really have to lose, dear?"

"How about my freedom when they lock me up for losing my mind?"

"You won't be here, Michael. I already told you that."

I stared at her dumbfounded. *"I won't be here?"* I muttered to myself, gazing at the floor as if it could respond to my question. I looked up at her. "Yeah, okay, I forgot that part. I'll be in a different universe?" I asked because I still needed clarity.

"Yes. Exactly right," she confirmed.

"And you and this *Madame* Druzella know for a fact that I will be going to a universe where I already exist and Cooper is waiting?"

She nodded and raised her eyebrows. Even she knew it sounded like the rantings of a lunatic. "Bit much, huh?" she agreed.

"Yes, Mom. A bit much for sure."

"But you'll consider it?" she asked.

I nodded. Insane for sure, but why antagonize her about it? She knew how this all sounded. I went over the plan she'd laid out for the third time. "I wait precisely seven days. Drink the concoction at midnight and then . . . that's it?" I asked. "Nothing more to do but those steps?"

"Just go to bed in your old room and be sure to open your mind. You have to believe and you have to want it to manifest. Other than that, you'll be good," she stated.

"What's in the potion?"

"A few things, but dried marigold petals are the main active ingredient," she answered. "You know, to attract the dead," she added without hesitation. "And no," she added after seeing my face. "Trace amounts of marigold petals are not toxic to humans. It can be to household pets, but not us."

"So don't give any to the cat across the street?" I asked, thinking of the creepy feline I'd seen three times now, wondering if it was cruel to think I might like to poison the fucking animal.

Mom had a confused look on her face. "The new neighbors don't have a cat, Mike," she corrected. "Marleen is allergic to cats."

"But it was in their ho . . ." I stopped before saying *house*. "You sure?"

"Positive," she said. "I haven't seen a cat on our block in years. Come to think of it, that is strange."

It was just after dawn and Mom's eyes closed for several minutes, the quiet convincing me she was asleep. I heard a car in the driveway and confirmed through the window that Mom's doctor, Marie Hollister, had arrived for

EVERYDAY IS LIKE SUNDAY

a house call. I headed for the front door to intercept her so the doorbell wouldn't wake the patient, but before exiting the room Mom called for me.

"Michael," she began, her hand reaching for me. I turned back and took three steps to her bedside, grabbing her hand. "You have to promise me you'll at least try. Please just humor me and give me that last wish. Can you do that?"

"Yes, Mom. I can do that," I responded. And I actually meant to honor the request. She was right, what did I have to lose? "The letter with your instructions is in your safe, right?" I asked, confirming where the items needed were located.

"Yes, honey. And my will. Do what you want with the house, dear, but make sure I am not buried with your father. That is absolutely key to this working. Cremate me, but do not bury me near Dad. Do you understand?" I nodded and blinked back a tear. She was getting ready to leave me. It was Saturday at eight A.M..

I leaned over her and kissed her forehead. "Don't go anywhere, okay? Marie is here. We'll be right back."

"I'll wait for you, Michael. You promise me and I'll promise you, okay?" she whispered, faintly squeezing my hand. "I love you, son."

"I promise," I whispered. "I promise," I repeated. Mom smiled, but I noticed the grimace contorting her face. This was the first time I'd seen her express the pain which cemented everything I dreaded. Mom was ready to give in.

"What time is it, honey?" she asked.

I glanced at my watch and struggled to see the time through the tears. A knot in my throat clamped down and helped me keep the sob inside. "Five after eight," I whispered.

"Sixteen hours, son. Make sure I last sixteen more hours," she whispered.

I heard the expected knock on the door. I knew Marie was coming for a house visit because Mom had summoned her for the final time.

I met Marie at the front door and stepped aside so she could enter the foyer.

"How's your mother, Mike?" she asked. She placed what I assumed was a medical bag on the floor and studied me carefully, most likely alarmed at the dark circles and dampness around my eyes. "And you. How about you?" she added.

"She says she's planning on exiting at midnight," I said. "The date is stuck in her mind, Marie." I stepped to the kitchen and waited for Marie to join me so our voices wouldn't carry down the hall and to Mom's open bedroom door. "Can she do that?" I asked after Marie joined me.

"Knowing Kathleen, yes. I wouldn't bet against her," she said. "She's outlived her prognosis, Mike. I'm sorry, but somehow she has lasted this long despite not accepting further treatment. Medically, it just doesn't make sense. It's as if she has something she needs to complete."

"If that's the case then what do you think her plan is? I mean she can't pick a time to die can she?"

Marie opened a cabinet for a mug and headed for the Mr. Coffee coffeemaker. Even though she was a visiting doctor today, she had been a guest many times before so she was comfortable helping herself. "Here again, Mike," she began, her back to me. "This is not a medical explanation or based on facts, but folks decide when they want to expire all the time. Being an oncologist I see this quite often." She turned around and faced me. "People at the end of their life make the decision that they're done and it simply happens."

"I'm not ready, Marie," I admitted, sitting at the kitchen island and placing my face in my hands. I rubbed the tiredness away and then stared at her. "First Dad and now Mom? This hardly seems fair."

"It isn't fair," she agreed. "Especially considering the type of folks your parents are, Mike. I don't get it either."

"Do you think my mother is rational, Marie?" I asked, seeking a professional opinion after the last few days of talking with Mom and listening to her outlandish ideas. Ideas that did not seem like they could come from a sane individual. "She's not taking opioids for the pain, but could the pain make her delusional?"

"I see zero indication that she's delusional. Even with her microdosing and the small amount of THC she ingests in the form of edibles, they'd have no discernable effect on her mental abilities. Why do you ask?"

"Just curious, I guess."

Marie reached across the island and held my hand. "Kathleen is an extraordinary woman, Mike. If she seems a bit, shall we say, spiritual or contemplative about what might be on the other side of this existence, you'd be surprised how common that is. Besides, who are we to question?"

I glanced toward the hallway and lowered my voice. "She's been talking about some unusual ideas concerning life and death," I said. "I guess I'm worried about her mindset."

"Don't be. Her train of thought is quite common. And trust me, your mom is as sharp as she was the day I met her back when you and my daughter were toddlers."

Her assessment of Mom's thinking alleviated the nagging feeling that I wasn't speaking with a lucid woman. "And she expects to pass at midnight or shortly after. What are your thoughts?" I asked.

"Well, then I expect she will. Your mother has lived a month longer than I would have assessed another patient in her situation. Of course, I'm not surprised."

"You're not?"

"Your mother is . . . how can I say this?"

"Weird?" I interjected.

Marie laughed out loud. "Different. Informed. Resilient. But weird? Not a chance. If Kathleen was offering me advice or insight into her beliefs, I'd drop everything and listen. Your mother is connected, Mike. Don't ask me to explain what the hell that even means but all of her friends sense that about her."

"Thank you, Marie," I said, feeling better. I was still confused and questioning reality, but hearing an educated woman of science admit there could be more to life than scientific facts had helped.

"Let me end with this, Mike," she began. "If there *is* something more after this life, I hope your mother is in my universe again."

I was surprised by Marie's word choice of *universe*. Her kind words about my mother were the same as I'd heard for most of my life. My mother was unique and well-loved among her friends. Things she did that I may have found odd when I was growing up didn't seem to faze her friends. Marie was a doctor for Christ's sake and she thought Mom was normal, so why couldn't I accept my own mother's views on our world, even if they did seem highly unusual?

"Are you going to leave something for Mom's pain in case she needs it?" I asked, interrupting the silence.

"Yes, but I don't expect that she'll take it. She's stubborn and insists she wants the full experience. But yes, I'll leave you with morphine in case she changes her mind."

"What's next?"

"I'm sorry to say this, son, but your mother is going to pass very soon." Marie released my hand, placed her mug in the sink and then came around the kitchen island to give me a hug from behind. "Her breathing will become shallow and there will be longer intervals between breaths. I can stay until then if you'd like."

"Please just check on her now and then set me up with the morphine. I'd like to be alone with Mom after that," I stated. "One other thing, Marie. What do I do when she passes?"

"Call the funeral home. They'll take it from there and I'll forward the cause of death directly to them and the county."

Her words seemed so clinical and unfeeling but I understood that Marie had experienced this many times in her career. Her presence was beyond the normal practice of medicine so I appreciated her and knew her directness came from a good place.

"The transition will be difficult for you, Mike, but keep in mind that Kathleen is suffering terribly. Personally, and I mean this in the best of ways, I'm relieved your mother will no longer be in pain and will be free to move on to her next journey, whatever that is."

Her kindness was appreciated and her assessment of the end of life surprised me. "You believe there's something after this life?" I asked.

"Let's just say I hope there is," she responded. "I can't imagine a universe without Kathleen."

She turned and headed down the hall. "Me neither," I mumbled.

CHAPTER FOURTEEN: Mike

Twelve years ago

"What?" I asked, catching Cooper staring at me again. We were in his bedroom doing homework. We went to the gym after school and hadn't showered yet so I was still in my old gray sweats and he was in his boxers.

"Nothing," he answered, looking away and relocating the cursor on his laptop, pretending to get back to our assignment.

"You were staring at me again, dude," I protested.

"Am not."

"Are so," I responded.

"I'm not," he whined. "I was just noticing how big your arms are getting," he admitted.

"So . . . that means you were looking at me."

"I'm just jealous, is all, Mikey."

"Of my arms or that Jennifer gets to touch all this?" I dared, alternately kissing both biceps.

"Never mind," he mumbled, instantly shutting down at any mention of my girlfriend Jennifer who was the hottest girl at our school.

"You like her, don't ya?" I asked, needing his approval for some reason. "You think she's hot as fuck, right?" I pushed.

"Not my type," he answered with a shrug, which immediately annoyed me.

I wanted my best friend to see my girlfriend the way I did: perfect. "Why? Because she doesn't have a dick?"

"Don't be crude," he said, frowning at me. Cooper was like that. He wasn't a prude, but he was classier than I was. "You know I like guys so stop busting my butt, will ya?"

"Butt, huh?" I teased. "That's a naughty word. I'm telling your mommy, you bad boy."

"Buzz off. You're hurting my feelings," he confessed, which caught me off guard.

I enjoyed ribbing my best friend but never wanted to hurt his feelings. I slid off of the bed and walked to his desk where he had laid his head down, staring at the opposite wall. I placed my hands on his neck and gently massaged him. "I'm sorry, buddy. I get crude sometimes and don't know when to stop my shit talking."

"It's okay," he mumbled into the crook of his arm so I barely understood his muffled voice. He turned to face me, his head once again resting on his arm. "Can I tell you something?" he asked, gazing at me with large blue vulnerable eyes that always grabbed me by the heart and squeezed so hard I felt my knees shake.

I tugged at his shaggy hair to get him to sit up. "Always," I responded. "Something got your panties in a bunch?" I teased.

He sat up, leaning back in his wooden chair, glaring at me. His eyes were wet. "See?" he asked, gesturing a hand toward me. "Like that."

I took a step back, a little pissed at him for pointing out what I assumed was a flaw. "Like what?" I dared, crossing my arms.

"Oh, and now here you go with the arm crossing and daggers."

"Jesus, dude. What am I, your boyfriend?" I spat. "You sound just like Jen lately. Both of you bitching about how I act."

"Stop comparing me to Jennifer," he stated. "I hate that."

"Stop acting like her then," I argued. "She bosses me around all the time and then I get the same fucking attitude from you, Coop. And . . . I hate that!" I emphasized.

"Then get a different girlfriend. Or maybe a different best friend."

I stepped closer and leaned over him, inches from his face. "What the fuck is wrong with you lately? I don't need a new best friend and you know it. I love you just fine and that's all there is to say," I stated. "And you love me too, right?" I asked.

He didn't look at me.

68

"Right?" I repeated, raising my voice and uncrossing my arms.

"Maybe too much," he mumbled.

"What the fuck did you just say?" I asked, not sure I'd heard him correctly. "Did you just say too much?"

"What if I did?" he asked.

His question made me start to rethink who we were to each other. He was my everything and I didn't want to lose him. Maybe I was being unfair when I required him to want what I wanted. It wasn't like Cooper to ever question who we were to each other. He was my everything and I would never accept that he didn't feel the same way. Maybe it was an unfair requirement that I had of him. "Take that back, Coop," I demanded. He ignored me. "Take it back right now," I said, feeling a panic I hadn't ever felt before. What the fuck were these feelings coursing through my veins that were rushing in and destroying my heart? I suddenly felt fear that I could lose him and I couldn't make sense of what was happening between us.

"It's the truth," he said defiantly. "I think my feelings for you are unhealthy sometimes."

"No, they aren't," I argued. "We're brothers, Coop. Besties, shit like that."

"Except one difference, Mikey, I like you more than that."

"No, you don't," I stated. "You're just confused. It's okay, buddy. I can be cooler if it helps."

"What would help right now is for you to go home," he said, turning away. I reached for his chin to turn him back to me but he swatted my hand away. "Just go, Mikey."

"Fuck that!" I hissed. "You're going to tell me what the problem is, dude, and you're gonna spill it right now."

Cooper pointed to his bedroom door. "I just did and you still don't get it, so go, please?" I reached for his shoulder but he pulled away. "Now," he added with a raised voice, something he rarely did.

I pulled my shirt on and backed toward the door. "I'm leaving unless you take it back."

He didn't.

He also didn't stand in his bedroom window to wave goodnight to me.

While I stared at his dark window, I began to think of my best friend, my everything, as someone more. If only I had recognized what was happening to me. If only.

CHAPTER FIFTEEN: Mike

Marie visited with Mom for more than an hour. I remained in the kitchen listening to muted whispers of their distant conversation, unable to make out the words they exchanged. I rested my cheek on the cool marble island, staring out the French doors to the backyard. The weather was sunny and life was going by as life always does, regardless of what you're going through. I wanted time to slow down or better yet stop so Mom's imminent death would be delayed, but that wasn't how the world functioned.

Marie suddenly appeared in the kitchen and cleared her throat, interrupting the quiet. "I have to leave now, Mike," she announced.

I sat up when I noticed her red eyes.

"Everything you need is in the room," she added.

I nodded, unable to form words.

"Call me if you need anything else or if you just want me to be here," she added.

I nodded again and struggled to keep my emotions in check

Her job had to suck, and this was a close friend of hers. There was a reason that doctors were advised not to care for family or close friends, but Mom had insisted Marie be by her side. Marie, of course, couldn't say no to Mom. Who could?

"Close?" I asked.

Marie understood what I meant and nodded, new tears glistened in her eyes before she looked away.

I stood and made my way to her. "Thank you," I choked out. "For everything." We embraced and I felt her chest heave as she stifled a sob. "I'll call . . . when . . . well, you know," I said.

Marie turned away and headed for the front door. She paused and turned around, appearing to have something to add but only shook her head before opening the door and stepping outside.

After the door closed I stood looking around the kitchen wishing Mom was there in her daisy-print apron, fussing over a meal or sharing one of her positive stories about our wonderful world. The house was quiet until a tray of ice dumped into the ice maker's storage bin, startling me. The fridge, like everything else, kept pace with the passing time. The clocks moved forward one tick at a time, yet I remained frozen in my grief.

I didn't want to go down the hall to what awaited me. I wasn't ready and walking into Mom's room said I was. The doctor was gone. The goodbyes were said and I would be the last attendee to my mother's final moments. Unlike the surprise of Dad's death, I would be here for Mom's. I'd be able to say all the things I wasn't able to say to my father, yet I wasn't really sure I preferred confronting death this way.

As I made my way down the hallway I'd breezed through thousands of times before, I paused and took the time to view the family photos that Mom had proudly put up over the years. There were the baby photos of me; some taken by my folks, others done professionally where the photographer added even more blue to my eyes and made my cherub-like cheeks a bit rosier as well.

In many of the photos, Mom and Dad appeared so young, their youthful faces smiling at me as I slowly walked down the hall. My toddler pictures morphed into the organized sports images. Me at six playing T-ball with a beaming Dad who was our coach. Me at eleven with a broken arm from Pee Wee football. Mom tried her darndest to prevent me from playing such a violent sport again but further down the hall were the junior high and high school football pictures that showed she hadn't been successful in that endeavor.

There were pictures of the homecoming pregame for seniors with Mom by my side at the stadium. Mom came out again and escorted me at halftime for the crowning of the homecoming king. I'd won and Jennifer was of course crowned queen, happy as hell when she was able to drag me away from Mom and get me to herself for the rest of the pictures. I guess I should have known then that her and Mom weren't destined to be close.

I paused at the open door to Mom's room even though the hall of memories continued beyond her bedroom door. There were the ones from college life and holiday family pictures of me, my mom and Jennifer that eventually lead up to our wedding. I recognized the irony of Mom's door being the divider in my life; telling me that I shouldn't look further down the hall at my past for directions to my future.

I took a deep breath and glanced at my watch. The time was five minutes to noon on Saturday, August 29th. Before entering her room I noticed a picture of my parents that Mom had hung right outside their bedroom door. I'd walked past it numerous times but I'd never studied the photo. We had visited the Oregon Coast two years before Dad died. I had taken the photo yet never noticed what stood out so clearly in the image that day.

Anyone who has visited the Washington or Oregon coasts knows that the weather is often cool even in the summer, and that the sun can disappear for days behind thick clouds. In the photo, Mom and Dad have their backs to the ocean with their arms entwined while Mom leaned against Dad's shoulder. Behind the thick clouds the sun was low on the horizon and appeared as a glowing outline of a circle of light. Another bright illumination was centered behind Mom as if she had a halo made of subtle beams streaking from her head into the clouds, framing her happy face. She looked ethereal. There was no other way to describe it.

I spoke to myself, "That's where you're going, isn't it?" The realization that she was indeed a special being filled me with warmth.

"Michael?" she asked from within the room. "Who are you talking to?"

I entered and made my way to her bedside. "Myself, Mom," I confessed when I reached for her hand. "I was admiring the picture of you and Dad at the beach."

"Can you bring it to me?" she asked. "That one is my favorite. How about we place it here on the dresser so Dad can join us? His presence always invigorates me."

"Good idea," I admitted, heading for the door. I retrieved the framed photo and propped it up on the dresser at the foot of the hospital bed.

"Your dad loved that picture," she stated, struggling to sit up in bed so she could see better.

I pushed a button on the controller that raised the head of the bed. "He used to say the ocean was my happy place, a sort of heaven for me, and that I shined whenever we visited."

"Do you believe in heaven, Mom?" I asked, happy to reminisce about the fond memory.

"Good question, son. Heaven does sound like an idyllic place to be but I'm not convinced to tell you the truth." Her answer didn't surprise me. Mom was well versed on this topic and she'd always stated that there were too many holes in the theory where a God was in charge.

"You do seem to be connected to a higher plane in that picture. I never noticed before."

"What do you mean?" She squinted, her eyes remaining locked on the picture fifteen feet away. "Bring it closer. I want to look at it," she said.

I brought the frame to her and placed it gently in her shaking fingers, making sure she could grip the photo with both hands.

"See that?" I asked, tracing the glowing circle around her head with my finger. "A halo, perhaps?" I asked. "What is that, Mom?"

She remained silent and continued to gaze at the image before turning toward me. "That wasn't there before," she stated. "I have looked at this photo every single night before going to bed since I put this photo up on the wall, especially after your father died. I swear to you that I have never seen that pattern of light before now," she insisted.

"Are you sure?" I asked, leaning over her and looking closer. "I've never noticed it either. Can I see? Could it be a lens flare?" After she handed me the photo I tried to use the lamp on her nightstand to examine the unusual light but when I ran my finger across the beautiful halo it disappeared. I damn near dropped the frame in my shock.

"What?" she whispered, questioning my reaction.

74

"It's gone," I whispered, handing the picture back to her. "See?" As soon as I handed the frame to her, the circle of light returned around her head. "What the . . .?" I snatched the photo out of her hands and held it under the lamp again. "Impossible," I muttered.

The lamp had to be creating an illusion by reflecting off the glass. What other explanation could there be? I hurried to the bathroom and turned on the overhead heat lamp, studying the framed photo beneath the brightest light in the house. The circle of light wasn't there either.

I walked back into the bedroom, perplexed by the mysterious halo.

"Did you see it in there?" Mom asked.

I shook my head with my mouth hanging open, gobsmacked. Were we both going nuts?

"Try under that one," she suggested, gesturing to the matching nightstand lamp on the other side of her bed.

I made my way around the bed and turned the lamp on, nervous about what I might see. Mom tried to lean closer but couldn't move due to the pain so I lifted the lamp and brought both to her. The circle of light around her head was as plain as day.

We looked from one another and back to the picture. "Your father slept on that side," she said, nodding to where I was kneeling.

"No fucking way," I declared. Mom frowned at my language but I was too preoccupied to care about my outburst because I was hurrying back to the first lamp. I moved the lamp on Mom's side of the bed over her again so we could both study the image. The light was not in the picture. "Impossible."

"He's here, Mikey. Dad is here for us."

The tingling sensation of goosebumps crawled all over me after hearing Mom state Dad was there with us. Is he standing right next to me? Is that why I feel this chilling sensation spreading up my spine? Something very strange was happening and I was so freaked out I could feel the hair standing on the back of my neck. Maybe my mother wasn't crazy.

The lamp in my hand flickered before suddenly turning off with a pop. "Dad?"

CHAPTER SIXTEEN: Mike

Twelve Years Ago

A week went by before Cooper went back to his usual loving self. Of course, I'd gone out of my way to be attentive and mindful of what I said around him. The fact that he had admitted that he liked me as more than a friend had occupied my thoughts for the past several days. I wasn't exactly sure how to respond or if it was true.

"Did you see the new senior that transferred from Boise?" he asked.

I had and wasn't impressed. "The dude all the girls are in a flutter about?" I asked, punching one of my pillows on my bed for some reason. "Seems like a regular enough schmuck to me," I added. I already couldn't stand the new dude because I'd spent lunchtime listening to Jennifer and her cheerleader pack of she-wolves drooling over him.

"His name is also Mike. Mike Hastings," Coop reported. "I'll call him New Mikey if we become friends," he added.

"The hell you will," I stated. "Not while I'm in a room with ya, ya won't."

Cooper grinned at me. "Sore spot for ya, buddy?" he asked. "Jennifer and her glam squad seemed all excited about 'Mr. Buff.'"

"And you won't be calling him that either," I insisted, glaring at him as he relaxed on my bed while tossing a small rubber ball in the air and catching it on every return. "He looks gay to me," I added, thinking that was a proper putdown.

"Wow," Coop said, sitting up and throwing the ball at me.

I dodged it and glared some more.

"So tell me, macho, what exactly does gay look like?"

"Like him," I blurted, bouncing off the bed and heading for the bathroom, dropping my boxers as I made my way to the shower.

Cooper hustled after me, stepping out of his shorts and boxers, thinking nothing of the fact that we were talking about gay guys and the two of us were about to shower together for the millionth time. *"So hold on and wait for me, tough guy,"* he hollered when I cranked the shower on. Coop stepped past me and leaned against the tile, massaging the bar of soap to create suds. My eyes moved to his cock and that new feeling washed over me. I quickly turned around.

"Do my back," I said.

Cooper stepped behind me like he always did. In fact, I felt the tip of his cock brush my ass cheek. Again, the rush of adrenaline surged through me and straight to my dick. It was getting hard.

"Hey," I began. *"Can you step out for a second?"*

"What for?" he asked, dragging the bar of soap over my ass crack before squatting and sudsing the back of my legs. *"I'm almost done."*

"Then step out, okay?" I asked, panic in my voice.

Cooper stood and grabbed my shoulder, spinning me around to study my face. *"Are you okay?"* His eyes shifted down my body and then widened. *"What's go . . .?"* His baby blues returned to mine. *"Oh, shit. Yeah, yeah, okay."*

"It's nothing, dude," I defended. *"I was just stroking it with the soap,"* I added, trying to talk my way out.

Cooper stepped out and shut the frosted glass door. *"But you didn't have the soap,"* he argued. *"I was soaping your back,"* he added, making the situation even more awkward.

"I meant shampoo," I lied.

"It's all cool," Coop yelled from the bedroom.

I had a full erection and even after being caught, it wouldn't deflate. Terror set in as I fumbled to rinse off quickly. As soon as I stepped out of the enclosure, Cooper entered the bathroom to finish his shower when he saw my raging boner still at full attention.

"Looks like someone's happy about something," he teased. *"Damn, Mikey, that's gotten huge."*

"Stop fucking looking at me, Coop," I vented, cupping my junk with both hands

to conceal it.

"Can I touch it?" he asked, stepping forward. "Not like sexual or anything, but I've never touched another guy's penis, and since we're buds and all."

"No fucking way, dude," I hissed. "That's fucking gay."

"Exactly like me," he quipped. "I just want to feel it. You're huge."

As embarrassed as I was, I enjoyed his describing my dick that way. I particularly liked that he thought it was huge, his words not mine. "You can look, but no touching," I stated.

"I've seen your penis a thousand times before, so what's the big deal suddenly?" he asked.

"The big deal is that you might like touching me," I argued, moving my hands to my hips and liking the shape of my boner from my angle. It was big.

"I already like it," he said, not taking his eyes off of me.

"This is weird, dude," I said, feeling uncomfortable and horny at the same time.

"I could touch it and if you liked how you feel then you could tell me what to do next," he offered, eyeing me carefully. "You know, only if you like what I do."

Cooper's tone and his words were unlike any I'd ever heard before. He was seductive and very convincing. I was mesmerized by him and had obscene thoughts about shoving my cock down his throat, maybe fucking his ass. What the fuck was I doing?

"Back the fuck up, dude. No guy is touching my cock even if you are my best bud," I stated. "You're pretty as fuck, Coop, but un-uh, no way."

He appeared crestfallen, but quickly recovered and began to laugh. "Just joshin' with ya, Mikey," he said. "You ain't my type anyway."

That didn't sit well either. "The fuck I ain't?" I hissed. "I'm every gay dude's dream. And the ladies too," I added.

"The new boy is buffer and rougher from what I can tell," he said, turning and walking out of the bathroom.

I hurried after him, wrapped in a towel as my dick deflated along with my ego. "Rougher? What the fuck does that even mean?" I raged, grabbing his arm and yanking him around. The moment I touched his soft naked skin, I felt the urges reignite.

"You know what I mean," he began. "He has a bad boy edge to him. I kinda like

78

that in a guy."

"The fuck you do. You like boys like me. I mean . . . men like me," I declared.

"But men like you, don't like boys like me," he quipped. "And the jury is out on New-Mikey and what team he plays for."

That was a tough night for me and I'll never forget fearing that Cooper could like another boy.

CHAPTER SEVENTEEN: Mike

"Hello," I said, picking up my cell phone before the humming vibration woke Mom.

"Hi, Michael." It was my soon-to-be ex-wife, Jennifer. "Marie called my folks and they called me," she began. "How's your mother?"

That was Jennifer's way. Get right to the point of every situation and conversation. No time or effort spent on small talk, catching up, or an exchange of *fuck-you's.*

"Anytime now," I whispered, getting out of the chair so I wouldn't wake my sleeping mother and making my way to the hall.

"I'm sorry, Michael. I just wanted to check on her," she stated. She was back to formal names and made no effort to conceal the fact that she was eating something while speaking with me. "I won't be able to make it to the funeral," she added. "My new job has me buried."

The use of the word buried was lost on her considering what I was facing at the moment. The reality was she probably would have missed the funeral even if we were still married. She didn't do funerals. That and she avoided Idaho Falls like the plague. I believed she didn't like *that* girl. The one who grew up here. Not to mention she'd still be seen as *high-school* Jennifer who was the bubble-headed blonde, not the more glamorous, uber-successful woman she was today.

"I understand," I lied, tapping the wall lightly and counting the seconds with my fingers until I could hang up. "I'll let Mom know you called and were concerned," I lied again. There was no way in hell I wanted to soil the last hours I had with my mother by reminiscing about a failed relationship with the former beauty queen of Idaho Falls High School.

"I wish I had more time," she said. "You know, work and all."

"Mom will understand, Jen. You're busy. We get it," I said, a bit harsher than I intended to sound. "Take care," I added.

She wasn't finished. "My parents said you haven't called or stopped by to see them since you got back in town, Michael," she quickly added, interrupting my desire to end the call.

I hated how she butchered my proper name with her guilt inflicting tone. "Perhaps after . . .," she stopped mid-sentence.

"Perhaps after what, Jen? After Mom dies?" I asked, finishing her sentence for her. "So maybe *I* can have a little family reunion with *your* parents?"

"Don't be difficult, Michael," she said.

"Don't be gross, Jennifer. Why don't *you* visit them instead? Oh wait, you're too busy," I hissed.

She'd hit a nerve.

"I sincerely hope that you never have to deal with what I'm dealing with right now. So do me a massive favor and fuck off." The phone went dead. I hadn't hung up. I guess I wouldn't be stopping by her parents' house after all.

I made my way to the kitchen and opened the fridge, staring at the contents like something inside might improve my mood. I'd bought a case of beer and hadn't touched a single bottle since arriving a couple of weeks ago. Maybe I hadn't been addicted to the beer as much as I was to the numbness provided while living my dull life in Seattle. A life I'd wasted over the past ten years because I just trudged through it. My life choices weren't Jen's fault. I knew that, but admitting that I'd failed in our relationship still hurt. She deserved more honesty as much as I deserve more respect.

The fact was that after Cooper died, I allowed my life to be influenced by external forces like parents, friends, and Jennifer. *"Let's go to UW now that you're not going to WSU,"* Jen had suggested right after Cooper's funeral, his corpse barely cold in the ground. *"I never wanted you to go to college without me,"* she'd added. So, of course, I went to the University of Washington in Seattle.

"I'd at least get engaged before she wises up," a high school football buddy who'd joined us at UW advised one day while we worked out at our frat house. *"She actually wants you for some odd reason, dude,"* he'd quipped, and then added. *"We all know she's out of your league."* I didn't ask her to marry me immediately but I eventually did and she'd said yes. Now I look back and wonder why I wasn't more thrilled that she had wanted me.

"If Jennifer thinks it's best for you to stay in Seattle after you graduate since you have a life there, I support you," Mom had agreed. *"Jennifer is ambitious, honey, but I bet that can be a good thing,"* Mom had added. I doubted she honestly felt that was true. Mom knew Jennifer, and she knew me. She knew it wouldn't be a *good thing*.

I wasn't a live-or-die-for-a-job fella. I was a diligent and hard worker, but running the show wasn't my career goal. I preferred collaborative scenarios where teams flourished. That should have been another clue that I wasn't a good match for my ex. If you weren't in Jennifer's shadow, you were outshining her and that wouldn't be tolerated. I had made sure to stay in her shadow but I guess her sun had outgrown our universe.

But I'd dutifully gone along for ten years, and truthfully would most likely still be there if Jen hadn't discovered Cooper's letter. The beer, the complacency, relinquishing control to my wife, and walking through life in an aimless stupor was who I'd become. Every single thing I doubt would've happened had Cooper lived.

Not anymore though.

I wanted to finally live and accept the parts of me that I kept hidden since childhood. I'd be alone, but that would force me to rely on the person I should have relied on all along: myself.

I closed the fridge before I gave into my desire for a beer. I wanted clarity for the next several hours in case my mother passed away and drinking would hinder that. The digital clock on the microwave read twenty-five minutes past five in the afternoon.

Mom was sitting upright and staring out the window when I entered her bedroom. "How'd you do that?" I asked, pointing at the bed she'd raised on her own.

She lifted her hand and showed me the controller. "I can push a button, Michael. Besides, I had a boost of energy after Dad's trick."

"I can see that. Hungry?" I asked, unsure of what else to say. "I can make you some soup."

"I'm tired, son. I think I'm ready," she whispered, a slight cough escaping her lungs. "What time is it?"

"Almost five-thirty," I answered, looking at my wrist even though I'd just seen the time in the kitchen.

She gazed toward the closet and jutted her chin out. "Grab a blue box from the top shelf in my closet," she stated.

"Why?" Dread crawled across my skin, slow and ominous before setting up shop in my gut. I wasn't fond of the shift of tone in her voice. I knew this version of Mom. This was the *I'm-in-control* Mom, so do as I say. "What's in the boxes?"

"Important stuff," she gasped, raising her hand to point again and grimacing in pain.

"You're hurting, Mom. Can you at least take a little morphine?" I encouraged.

She narrowed her eyes at me, once again being *in-control* Mom.

"*We* are doing this on *my* terms, Michael. Time is precious and I want to share something with you before my departure," she announced.

"How about we tackle that tomorrow?"

"I won't be here tomorrow," she stated. "We will enjoy this now and then we can be free to chat until I move on from this plane of existence."

"I prefer you stay in this plane with me," I choked out, glancing at the closet. I didn't want to get the boxes. I couldn't accept that she was ready. How could she be ready? I sure as fuck wasn't.

The room was silent while Mom waited for me to comply. She couldn't be unkind. Her path forward was one of patience no matter how strong the headwinds trying to force her backward were. She never looked back. She never complained about the past. Mom had zero interest in what *had* happened and was far more curious about what *could* happen.

"You promised," she reminded me. "And now is the time to hold up your end of that bargain."

I walked to the closet where four blue cardboard boxes sat on the top shelf. The boxes looked like they held fancy hats or winter sweaters, but I feared it held instructions. Death instructions.

"The first one on the left," she said, pointing a shaking finger above my head.

I placed the box beside her on the bed and removed the fitted lid. A sealed note with my name scrawled across the front was on top. "I thought this sorta stuff was in the safe," I stated.

"These items are personal effects," she explained. "Things I saved from your childhood that I want you to have. The letter on top is for after I'm gone."

I removed the letter, noting a handwritten date in the corner where a stamp would normally be that was dated August 30th.

"For tomorrow," she said.

I didn't protest the date. Why bother at this point? Under a baby's blanket were other short notes clipped to pictures. There were baby clothes and two pairs of baby shoes. A ceramic circle of my hand print that I'd made in kindergarten stood out like a beacon from my childhood. She'd saved it all. Every important moment from her only child's life had been beautifully preserved and labeled.

I picked up a polaroid of a very tiny me. I appeared to be about three years old wearing a suit with black shiny shoes and a bow tie. There was a rabbit in a wooden wheelbarrow beside me. I was obviously fascinated by the bunny and was pointing to it with chubby fingers to whomever was taking the photo.

The note attached read: *You were almost three in this picture on Easter morning. Dad and I borrowed the rabbit from grandpa so you could have him for the day. Sadly, grandpa ate him the following week.*

I burst out laughing at the last sentence, until I began to weep. Sniffling, I set the picture on the bed and reached for another. Tears fell freely as I sifted through photos and memories, digging through the layers of my boyhood.

Another note read: *You were five and had finally figured out how to ride a bike without training wheels. Dad took them off and forced you to learn. Of course, you fell several times. Your father was impatient and I didn't forgive him for three days after that.* I was sitting on a bright blue bike and grinning extra wide, my sneakers barely touching the driveway in front of the house we were currently in.

I lifted my eyes to my mother. "Is everything here?" I asked.

She smiled and nodded. "That box is from your birth to age five. The others are the years following."

"You seriously saved everything?" I asked, smiling through my tears.

"What else would a mother who has only one kiddo do?" she asked. "I put all I had into you, honey. Dad and I were always so proud of you. I am still proud of you," she added.

"Can we go through them together?" I asked.

"They go all the way until you leave for college," she warned.

"I've got time if you do," I said. "You can remind me of all the good times, Mom."

"Watching you grow up was all good times, son."

We finished box one and then I retrieved box two that was labeled *ages five to ten.* There'd be two more boxes after this one. I planned to take my time so Mom and I could relive my childhood. I was selfishly doing my best to extend my time with her. What Mom had done was provide me a wonderful gift full of memories. Memories I didn't recall but now I would cherish forever after they'd been retold to me by the woman who'd meticulously recorded them.

The time was 7:17 P.M. on Saturday, the 29th of August.

.

CHAPTER EIGHTEEN: Mike

I sat beside my mother and watched the digital clock on the dresser countdown the last moments of her life. In my head, I counted silently to myself, attempting to time my count with the change to the next minute. Digital numbers are fascinating to observe on a clock. I stared at the numbers and envisioned how a 3 would turn into a 4. Wondering which hashes of the digital number would disappear as it morphed into the next number.

The quiet room lulled me into thinking that Mom was simply asleep and that I could wait until she woke so we could continue our trip down memory lane. However, her breathing was shallow and the rising of her chest with each breath was becoming less frequent, just as Marie had described. Once again I stared at the clock, timing the intervals of the changing numbers to the rise of Mom's chest. The time was 10:48 P.M..

Her face grimaced when she was jolted awake from pain. "Michael?" she gasped.

I stood and leaned over her, holding her hand in mine. "I'm right here, Mom."

Mom's eyes popped open and she did her best to smile through the agony of what life had dealt her. "I'm not going to lie, Mikey. This shit hurts."

I believed her.

I had two choices. Either laugh at her cussing, something she never did, or cry because I hated to see her suffering. "Can I give you some meds?" I asked, stroking her face. "Just something to ease the pain, Mom."

"Absolutely not," she stated. "We have important stuff to discuss."

"Can we not do that right now?" I implored. "I love you and you love me. We know that without question so why don't we talk about something pleasant? Tell me how you met Dad?"

"Ask him yourself," she answered. "He's in the corner."

I immediately moved my eyes from one corner to the next when the lamp with the burnt out lightbulb on his nightstand suddenly turned on.

"See?" she asked. "You need to open your mind, son."

"How am I supposed to do that?" I asked, exasperated by her insistence of the unnatural even though I'd just witnessed some paranormal activity. "I'm not convinced," I added.

"Come closer," she urged. "Listen to me carefully." I sat on the edge of the bed and leaned closer to her. "I'm going to give you an example of how you can believe that there are extraordinary things in our universes, and you can experience them. In fact, you already do," she stated. I suppressed the desire to roll my eyes.

She closed her eyes and gasped for air because she had spoken too quickly and needed to wait for weakened lungs to replenish some oxygen.

I waited, thinking she may have dozed off again. "Mom?" I whispered.

"Listen and allow yourself to be open," she advised, her eyes squinting open, registering the effort she was making to force through the pain. "You have to believe or what's possible can't happen for you."

"I'm listening," I responded. And I was.

Her explanation took a long time as she struggled for breaths between sentences, but in a nutshell, I understood her loud and clear. Mom explained that I already participated in parallel universes every time I envisioned myself doing something different. Perhaps a different job, maybe having a talent that I didn't currently possess.

Her idea was that if you could envision being or doing something else, or imagine the type of life you could have, then you were tapping into your parallel life. *"Your imagination can give you the doorway to tap into your intuition,"* she'd declared.

I sort of knew what she was trying to explain because I often thought about what could have been when I wondered what my life would be if I had chosen to be a doctor or maybe even a teacher. I would imagine caring for others, treating my mother's illness, the prestige that life might offer. The visions were always full and detailed. I hated to admit that I assumed we all had fantasy visions during sex. The act is pleasurable, but how many times in our minds did we insert other participants in place of our partners? Role playing in our minds can create satisfying details. Her belief was that our imagination was our doorway to our intuition and the way to access other dimensions which are our parallel lives.

Knowing that I was a man of computer science and held strong beliefs in provable theories, Mom brought up a young Princeton University doctoral candidate named Hugh Everett III. In 1954 he came up with a radical idea that parallel universes exist exactly like our own universe. These universes are all related to ours; in fact, they branch off from ours and our universe branched off from others. Mom quoted string theory research that suggests that parallel universes can come in contact with each other. Therein was where she and her medium Druzella believed meditation could transport us to a parallel universe when these branches meet.

"I am convinced that if you meditate *and* if you envision going to another universe, it can happen," she stated. "The alignment of stars and planets affects everything and with Druzella's assistance, I can deliver you there. My potion, Druzella's charts for you and Cooper, which have never been aligned better, and your belief will make it happen."

I couldn't believe my next words. "I'll try."

"Thank you," she whispered. "One more request before I go," she said, causing my heart to thump painfully.

I nodded and desperately held onto her hand, hoping I could transport both of us to one of those parallel universes.

"Ask away," I croaked, unable to compose myself any longer.

"First off, give me a *very healthy* shot of the morphine and then tell me about you and Cooper, honey," she requested. "Tell me what you imagine the two of you are doing in a different world? Where are thirty year old Cooper and you living?"

Suddenly I didn't like the thought of her taking the drug. I didn't like the implication. "Are you sure?" I asked, reaching for the prefilled syringe on Dad's nightstand. The moment I lifted the syringe off of the nightstand, the light turned off.

Mom smiled through her pain. "See? Dad is waiting for me."

I gave her the shot, trying to pass off the lamp as faulty wiring since it was old.

"Now, where were we?" she asked, pausing to catch her breath. "Oh, yes, I've always known you boys were destined to be together," she explained. "And because of that, I have so desperately wanted the two of you to be reunited again. Now tell me, son, where are you and your beloved Cooper in your vision?"

I decided to share a desire that I often had. Why not? If Mom and Dad were about to be reunited, why couldn't Cooper and I?

I climbed in the bed and laid on my side, facing Mom. My left hand held her right while the other was tucked between us. I'd been doing this for as long as I could remember when I needed a dose of her love. Mom was always a safe haven for me and I needed her strength now more than ever.

"Well, let me see," I began, gazing at the streetlights outside. "I think we're right here in Idaho Falls. You live next door to us. Maybe still in this house and Cooper and I are next door in the Taylor's house. You've planted a huge row of marigolds between our driveways just to piss me off," I said before adding, "and God willing, you aren't summoning the dead anymore." I chuckled at my joke as I set up my life with an adult Cooper. "We'd still be over on Sunday mornings of course. We'd be married, Mom," I whispered. "We'd be happy and I would tell him I loved him every single day."

I choked up and paused. The thought of that life sounded amazing and I wished so much for another chance with him. I stared at the wall behind Mom before glancing down to her chest. I waited. *One, two, three, four,* I counted in my head. Nothing.

"Mom?" I cried, sitting up immediately and nudging her shoulder. "Mom?"

It was extremely difficult to see through the wall of tears, but I squinted to make out the numbers on the clock that sat on the dresser at the foot of the bed. It was 11:59 P.M. on August 29th. Mom suddenly took another shallow breath. I watched through tears as she faded away, hopefully to Dad who was waiting on the other side.

One, two, three, four, five. Nothing. Mom had ceased breathing. *One, two, three, four, five.* And then it was 12:01 A.M. on August 30th.

Mom was gone.

Just like she'd wanted.

I moved closer and draped my arm around her, bringing her empty body closer and hoping for her soul to find my father while I gently wept.

I was alone.

* * *

After several minutes I got up and made my way to the kitchen to find my cell phone. The house was eerily quiet. Even our home knew she'd moved on. Regardless of my wishing for a miracle, Mom had made her decision and left on her terms. There couldn't have been another way for her to die. Strong willed and so incredibly in tune with her surroundings, she'd made the final move.

The funeral home's number was on a notepad alongside Marie's number. I placed the two calls and then opened the fridge. If there was ever a time for beer it was now, but I couldn't bring myself to grab a bottle. For some reason I doubted I'd ever drink beer again. Instead I reached for a bottle of water then let the door close. Turning, I headed for the French doors that opened to the back patio. I flipped on the patio light and stepped outside. I needed to see her marigolds and inform them that she'd abandoned them too.

The periphery of the patio was pitch black, hiding the corners of the deck that disappeared into the shadows and around the side of the house. My eyes scanned the edges of the deck through tears of grief. *What should I do now?* And then I noticed two yellow circles glowing through the darkness inside the faint outline of a black cat.

"What do you want now?" I muttered.

90

The cat sat motionless while we stared at one another.

"What?" I pleaded.

The patio light flickered, causing me to glance over my shoulder at the door. When I turned back, the cat was gone.

CHAPTER NINETEEN: Mike

Eleven Years Ago

My senior year started a few weeks after the tragic death of my dad. The loss of him that summer was devastating and I'd leaned on Coop to help me with the hurt. He was there for me from day one. He was also there for Mom. If it hadn't been for his family stepping up like they did, Mom and I may have crumbled from the loss.

Cooper and I had turned seventeen that July. We both felt like grownups as we pondered what being seniors actually meant. I particularly felt thrust into the role of being man of the house even though my mother was more than capable of running things. Mom had always been head of our household but now I felt the pressure to be more supportive.

To help distract me from my grief, I filled out college applications with Cooper. We were both hoping to be accepted at Washington State University which was just across the border. Jennifer complained about me wanting to be with Coop in Pullman, instead of with her in Seattle.

"What is it with you two?" she griped. "Personally, and this is just my opinion as your girlfriend, I think it's time for the two of you to move on from this . . ." She needed a moment to define our closeness. "This . . . what should I call it?" she continued. "Well, I dunno, but it's weird. You know, the closeness and all," she explained.

"You think our friendship is weird?" I asked. "Coop is like a brother to me."

"And I am like your future," she countered. "You two will soon be eighteen and he needs to go his own way so we can go ours."

"That ain't happening, Jen," I insisted. *"Not in this lifetime anyway."* I stole a French fry from her tray and stuffed it in my mouth. *"He ain't with us right now is he?"* I argued.

"Surprisingly." She slapped at my hand when I went in for another fry or five. *"People are talking about you two."*

"Bullshit!" I hissed. I'd heard chatter over the years but Coop and I never ran from the gossip. He was an out gay guy and I had the hottest chick in school. *"That shit has been batted around for years, Jen. Even if I were gay, I wouldn't give a shit telling anyone. You missing anything from me?"* I asked.

She blushed, knowing exactly what I was talking about. She pulled the straw in her milkshake toward her and sipped on it as she raised her eyes to me and smiled. *"No,"* she admitted.

"Well, good then," I stated. *"You lemme know when I'm not a good boyfriend."*

Jen giggled and tucked loose strands of her blond hair behind an ear. She was stunning to look at and she knew it. I wasn't the type of boyfriend that followed her around school or hung out at her locker while other dudes fawned over her. That was why she chose to be with me. Jealousy wasn't one of my problems in regards to her because I was smart enough to know my indifference was what kept her interested in me. She hated guys that drooled over her even though their attention fed her ego. Most guys my age never understood that playing it cool worked better with girls. Besides, the only jealousy I felt was because of Cooper and the new guy who had moved to town at the end of our junior year.

"Is Cooper with Mike Hastings today?" Jen asked. *"The rumor is they're dating,"* she added.

I knew she was studying my reaction so I did my best to keep a calm face. *"So now people are saying they're boyfriends? Not him and me?"* I quipped. *"I'm not sure where he is,"* I lied. *"Cooper doesn't tell me where he is every five seconds."* He actually did but she didn't need to know that. Coop and I texted constantly and updated each other throughout the day. Perhaps it was a bit much but we were close like that.

"Hmmm," she mused, raising an eyebrow and still studying me. *"He is sorta cute though. You know, Mike Hastings."*

"I know who you're talking about," I fumed. So much for my nonchalant

reaction to her line of questioning. "Rumor has it he's not gay," I added for clarity.

"But I heard that Cooper is highly persuasive," she countered, quoting the air with her perfectly painted fingernails. "I don't suppose you've ever been persuaded have you, Mike?"

I glared at her and leaned forward so the nosy old geezer next to us wouldn't hear me. Grampa had been staring at Jennifer and her low cut midriff top since we walked in. "I might be if you don't give it up soon," I said.

Jennifer attempted to slap my face so I leaned back. She turned fifty shades of red. "Stop," she giggled. "He's listening," she added, gesturing to the older man next to us who was munching on his Big Mac.

"I ain't gay if that's what you're asking?"

"I know that, silly, besides I'm saving myself for marriage." Jen pulled the lid off of her cup and dipped a fry into the milkshake. She moved the fry to her lips where it lingered for a moment before she licked off the cool dessert. "Mmmm," she teased, taunting me. "Tasty."

"I wouldn't know," I quickly complained since I've been wanting her to suck on my cock since we first started dating. "I got something bigger than that fry," I added, grinning at the dude next to us as he perked up after hearing my wisecrack.

"I don't do that," she declared. "That's gross and us cheerleaders will not be partaking."

"Partaking?" I asked, acting all offended. "Who the fuck are you? Mother Teresa?"

"Maybe Cooper will suck your wiener," she said, daring me to react. "I bet he'd just love that."

"I'm sure he would," I agreed. "And if you don't, I might just have to give in to him."

"Well, Michael. Don't plan on oral sex from me," she began. "That is not happening in this lifetime or the next one."

She'd gotten under my skin, but it wasn't just her pointing out that Cooper and New Mikey were spending time together. Their friendship shouldn't have bothered me. I was dating the best girl in school so why should I care if they might be dating or fucking?

That was the problem, I did care. Yes, I was dating the girl every guy wanted.

94

Yes, the make out sessions were good. Maybe a bit vanilla, but I was still young. I desired all physical contact with Jen but lately I'd been thinking about my feelings for Cooper and how I desired him too. I wasn't sure if my desire for my best friend was just because my girlfriend wasn't putting out.

I was embarrassed to admit that recently I'd fantasized about having sex with Coop when I jacked off, and my fantasies were very confusing. On one hand I had Jennifer. On the other hand, I was confused about why I imagined being with Cooper when I masturbated.

But the craziest development was that I envisioned a future with him, not with the girl I claimed to love. My secret feelings for Cooper were driving me insane and I didn't know how to face the truth. I loved Cooper, but that was because we were like brothers, right? My feelings for my best friend were normal, weren't they? I wasn't so sure anymore.

He'd admitted how he felt about me a coupla times and even though his confession made me happy, I didn't know what to do with the information. Part of me wanted to experiment sexually. Maybe I would like it with Coop. But then again, I was still attracted to Jennifer. Being with her was an easier choice for me, but the thought that Cooper might find another guy tore me up inside.

CHAPTER TWENTY: Mike

Day One After Mom's Death

The neighbors stood silently on the sidewalks when the hearse pulled away with Mom's body. They'd known she was gravely ill because my mother kept no secrets about her health situation. *"I don't want them to find out after. That'd be too upsetting,"* she'd said. *"Besides, I've known these wonderful people for years. I hope to see them all again,"* she'd added.

The doorbell rang nonstop all day as mourners dropped by with casseroles and baskets of marigolds. Even they knew about Mom's obsession with the stinky flower.

"I'll fly there right now if you need me," Brandt had offered. *"I mean it, Mike. Right this second. Just say the word."*

A couple of coworkers emailed their condolences. The office secretary even sent flowers. The house was filling up with reminders that I didn't have a mother anymore. This time felt different from when Dad died. Mom ran point on that one despite being the surviving spouse. I didn't worry about what to say. Mom handled all of that. Who will handle my grief from now on?

Day Two

If my mother was anything, she was organized. The safe held exact instructions on what to do after she died. She even noted that the freezer in the garage was full of meat and what to do if I didn't stay in town. And of course, she wanted everything in the house donated if I decided to sell.

There was a sealed box with a letter taped to the top. *Open on the seventh day* was handwritten on the envelope. I picked up the small container and found it to be lighter than I had anticipated. I shook the box gently and felt something solid moving against each side.

I had a few days to keep a promise or to chalk everything up to the musings of a spiritual creature. I closed my eyes and tried to visualize my mother. It was only day two and I was desperate to be able to recall her face upon request.

Day Three

"Are you sure, Mike?" Brad McPherson asked. "I sold your folks the plots so they could be side by side." Brad and I had gone to school together. His father owned one of two funeral homes in town. "The extra large headstone was designed for both of them," he reminded me.

"She changed her mind, Brad. Cremation only and then please deliver her remains to me," I stated, a bit harsher than needed.

"It'll be hard to sell the other plot," he pushed. "I'm not sure we can refund any unused final care expenses."

"You think I give a fuck about a refund?" I hissed.

Day Four

On day four I couldn't control my anger. I'd been sad for the first three days as I tried to find comfort in the fact that Mom wasn't suffering any longer, but the bullshit offerings from guests that stopped by our house did little to quell my agony. How could I be happy about Mom's liberation from pain when I was currently buried in my own? I knew I was wrong to wish her here after the battle she waged, but I hadn't come to grips with her passing. I didn't have to, so fuck off people.

Day Five

"Nice of you to find the time to call, Jennifer," I stated, seething that my ex gave zero shits about me losing my other parent. "Finally had a break, did ya?"

"Don't be morose, Michael. I was in London on business."

"Phones don't work in London?" I inquired. "Never mind. What do you want besides this phony condolence call?"

"That's rude, Michael," she stated before continuing to the real purpose of her call. "I'm calling about the investment account at Fidelity," she revealed. "As you know, even though it's a joint account, I contributed most of the funds."

"Send me the form to sign." Click.

Day Six

"We love you, Michael," Charla, Cooper's mother, spoke on the other end of the call. "Oh, honey, I wish we were still across the street from you," she added. "I just want to hold you right now."

"Thank you, Charla," I said, choking up at the first genuine words of comfort I've received. "I wish you were here too, but I understand. As it turns out, Mom didn't want a funeral so there's no reason to come back."

"Roger and I would if you need us, honey. Just say the word."

"I miss him," I said softly. I knew she'd understand who I meant. "He always knew how to get me through stuff like this." It felt odd to revert to my boyhood when I spoke to Cooper's Mom, but she had that effect on me. She was like a second mother.

"Funny you thought of our Cooper," she began. "He's been on our minds so much lately. Maybe losing Kathleen and all the memories of our life there have caused us to think about him, but we feel his presence lately."

"Me too," I admitted. "He was my everything." I was shocked the words came out the way they did.

"We know that, Mike. You were his."

After more small talk and the exchange of *I love yous* we ended the call. Cooper's parents knew their son was gay and always supported him. I believe her comment of *'you were his'* was her way of saying they knew how Cooper had felt about me.

I wanted–no *I needed* another chance with Cooper, but was I willing to step into Mom's fantasy world? Could I suspend a lifelong belief that strange occurrences and unexplained phenomena were people's ways of wishing there were outside forces that might be real? Mom had always encouraged me to open my mind. Could I?

According to Mom and Druzella's *out-there* plan, I had one day left. Day seven at midnight. The clock was ticking and I had a decision to make. Perhaps I should open the box in the safe and see what lies within. If there were assurances that the potion or concoction inside wouldn't truly harm me, why not humor my mother? After all, I had promised.

CHAPTER TWENTY-ONE: Mike

I t was Sunday. The seventh day since Mom died and the last opportunity to follow her instructions. I still hadn't opened the contents of the mystery box. The clock was ticking and I had to decide. Glancing at my watch, I noted that I had little time left to make the strangest decision I'd ever been faced with. I still wasn't convinced that I could do this.

I'd moved back upstairs to my bedroom and replaced the original furniture in Mom and Dad's bedroom after the rental company picked up the hospital bed. Dragging the mattress and box spring for a king bed by myself was no easy feat. The headboard and rails had been stored against the wall of their bedroom so thankfully those parts didn't need carrying in from the garage.

I was surprised at how easily I recalled where Mom had kept her knick-knacks and how she displayed them. The only change I'd made was that I left their picture from the hallway on the dresser where we'd left it the week before. Picking the frame up, I examined the photo closely for any signs of the halo flare we'd spotted around Mom's head. There was none. The background was the same cloudy day I remembered from when I took the picture over a decade ago. The mysterious light, like my mother's presence, had vanished. The discovery did nothing to encourage me to follow through with Mom's request.

Mom had a comforter on their bed that matched the wallpaper behind the headboard. Broad green banana leaves that were similar to those in Blanche Devereaux's bedroom on *The Golden Girls* were everywhere. The comforter set had all the matching pillow shams and decorative pillows. The print was ghastly and if I decided to keep my childhood home, they'd be the first items to go.

The possibility of a move to Idaho Falls had occupied my mind since I'd returned home weeks ago. Why not? I could live anywhere while working remotely and since I was closing in on a divorce, I had the opportunity to come home. But the sad reality was that I had no one left in Idaho except a grandfather who didn't recognize me.

The mortgage was paid in full thanks to Dad's life insurance payout eleven years ago, and I had a couple of hundred thousand from Mom's policy due to me whenever I sent them the death certificate. The thought of financially benefiting from her death did not sit well with me, but I figured I could give most of the money to several of Mom's favorite charities. Like everything in her will, she had a detailed list of the ones she supported. The list was her way of saying, *"In case you're uncomfortable with the money. . ."*

I tried busying myself while I paced around the house. Spending twenty minutes in the hall adjusting and leveling pictures on the wall of family history, but the pending time of no return was marching closer as I procrastinated on the decision. I emptied the dishwasher of dishes from the last few days. Dishes Mom would never use again. Everything I touched, everything I held in my hands were reminders of my childhood. Souvenirs from family vacations, furniture Mom had picked out when I was a ninth grader. From the rugs to the wall art, everything had her handprints on them. If I did stay here, could I live in a museum of my past?

I wandered upstairs and to my bedroom. Mom had never redecorated my room after I'd left for college in Seattle. Even now, memories from high school were everywhere. Stuffed animals given to me by Jennifer, trophies from sports, old Sports Illustrated magazines, and a free calendar from 2013 that was still on the wall by my desk was open to August. I'd never been able to touch the calendar after Cooper had drowned, and I still refused to take it down.

The poster of Tom Brady still bore the darts Cooper and I had thrown at it for years. We were Seahawk fans because of how close we were to Seattle,

EVERYDAY IS LIKE SUNDAY

and nothing had delighted us more than winning a Superbowl and hating Brady. The two darts that lodged perfectly in his eyeballs still remained from the last time Coop and I had taken aim. After two bullseye hits, we never touched the darts again.

My cell phone buzzed with a text. Brandt's name illuminated the screen so I picked it up.

Brandt: Thinking of you and hoping you're okay.

Me: The reality is starting to sink in, buddy, but thank u for reaching out.

I watched as the bubbles signaled he was typing a response.

Brandt: Do you need anything? A shoulder? A kind voice?

Me: Can I call?

Brandt: Of course.

I'd only known Brandt for a couple of years but after revealing my dilemma about Cooper and the letter he'd left, Brandt had proven to be a good listener. I'd told him my entire history that night at the bar after Jennifer and I split, and he didn't judge the hesitancy I had regarding my sexual status. He offered to support whatever decisions I made, even if I chose to remain in a place where I'd be questioning my sexuality forever. He'd been fair and unbiased with his opinions. Of course, he'd encouraged me to be open to the possibility that I may be gay, but he didn't insist I was. He'd been a good friend that night at the bar and I trusted him. Perhaps he could shed light on the crazy predicament I'd found myself in.

He picked up after the first ring. "Hey, my friend. How are you?"

"Getting there," I answered. "I'm not sure if I'm accepting her death because I knew Mom was so sick or if the fact that I'm all alone now hasn't hit me yet."

"You're not alone, buddy. You've got me," he reassured. "But I understand. Well, maybe not completely since I still have both of my parents," he added.

I decided to rip the Band-Aid off immediately. "Do you have time to listen to another story?" I asked. "Warning though. This one is weird as fuck."

Brandt laughed on the other end. "I love weird, dude. Bring it on."

"You sure?" I questioned. "My tale will force you to question reality."

I stared at the ceiling of my bedroom while resting on the bed. Dozens of small discolored circular spots from when Cooper and I would lie on the bed and toss a rubber ball up at the ceiling dotted the white surface. I loved lying side by side talking, throwing and catching the ball while sharing our day with each other.

Brandt's response brought me back to reality.

"That sounds like a good thing because I'm sitting here questioning why I'm home on a Saturday evening with no plans for a date or a casual hook up," he complained. "Now that's a fucked up story. So hit me with yours, dude."

I'd already told him about my childhood with a mother who believed in the afterlife and spiritual journeys so he knew the backstory. "Remember when I mentioned that my mother claimed she was connected to my friend Cooper and that she had premonitions that he was still present in her life?"

"Yep. Hard to forget something like that," he answered. "And I told you I had an aunt that could do the same shit. My family ostracized her, but I believed that woman had connections. She knew shit, man; and I'll never question her."

"Well, about that," I began.

I proceeded to tell Brandt the entire story about Mom's hairbrained idea: the book on parallel universes, her medium, Druzella, and the cat I kept seeing. I told him about the seven day wait, not burying Mom in the plot next to Dad, the halo ring in the picture, flickering lights, the entire list of unexplainable events. He made small noises as I told my story by adding a *hmmm* or a slight gasp to let me know he was fully engaged. I finally told him about the box and the instructions she'd given to me, but how I still hadn't opened it.

"I have less than six hours to shit or get off the pot," I said, waiting for a response. There was complete silence for ten or fifteen seconds. "You still there?" I whispered, thinking I may have finally convinced him I was one fucked up acquaintance.

"I say you fucking do it," he urged. "Oh yeah, dude. You abso-fucking-lutely do that shit."

"Am I crazy?" I questioned. "Was my mother?"

"Yeah, probably on both counts, but you also don't fuck with the universe, man. I believe in that parallel shit. That stuff is real."

"So you'd follow the instructions?" I asked.

"As long as you know that potion your mom conjured up with her psychic friend is safe, I would."

"She said the powder is made from all-natural plant based ingredients. I trust my mom on that," I stated. "So, you'd do it?"

"Hell yeah!" he declared. "Without a doubt." Two seconds went by before he added, "Do you think you'll know if you're in the other universe? Oh shit. Will I still know you in this one?" He was dead serious.

"I never thought about that," I admitted. "That would suck, right?"

"I'll miss you, dude, but I still say go for it," he said. "And just in case nothing happens, we'll still have one hell of a story, won't we?"

"I'm desperate for even the slimmest chance she knew what she was talking about," I confessed. "I think I'm willing to do almost anything for a chance to see him again. I'm crazy, right?"

"Maybe you are, maybe you aren't," he began. "But what if she's right and you get that second chance?"

Perhaps Brandt went along with me because he felt I was grieving. He could have been an asshole and told me I'd lost my mind, but he wasn't. I was grasping for straws and encouragement.

"I'm going to open the box," I whispered. "I am actually going to try."

"Good for you, and if I don't get a text from you tomorrow, I'll know it worked," he said, without any sarcasm or judgment. "Holy shit, dude. What if it fucking works?" he added.

I couldn't believe I said what I said next. "If you don't get the text, then it worked. Wait a second," I said, pausing to think about the possibilities. "Or if you get a text but it isn't about this, then it worked. Is that how it would go in a parallel universe?" I asked.

"I don't know, man. Will you even remember your life here?"

His question scared me. Do I get to keep my memories? "I have no idea. It's not like I've done this before."

"Maybe you should try and send yourself a message so you know what's going on? Wait, I've got an idea," Brandt continued. "You're a computer geek, right?"

"I'd like to think I'm not an actual geek, but yeah, go on."

"Do you remember your email address when you were a teenager?" he asked.

"Yes, of course. I used a goofy name that Cooper and I made up for one another."

"Get this, dude. I know its fucking nuts but listen. What if you sent yourself an email to that address from your current address?" he suggested.

"That won't work because of the time differential. We can't email the past . . . I . . . don't . . . think," I answered, my mind reeling.

"Could you manipulate the internal time on your computer? Maybe convince it that you're emailing from before a particular date?" he asked. "You write code, buddy. It has to be possible."

"Who the fuck knows but I could try," I said. "To my knowledge, maybe it's been tried, but no one has gone back to receive an email from the future, have they?" I asked.

"Oh and wait a second," he urged, full of excitement at a possible new idea. "You need the email to include a picture of you holding a newspaper with today's date or some kind of proof."

"Jesus, Brandt. You're practically a wizard at time travel," I stated.

"I saw *Back To The Future*, dude. I took notes and shit," he bragged, laughing at our sixth-grade-boy plotting. "And should I bring this shit up to the Mike that remains in my world?" he asked.

"He might think you're nuts," I responded.

We discussed the craziness of the conversation but he encouraged me not to chicken out. "A promise is a promise, Mike, and this promise was made to your mom," he'd concluded right before we ended the call.

The idea about an email to the past with some kind of proof fascinated me. Was it possible? Was any of this crazy shit possible?

I was definitely going to try.

CHAPTER TWENTY-TWO: Mike

Eleven Years Ago

A round midnight, the sound of a car parking across the street pulled me from my bed. I'd been lying in the dark since ten thirty, waiting for Cooper to get home. He'd texted that since Jen and I were on a date that he was going to the drive-in with Mike Hastings. Jen canceled because of a sore throat but I didn't tell him that so he went to see The Avengers without me. We'd talked about going together since we both loved action films, but he'd chosen to go with Hastings because I'd had plans.

I hid off to the side of my open window so I could watch them. I didn't like the thought of Cooper kissing Hastings but it was his right to be happy like I was with Jen. Just moments after arriving, Cooper hopped out and Hastings roared off in his parents' Honda Civic. Cooper stood under the streetlamp watching the car disappear around the corner with his shoulders slumped in sadness.

I held my cell phone flashlight under my face and waved at him from my bedroom window. He touched his chest and then pointed at me, asking permission to come over so I nodded and waited. I heard Mom and him talking at the foot of the stairs. She wasn't surprised to see Coop in our house at odd hours of the night. The way he trudged up the stairs told me that he wasn't in good spirits.

"Hey, buddy," I greeted after he closed the door behind him. "How was the movie?"

"Movie was okay. Company not so much," he admitted. Cooper kicked his sneakers off, and then pulled off his T-shirt and jeans before rolling over me to his spot closer to the wall. We had our sleeping positions ever since he'd been spooked *when we were eleven years old and he asked me to sleep closer to the door. Even then I'd been his protector.*

I had a million questions about Hastings, but waited for him to spill the beans. We lay in silence until he rolled over to face me and rested his hand on my chest.

"I hate being gay," he muttered, snuggling closer to me even though it was hot for April. "Guys are mean sometimes."

His announcement got my shackles up because I was concerned that Hastings had hurt him. "Did Hastings lay a hand on you?" I asked. "I swear I'll . . ."

Cooper slid his hand to my mouth and shushed me. "Calm down, Mikey. Hastings didn't lay a hand on me. I'd be so lucky."

"Then what?" I grilled, ready to defend my best friend. "Did he call you names?"

"I thought he liked me that way," Cooper said. "You know what I mean, like he asked me to the drive-in and stuff. What straight guy goes to a drive-in with another boy?" he asked. "Well, other than you," he added, laughing.

"He tell you he didn't like you?" I asked. "Did you ask him if he did?"

"He said he liked me as a friend. He friendzoned me ten minutes into the movie."

"That's not so bad, right?" I asked. "He seems cool enough to have as a friend and shit." I said the words but didn't mean them. I preferred they weren't friends and had felt shitty ever since the admission had crossed my mind. I didn't have exclusive rights to Cooper's friendship but still didn't want him having such a stud as a friend. I couldn't explain my jealousy. What if he liked Cooper and took him away from me?

"It's what he said after he friendzoned me," Cooper said quietly. I waited for him to explain further but he didn't continue.

"What happened, buddy?" I whispered. "No judgment."

Cooper let out a long sigh. "He asked me to suck his dick. He said we could be friends and on the down low. He said he wouldn't do stuff to me but I could suck him off and he wouldn't tell anyone."

"Jesus," I muttered.

"And when I said no he grabbed my hand and pressed it against his crotch. 'See what you do to me,' he said."

I gently squeezed Cooper's hand that was on my chest. "Asshole," I stated. "I'll kick his ass for you."

Cooper continued, "Then he said he thought all gays wanted to suck straight guys' dicks and he was totally fine if I blew him a few times a week until he got a girlfriend. Maybe even after in case she didn't suck dick," Cooper explained. "He even asked if I was blowing you."

I pushed Cooper's hand from my chest and leaped out of bed. "What a fucking creep!" I raged. "Fucking asshole! I will fuck him up."

"He didn't actually like me as a boyfriend like I'd hoped he did," Cooper said, biting his lower lip. "And I would have sucked his dick if he had."

"The fuck you would've," I raged further. "He doesn't deserve you, Coop. What a fuckwad." I sat on the edge of my bed facing away from Cooper. I was angry and sad that my best friend was hurting. "But he didn't hurt you, right? Not physically or anything?" I asked, turning to face him.

Cooper slid a hand across the bed toward mine, forcing his fingers underneath mine. "No, he didn't," he answered. "But, Mikey, it just sucks that I'm good enough to suck his dick but not good enough to kiss and stuff."

"Yes, you are," I whispered. "I think you are anyway."

"I wished I had a boyfriend like you, Mikey. A guy that makes me feel the way I feel when I'm around you," he said. "I want to be safe and cared for by a guy that's handsome like you."

"You will, Coop."

He pulled me back on the bed and played with my hair while my head rested on his bare stomach. It was a typical gesture between us that I didn't recognize was something I needed until he was holding me. I listened, defended, and made it clear I was there for him, then he always showed me what I meant to him by comforting me back.

"I really liked him," he admitted.

"I know you did, buddy. I'm sorry it didn't go your way this time," I said, even though my words were untrue.

I wished nothing but the best for Cooper, but secretly I was pleased that Mike Hastings wasn't the guy for him. The thought of a guy like Hastings who was all muscular and good looking being with Coop didn't sit well with me. I knew I was being unfair, but I wanted Cooper all to myself.

Perhaps I wasn't a good friend.

CHAPTER TWENTY-THREE: Mike

T he small box sat on the kitchen island, reminding me that I had three hours to make a decision. I paced back and forth in the kitchen, stepping through the open French doors and staring at the dark backyard while I pondered my sanity.

"She was losing it," I whispered, turning to face the kitchen. I'd cleaned the place top to bottom. I'd wanted the house to be perfectly clean in case I went to the other side and if there was a replacement who would want to sell. "I'm not doing this," I muttered, still fighting a desire to keep my sanity intact.

Again I turned and stared into the yard, the darkness offering no argument to support why I should do as I'd promised. Mom would never know either way. I wanted to call Brandt again and ask him if he still thought I should go through with mom's crazy plan, but he texted an hour ago encouraging me to keep my promise and reminded me to take a picture for proof.

I walked to the island and stared at the envelope on the box. Mom's handwriting said to read before opening the box. I held the envelope in my hand, my heart racing.

She was crazy.

I was crazy.

Her idea was fantastically crazy.

You can't do this, I heard my inner voice speak. *And you don't have to, Mike. She's gone.*

I felt a chill run up my spine like I was being watched by someone, the unnerving feeling causing me to jerk around. The black cat was sitting in the open doorway watching me intently, judging me. I should have jumped out of my skin with fright but I didn't. The animal kept studying me without moving a single hair on its body.

I set the envelope down and walked to the sink for some water, pretending that I wasn't surprised by the strange beast. With my back to the feline, I bent over and took a long drink directly from the faucet. I didn't want to dirty a glass after all the work I just did. When I turned back toward the French doors, the cat was walking past me toward the hallway. I followed the animal down the hall and into Mom's bedroom. The cat jumped onto the dresser and sat beside the picture of Mom and Dad on the Oregon coast; the one where Mom had the mysterious halo of light around her head.

I stepped closer to the photo carefully, aware that the cat might leap off the dresser. I jumped back, almost tripping on the throw rug near the foot of the bed. "What the . . .?" My pulse quickened and I felt as if I might pass out. "No fucking way."

When I stepped forward again, the cat jumped off the dresser and waited at the doorway. I picked up the photo and studied the picture. Both Mom and Dad's heads were surrounded by circles of light. The halos were as real as the Pacific Ocean behind them.

I stared at my reflection in the mirror above the dresser and then slowly turned the picture to face it. There were no halos in the reflection of the picture, but there was one around my own head. "Jesus Christ!" I yelped, dropping the frame on the dresser top.

The cat was gone when I backed out of the room, feeling like a million little spiders were crawling all over me. I was freaking out and struggling to catch my breath.

I was losing my marbles. The self-diagnosis would be hereditary lunacy.

There was no way that what I just saw could be real. But hadn't the cat led me to the bedroom? The mystical creature somehow knew. Where was the little fucker now? I rushed down the hall and turned the corner to the kitchen.

The cat sat on the kitchen island next to the small box and the envelope. "For fuck's sake, I'm gonna," I said.

The sleek-coated creature leapt from the island and sauntered out the French doors then stopped next to a planter full of marigolds.

"I will," I insisted.

The feline disappeared into the darkness.

I took cautious steps toward the envelope. I will keep my promise.

The envelope held the final letter from Mom. She told me that the letter was the step-by-step instructions and to keep an open mind. I carefully read it:

My Dearest Son,

So, you've opened the letter. That's a good sign that you will let your mother try her best to give her child one final gift: the gift of love. I've always understood that Cooper held your heart. To me, his death extinguished your zest for life. I want to correct the injustice of his premature death because a mother's love knows no boundaries, even those between universes.

I believe that I can remedy that pain and find you the one resolution that will offer you an opportunity to truly live and love again. Of course, I understand that my idea seems impossible, but when a person fortifies love with sincere desire, all things are possible. Why not take the risk and humor me? I want to see you happy and living life again. So, maybe I am crazy, but in our billions of universes, crazier things have occurred, so why not this?

The following instructions are direct and simple—the exact way that your scientific mind works. Take the chance. Suspend reality for once and dream with me.

I love you to infinity and maybe even further,

Mom

1 – Take the vial in your bedroom before midnight on the seventh day, but not a minute past.

2 – Remove the calendar from your bedroom wall that is still open to August 2013.

3 – Choose a month in the calendar that's at least thirty days to six months before the day of Cooper's death, and then hang the calendar where it was with the month you chose displayed.

4 – Mix the contents of the vial with water and place it on your nightstand.

5 – Strip off all of your clothes and lie on your bed.

6 – There is a mild, all-natural sedative in the ingredients.

7 – This will only work if you can truly convince yourself that you want this. You have to want to see Cooper again. The desire must come from the deepest part of your heart. You must envision being with him again in a universe where he is alive.

8 – Drink the potion.

9 – If you wake up the next day and nothing has happened, thank you for trying and trusting my wish for you. If this works, have an amazing journey. I loved you in this universe and will always be with you no matter where you dwell. Look for me, son. You'll know.

The time was 10:15. An hour and forty-five minutes to go. Now that I knew Mom expected to send me to a time before Cooper drowned, it was time to send an email and then to open the small box.

CHAPTER TWENTY-FOUR: Mike

After reading Mom's instructions, I found my old laptop hidden at the bottom of my closet. After dusting it off and turning the old machine on, I changed the date and time to July 1, 2013. I signed into my email and attached a photo of me holding a copy of The Post Register, the local newspaper in Idaho Falls. I'd circled the date and held it near my face. If Mom's concoction could propel me to the past of a different universe, then couldn't my email do the same?

I tilted the tiny box from side to side several times and listened to the familiar thuds. I assumed it was the small vial mentioned in Mom's note. After opening the box, I saw a glass ampoule next to a small royal-blue sack with gold tassels that were tied in a loose knot. I held the miniature bottle up to the light and saw finely ground particles. I figured the small bits were marigold. Mom didn't leave a list of the other ingredients of the potion.

I hadn't expected the silk bag. Loosening the knot, I opened the small sack and dumped the contents onto my palm. A recognized the silver necklace looped through a ring. The piece of jewelry was a ring that Cooper and I had given Mom on Mother's Day the year after Dad passed. The three stones were ruby, the birthstones for Mom, Cooper, and me since all of us were born under the sign of Cancer. Cooper and I had gifted Mom the ring to symbolize our connection and love for our shared mother. A fact I couldn't dispute as they had always been close.

I peeked inside the bag and retrieved a piece of paper that simply read: *wear the connection.* An epiphany washed over me. *She knows what she's doing.*

I poured the vial's contents into the glass of water and stirred the mixture until it dissolved before bringing the glass to my nose for a quick whiff. "Shit," I muttered. I dared another smell. "I can't swallow this swill," I protested to the empty room. The digital alarm clock read 11:57. I had to drink it, and fast.

I stared around the room, double checking the note to make sure I didn't miss anything. "The calendar. Shit," I gasped before leaping across the room. *Not more than six months but at least thirty days before.* I should have given the time frame more thought but had forgotten about the instruction. I leafed through the old calendar, thinking of the email I'd sent to July, letting my thumb make the decision when it landed between the pages for June 2013, two months before he drowned. I quickly hung the calendar on the nail then hustled back to the nightstand.

The mixture was murky and still smelled like death thanks to the marigolds; an odd thought considering the desired goal of the concoction.

"You have to truly want it," she'd said from her hospital bed. *"Envision a life with Cooper in a world where you both are."* Mom's words haunted my mind.

I wanted to believe. I wanted to live in a world with Cooper again. I had to.

"Envision living in a world with him again," I whispered, reaching for the glass. I pinched my nose closed and chugged the vile liquid, struggling to keep the lukewarm potion down.

11:59 P.M..

Several seconds passed.

Nothing. *Shit!*

I felt normal, if not a bit disappointed while sitting on my bed in my birthday suit. I shifted on to my bed and relaxed with my head on my pillow, the necklace wrapped around my wrist while I clutched the ring.

The numbing sensation began simultaneously in my feet and at the top of my head as it raced from both ends toward my center.

I wanted to scream but it was too late.

"You have to want it to happen. You have to believe. Envision a world with Cooper in it."

My mind fixated on Mom's voice that invaded my mind in a soothing tone. I felt her hand in mine as my father appeared in what seemed like a tunnel in the distance, smiling and waving.

My thoughts drifted to the hole in my heart. A void I had lived with for a decade since Cooper's death. Focusing on my best friend, I felt like the hole had been ripped open, manifesting as physical pain that made me cry out. The memories of losing him swept in like ocean waves crashing against the shore during a winter's storm, reminding me of how I couldn't live without him for even one more moment.

And then, there he was.

Cooper's smiling face hovered above me when his hand covered the hole in my heart.

"Are you real?" I whispered.

"Are you?" he answered, his mouth not moving.

I imagined waking up on a Sunday morning, wondering if Cooper was downstairs with Mom and Dad yet. I'd wait until he got bored so he'd come upstairs and flop on the bed with me, complaining he was hungry so I needed to get my butt outta bed. He never used words like ass. It wasn't his style. He'd slide under my arm, almost like a snuggle session but not quite.

"I love you," I admitted.

An impossibly loving embrace pulled me out to sea and I relaxed as Cooper and I planned another Sunday. His favorite day of the week.

CHAPTER TWENTY-FIVE: Cooper

Maybe Ten Years Ago

"Good morning, Mrs. H.," I said, after I burst through the back door of the Hill residence. I motioned up the staircase just off the kitchen. "Still sleeping?"

"He is," she confirmed. "And as always, impeccable timing on your part, young man. Breakfast is almost ready."

"Of course it is. Today's Sunday. Besides, I smelled the bacon from across the street."

"Let's give Mikey a bit more rest. He worked late last night," she responded.

That didn't work for me. "No way. He promised me we'd go to the mall to meet a friend."

"Still can't talk your folks into a car?" she teased.

"No. They're still sticking to the idea that once Mikey has one, I can have one."

Mrs. H. opened the oven and removed homemade muffins. She dropped the hot tin suddenly. "Ouch," she uttered. "That wasn't smart."

I rushed to her side and looked at her hand. Two fingertips were red from the burn so I pulled her toward the sink and ran cold water over them. "Under this," I encouraged. We stood at the sink for several seconds, me still holding her hand under the cool liquid.

She fixed her eyes on me. "I shouldn't admit this, son, but I tell Mikey the same thing about his potential car."

My eyes widened when I put two and two together.

She was nodding and grinning. "Oopsie," she giggled. Mikey's mother had the best laugh. More of a girlish giggle really. It fit her quirky personality.

Mrs. H. had the best disposition in my opinion. She was a constant brightness in a world that always tried to dim people. I told Mikey all the time that he was lucky he had a mom like her. Don't get me wrong, mine was awesome too, but Mikey's was different. She always believed something great was about to happen and her enthusiasm was contagious.

"You're telling *me* . . . that . . . ," I began, sensing a conspiracy.

She was nodding again.

"This whole time our parents conspired against us?"

"Don't tell Charla I caved," she begged. "I broke the mom code."

"You're in big trouble," I ribbed, removing her hand from under the water and checking the redness. "Looks better. Feel okay?" I asked.

Mrs. H. gazed at me with glistening eyes. "You're always so sweet, kiddo. Always a ray of sunshine."

I dried her hand with a hand towel.

"Can I admit something to you?" she inquired. "To explain why we're dodging the car purchase?"

"There's an actual good reason, huh?" I quipped. "Your two handsome boys being carless, isn't that enough?"

"Unfortunately, yes," she said, looking disappointed in what she was about to share. "I can't afford one since Mike's dad died, son."

Her usual joyful face was crestfallen. It was rare for Mikey's mom to show negative emotions. If she thought *I* was a ray of sunshine, *she* was the sun itself.

"And let me guess, Mom and Dad don't want me to have something Mikey doesn't have?" I surmised.

Mrs. H. squeezed my hand and nodded.

"Good," I stated. "Me neither."

"So, this can be our little secret?"

I pretended to lock my mouth and throw the key over my shoulder. "Mikey and I don't keep secrets," I reminded her. "But for you, Mrs. H., anything."

She held the sides of my head and kissed my forehead. "I love you," she cooed.

"Ditto," I responded. "Now I'm waking him up. I'm hungry."

She glanced at her watch. "It's nearly ten. Go ahead."

It took me exactly four seconds to take the fourteen steps to Mikey's bedroom. I burst through the door and was about to pounce on the bed and annoy him, but he was already awake and sitting up.

I stood in the doorway and watched him stare straight ahead with glassy eyes. He was completely naked except for something shining in his hand. He seemed disoriented when he slowly gazed down at his hand, confusion contorting his features. I wondered if he'd awakened in a trance like one did after a hard sleep, and that he needed a moment.

"Mikey?" I quietly called so I wouldn't startle him.

He turned to me, his eyes staring blankly.

"You okay?" I asked.

He blinked before he focused on me, his brow furrowing like he didn't quite understand what was happening. "Are you real?" he asked before rubbing his eyes. He searched the room while his hands ran over his chest and arms. "Are Mom and Dad here?"

CHAPTER TWENTY-SIX: Mike

"What's with you?" Cooper asked. "Of course, I'm real, you dodo bird. I'm as real as your butt-naked self."

When Cooper stepped toward me, it suddenly dawned on me that I was on top of my bed naked in my same bedroom but it was daytime instead of midnight like it was only a moment ago. A moment ago, a day ago, I was unsure of how much time had passed. But with one big difference: Cooper stood before me.

I panicked as I looked around the room feverishly searching for something I could tether my reality to. *Was I . . . was I awake?*

Cooper grabbed the folded blanket at the foot of my bed and tossed it over my lower body. It was definitely Cooper or a version of Cooper, someone who looked exactly like Cooper. I pinched my arm and closed my eyes for a second. *Jesus Christ. She fucking did it. She actually fucking did it. This cannot be real.*

"What's wrong, Mikey? You look weird," he said, moving his hand to my forehead to test my temperature. Typical Cooper. Always taking care of me. "You're not warmer than usual," he noted.

"I'm . . . I'm fine," I whispered hoarsely, clearing my throat. "I guess I wasn't expecting you."

"It's Sunday, silly butt. Where else would I be?"

Dodo bird, silly butt? Yep, this was definitely Coop. "Yeah, I mumbled. "Where else would you be?"

"You want me to get your mom?" he asked, his hand reaching for mine gently. I'd forgotten how loving and attentive Cooper was. His love for me was as clear as a summer's day. "Why do you have this?" he asked, lifting my hand higher.

I diverted my eyes to my hand and focused on my mother's ring. "I . . . I . . . well," I stuttered.

He removed the necklace from my hand and the silver chain and ring sparkled in the morning sunlight when he dangled them between us. "Did you add this chain?" he asked. "Did I forget her birthday or something?"

"That's not until July," I whispered, staring into his sweet eyes and realizing just how beautiful he was. "Just like ours," I added. My God, he was beautiful.

"Then why?" he asked, holding the ring and staring at me. "Does she know you have it?"

"I bought the necklace," I said, terrified of what I could and couldn't say in my current predicament. *This was one hell of a dream.* "I was going to tell you," I defended. "I figured Mom would like to use a necklace so she doesn't lose the ring when she's cooking and stuff. You know her, taking things off and losing stuff," I added.

Cooper looked at me and then back to the necklace. "Hmm," he mumbled. "I bet she would too. Wanna go half-sies?" he asked.

He dropped the necklace and ring into my open hand and stepped to my dresser, pulling out a pair of boxers and tossing them at me.

"Thanks," I said, unsure of my next move. I slid the boxers under the blanket and slid them on.

His eyes narrowed. "Why'd you do that? You're acting goofy, Mikey," he stated, approaching me again and sitting next to me on the edge of the bed. "I've seen your wiener a bazillion times."

"I was surprised is all, I guess."

"Everything okay with you and Jennifer?"

Jennifer existed here too?

"Uhm, yeah," I said. "I'm just tired."

Cooper studied me carefully, suspicious about something. "Are you hiding something from me?"

"No," I said, feeling closer to him than ever before. Our connection felt more intimate, like what we shared was real and important. I hadn't noticed the feeling before. How had I missed the sensation he gave me? "I wouldn't do that."

He stood up. "Okay then, mister. I'll meet you downstairs. Hurry your butt up too." He headed for the door but stopped before exiting the room, turning back to me. "And you're sure you're okay?" he asked again.

I nodded, holding back tears of joy. "I'm fine, Coop," I whispered. "Thank you for caring about me."

"Anything for my bestie," he said with a wide grin on his beautiful face. "Now hurry up."

He stepped out, gently bringing the door to an almost shut position.

How had I not known how I felt about him all those years? How was it possible that I didn't understand my desire for him? He was my everything back then and I never understood. And here I was. Back then. Back here.

CHAPTER TWENTY-SEVEN: Cooper

I paused at the top of the stairs, turning back to Mikey's room. Something wasn't right. I wasn't an expert on much but I knew my best friend inside and out. Mikey was my person. We shared a connection unlike any I'd witnessed in my nearly eighteen years. Something was off and I'd get him to spill the beans eventually. I shrugged and exhaled, then headed down the stairs, two at a time.

"One of you boys is going to slip and fall one of these days," Mrs. H. said. "Be careful on those stairs, Cooper."

"Yes, ma'am," I replied, scooting into one of the four chairs. The missing place setting wasn't lost on me. I missed Mikey's dad too. It hadn't gotten past me that he'd just asked if his dad was here. He must've had a bad dream. Mr. H. was the best father and Mikey had been a mess right after he died. His death was less than a year ago and Mikey seemed to be in a better place, but maybe he was still grieving. I'd ask him later.

"You wake him?" she asked, setting a plate of scrambled eggs next to a two-pound pile of bacon.

"I think he might be sick," I said. "But his forehead was cool," I added nonchalantly, like I was a medical expert and chief of all things Mike Hill.

"Were his eyes red?" she asked with her back to me while she put a frying pan into the sink when she referred to Mikey's allergies.

"Nope. All clear," I replied. "No sniffles either. Spring is pretty much gone so we're clear of the pollen," I added, giving both a seasonal update and an allergy status.

Mrs. H. turned around and looked at me. Leaning back against the sink she shook her head from side to side. "You are really something, Cooper." She brushed a crumb from her floral blouse and then moved to my side of the table. She leaned over my shoulder and wrapped me in her arms. Her smell matched her blouse, floral. "He loves you just as much, Cooper," she whispered in my ear.

"You sure?" I asked, needing confirmation.

"I'm positive. A mom knows these things about her son."

"Just not in the same way," I reminded her, squeezing her arms tightly. "Not like I wish he did anyway."

"Maybe not the same, son, but sometimes one doesn't understand everything about our choices early in life. Why don't we just continue loving him and let him find his way?" She stood and was rubbing my shoulders when we heard footsteps on the stairs. We both turned in unison.

Mikey smiled sheepishly at both of us. "Good morning," he said, heading for his usual spot across from where his dad normally sat, but he stopped halfway and went to his mom. He pulled her into his arms and hugged her. I could see Mrs. H's face from my angle and she looked taken aback for a second. Mikey pulled away and held her at a short distance. "You look pretty, Mom."

"You don't get any more bacon than I do," I quipped, wondering what was happening. Mikey and his mother were close, but I hadn't seen them hug in months. I stood and moved him out of the way before pulling Mrs. H. into a bear hug. "I love you just as much," I said, scrunching my face at Mikey as he watched us.

Mrs. H. pulled away and swatted her hands toward both of us. "Well, well, well. This is certainly a mother's dream come true. My two handsome boys showering me with their affection," she stated. "And you say I look pretty?" she asked. "You still don't get a car," she added, winking at me. "Now sit down and stuff your faces."

"I love you, Mom," Mikey said, pulling his chair out and sitting down, not taking his eyes off of his mother. "I mean it."

I watched his mother light up like a Christmas tree. He was sincere and his words were so pure. Mike had confidence that I envied and was heartbreakingly handsome in my eyes. A lot like his father, he was tall with broad shoulders, blonde with gold-tinted skin that would soon be bronze as summer was nearly here. We were about to turn eighteen and he was practically a man compared to me.

"You're filling out, Coop," he'd said last week when we showered at my place after a workout. *"I'm taller now but your dad is tall too, so you'll grow some more. You'll see, buddy,"* he'd added, squeezing my biceps and pulling me against him tightly even though we were naked. No wonder I was so crazy about him.

"Well, thank you, honey," Mrs. H. said, waking me from my memory of us showering and from falling deeper in love with my best friend. "And I love you too. And you too, Cooper," she added, handing me the bacon platter.

"What are you burning today, Mom?" Mikey asked her, motioning toward her ever-present incense. "I like this one," he added, smiling at her and dishing up some eggs onto my plate while I held the plate of bacon, questioning his newfound interest in Mrs. H's unique approach to the spirit world.

Mrs. H. raised an eyebrow and crossed her arms, looked at me and smiled before turning back to Mikey. "Honey, are we feeling okay this morning?"

"Yeah, honey," I teased. "Something doesn't seem right," I pointed out, nodding in agreement with his mom.

"You look pretty, and the incense is nice," he defended. "And I'm happy," he added.

Me and his mom looked at each other because we were two peas in a pod when it came to taking care of Mike. "He's happy," I mimicked.

"I heard," Mrs. H. added.

Mikey began laughing. His mood was contagious and we joined him. At first he appeared pleased, but his laughter suddenly turned into tears and weeping. He brought his hands to his face and leaned forward, crying harder until his mom stood up quickly and went to his side.

"Michael, honey?" she asked, trying to remove his hands from his face.

He gave in and leaned back in his chair, letting out a huge sigh when he caught his breath, his face a tear streaked mess.

I was stunned by his outburst. I was right. Something was wrong.

"What's wrong, honey," she asked, reaching for my napkin and dabbing his face.

He stared at me and then at his mom.

"Mikey?" I whispered. "What's up?"

He opened his mouth but words wouldn't come out. He took a drink of water and wiped his eyes, taking a moment. He let out a nervous laugh then cleared his throat. "I'm happy, is all," he said softly. He stared at the empty seat across from him. "But I miss Dad. I hoped he'd be here too."

Mrs. H. looked surprised by his statement. Mikey hadn't spoken much about Mr. H. since he'd died. "You hoped he'd be here?" she asked.

Mikey just kept staring at the vacant chair.

"Oh, honey, I wish he was here as well. Your father is with us in spirit though. I know he is and always will be, son."

Mikey reached for his mother's hand. "I know he is too, Mom. I really think he is."

"Thank you, son," she replied. I noticed her tilt her head slightly. She was as surprised as I was. Mikey didn't talk much about spirits, incense or any sort of mumbo-jumbo his mom believed in. He wasn't unkind about it, but he and his dad had had a running joke about the odd woman they shared a house with for as long as I could remember. He usually had a wisecrack whenever she brought up something he found a bit too out there.

"Sage, right?" he asked. "Dad liked that one, didn't he?"

"Yes. Yes, he did," she answered. "Everything okay, son?"

"It's perfect, Mom. Like every Sunday with you and Coop."

I wasn't convinced he was perfect though. Something about Mikey was different and I was hell bent on finding out what that was.

"How was work last night?" I asked.

He hesitated and looked toward his mom. "You know . . . busy-ish . . . type, sort of thing," he stated, unsure about his own words. "Nothing special really," he added, reaching for more bacon and smiling nervously at both of us.

"I didn't see you come home last night," I said. "Did I miss Jen dropping you off or did you stay overnight with her and then come home early this morning?"

"Hardly," Mrs. H. interjected. "There is no staying overnight at Jennifer's house. You boys are still seventeen and I make the rules."

"I walked home and used the backdoor," Mikey interrupted the lecture, ending the discussion about sleepovers at Jen's. "I forgot to wave at ya, Coop. Sorry, bro."

"Okay, yeah," I agreed, even though I knew he wasn't being truthful. I knew he was hiding something because Jen had texted me at half-past midnight looking for him.

Mikey yawned and stretched his arms high over his head, exposing his ripped abs and a happy trail I wanted to hike. I constantly had dirty thoughts about him even though I would never act on them. Mikey thought I was somewhat pure, old fashioned, and shy. Most of that was true, however I still had dirty and sexual thoughts about us all the time. Those thoughts conflicted with the guilt in my heart about my feelings because I also deeply loved him and wanted to tell him the truth.

The love that Mikey had shown me my entire life through how he took care of me and protected me had always been enough for me. I sometimes felt like I was in his shadow, but he always respected me and treated me as his equal even though he was better at practically everything. He was more popular but still made sure to always include me.

Sometimes I think he was better at loving as well. He was direct, honest and unmoved by people that questioned who we were to each other. In my opinion, his approach was a risk considering his popularity, but he never cared nor did he defend himself against the chatter. He'd once told me that what we shared was far more important than a bunch of bullshit chinwag. I think he'd heard his dad use the word chinwag. It was an odd choice, but definitely something Mr. H. would've busted out.

"Okay, all," he began and started to clear the table. "I'm gonna take a nap for a bit. Late night," he added.

I quickly stood and motioned for his mom to sit back down. "I got this, Mrs. H.," I said. "You relax and I'll clean up. Mikey, I'll be up in a few."

"Ummmm, I'm kinda tired, Coop."

"Ummmm, and I don't care," I replied. "Be up in five."

Mikey shrugged his shoulders and then headed to his mom's side of the table where he kissed the top of her head. "Thanks, Mom. Great meal. Next Sunday can we make Dad's fave?"

"Biscuits and gravy?" she asked, furrowing her brow in question.

He nodded.

"I've asked you a million times if you wanted biscuits and gravy, Michael."

"Yeah, I know, but I've been thinking about Dad quite a bit lately. Can we?"

"Well of course, honey," she answered.

"Do you remember that time I smushed his face into a plate of it?" Mikey asked out of the blue. "He was so angry." Mikey laughed out loud and made a show of wiping his eyes with his fingers and then his mouth like he was his father with a face covered in goo. "And . . . and . . . then . . . " he could barely continue due to his laughing. "And then Dad licked his lips and went . . . *mmmm,* before throwing a biscuit across the kitchen at me."

Mrs. H. teared up at the memory, smiling as the dam finally broke and cascaded down her cheeks. "What made you think of that, honey?" she asked.

"I dreamed about Dad last night, Mom. He was happy and waving at me."

Mrs. H. sat up straight, her mouth agape. "You did?" she asked. "And where was he?"

"I'm not sure, but definitely some place nice, I think. He waved like all was good," he said, smiling. "Seeing him was really nice."

"Thank you for sharing that with us, son."

With that, Mikey headed upstairs.

Mrs. H. and I turned and stared at each other, neither of us quite sure what we'd just witnessed.

CHAPTER TWENTY-EIGHT: Mike

I stared out of my window in wonderment. The street where I lived looked exactly the same. Literally everything was as I remembered. The decorations, the smells, the posters on my childhood bedroom walls, Mom's incense wafting up the staircase filled my brain with nostalgia and longing. I'd wondered whether Cooper would look or be the same. He was still seventeen. Apparently, I was too. On the outside. But I had a secret. I was twenty-seven on the inside.

Walking into the bathroom I leaned closer to the mirror above the sink. "Holy shit," I whispered, touching the skin around my eyes. "You're actually seventeen again." I widened and then relaxed my eyes again. Not a single crow's foot. I looked amazing.

Mom hadn't mentioned the possibility that I could land in another dimension and remember where I was from. Was I supposed to remember everything? But then again, I'd never read a firsthand account from anyone who had actually achieved interdimensional time travel, but if they existed I'm quite sure it'd involve more than drinking some marigold juice. Who exactly was my mother and where'd she get this gift? Who was Druzella for that matter? How on earth had those two loon-boon spirit heads come up with this trick?

Now that same mystical creature was downstairs acting like nothing out of the normal was happening. She didn't know. Should I tell her? If I did, would she believe me? Knowing the old Mom and now this Mom, she probably would. I blinked my eyes over and over again. This shit could not be real, but every time I opened them, the seventeen-year-old me was staring back from the mirror.

I questioned how the necklace with Mom's ring traveled with me. When I was downstairs eating breakfast I casually checked the kitchen for any evidence that adult Mike had been there. There was no wallet, car keys, or cell phone of his anywhere in the kitchen. The kitchen was similar to the one I'd been in a day ago except that the French doors weren't in yet. Mom had those installed two years ago in the future after wanting to invite her garden into her kitchen.

Mom looked amazing, especially compared to the last few months of her life. I wondered if the cancer was growing in her yet. I had wild thoughts like wishing I could have returned to an even earlier date and talked Dad out of going to work that day. My mind was in overdrive as I considered the consequences of being here. What could I affect? What should I change?

Suddenly the bathroom door burst open and Cooper stood in the doorway with his arms crossed. "Okay, mister. What the heck was all that about?" he asked, moving to my side while I returned his gaze in the mirror.

"What was *what* about?" I delayed, knowing full well what he meant.

"*Nice sage, Mom. Wasn't that Dad's favorite, Mom. You look pretty, Mom,*" he mimicked.

"Well, she did."

"I know that, Mikey, but clue me in next time we're going on an all-out schmoozefest. I want some credit too," he said. "Now tell me, what are we after?" He ran his hand across the back of my neck, smoothing down some fly-away hair along my neck line. "Let me trim your hetero hair," he stated, opening the top drawer for the hair trimmers.

"You still call it hetero hair?" I asked, forgetting that I needed to try and act like everything he said was normal.

"Of course I do, silly. Only straight guys like you allow bushy hair to grow along their necks. It's gross and you know I hate it."

Cooper rubbed against me, holding my hip while he buzzed along my neckline. He blew the falling hair, then swiped across my back. His touch sent fire ripping through my body. I'd forgotten what his touch felt like from all those years ago. Years which had evaporated, but now I was reenacting, reliving, re-*something*-ing again.

"Do I need a haircut?" I asked, hoping to prolong the feeling of his touch. He spun me around gently and moved the bangs of my long hair to the side. After mussing the top, he smiled.

"Nope. You look great, Mikey," he replied before tossing his tank top to the corner and tugging his sweat pants down. He had a pair of tight Calvin Klein's on. The waistband rested just below his sharp obliques and small waist. I had an urge to drop to my knees and suck his cock, but how would I explain the change of heart? Even though that was what I desperately wanted, I was still as inexperienced as he was. I hadn't had sex with a male. "Let's shower," he announced. "And then I need you to take me to the mall in your mom's car," he said, stepping back.

Cooper pulled his briefs off and headed for the shower, his round and adorable butt cheeks moving slightly when his lean legs stepped away. I swallowed hard. Seeing him again after all these years with the fresh eyes of a man who'd discovered far too late how much he loved and desired him was overwhelming. His naked body was stunning to look at. He was beautiful and perfect in every way. Why had I been so blind before?

"I'll wait," I croaked, looking away when he stopped short and turned around, his cock on full display. "Go ahead," I urged, keeping my eyes diverted while gesturing for him to get in without me.

"Wait for what?" he asked, turning away from me and adjusting the shower's spray and temperature. "I'll warm it up first. Gimme my toothbrush."

"No, go ahead. I'll wait till you're done," I said, fumbling to locate his toothbrush.

"I don't think so, mister man," he stated, stepping closer to me with his front fully displayed again. My heart skipped a beat as my throat dropped to my stomach. His cock was gorgeous with a light dusting of blond pubic hair above it. The rest of his entire body was as smooth as silk. "Come here," he said, reaching for my gym shorts and holding my hips while looking up slightly as if he was waiting for me to move my hands out of the way.

I moved my hands so he pulled my shorts and boxers off in one swift

CHAPTER TWENTY-EIGHT: MIKE

movement as he kneeled, then tapping each ankle to get me to step out of them. His head was looking down at my feet but was only inches from my cock. My breath hitched as I fantasized about grabbing the sides of his head and forcing him to suck me off. He used my arm to pull himself up. He was standing mere inches from me.

"Thanks," I mumbled.

He wrinkled his nose and his eyes scanned my face carefully. "What is going on?" he asked softly. "Are you hiding something?"

Tell him you love him. Tell him you always have. Beg him to be yours forever and ever. Kiss him you fool. "I guess I'm just tired, Coop."

Cooper wrapped his arms around my neck and pulled me closer. "I'm always here for you, Mikey. No one loves you like I do. No one," he repeated.

I buried my face in his neck and inhaled his nostalgic smell. A scent that had occupied my deepest memories for years. The smell, him, his touch, everything was exactly the same.

The only difference was that now I knew I was in love with him. I had a ten-year head start on my maturing love for him. I had a decade of rehearsing what I would say, what I would do if ever given the chance to see him again. But here I was, wordless.

CHAPTER TWENTY-NINE: Cooper

I tugged on Mikey's hand, dragging him to the shower. "What, you don't wanna shower together anymore?" I asked, ignoring whether he did or didn't. That was how I treated my best friend. I assumed he'd do whatever I wanted and I'd do the same. I already admitted I wished he liked me in the same way and he seemed cool about it, but he didn't know what I truly wanted. But I didn't want to be *that* friend. The creepy, pushy, nag at you until you give in to my wants, friend. Of course, I wished Mikey saw me in a sexual way but he didn't.

"I do," he said, waiting for me to step under the water first like he always did so I wouldn't be cold. It was the middle of June, but he was always thinking about my welfare first. Mike squeezed shampoo on my head and began sudsing my hair. I stepped back, my ass against his front side, my head tilted back so he could massage my scalp. "Are we getting too old to be showering together?" he asked.

"No," I answered immediately. "Why would you ask that?"

"No reason I guess," he said, moving my head under the spray and rinsing my hair. "It doesn't strike you as a bit odd?"

"Strike me?" I parroted. "Who are you? An English professor? Why are you talking like your Dad all of a sudden?" I asked, turning around.

He pushed my dripping bangs out of my face and grinned at me.

"Seriously, Mikey. You've been acting weird all morning."

"I'm just hoping you don't wanna stop doing stuff like this."

"Really?" I asked. "Because to be honest, I've been worrying that maybe you were the one that wanted us to stop showering together and having sleepovers."

"Well, I don't," he said.

"Turn around," I said, twisting him around and adding shampoo to my hand. "What if Jennifer knew?"

"I wouldn't care if she did?" he admitted. We omitted certain things that we did as friends. Showering together and sharing a bed three to four nights a week were two of them. "I suppose it'd sound weird if folks knew though, right?"

"Yeah, I suppose. And then there's Hastings," I added. "He might get jealous if I told him."

Mikey spun around and swiped shampoo out of his eyes. "What the fuck does Hastings have to with anything?" he demanded. "I thought he was mean to you and that he wanted you to blow him on the down-low. Are we talking about the same Hastings?"

"Do what?" I asked, laughing while I washed my armpits with the bar of soap. "No one's blowing anyone . . . at least not yet anyway," I added.

"He practically tried to rape you at the drive-in," Mikey hissed, anger spreading across his face like a prairie fire in a strong wind.

"No, he didn't."

"Yes, he did," he insisted. "You said he did."

"Exactly when did I say that, Mikey? Michael isn't like that."

He turned the water off and stood staring at me like I was a stranger to him. "You call him Michael?" he asked. "I hate that fucking name."

"That's what Jennifer calls you," I argued.

"The fuck she does!" he raged, shoving me out of the way before he stepped out of the glass enclosure. "I hate it when she calls me that. Always bitching about her job and my beer."

Mike leaned over the sink with his head slumped when I walked cautiously toward him. What the heck had he just said? What was he talking about?

"Mikey?"

He turned around, red-faced and angry. "What?"

"You're angry at me. Yelling too," I stated. "Have I done something wrong?"

133

"I don't want you talking to Hastings anymore."

"But you like Michael. What happened? Why?" I asked, confused by his behavior.

"And stop calling him Michael. If you need to call someone Michael, call me Michael," he insisted. "I'm your Michael, dammit."

"You're Jennifer's Michael and you're my Mikey," I reminded him. "Remember, you hated that I was going to call him New Mikey. We all laughed about it and you guys agreed on this arrangement."

"That was when he was straight."

"Have you gone insane? Michael isn't straight," I said.

I watched his face when I told him Michael Hastings wasn't straight and it was as if he actually didn't believe me and had never heard it before. I knew my best friend and I could tell when he was serious. This wasn't a joke to him.

"You said he was straight and that he wanted to be on the down-low, Coop," he whispered. "He wanted blowjobs."

I walked over and grabbed his hand. "I didn't say that, Mikey. Honest, you know I didn't say that."

His eyes filled and he stared past me and at the wall behind us. I could see his shoulders slump forward in his reflection in the mirror. He turned slightly and looked pleadingly at me. "He's gay like you?" he whispered.

I nodded.

A single tear escaped one of his eyes. "Do you like him like that?"

"I do," I admitted. "Maybe. I'm not quite sure, but probably, yes." My answer was unsure because Michael Hastings sent mixed signals about his sexuality.

"Okay then," he said. "I . . . I understand." He seemed defeated by the news that Hastings was gay even though I swore we've discussed it before. He'd been in support of me exploring something with the new guy at school when I mentioned I thought Hastings was cute. "Can you give me a bit? I'm really tired, Coop." I let go of his hand and he turned toward the mirror, facing me in its reflection. "I guess I forgot."

"It's okay, Mikey," I soothed. "But can I ask you something?"

134

He nodded.

"Are you really drinking beer?"

"No. I was . . . I was, you know. I was joking about that."

"It'd kill your mom if you were," I reminded him. "You know, the drunk driver and everything."

"What drunk driver?"

Something was way off with Mike and I knew I should tell his mom but I also understood that we always had each other's backs. We didn't squeal on one another. I quickly dressed because I was running late without a ride from Mikey. "I'll text you in a coupla hours, Mikey," I said. "I need to ask my mom to give me a ride. I'm meeting Michael at the McDonalds at the mall."

He followed me out of the bathroom and climbed onto his bed, ignoring me as I left the room even though I'd waited for a goodbye from him. I kept my promise in regards to having his back and did not mention a thing to Mrs. H..

Something wasn't right.

CHAPTER THIRTY: Mike

Not all was as I'd remembered. This particular universe that my lovely mother had apparently sent me to had some differences. I had better continue cautiously because I could believe events have happened when they in fact did not.

Cooper must be thinking I'd lost my frikkin mind with the way I reacted to unexpected news. Here's what I knew thus far: Hastings was gay in this realm, I was still Jennifer James' boyfriend, and it sounded like a drunk driver had killed my father, not a person who'd fallen asleep at the wheel of a car and ran a red light. And that I didn't drink beer when I was seventeen.

How was I supposed to navigate this life when my brain was full of memories from a life I'd already lived? I suddenly realized that my mother probably hadn't thought that alternate universes offered alternate outcomes, alternate choices and decisions. What if Cooper didn't want me in this one? *Jesus! What if he hadn't been here?*

The calendar on the wall was turned to June just like I'd done when I'd been standing in this room a few hours ago, but somewhere else. Wrapping my head around the entirety was impossible. I pinched my skin for the tenth time that day. Either the pinching was part of the dream or I was actually here, looking like a young adult once again.

I stood and closed my bedroom door all the way, wanting to look at myself in the full-length mirror that hung on the backside of the door. My hands ran over my stomach to where a scar should have been after having my appendix removed at age twenty-two. The scar wasn't there; the skin was smooth and perfect.

My abs were a clearly outlined six pack with jutting obliques that pointed to a full and thick cock. A cock that in this world had yet to experience sex, but it wanted to. I could feel the desire warming in my crotch as I thought about being inside Cooper. Burying my length in his ass or his throat, whichever he'd prefer. I knew I'd prefer both. The crazy thing was that I didn't have those nasty thoughts the first time around. Would I be able to communicate how I felt now that I knew what I wanted from Cooper?

I liked my shaggy blond hair and smooth young face. I'd forgotten how I'd looked as a youthful, non-stressed, athletic boy. I was powerful, muscular, and naturally fit thanks to my good genetics. I felt weird staring at myself and admiring who I was, but I'd forgotten I had been a good looking young man.

In my twenties, I, like many my age, began to notice flaws. Of course there was the aging, and the aches that hadn't been there before. It was natural to dread the passing of time. I'd been getting closer to thirty in another universe. What a trick for the beauty business this would be. *Fuck Father Time* could be the headline. You can swap realities, baby, and restart life from any age. Just drink the marigold juice.

"Fuckin' stupid," I huffed, twisting and checking out my bubble butt from another angle. "Damn," I whispered. "Not bad, Mikey. Not bad at all."

"Michael?" A knock on my bedroom door nearly caused me to scream like a girl. "Honey? Are you going out today?" Mom asked through the closed door. "Are you decent?"

"Just a sec, Mom," I answered, rushing for my gym shorts on the bathroom floor. "Come in," I yelled, casually strolling out of the bathroom.

"Oh there you are, sweety. Why'd Cooper leave? He mentioned needing a ride to the mall at breakfast."

"He changed his mind," I lied, attempting to be wiser about what I said and how I said it. "I can check again if you think I should."

Mom walked around my room picking up our towels and placing them in the hamper she wished I'd use on occasion. "I thought I'd drive out and visit Dad today. It's been a minute," she announced. "You got me thinking about him."

"Would you like some company?" I asked. "Maybe grab Dad's favorite Frosty from Wendy's and then eat them in front of him. You know he'd hate that."

Mom looked surprised.

"He liked Frosty, right?"

"Yes . . . your father liked Frosty, Michael," she said, slowly enunciating her words.

You screwed something up, idiot.

"But *you* dislike going to visit your father," she pointed out. "And after this morning with your mention of incense and the biscuits and gravy, what is all this about, son?"

I sat on the edge of my bed and smiled. "I want to do better, Mom. I miss Dad and I want to talk with him like you do," I admitted.

"Are you sure, honey? I appreciate you putting in more effort, but you don't have to try to fool your mom about the stuff I talk about. Even your father thought it was a bit much at times."

"Dad and I joked around, Mom, but we didn't mind all that much," I confessed. "I sorta like having a goofy mom. You're unique," I said. "Even possibly cool. I'd say ahead of the rest."

"You're still not getting a car," she reminded me, giggling.

I loved my mother's giggle. The feeling of love that flowed to my heart was incredible now that I could hear it again. What a sound she made. Pure, kind, sweet and loving.

"About that, Mom," I began.

She adjusted the neckline of her blouse in preparation for another one of my begging sessions or another list of reasons why I just had to have a car before I went to college.

"I don't need a car."

"Well, you're right about that, young man, but why the change of heart?" she inquired.

"I'll be in Pullman for college in three months anyway. Classes are near the fraternity houses if Coop and I get in, so we can walk everywhere," I said. "I need to save for tuition anyways."

"We have your college money, son. Dad and I set a nice sum aside and I have some of Dad's life insurance money for the rest."

I walked to my desk, pulling the calendar off the wall. "I have a summer job and will save as much as I can." I leafed through the months until August came up. I stared at the small square box that read 30. My heart sank when I remembered the pain associated with the date. Mom would have no idea about either of course. She had no idea she and Cooper would share a death date in another universe. "I've got nearly three months to save. Prices are cheaper in Pullman too," I added, having decided to go to Washington State with Cooper instead of the University of Washington with Jen.

"Does Jennifer know you've decided on WSU?" she asked. Even in this world I sensed she understood my girlfriend was headstrong and determined.

"She'll deal with it," I stated, hanging the calendar back on the wall and wondering what Sunday of the month we were actually in. "What's the date, Mom?" I asked, turning to face her.

"You were the one looking at a calendar, silly," she pointed out. "It's the 13th. You have one week of school left and then it's your dad's and my twentieth anniversary actually."

I moved closer to her. "Oh, shit," I let slip. "Are you okay?" I asked, standing in front of her, a good six inches taller.

"When did you get so big, kiddo?" she asked, trying to dam the reservoir building in her eyes.

"I miss him too, Mom."

She stared into my eyes for what seemed like an eternity. I wondered if she could see into my mind and knew I wasn't of this world. But that wouldn't be possible, would it? But then again, this was my mother.

"You're different today, honey." Maybe she had uncovered my secret. "I can't seem to put a finger on what it is, but you've definitely changed," she began before grabbing my chin and gently turning my head side to side. "It's you and then it's not you." She shook her head as if to clear fog from her brain. "I'm losing my mind," she added, laughing at herself and dropping her hand to her side. "You're just a man, is all."

I reached for her and held her hands. "Are you lonely, Mom?" I asked.

Once again she seemed unprepared for my question. "Michael, honey. Why would you ask such a thing?"

"It's just us now. I guess I was wondering," I said, lowering my voice. "I worry about you."

"Then stop," she replied, tapping my wrist with a hand she'd freed from my grip. "You're a boy. These things are not for you to worry about."

"I could stay home a year or two and work instead," I offered. "Maybe give us both some more time to heal?"

"Fat chance, kiddo. Your father wouldn't want that. I won't allow it. You *are* going to college, young man," she declared. "I am a resilient woman anyway. Plus," she began, her eyes lighting up. "I had my charts read by this new lady, a fabulous spiritualist, and she says my Moon is in a wonderful new phase. Full of health and wisdom."

"Oh yeah? And what exactly is Miss Koo-Koo for Coco Puffs predicting?" I teased.

"Aww, so there he is," she joked. "That's the Michael I know and love. Her name is Druzella and she sees all."

I couldn't hide the smirk on my face. I was surprised I wasn't shitting my pants instead, but things were probably going to get weirder, so why the fuck not roll with it? "I bet she does," I agreed, hearing the name for what had to be the first time in this universe. Maybe not the first time in my former world, but here was the connection I'd wondered about. Maybe Druzella should check out *my* moon phase. I sure as fuck had a phase for her.

Mom headed for the door.

"Hey, have you seen my phone by chance?" I asked after her, assuming I had one somewhere around here.

"Nice try, smarty pants," she replied. "Come home at two in the morning again without permission and we'll see if you *ever* see a cell phone."

"But, Mo . . ."

She cut me off with a raise of her hand. "You might think you're a man and you might look like one too, but Momma still rules the roost, big boy, even if the rooster left the coop."

"Okay, that was weird, Mom. But what about texts or calls, I can't be without my cell phone," I complained, wondering what type I had in what I assumed was 2013 all over again.

"Mow the grass and straighten out the garage, son. Maybe when I get back from the cemetery I'll reconsider. Until then, use the landline if you have an emergency."

I laughed out loud. "You always been this tough?"

Mom pointed at my feet and then gestured her hand up and down my body a couple of times from across the room. "I don't know who this boy is today, but I'm still the mom. I have to be tough. Now get to it." And then she twirled around like a version of Stevie Nicks and exited the room.

"Yes you are," I whispered after her.

CHAPTER THIRTY-ONE: Cooper

"He's acting weird."

"You've mentioned that ten times already, Cooper," Hastings stated before leaning forward and placing the straw in his mouth. After a sip of Coke, he added. "So, why dontcha narrow it down for me?"

Michael Hastings was hot. He'd been the new kid last year and every girl wanted him the very day he'd arrived in math class. I was preoccupied with being lovesick over my best friend Mike Hill, so I hadn't noticed at first.

"I can't," I began. "I know Mikey so well that I can see when he's got something on his mind, but this was different. He looked lost," I added. "Like he was new to earth or something."

"New to earth?" he asked, looking at me confused or bored. Maybe both. "Like an alien?"

I waved a dismissive hand at him and turned to the parking lot in time to see Mikey's girlfriend, Jennifer James, getting out of her BMW convertible. Megan Wright, cheerleader, co-diva, and second hottest girl in school followed from the passenger side. The sight of them turned my stomach. I'd never met a pair so in love with themselves.

"I'll ask Jennifer," I said, gesturing outside and waiting for the gruesome twosome to walk into the McDonalds we were in. "She keeps him on a short leash. She'll know."

We stared as they sashayed through the fast-food joint, most eyes following them.

"Boys," Jennifer cooed. "Another date? Megs and I are *soooo* jelly of you two."

Jennifer looked ridiculously hot as usual. Her toned midriff was visible above a skirt so short I thought I could see her pubes. Hastings took a second look, making me wonder if he was actually as gay as he said he was.

"We're friends, Jen," Hastings corrected, sending an alert to my brain. Like I said, Hastings was masculine in that traditional square jawed sorta way but I wondered if he played both sides of the field. "Buddies. Right, Coop?" he added.

Jennifer feigned shock and covered her perfectly painted mouth. "Nobody is allowed to call him Coop," Jen pointed out. "That's reserved for Mike Hill."

I was surprised Jennifer knew my feelings about my nickname. However, she was correct.

Hastings was nonplussed. "Even if I was *Coop's* boyfriend?" he dared.

Jennifer looked from him to me, in search of a headline news story for her cheer gossip fest. "Is this true, Cooper?" she asked.

"Yeah, Cooper," Megan chimed in, right on cue as Jen's parrot. "Are you boys officially an item now?"

"We are not," I stated. And truthfully, I was as confused as they were.

Hastings came out after every girl in school chased him for two weeks. We were all attracted to his dark and brooding good looks. High cheekbones, a square jaw, full lips, and a nose almost too big. His jet black hair hung in waves and crowned his olive-skinned face.

"We are not, *yet*," he corrected possessively, giving me a look that once again made me feel a tad weak-kneed. But I knew I was in love with Mikey. I also knew Mikey didn't have the same feelings for me. I knew he loved me, just not in the way I wished; so here I was, finally giving other possibilities a shot.

"I think the two of you are so hot together," Megan announced, tugging at her miniskirt and flipping her hair back simultaneously, not an easy thing to do while trying to maintain a teasing pose in six-inch wedges. "Right, Jennifer?"

"Well at least it keeps Cooper from wanting my man," she stated. "*That* Michael is off the market. No offense, Michael," she added, looking at

Hastings.

"Why don't we quit with all the Michael references," I said. "You have Hill and I have no one," I added, glancing at Hastings and reminding him that two can play his game. I didn't want to play games but I also hated not having a guy of my own. If Mikey only felt the kind of love reserved for a best friend, I could accept that. Besides, Mikey and I were closer than any of these teenage fantasies.

"Just one more," Jennifer stated. "Have you seen *my* Michael today? Or better yet, last night?"

"I saw him earlier," I said, leaving out that he was acting weird.

"Cooper said he was acting strange," Hastings said, making my eyes widen. "Like from outer space or something."

"I didn't say outer space," I argued. "Just a bit off."

Jennifer slid next to me in the booth. Mimic Megan did the same and slid in next to Michael, her wide eyes telling me she was anticipating for Jennifer to make an all-important statement or perhaps drop a juicy piece of gossip.

"He didn't text me after he got off from work," Jen began. "I texted him like forty times until two in the morning."

"Sounds like he's sneaking around," Hastings added.

"Mikey doesn't *sneak* around," I defended. "Not his style."

"Then where was he?" Megan pitched in. "Sounds super sketch in my opinion." She interpreted the pause in conversation as her invitation to add more BS to the chat. "Missy Lyles' boyfriend did the same thing last month. Several disappearing acts and stuff like that. He was cheating with Symmie Johanson."

The comment woke Jennifer up from her musings. "You think?" she asked, pursing her lips. "That would be totally fatal to our relationship," she announced, regaining her confidence. "Michael would never be forgiven," she added, making sure to maintain her poise at the first sign of any news that could affect her status as queen.

"Mikey doesn't cheat," I reminded anyone listening. "Not even a possibility."

"You seem so sure, Cooper," Hastings added, gazing at me as he tested my allegiance to Mikey.

"Well, he wouldn't," I stated.

"Accept maybe with *you?*" Jennifer asked half joking or maybe not joking at all. "You seem to know everything about my boyfriend, Cooper."

"I know he wouldn't cheat on you, Jennifer. Period. With no one," I said. "And you should know that too," I added, glaring at her and daring her to add another shitty comment like the one she'd just dropped in front of our friends.

People had been suggesting that Mikey and I had something going on since we were sixth graders. The noise only got louder after we started high school and our close friendship was so obvious. Mikey never entertained the gossip and I followed his lead. We were each other's world and he didn't give a rat's ass if anyone didn't like it. I loved that about him. That, and so many other things.

"Then where was he?" she asked, looking directly into my eyes like she had the ability to catch me in a lie.

"He doesn't fucking cheat, Jen, and I don't know," I said firmly.

The other two sets of eyes watched us closely. The girlfriend and the best friend. Who held the most power?

I often wondered if Jennifer resented me. I held no ill will toward her even though I wished the roles were reversed; even if that meant I was the girl. Of course I was jealous of her. She was everything to Mikey that I couldn't be.

"I believe you," she finally admitted. "I'm not happy, but I believe you, Cooper. Now when are the four of us going on a double date?" She gestured between me and Hastings with her lacquered nails waving in the air.

"What about Greg and me?" Megan cried.

We all turned to Megan but it was Jennifer that went for the jugular. "That isn't going to last, Megan."

I watched as Megan withered like a spring plant in a severe drought. I wondered where Mikey had been. He hadn't been home by the time I finally fell asleep around two or three in the morning while waiting for our goodnight wave. *Where had he been?*

CHAPTER THIRTY-TWO: Mike

I waited until Mom was gone for at least ten minutes before I tore through the house. The cemetery where Dad was buried was on the other side of town so she'd be gone for a while. There was a closer one, but my folks had been friends with the McPherson family that owned the funeral home across town when they decided to buy their plots. I'd attended classes with their son Brad. Classes where I assumed I'd be bumping into him again. I'd been rude to Brad just a week ago after Mom died in the other universe when I got snappy about not burying her in the prepaid resting spot, but that hadn't happened here yet. This was getting fucking weirder by the minute.

I wanted to go through the house to see if I could note the differences in this universe. *Wouldn't it be trippy if Dad was a different man?* First stop was the hallway of family photos. Dad was still Dad. All of the pictures of my childhood were the same, but only appeared halfway down the hall. The main difference being that all of the photos stopped before any senior graduation pics.

It was odd to be standing in the hallway and being able to visualize where the images of my adult life had been displayed. Those pictures didn't exist here yet. This world hadn't seen me graduate high school or attend college either. No pictures of the university I'd attended after Cooper died. No wedding photos with my bride, Jennifer. None of it happened. Those years were waiting to be experienced.

"Mom," I whispered, wishing old Mom was nearby. "What the hell were you thinking?"

I stepped down the hall and imagined the frames on the wall from my memory. My nineteenth birthday. The used car Mom finally gave in and bought me the month before college. After Cooper died she purchased me a used car even though we'd agreed it was better financially not to. Graduation from The University of Washington. All of those memories should have been here. The second half of the hallway walls were devoid of pictures, along with nearly half of my life experiences.

I walked back to the beginning of the hall and studied familiar images from my childhood, each and every one exactly as I'd remembered. And then there was the one by Mom and Dad's bedroom door from the summer we'd gone to the Oregon coast before Dad died. Mom had hung it there after his funeral. This was the one I'd wanted to see. After close examination, nothing was different about the photo. There was no halo around Mom's head.

I peeked into Mom's bedroom and verified all was the same. The living room was an exact replica as well, down to the quilts and the spiritual knick-knacks Mom collected. There were Buddhas, crosses of varying shapes and sizes, Shinto images, the Yin and Yang of Taoism, Wicca representations, and many more I didn't recognize. She'd made sure to consider all of her options while not necessarily adhering to any one belief system. *"I'm open to them all,"* she'd said. She had books on positive mindset, yoga, meditating, and even a book on ayahuasca retreats.

But after carefully going book by book in her cherished collection, I didn't find a single one on parallel universes, particularly the one she'd insisted I read a few weeks back. I went through the bathrooms, the spare bedroom, Dad's old office, and even my own bedroom one more time. The rest was just as I remembered. This home was a carbon copy of my childhood home from my previous life.

I peeked out the window at Cooper's house across the street. It too was the same. A reverse layout of my house which was like all of the homes on our tree-lined street of nineteen-fifties bungalow houses. Charla's car was in the driveway but Roger's was not. Since Roger was usually home on Sunday, perhaps Coop had taken his Dad's car instead.

My next task was to check if Mom still kept a schedule of school events taped to the right side of the fridge. It was mid-June and school ended the following week and then graduation. I used the same calendar to keep track of my work schedule so I could make sure to ask for days off on special occasions. Mom allowed me to work two school nights a week and one weekend day. She was a stickler for homework and for family time, especially after Dad passed.

The schedule was in its usual spot on the fridge so I closely examined the days left in June. I was off today and had work Tuesday and Thursday next week. Looking closer, I noticed that Senior prom was that weekend. Our school traditionally had prom on the final week of school. Underclassmen had an additional week of class.

A note was written last week to remind me to ask for prom Saturday off, as well as a note Mom added that Jennifer was wearing a sky blue dress. I assumed this was so I could match. Mom was trying her hardest to fade heat from my girlfriend even back then. I marveled at Mom trying to keep her opinions about Jennifer to herself back then.

I had school tomorrow which should be a trippy experience then work on Tuesday, and prom in less than a week. This first week would be my test to see if I'm able to slide back into a life I've already experienced. Talk about déjà vu.

The front door burst open, startling me until I heard a familiar voice. A voice that after more than a decade, I adored and never forgot.

"Mikey?" Cooper hollered. "You home?"

"In the hallway," I yelled back, walking toward the entryway to intercept him.

I came around the corner and found Cooper standing next to Hastings. Hastings had his arm around Coop's shoulder. I couldn't recall ever seeing Hastings in my house, especially after hearing he'd been such a creep to Cooper on a *so-called* date at the drive-in. However, according to this Cooper, that hadn't happened.

"There you are," Coop said, moving from under Hastings' arm. The move hadn't escaped Hastings and he looked less than pleased. I might not have recognized his disappointment had I been my former seventeen-year-old self, but this version was a decade wiser and less forgiving in regards to his demonstrated possessive move for my benefit.

"Hastings," I grudgingly acknowledged, trying not to form an opinion at this early stage considering Coop corrected an earlier belief I'd held. "What are you two up to?" I asked, not really caring about anything other than I didn't like them together, especially right under my nose.

Hastings looked at Coop before proceeding, checking in as if he wanted to be the one to spring any news they had about me.

"Go ahead," Cooper said, looking warily at me.

"Your girlfriend is pissed," he blurted out.

"Not actually pissed," Cooper quickly corrected, frowning at Hastings which pleased me to no end. Cooper always wanted to make people look good when they weren't around to defend themselves. "Disappointed more than anything," Cooper added.

"I'd say she was pissed," Hastings argued. "Thinks you're cheating on her."

"She didn't say that," Cooper defended. "Not in so many words anyway."

Hastings glared at Cooper. "Yes, she did." He turned his attention to me. "She even asked Cooper if it was with him."

"That's absurd," Cooper retorted.

I noticed some things hadn't changed. Cooper loved using fancy words like absurd. I swore I'd never heard another teenaged boy speak that way.

"Trust me, if I was going to cheat, it *would* be with Cooper," I stated, testing Hastings reaction. "He'd be less of a pain in the ass," I added, turning back to the kitchen and tilting my head for them to join me.

I sat at the kitchen island while Coop opened the fridge for something to drink. Once again, I noticed Hastings watching Cooper move around my house with familiarity and the comfort to make himself at home. I wondered if Coop's behavior bothered him.

"I'll take her," Hastings said, watching our reactions, his eyes traveling back and forth to see what we'd say.

"Have at her," I remarked, probably too casual and unfeeling in my response. "I'll take Coop then."

Cooper stared at me with what appeared to be disappointment. I couldn't tell if it was in regards to my statement or the fact that Hastings wanted my girlfriend and not him.

"Damn, dude," Hastings said. "You obviously don't know what you have."

I glanced at Cooper and noticed he'd crossed his arms. I'd seen this move before, it wasn't anger, he was protecting himself from hurt. I was shocked how cavalier Hastings was in front of us considering Cooper liked him and I was Coop's bestie.

I gestured to Cooper before asking Hastings a direct question. "Wanna trade? I'm serious. I'll take him and you can have her," I said.

Hastings didn't answer my question. Most likely because I sounded as serious as a heart attack with more bitterness than intended. I had to remind myself that they didn't know why I was so blasé about Jennifer. How could they?

"Uh, thanks, but no thanks," Cooper muttered. He was upset and I'd hurt his feelings. I needed to shut up before I completed a trifecta. "I'm going home," he added.

"Want me to go with you?" Hastings asked.

"No. I'm tired and have homework to do," Cooper answered.

"How will I get home? We drove your old man's car," he said, suddenly realizing he may have put his foot in his mouth in regards to Jennifer.

"I suggest you call Jennifer." And with that, Cooper left the kitchen and walked out the front door. The slam of the door let us know he wasn't happy with either of our comments.

"Shit!" Hastings said. "Fucked that up, didn't I?"

"Looks like it," I agreed, sounding happier than I should.

That's when I heard Mom enter the front door before she came around the corner to the kitchen. "Why was Cooper so upset?" she asked, giving me one of her *this better not be because of you, young man,* looks. "He could barely speak when I ran into him in the driveway," she added. "Mike?"

I quickly looked at Hastings, needing a cover. "I think we may have teased him about something and he didn't like it, Mom. I'll apologize later."

Mom crossed her arms, but unlike Coop, this *was* her go to *I'm not happy with you,* move. "You'll apologize right now, young man. I mean it. You know Cooper is more sensitive than you."

"I know, Mom," I muttered.

"He loves you, Mike. You need to do better," she reminded me.

"Sorry, Mrs. Hill," Hastings said. He'd been watching my interaction with my mother and seemed shocked that Mom defended Cooper. "I'll be going now," he added.

"And you too, young man," Mom stated, glaring at Hastings. "That boy likes you and you better be respectful toward his feelings."

"Chill, Mom," I said, noticing Hastings withering in her presence.

"I will not chill. Neither of you deserve Cooper's friendship," she said. "And you certainly know better, Michael."

Hastings started heading toward the front door, a look of confusion on his face. "I'm gonna run," he said, glancing at Mom and then me. "Sorry, ma'am." Hastings hunched his shoulders and scurried out of the kitchen.

"That was harsh," I stated, gesturing toward the living room after we heard the door shut behind Hastings.

"You need to go over and say you're sorry for whatever it is you said to Cooper."

"It was just boys being boys, Mom," I said, standing from the island and attempting to move around her.

Mom stepped in front of me, clearly disappointed. "You are not this blind, son," she began. The corner of my mouth curled in confusion and surprise at her words. "Cooper is in love with you and I'm sure you know it's not just as your best friend."

"What are you talking about?" I asked, unaware that she knew about Coop's feelings. "Did he say that?"

"He doesn't have to," she said. "And regardless of your feelings, he is your best friend, Michael, and you will not treat him as anything less. Understood?"

"Can I go now?"

"No, you may not. What has gotten into you today?" she asked.

Her comment caught me off guard. Could she see that I was different?

Did she notice I had years of experiences and feelings coursing through my brain? "Nothing," I answered, staring at my feet. "I'll go over and apologize now."

Her face softened when she lifted my chin so I could face her. "Look, honey," she began. "I don't expect you to feel the same way about Cooper unless you really do, but you need to handle him more carefully."

"I'll do better," I said. "Honest, Mom. I will."

She hugged me and sniffed my neck. "You smell different," she said. She stepped back, still holding my arms. "What is it with you today?" she asked again.

"I'm just getting older, Mom," I said, chills running up my spine as she studied me. "Your baby boy is almost a man."

"That's not it, son, but trust me, mom's know stuff and we both know that I have that something extra, so you best be watching yourself."

I believed her.

CHAPTER THIRTY-THREE: Cooper

My father's voice carried up the stairs and through my open bedroom door. "He's up there," I heard him tell Mikey. "You must've really angered him this time, Mike," he added. "He didn't join us for dinner, so I know he's in a mood."

Mikey either didn't respond or he was quiet, but I heard steps on the staircase and figured either him or Dad were on their way up. I rolled over and faced the wall before the door opened.

"Still mad at me?" Mikey asked softly, walking across the room and nudging my shoulder. "Can I lay down with you?"

"You never asked before," I muttered.

Mikey lay on his back beside me and scooted as close to my back as he could, his hand between my butt and his hip. I was angry with him but I couldn't escape my longing for his touch whenever we were near one another. For as long as I could remember things had been this way. I just had to touch him, feel his presence, be in his space at all times. I figured he tolerated me because of our closeness, but as we aged I worried we were close to moving past that sort of boyhood friendship.

"I'm sorry," he whispered, tapping my butt with his hand. "I shouldn't discount your feelings or relationship with Hastings by saying off handed shit like that."

"It's okay," I said.

"No, it isn't, Coop. Truthfully, I don't know why you put up with me."

He knew why. He was just being nice and not saying it out loud.

"I'm just being a baby about stuff," I said. "Sometimes jokes hurt more when they come from you."

"Why don't you tell me shit like this then?" He rolled over and spooned with me, draping his arm over my hip and resting his hand on my stomach.

I wasn't exactly sure why I hadn't, but figured it was because I was afraid to lose him. If I nagged him too much I worried he'd get tired of me. "I don't know," I mumbled, enjoying his closeness and his fingers gently caressing my stomach through my T-shirt. "It's just . . . well, sometimes I think you forget about my feelings about being gay."

Mikey propped himself up on his elbow and looked over me, his chin digging into my shoulder. "I do?" he asked. "I sure as shit don't mean to, Coop."

"You told Hastings you'd trade Jennifer for me. I know you're joking but it makes me feel less than, Mikey," I began, trying hard to keep a level voice and to not start bawling. "I don't wanna seem like a consolation prize."

"I didn't mean it like that."

"You forget that most people don't treat me the way you do," I reminded him. "I'm sure I only escape the name calling because you're popular. If we weren't friends they'd be calling me fag and pansy like they do to Rusty Whitman."

"I'd kick their fucking asses," he stated. "So let 'em try."

"See?" I pointed out. "Just like that."

Mikey tugged on my shoulder and rolled me over when he readjusted onto his back again then lifted his arm for me to slide under. I scooted closer and rested my head on his shoulder. "I'm just saying I'd stick up for you, is all, Coop."

"Who sticks up for Rusty?"

Mikey instantly sat up and turned to face me. "Who's calling you a fag?"

"Nobody. That's my point," I said. "If we weren't friends and I didn't have your whole group of cool friends, I'd be toast."

"Bullshit!" he hissed. "Everyone loves you, Coop."

"Maybe, but if they do it's only because of you," I argued. "And don't get me wrong, I appreciate that we're friends, but if I'm supposed to accept that you really care and respect me, it sucks when you make a joke about being with me instead of Jen when we both know that'll never happen."

Mikey let out a breath, tapping my shoulder. "Not true, Coop."

"You don't get it, Mikey. People look to you to decide how they feel about others. Come on, you see that, right?" I asked. He shook his head like I'd just delivered the most ridiculous news he'd ever heard. "And my point is if you say stuff like you did in front of Hastings, why won't everyone else do the same? You minimized me."

"Jesus, Coop," he responded. "Why haven't you told me this before?"

"Fear I guess."

"Fear of what?"

"Losing our friendship, I suppose," I admitted. "Then what would I be at school? I'm not like you. People flock to you, Mikey. I just stand beside you."

Mikey turned to his side so he could face me, his right hand on my hip and his other reaching for mine. Our faces were mere inches apart. "That will never happen, Coop. Ever."

I began to cry. "You say that . . . but . . .," I began.

Mikey pulled me into his arms and held me. I let myself cry as all of my fears about losing my best friend surged through me. I hated that he joked about trading me to a guy who I had hoped could offer me what I've never had: a boyfriend. I knew Hastings was a replacement for who I really wanted, but at least maybe there was a chance that he saw me in a way that Mikey didn't.

"I didn't know you felt that way, Coop, but I still think you're wrong," he said. "I'm the one who is afraid of losing you. Trust me, I know what it feels like."

I pulled away from him. "How do you know what it feels like?" I asked. "And besides, I would never quit on you," I stated.

Mikey looked like he'd stepped on a landmine and didn't know whether to take a step forward or stay put as he stared at me. "I . . . I was talking about Dad," he stumbled. "Losing someone so close and all."

"Oh . . . oh yeah," I agreed, studying him closely. I'm not sure he noticed but he was holding my hand and gently caressing my knuckles. The connection felt amazingly intimate and different than how we normally were. We were pretty affectionate but this felt unusual even for us, and I couldn't quite figure out why.

He stared into my eyes like he had something more to say but was hesitant to speak the words. His free hand moved loose hair out of my eyes, his fingers lingering on my skin. Our eyes locked and my breath hitched.

I was probably imagining things but he seemed like he wanted to kiss me. There was nothing in the world I wanted more, but also knew I'd be terrified if we crossed that line. We held each other all the time, even showered together and washed each other's backs. If that wasn't intimate I'm not sure what was, but to kiss him?

He broke the stalemate and pulled his hand back from my forehead. "So do you really like Hastings that way? Like as your boyfriend?" he asked, looking past me, perhaps not wanting to hear my answer.

"He's the only guy who has ever asked me to hang out other than you," I said. "I guess that's something, right?"

"That's not what I asked you."

Our eyes realigned and he waited for an answer. Could I tell him what I truly hoped for? Maybe it was just a coincidence, but we both bit our lower lips at exactly the same time. "I'm not certain he likes boys exclusively like I do," I said, still dodging his real question. "He's handsome and he asked me to prom," I added, running out of ways to avoid admitting I was desperate for someone to see me as a potential person to love. "He's funny too."

"I know you, Coop, and what you just said doesn't sound like the you I know. How does he make you feel?"

My eyes widened at his question. *How did Hastings make me feel?* Better question was when did Mikey start talking like Oprah? He was definitely acting weird, almost like an adult. Normally he would've made fun of Hastings, told me to blow him or some dumb jock comment, but he was suddenly acting like a mature person.

"He doesn't," I whispered, admitting the truth. I felt nothing real toward Hastings and after his comments about Jennifer and how hot she was, I knew he didn't see me that way either. Neither of us had our breath taken away by the other.

"Nothing?" Mikey pushed. "You feel nothing?"

"I was lying to myself, Mikey. I just want to have someone for once," I confessed. "Is it so bad to just want to be loved?"

"No. I feel the same," he said.

I was stunned by the admission. "But . . . Jennifer loves you," I protested. "And you love her, right?"

"We don't really love each other," he stated, shocking me. "People like us are supposed to be a couple in high school, Coop. It's all bullshit optics."

I swear I wouldn't have recognized him if we weren't right in front of one another. This was definitely Mikey, but a stranger version for sure.

"This has been the oddest Sunday I can remember," I said. "Are you okay, Mikey? I don't wanna hurt your feelings, but you're acting differently."

He lifted his brows and grinned. "Well, get ready, buddy," he began, pushing away from me. "Like you always say, every day is like Sunday. It doesn't get better than this." Mikey leaned in and casually kissed me directly on the lips. "See ya tomorrow?" He stood and headed for the open door but stopped before leaving and turned toward me. "Am I forgiven?"

I nodded, too confused to speak.

CHAPTER THIRTY-FOUR: Mike

Even in this universe, Mom was an amazing mother and still did all of my laundry. When I woke up Monday morning, I went to the dresser and pulled out clean boxers. A lower drawer held neatly folded Levis and in the closet ten to fifteen assorted graphic T-shirts hung in a row. I reached for a white North Face shirt, held it to my nose and noticed Mom still used Downy. I pulled the T-shirt over my head, admitting how good it looked on my trim body when I checked myself in the mirror hanging on my door. Levis hugged me in all the right places as well. Stepping into some well-worn Nikes, I headed down for breakfast and my cheerful mother.

My mother generally rose hours before I did, even on school days. She practiced yoga before meditating to prepare her for setting up her chakras or something like that. She hardly ever wore makeup and usually kept her blonde hair pulled back in a ponytail. Her routine must be working because she looked a decade younger than her true age.

"Omelet okay, son?" she asked after I showed up.

The kitchen smelled like incense of course and she had her new-age music playing softly in the background. *All was good in her universe.* I laughed at my internal joke, not realizing it was out loud.

"What's so funny?" she asked, turning to face me.

"Just glad to see you never changed, Mom," I admitted, sliding a chair from under the table I'd eaten off of my entire life. The table, like Mom's decor, hardly ever changed: white farmhouse chic with a different table cloth every week. I tucked into the cheddar cheese with spinach omelet she placed before me. Swallowing quickly, I inhaled deeply when I noticed a familiar scent. "Is that the smell that sets your day up for success?" I asked, motioning to the slim and scented smoke trail rising to the popcorn ceilings.

"So," she began, albeit suspiciously. "You *do* listen when I carry on about my life enhancers."

"Hey, as long as you're happy," I stated, shoving a heaping forkful of hash browns into my mouth. "Oh yeah, I wanted to ask you about your books," I mumbled, my mouth still half full.

Mom sat down across from me, shaking her head in disappointment because I was talking with food in my mouth. While adding oat milk to her ethically sourced coffee she asked, "Which one, honey? Do you have a school project you need help with?"

"I didn't see a book on parallel universes," I said. "Do you not believe in that stuff?"

"Truthfully, I haven't read up on it," she admitted, blowing on her coffee before taking a sip. "But you know me, I'm open to all possibilities." Mom pursed her lips and looked like she was trying to remember something important. "You know what?" she began. "I did read something a while back at the library about déjà vu and the connections to parallel universes. So, there could be something to it actually."

"Wouldn't that be weird?" I asked. "Kinda freaky, dontcha think?"

"Oh, not really, I love the idea of it," she stated. "Imagine the limitless opportunities we'd have." She closed her eyes and smiled. I knew she was thinking about Dad. "I'd like that, son. Eat up and I'll take you and Cooper to school. I feel like going to the library."

As soon as she said she was going to the library, I wondered if it was because of my question. I suddenly realized that maybe I should be more careful about asking questions or making observations about things I may have known in my former life.

That was the thing about Mom that I admired the most. She never poo-pooed other folks' ideals, traditions, or beliefs. Instead, she immediately explored their rituals and educated herself about them. "Lemme know what you find, Mom."

I stood and placed my plate in the sink, running water over it before deciding to wash and dry the plate before placing it in the designated cabinet.

Mom watched me the entire time. "Have you seen my son?" she asked, scratching her chin in amusement.

"What?" I questioned, leaning against the counter. "I can help out around here more."

Mom stood and came to stand in front of me. "Okay. I'll stop," she stated. "I'm not going to tease you about this . . . this . . ."

"Change?" I said.

"So," she began suspiciously. "This is intentional?"

"I appreciate you, Mom. That's all it is."

"Maybe my magic is working on you," she said.

"Oh, trust me, I think it is," I quipped.

* * *

Twenty-seven years old and walking down the halls of high school again. Was it trippy? Trippy as fuck. Absolutely nothing had changed in these hallways. The long and narrow space was still loud, buzzing with energy, and full of teenage shenanigans. I couldn't believe I used to participate in all of the crazy.

"Wassup, Hill," Jonah Selmer asked after smacking my shoulder. I'd forgotten how handsome he was. Jonah was actually a sweet guy back then too. He turned into a predator after we graduated, but I won't be letting him know about his future. *Why bother?* I guess getting caught hiding cameras in the women's locker room at the local gym, and then storing unauthorized videos on his personal computer didn't appeal to his wife all that much. Rae-Anne Tilton had found the videos one night because her husband accidently forgot to log out. I was tempted to give her a heads-up to save her the embarrassment.

As I walked through the building and recognized kids from my past, I became overwhelmed by the memories of them as adults. I hadn't planned on this side effect of time travel. Was that what it was? Time travel? Had Mom even thought about the possibility that I could be my matured self while in this universe? Seventeen in physical appearance, twenty-seven in my head? After being at school for five minutes I was reeling.

"You're in trouble, mister." The unmistakable voice of Jennifer hit me from behind, I turned around and found my drop-dead gorgeous girlfriend scowling at me. "Big time," she added, flipping her hair from her shoulder and leveling her gaze at me.

"Mom took my phone," I said, calm as a cuke. "Still don't have it back."

"And landlines don't work?" she asked, still riding my ass like only she could, a practice she'd perfect over the next decade.

"Land what?" I stupidly asked, before understanding I was in 2013 again. Mom still had one too. I think she dropped it when I was in college. "I forgot," I stated.

"How convenient, Michael."

God, I hated hearing my full name roll off of her tongue. This was going to be tough.

"I'm sorry, Jen." *That sounded familiar.*

Old feelings about my ex-wife were unfairly ripping through my mind. I was angry and full of contempt for how self-absorbed this woman had been. The problem, however, was that this seventeen-year-old Jennifer was not the focused, unrelenting woman I would divorce ten years from now.

"You should be," she said. "I could've needed you Saturday night. Maybe I could've died or something."

I pulled her in for a hug. *Remember this is high school Jennifer, Mike.* "That's a bit dramatic, Jen, but you know my mom and her rules," I reminded her. "Mom is disciplining for two now that Dad's gone."

"That was almost a year ago, Michael. Can't she read one of her quack books and just move on?"

Her comment did not sit well with me. My eyes narrowed and she jumped back like I was about to strike her. I grabbed her shoulders. "Do not speak about my mother like that again. You hear me?" I hissed.

Her face turned red and she quickly looked around in case a witness had

162

seen my overreaction. After composing herself and letting out a huff she responded. "How dare you speak to me like that, Michael," she whispered. "I . . . well, I . . .," she stammered. "I just will not be spoken to like that," she concluded.

I was raging inside and couldn't stop myself. "Do not call me Michael and don't ever speak about my mother unless you have some good shit to say for once," I insisted.

"Don't call me then. I don't care," she huffed. "You're being mean to me, Michael, and you know I have an assembly later. How can I look my best if you're being so mean?"

She was definitely the seventeen year old princess I remembered. I needed to calm down. "You look amazing, Jen. You're the hottest girl in school," I added, shifting gears after remembering how fragile Jennifer could be back then. Funny thing I never felt that way about her the first time around. In fact, no one at our school had.

She smiled seductively, a trick that used to kill me with desire. "I do, don't I?" she half asked, half declared. "Okay, then," she began, kissing my cheek. "Gotta run." And with that, she flounced away, heading for the row of lockers that all the cheerleaders claimed every year. Locker numbers one through eight. Number 1 was assigned to the head cheerleader who was queen of everything, and every student knew that it belonged to Jennifer James.

I watched as she sashayed through the hall toward her squad like nothing had just happened between us. Like a fart in a skillet, she couldn't be contained. She had the memory of a goldfish. For Jennifer, being on top was her priority. I knew she hadn't heard a thing I'd said about Mom, but she had heard that she looked amazing and that's what counted in her world.

I reminded myself that it would be horribly unfair to judge Jen for things she hadn't done yet or ever because I didn't know how this journey would turn out. I had an unfair advantage over her now and truly didn't want to capitalize on that fact. Were there times when we were married that I would have killed for this opportunity? Of course, but this was entirely different.

But I knew one thing for certain, I wouldn't be able to fake my way through a relationship with her.

This universe was going to test me.

CHAPTER THIRTY-FIVE: Cooper

Jennifer was going on and on about how mean Mikey had been before first period. Apparently he'd crossed a line when he hadn't even walked her to class like she'd expected. "He's acting totally weird," she noted, opening the tiny compact mirror that was permanently attached to her hand and checking her painted lips. "Do you like this shade of pink, Cooper?" she asked, turning back to me and puckering up. "Michael refuses to give his opinion of course, but I know you will. We're practically the same person."

That woke me up. "How's that, Jennifer?"

"We both like pretty things, is all I meant," she replied, leaning closer. "You *get* us girls. Unlike the *normal* boys."

I knew exactly what she meant. "Thanks for the compliment," I stated, trying to remain friendly.

I really wanted to like Mikey's girlfriend, but she tested my limits; and I saw myself as a fairly patient person. Jennifer James was born beautiful. She started kindergarten beautiful. And middle school, yep, still beautiful, but high school? Holy smokes. That was when she blossomed into a goddess. Lush blonde hair that cascaded in perfect waves of shine down her back. She had perfect teeth. She possessed an impossibly tiny waist that popped into a round bubble butt. Her soft, flawless skin glowed like God had personally touched her and pronounced her his successful creation. All that perfection and I still didn't really like her that much. I tolerated her. For Mikey.

I watched the cafeteria door open and close, anticipating Mikey and Hastings coming through at any moment. I needed someone to rescue me from Jennifer's endless babbling. Hastings and Mikey shared chemistry class just before lunch period, so they often walked to lunch together. I sensed that Hastings liked Mikey more than Mikey liked him, but overall they were buddies even after Mikey's recent confusion about Hastings' gay status.

I noticed Hastings walk in alone and look toward the table reserved for the cool crowd. Even though I sat here, I never felt comfortable. In fact I was an imposter; slipping through geek-prevention security measures because of Mikey.

Hastings slid onto the bench next to me, ogling God's gift to the universe, Jennifer James. "Hey," he said to me while still eyeing her.

You're gay right? I wanted to ask out loud.

"Mikey was behind me," he said to Jennifer.

"He better be," she stated. "I'm up to here with my boyfriend and his antics," she huffed, raising her hand above her head to an imaginary bar of *having had enough*.

This comment seemed to pique Hastings' interest more than I thought it warranted. He perked up immediately. "Trouble in paradise for the pretty people?" he asked, tapping my knee with his under the long table. "That'd be such a shame, Jen," he added, leaning across the table and acting all surprised by her pronouncement.

"I'm sure it would be, but I'm totally over his behavior this past weekend. I deserve so much better. Right, Cooper?" she asked.

I nodded like I cared, but Hastings wasn't done applying for the possibly-soon-to-be-open position of *Mr.* Jennifer James. "What would you do then?" he asked. "I mean if it happened. You know, a breakup."

Mikey would puke if he could witness this, not that he'd care all that much.

"I'd be the most wanted bachelorette at school is what would happen," she said, with zero hesitance. "I'd probably get a TV show."

"That's a fact, Jennifer. Amen to that," he added.

Just as I was about to gag, Mikey walked in, surveyed the room, and witnessed Hastings barely staying on his side of the table while his girlfriend held court. For just a flash, I saw a look that said he wanted to turn and exit the cafeteria, but he didn't.

Mikey sat down on Jen's side of the table, but not directly beside her. "Hey, Coop," he said, barely acknowledging Hastings and Jennifer. "Hastings," he said in a way that sounded dismissive to me. His eyes were sad when he redirected them toward his girlfriend. "Still pissed?" he asked her.

"What do you think?" she snapped, turning away.

That was apparently the wrong answer. Mikey stood up immediately. "Okay. Whatever," he said before walking off.

"Uh-oh." Hastings said, raising his eyebrows and looking like the wolf that just discovered the farmer left the sheep unattended. "He's pissed, Jennifer."

"Go after him, Michael," I urged, trying to get Hastings to stop drooling over my best friend's girl.

"Screw that," he answered. "Our friend Jennifer here is the one that needs our support." If Hastings, my supposed love interest and prom date, was any more transparent he'd have been made of glass.

"Then I'll go," I said, pushing away from the table and standing. "He's just tired," I added, sharing my assessment with Jennifer, not Hastings.

"Yeah, you do that," Hastings said, barely acknowledging that I was there.

I rushed after Mikey who had cut through the exit and was already outside and was walking toward the football field.

"Hey, Mikey. Hang on," I hollered after him. I jogged to catch up when he went under the metal bleachers and disappeared into the tangle of aluminum support bars and oversized bolts. I followed him under the bleachers. "What's wrong?" I asked, catching my breath and pulling at his shoulder to get him to face me.

We stood quietly, staring at one another. He had his hands deep in his jean pockets, a sign he was angry at something or someone. "I'm fine," he finally said.

"No, you aren't," I corrected. "You haven't been fine for two days."

He stared down at his Nikes. "What do you know?" he snarled, digging his hands deeper into the pockets of his tight Levis which caused the low waist to ride even lower.

Not that I was complaining since his abs made an appearance on his lean stomach. *God, you're so cute.*

"I know *you,*" I reminded him. "And I care about *you,*" I added. "And I'm here, ain't I?"

He looked up from the staring contest he was having with his feet.

I looked both directions to see if we were hidden.

"You never used words like *ain't,*" he stated.

I didn't know what he was talking about. "Since when?" I asked.

He quickly looked away, sighing heavily before returning his gaze. "You sure?" he asked, distress on his face as his forehead wrinkled like baked mud on a ninety-degree day.

I stepped in front of him. "Just tell me what it is, Mikey," I said.

He looked away. "There's nothing to tell you."

I reached for his belt and slid a finger under the leather then pulled myself even closer. "This is me, Mikey. We tell each other stuff. Remember?" I asked softly. He didn't move my hand away from his waist even though we could've been caught in a compromising position if someone approached.

"You wouldn't understand," he mumbled. "And besides, you like that guy."

"Hastings?"

His chin fell and he frowned. "Yeah, and he's just such a . . . such a . . ."

"Creep?" I asked.

"Not the word I was gonna use, but yeah, since you said it."

I glanced behind me wondering if maybe Hastings had left the cafeteria and came to check up on me. He hadn't. I returned my focus to Mikey. "He doesn't like me that way," I confessed. "I thought he did. At first anyway."

"He sure seems to like Jennifer," he said.

"You noticed, huh?" I asked.

He nodded and looked past me and toward the cafeteria. "I don't think either one of them cares that we left, Coop."

He was probably correct but I didn't care. "I can't force you to tell me what's up," I began. "But is it me?"

What he said next surprised the heck out of me. "Actually, it is."

"Okay," I replied slowly, worried I'd been the cause of his unusual behavior over the past couple of days. "Did I do something wrong? Are you angry that I called you out last night about my feelings being hurt? I can try harder," I said. "I was out of line," I added, fear rushing to my gut like it always did when I thought I'd disappointed him.

"Just stop, Coop," he said, grabbing my hand that was holding his belt. "Look at me."

I lifted my face from where I'd been gazing at the strong hand that held mine so tenderly, fright overloading my every impulse. I wanted to run, to faint, or even die. I'd never survive if he said we couldn't be friends anymore. "I'm sorry, Mikey," I whispered.

"Please stop doing that."

"Doing what?" I asked. "I said I was sorry."

"Stop acting like you've made a mistake, Coop. You always acted like this," he stated.

I looked into his blue eyes and knew that this Mikey wasn't the usual Mikey. This boy seemed more like a man. *Yeah, that had to be it.* He was growing up and I was holding him back with my childish ways. He needed to grow past me and he'd finally figured it out. There'd be no more sleepovers, no more cuddling, and no more showers together.

As hard as I tried, I couldn't stop the tears. Mikey had always been my everything. Of course, I had to learn to accept that he would never feel the same about us. But I loved him with all my heart; like the boyfriend I wished I had. Heck, even his mother knew that. I'd told her after Mikey and I had an argument and didn't speak for two days. I was a mess but still came to his house every night and hung out with Mrs. H. while he ignored me.

"Can I still sit with you at lunch?" I asked, tears sliding down my cheeks.

"Listen to me, Coop," he said, wiping my face with his hand. "I think you're assuming something."

"I need to act more manly, right?" I asked, barely containing the hurt in my voice. "You're tired of me looking at you with puppy-dog eyes. That's it, right? I can do better, Mikey," I cried, choking on my words. "And now Hastings doesn't want me either," I sobbed, trying to hold it together as my life was shattering right in front of me.

169

He crossed his arms, shaking his head. "Are you done yet?" he asked. "Can I get a word in now?"

I nodded and sniffed out loud, a moment away from a complete cry-a-thon.

He lifted my chin. "I'm feeling the same way about you, Coop. I mean if you like me like a boyfriend that is."

"You . . . you . . . what?"

"I love you like that too and I'm tired of denying how I feel about you."

I turned toward the school and then back to him, only to turn to the school again. *What did he just say? Where were they? Where were Jennifer and Hastings?* I was afraid to turn back to Mikey, but I did. Surely I'd been exposed to some illicit drug in the cafeteria and was suffering from a contact high. "You love me? Like more than a friend?" I asked.

"Yes. Yes, I do," he said, nervously dragging a shoe across the gravel.

"But . . . but, what about Jennifer?" I asked. "Uh. . . and Hastings if he actually likes me?"

"We might have a problem, Coop."

And once again, I turned toward the school, noticing how clearly I could see the school grounds even though I couldn't see into the bleachers when I chased after Mikey. The football field nearby was empty since the season was long over with. The wide concrete sidewalks around the school were crowded with kids hanging out enjoying the warmer spring weather while sitting on the grass with their lunch. I noticed a few guys talking near their cars in the student's lot, most likely comparing engines or horsepower, or things I didn't care about. Two monitors kept careful eyes on everyone. Suddenly I realized that all the people were going about their business and hadn't noticed us. They hadn't heard Mikey say what I've always wanted him to say.

I turned back to Mikey. "You're not teasing me, are you?" He shook his head. "For real, real?" I asked.

"If you want to give me a chance."

All I could manage was a nod. I nodded over and over and over again. It was difficult to see Mikey through welling eyes, but he was there. Right there. He said he loved me like I loved him. I wasn't daydreaming this moment.

"I'd like that."

CHAPTER THIRTY-SIX: Mike

I caught Cooper staring at me from the rearview mirror. Him and Hastings were in the back of Jennifer's car while I drove us to the local tux shop for final fittings after school. The afternoon had gone by painstakingly slow after my admission to Cooper under the bleachers. We had one class together after lunch where we just stared across the room at each other while we sat with our lab partners in biology.

* * *

"What are we going to do?" Cooper had asked after I told him how I felt about him. "I mean, we have to go to class, we're gonna see them."

"Come here," I'd said, pulling him close, and keeping an eye on the area around the bleachers. I leaned into his neck and inhaled a familiar scent that I'd never forgotten even after all those years. He smelled fresh with a mild hint of a musk cologne he wore: sweet yet masculine.

"I don't want to hurt anyone," Cooper said, relaxing into me. "Plus, I'm afraid you're not certain about this, Mikey. What . . . what . . . what if you change your mind?" he stuttered.

"Does this help?" I gently touched his chin and lifted his head to face me. "I want to be with you, Coop, and I will not change my mind. I promise."

I slowly closed the distance, causing his eyes to widen before shutting after I pressed my lips gently onto his. I tenderly flicked my tongue across his lips, encouraging him to open for me. His chest heaved and I felt a tremor travel through him before he relaxed into me; allowing me to do what I had anticipated he would, to let me lead the way.

My tongue moved past his soft lips and his velvety tongue met mine, testing the feeling. The kiss wasn't my first but I assumed might be his because he'd never shared whether Hastings and him had kissed. My first kiss with the boy I have loved forever was different from the ones that came before him. Coop felt masculine and more solid than Jennifer had at any age, and she was always fit.

For the first time in both my lives, I felt like I was finally home.

I pushed harder, more aggressively when he opened his mouth wider and let me explore the incredible emotions blazing through my brain, invading my heart, and waking up a sexual desire I'd never experienced before.

Soft moaning escaped from him while I devoured his silky mouth by darting and swirling my tongue against his. I inhaled everything about him. A kiss would never get me close enough to him no matter how hard I pressed or how deep I probed. I wanted, no, I needed all of him.

Cooper moved his hands from his sides where they had been dangling while we kissed and placed them on the sides of my face before standing taller on his toes and meeting me forcefully, causing our teeth to clash.

A low and guttural noise emanated from me as my cock swelled uncontrollably. I pulled away and stared into his eyes. "Fuck," I swore. "I never imagined it'd be like this after all these years, Coop."

He smiled sheepishly. "I believe you."

* * *

"Oh my God," Jennifer shrieked. "Turn that up. It's Taylor Swift's new song."

"We Are Never Ever Getting Back Together" blared through her sound system in her far-too-expensive-for-a-teenager's BMW.

"She's country though," Hastings complained from the back seat, a sour look on his face when he made gagging motions behind Jennifer. "I give her fifteen minutes and she's over," he added.

"I don't care," Jen stated. "This is my anthem if Michael ever screws around on me."

"She'll never be *Britney* big," Hastings threw back at her. "Or even *Lady*

Gaga big."

Hastings just convinced me that he was truly gay. I didn't have the heart or the nerve to tell them that Taylor Swift was the biggest music star on the planet in 2023.

There was an odd silence in the car while we drove to the mall after the Swifties calmed down. Our eyes locked and I smiled at Cooper in the mirror when he rolled his eyes in amusement. Perhaps Hastings' and Jen's chat about Taylor would finally convince him he was going to prom with an actual gay guy. Prom was not high on my lists of moments from my past to relive, especially in this version where Hastings would be escorting Cooper.

I kept thinking about the secret between Coop and me. We shared a kiss. I had an additional secret I'd never be able to reveal to anyone. I couldn't fathom how or when I'd ever be willing to try and convince someone I was not from this version of time. Odds were that this would end up being my new space, universe, time, whatever the hell my mother had managed to pull off, and I would live here from now on which was a sobering truth indeed.

What did that actually mean for me? Was I going to relive another ten, nearing eleven years all over again? Would this be how I find out what Coop and I would become? Would I watch my mother die again? What could I do in this world since I knew so many things already? But more importantly, what would change by me simply being here?

Did my mother and I change this future? I had the advantage of maturity. How on earth could my love for Cooper mature and grow organically when I had a decade-long head start? He was only seventeen. So was I in this realm if we were speaking about my physical body, but I was twenty-seven in my experiences. Twenty-eight in a few weeks. Was this even fair?

Cooper smiled at me again and my heart ached to touch him. I had a physical reaction to him and desperately wanted us to be alone so I could show him how much I loved him.

"What are you grinning at?" Hastings asked Cooper. "Everyone is dead silent and boring as hell and you're sitting back here smiling."

"Nothing," Coop replied. "I'm excited to try on my tux. I've never been to prom."

"Excited for all this, huh?" Hastings asked, moving his hands over his body and writhing like a bad Elvis impersonator making me want to smash his fucking face in.

"Oohhh, sounds like a prom-night love session to me," Jen chimed in. "Maybe we can share a hotel room?"

"That ain't happening," I barked, checking on Coop in the mirror.

He'd stiffened up when Hastings grabbed his hand and set it on his crotch.

"Break it up, Hastings," I said, eyeing him now with an adjusted mirror, perhaps glaring a bit too harshly.

"You got yours up there," Hastings quipped. "Leave me and mine alone."

"I'm not yours," Coop said, pulling his hand away. "You don't see a ring on this hand do ya?"

Jennifer shrieked in laughter and attempted to high five Coop but he ignored her so she praised him instead. "That's how it's done, Cooper," she agreed. She waved the promise ring I'd given her in front of us. "This is how you take someone off the market, Michael Hastings," she said, using his full name whenever the two Michaels were together.

"Glad to see you two lovebirds made up," Hastings stated, convincing no one he meant what he said.

"Let's change the subject," Cooper said, turning his attention to Hastings. "You know," he began hesitantly. "If you want . . . well, we don't have to be like on a real date or anything for prom, Michael," he added. "You know, just in case you want to check out the scene and stuff."

"Peeling off are ya?" Hastings replied. "I asked you to prom, pretty boy, and you said yes, *so we is going.*"

Hastings' voice irritated the fuck out of me. His attempt at ghetto slang made me want to punch the windshield. *Lay a hand on him at prom, fucker, and see what I do.*

Cooper seemed resigned to his prom date even though I got the signal loud and clear, he wanted out. Coop wasn't an unkind person. He'd most likely fulfill his obligations and I'd also have to deal with it.

The *youngish* man at the tux place rushed over and greeted us after recognizing the three of us had Jennifer in tow. I recognized him as a hometown hero from a dozen years back when he won a regional basketball game with a last second winning shot. He dined off that event for years. He ogled Jennifer like a hungry wolf, and I figured he should find a more tactful way to communicate instead of eye banging her like she was a piece of meat. "Which of you low-lives has the honor of taking this beauty to the dance?" he asked, as smarmy as a used car salesman.

Jennifer slid her arm inside mine and smiled sweetly. "This one," she purred, knowing when she had an audience. "Those two are each other's dates," she added, thinking he would find her so worldly and diverse minded.

"How about they have a three way and I take you myself?" he asked, looking like a pervert in his ill-fitting suit and oversized rental shoes.

"How about you date in your own species genome," I growled, knowing I was reacting as a nearly thirty-year-old man and not a dumb teenage boy who probably should've laughed at his entirely inappropriate jokes.

He winked at Jennifer like the gross human he was. "Well, looky here. A real tough guy smarty pants you got there, girly."

"Just get our tuxes so we can try them on," I stated, ready to lose my shit like a grumpy old man who'd heard enough. I'd better wise up quickly and do better at acting like a teenager.

Too late. "Chill, Mike," Hastings said. "When did you get all old and shit? You sound like my old man."

"Fuck off, loser," I hissed under my breath. I felt Cooper's hand on my lower back when he walked past me in his attempt to calm me down. He understood me and could sense my emotions so well. The realization was an eye opener that I never would've figured out when I was actually seventeen. He understood me and was attuned to my body language. He had my back and was already looking out for his boyfriend.

The word boyfriend sounded strange as I rolled it around my brain for a moment. I loved the idea of us being boyfriends. Him belonging to me, me to him.

The fittings went well. I wasn't happy that Hastings barged into Coop's dressing room and insisted on sharing the tight space with him. The idea of a *stripped to his briefs* Coop anywhere near Hastings made my blood boil. We finished the fitting and left the mall after getting Orange Julius drinks.

"I'm still grounded, guys," I said, pulling in front of my house. "Sorry, but you guys are on your own." I jumped out of Jen's BMW and held the door for her while she walked around to the driver's side. Surprisingly, Cooper got out as well.

"Shotgun!" Hastings yelled.

"I'm going home too," Coop stated. "So you can have shotgun."

"Leaving me all alone with your lady, Hill?" Hastings asked, grinning like an idiot.

I noticed the pained look on Coop's face. He was embarrassed and I hated to see him sad.

"I trust you, Hastings," I replied, trying a different tactic for now. "But I trust Jennifer more," I added, covering all of my bases.

"That's your first mistake, bro," he said, sliding into the passenger seat without a goodbye hug or any words for Coop.

"You still owe me, Michael Hill," Jen said when she stood in front of me and crossed her arms. "And I'm not completely done being upset either." She kissed her fingertips then touched my nose. "See ya tomorrow."

"Yeah," I answered, preparing to close her door after she adjusted her seatbelt.

Before I could get the door closed, Hastings had one more snarky comment. "Don't you two boys do anything that we wouldn't do."

Jennifer gasped and spun around to face him. "As if," she shrieked, sounding exactly like the chick from the movie *Clueless*, her all-time fave. She fancied herself the latest edition of the movie's character Cher.

Cooper and I stepped back when they pulled away from the curb and watched them drive down the street. "That was awful," Coop said. "They totally know."

"No, they don't," I insisted. "*We* barely know."

I stood with my hands in my pockets as I was prone to do when nervous or pissed. A behavior Jennifer had pointed out more than a few times when we were married. I hadn't grown out of that move even as an adult later in life. And then I realized something important. I now had the chance to work on improving what I felt were my shortcomings or bad traits I had developed at this age. *Why not?* Something told me I'd have the time.

"Even though I tease you about it, I think you look cute when you do that, Mikey," Coop stated, smiling at me.

"This?" I asked, wriggling my hands in my pockets.

"Yes. You look so boyish and mischievous. I like it."

So much for change.

CHAPTER THIRTY-SEVEN: Cooper

We stood staring at one another on the sidewalk after Jennifer and Hastings drove off. Mikey doing his best to keep his cool with his hands buried in his pockets.

"You comin' in?" he asked, kicking at the curb nervously.

"Should I?" I asked, realizing that everything had changed between us, and for the first time in our lives, we felt like strangers.

"Feels odd, don't it?"

"Sort of," I admitted. "I finally got my wish and now I'm not sure I know what to do," I added. "I'm kinda nervous now."

"Me too," he confessed. "But I still want you to come in."

"Are we really going to do this, Mikey?" I asked, looking across the street at my house and feeling a strong pull to run to my room.

"I'd like to, Coop," he answered. "And if it helps, I'm scared shitless too," he acknowledged.

"Really?" I felt a bit better at his admission.

"I'm just as new to this as you. Heck, I'd say even more so," he said. "At least you've been gay longer."

"Are you gay now?" I asked, truthfully wondering what happened in a day and a half, and how that was even possible.

"I want to be with you. I know that for sure," he admitted. "Why don't we go to my room and talk?"

"Sure," I responded, taking another glance toward my house.

Why was I so terrified of him suddenly? This was exactly what I wanted and he was offering himself up on a silver platter, but I felt unexpected fear.

Mikey turned and headed for his house, stopping on the front porch and glancing back at me.

I hadn't moved an inch because I was frozen with anxiety.

He made his way back to the sidewalk. "You're afraid, aren't you?" he asked, reaching for my hand.

I nodded and gazed into his eyes. He seemed calm, even mature. Maybe that's where my fear came from.

He seemed to recognize my anxiety. "Are you more afraid of me or of what happens next?"

"Maybe a little of both?" I answered.

"I see," he said softly. "Wanna call it a night then?"

"I think I do," I said. "I'm sorry, Mikey, but I'm confused by all of this. The kiss. Your news. Them," I added, gesturing down the street in Jen and Hastings' last position. "Going to your bedroom. You. Us."

He squeezed my hand. "That's a lot of worry, Coop, but I get it, and that's totally fine with me. I understand you might need time and like I said, I totally get it."

"You seem so calm about all this," I said. "Such a big change and I guess I'm still in shock. You know, happy, but confused. All at the same time," I said. "I probably sound like a baby."

"You sound like Cooper to me," he replied. "I wouldn't want you to be anyone else."

I was stunned by his relaxed demeanor. Shouldn't he be freaked out by being with me the way I wanted? The sudden shift had me worried because he even sounded different. He was calmer, cooler, and strangely wiser. I tilted my head and stared at him in amazement.

I pointed at him. "That. Right there, Mikey," I said.

He looked behind him, letting go of my hand when he twisted around. After realizing what I must have meant, he turned back. "Am I doing something you don't like?" he asked, shoving his hands back into his pockets.

"No, not exactly," I said. "There's just something unusual about the way you speak lately, and the words you choose. I can't put my finger on it."

Mikey seemed nervous. He went white for a second and appeared to be on edge. "You keep saying that, Coop. You're acting like you don't know me or something."

"I can't shake it," I admitted. "There's just something there. Not bad," I quickly assured.

"What? You don't like me now?"

"No, of course I do. You know I want to be with you, Mikey, but if you're hiding something, you need to tell me."

He threw his hands in the air and let them fall against his hips. "I'm not," he whined, instantly sounding like himself again. "I just . . ."

He went silent and we stared at one another. The seconds felt like eons, glaciers could have formed during the uncomfortable hush, so I finished for him. "Lemme guess, you *just* can't do this? Is that what you were gonna say?"

"No. That's not it. I wouldn't have said I could earlier. That's not what this is about, Coop," he began. "Yes, of course, *maybe* I am different." Mikey moved his hands around wildly as he tried to articulate his thoughts. "This, us, everything, it's all gonna be different." He pointed to me and then back to himself, pressing his finger against his chest. "We're different. Our love is different, so yes, naturally I want to be different."

"Okay. I think I understand."

"What the fuck is this, Coop? I'm really trying here, and I finally gave in to you and now you wanna give me shit about it?"

I hadn't seen that comment coming. "You *finally* gave in to me?" I asked quietly.

His hands went to his face, most likely to hide his anger with me. "God!" he yelled. "That's not what I meant."

"But it's what you said?" I replied. "It is *exactly* what you just said," I repeated.

"Fuck me," he moaned, leveling me with a defeated glare. "You're just like . . ." He stopped in his tracks.

"Like Jennifer?" I accused.

"Fuck no," he stated. "What are we doing, Coop?"

I turned away from him to gather my thoughts, making an attempt to control the fear that he wouldn't love me like he said he would. For the first time in our friendship, I felt powerless.

I took a breath and faced him once more. "I don't want to feel like I forced you to *give in* to me, Mikey," I stated, more aggressive than I'd intended. "So how about *no thanks*? I think I'll pass."

"You can't pass on us, Coop," he said, stepping toward me. "I've waited too long for this."

My eyes saucered. *"You've* waited too long?" I questioned. *"You*? It's you who had to wait?" I raged. "Bullshit, Mike! That is total bullshit."

My harsh words and the fact that I'd cussed stunned him and he staggered back in disbelief. "Alright, Coop. Yeah. Mmm-hmm, yeah," he stammered, his eyes frantically moving around the neighborhood like a trapped animal. "Oh yeah. Okay. So now you don't want me, is that it?"

"I didn't say that," I defended.

"You don't like this me? I'm weird? I'm different? Is that what I'm hearing?" he raged. "Maybe Hastings is better for you? Is he who you want now?"

"Who I don't want is this," I said, gesturing to him and his out-of-bounds accusations.

"Well, that's just perfect," he steamed. "Then that is exactly what you'll get."

Mikey skulked back up the sidewalk and slammed the door behind him after he entered his house.

So much for being mature and wise.

CHAPTER THIRTY-EIGHT: Mike

"Michael? Honey? What's wrong?" Mom asked after I barged through the front door, slamming it hard and cursing like she'd never heard before.

Mom was sitting in the middle of the living room while a hypnotic, calm voice was urging her to relax and center her stress into a circle that she could push away from her mind. *Fuck that!*

I stormed past her, blinded by fury as I tried to wrap my mind around what had just happened on the curb.

"Michael!" she called, raising her voice and most likely expanding her stress circle. "I asked you a question."

I was halfway up the stairs seeking another door to slam. "I'm fine!" I yelled. I got to the top of the staircase and stopped, turned around and added, "And I'm not accepting company or calls." *Mature for sure.*

I decided not to slam the door, instead choosing to pathetically pace back and forth in my bedroom, stopping every other lap to peer over my desk and out my bedroom window at Cooper's house.

"I'm so fucked," I grumbled. "So goddamned fucking fucked."

I headed toward the door, wanting to scream at the person who had caused my problem. *"Oh, yeah, she said,"* I muttered. *"Go drink this stupid potion. Find him in another universe. Be fucking seventeen again.* Fucking bullshit," I hissed before slapping the closet door.

"Michael?" It was my mother's voice outside my bedroom door. "Honey? Bad day?" she asked, her voice slightly muffled by the wooden door. "Can I do anything?"

"You've done quite enough, Mom, so thanks a whole hell of a lot," I stated, forgetting I wasn't twenty-seven in this world and was speaking to a mother who had zero idea what the fuck was going on.

"That is quite enough from you, young man. Do not take your anger or disappointment, or whatever this behavior is, out on me."

"Arrgghhh!" I yelled, squeezing the sides of my head and wanting to smack something. I was normally a calm individual so this outburst caught even me by surprise. Was I acting calm? Not exactly. Did I have a good reason to be pissed off? Possibly.

Then it hit me. I was stuck here. I was a soon-to-be thirty year old man who was stuck in the past and had no plan for what came next. Mom hadn't thought through my journey to the unknown. I'd kept a promise that was ridiculous at best. I was so royally screwed they should crown me king of the idiots.

"Dammit," I hissed.

"Enough of the language, Michael."

"Come in if you want," I said, opening the door in a huff and then heading for my desk to sit down. After pushing two books to the floor, I laid my head on my folded arms on the top of my desk.

"Take a breath, Michael," she suggested, coming up behind me and rubbing the back of my neck. "Carrying on like this will not solve whatever it is that has you so upset."

I inhaled deeply. "I know, Mom," I agreed, forcing myself to remember I was her teenaged son, not the man she'd presented this fucking idea to over a week ago. Not only was *that* woman not available to take a call, she was dead. I had the option to love and respect the one behind me.

"Wanna talk?" she asked.

"Not really," I said, resting my chin on my hands and looking out the window toward Cooper's bedroom. "I had a tough day. I'm being stupid, is all."

"Well, that's certainly not true, son. You carry a 4.0, work part-time, cheer me up when I'm down. I'd say you're an intelligent person."

I moved a hand to my shoulder, offering her to take it. "You're supposed to say that, but thanks, Mom. I guess I'm feeling lost or something."

"Lost is certainly an unusual word choice, honey," she said. "Is this about college? Work? Dad? Are you and Jennifer having a disagreement?"

I understood that my mother wasn't the biggest fan of my girlfriend in this universe or the other, but she would always support me. "Do you like her, Mom?"

"Jennifer?"

"Yeah. Do you like her? Do you think she's a good person?" I asked.

Mom walked to the other side of the room, fussing with her hair and most likely putting on her mom face so she wouldn't reveal her true feelings. I didn't know any of this to be true of course, I based it on future knowledge which wasn't fair to her.

I stood up, straddling the chair like a horse and leaning over the back so I could face her. Once again using my arms as a cushion for my chin. "Forget I asked. Never mind."

Mom leaned against the wall and was quiet. After a minute or so she asked, "How do you feel about her, Michael? I think that's the more important question."

I spoke too quickly. "Indifferent," I acknowledged.

Her eyebrows raised in surprise. "I see someone has been reading up on interesting emotional descriptors. *Lost? Indifferent?* Those are a couple of unusual choices for you to use."

"I guess I don't care if she is or isn't my girlfriend," I admitted. "She didn't really do anything wrong," I added, which truthfully she hadn't in this universe. "I just can't imagine a life with her; not like long term or anything."

"You're seventeen, son," she reminded me. "I'd hope you couldn't at this age, but that doesn't mean the two of you can't grow and mature, finding a mutually loving place as you grow together."

"You always stick up for her," I said, picking at a small scab on my arm that I was noticing for the first time. "Always so nice too."

Mom tapped on her head and laughed. "Let's just say your old mother is smart. Just in case you marry her."

I wanted to say *not a fucking chance of that now that I get a do-over*, but that was mean and she'd never understand the reference to a do-over anyway.

"Do you have a minute?" I asked, deciding on feeling her out about what the real issue was.

In typical *I'm a yoga fitness queen* behavior, Mom crossed her legs as she squatted into a seated position and placed her hands on her knees. "Sounds serious, Michael, and I've got as much time as you need."

"Oh, you're just loving this aren't you?" I teased.

"Maybe," she giggled.

"I'm about to admit something to you that may come as a total shock, Mom, so I'm warning you."

Her face fell faster than an overloaded elevator with a broken cable. "Nobody better be pregnant in this chat," she said, actual fear evident on her face.

"Not likely. I'm a virgin, Mom."

She let out a massive breath and bent forward over her crossed legs to kiss the floor.

"Okay, that was weird. Even for you," I said.

"You're still a virgin?" she asked, her once petrified face turning to amusement, relief, or maybe both. "I'll admit, I wondered," she added.

The conversation felt gross so I didn't answer her follow-up *you're still a virgin* question. "This is about someone else," I stated, thinking I might be confusing her, like when someone asks questions for someone else when it's really for them. "But it's also about me," I quickly corrected. "Just not me and Jen."

"Okay."

I went straight to it, pardon the pun. "I think I might be gay," I said matter-of-factly. "Actually, I am gay," I clarified.

Her face didn't register shock, disappointment, or any of the expected reactions. Of course, this was *my* mother. There wouldn't be any condemnation or lectures about disgraceful lifestyle choices. Mom had the adage that all love was good. If it was love, and if that love was pure of heart, it was a good love.

"I'm so happy you're able to trust me with your true self," she said.

"I think I might like someone," I stated.

"And am I to assume that I'd be correct about whom you may be feeling this way?" she asked, doing her absolute best to check off in her mind the most thoughtful and kind words she could employ in our discussion so as not to offend me.

"I think you can guess."

"And does he know you're having these feelings?"

"Yes, I told him today," I said, pushing my hair out of my eyes. I needed a haircut but apparently this shaggy look was all the rage for high school boys. And that's what I was, a high school boy. "I may have freaked him out," I admitted. "Said some dumb shit."

"First off, Michael. What's with the language? You are not an adult and this is my house, so knock it off please."

Being spoken to like a teenager by your mother was a strange feeling when you went through it once before and hoped you'd picked up a lesson or two along the road all these years later.

"Sorry," I whispered.

We stared at each other, her studying me carefully. I knew what she was doing too. This was her deciding in her mind about how to proceed. This was the mother who was careful about every serious conversation she had or decisions she made. My mother hated when parents demanded their children be something they aren't or attempted to dictate their lives.

"Seems like you're serious, son," she began. "And of course, I'll support any decision you make if the commitment from you is there."

"Thanks," I whispered, still staring into her green eyes, eyes Dad had said had the power for life or death depending on how she looked at you. Today, her gaze was brimming with love. I'd come to expect that from my mother. Witnessing her amazing capacity for love for the second time as a child made the pain of her death hit me suddenly.

I gulped down my emotions and blinked back the tears. "Remember how I said I felt indifferent about me and Jen a couple minutes ago?" I asked.

She nodded.

"I feel differently about Coop. I don't know when it happened, Mom." *That was a lie, I knew.*

"Different than you did yesterday or different than you do about Jennifer? Because this seems kind of sudden, Michael. Unless, of course, you've been thinking about everything for a while."

"I've been thinking about it for a really long time," I said, and that was the truth. *A decade or so was a long time, wasn't it?* "And I fuc . . . I mean, I messed up pretty good out there earlier." I jacked my thumb to the front yard.

"Yeah, I didn't miss your mood when you came in," she stated, nodding, inflating her cheeks before letting the air out slowly while she thought about my words. "What exactly did you say to him?"

"I told him I was finally *giving in to him.*"

Mom's eyes widened and she exhaled, sucking in her cheeks this time. She was surprised by my indelicate comment too.

"Bad, right?" I asked, biting my lower lip.

"Yikes," she said, shaking her head slowly. "Not your finest hour, Michael. Is that what you're doing? Are you giving in to him?"

"No, of course not. I was just mad because he wasn't listening to me."

"Listening to you about what?" she asked.

"He was saying I've been acting weird or grown up all of a sudden. He thinks I'm hiding something because I've been odd these days."

"Are you hiding something?"

She was good at the mom-speak. I'd forgotten what a master she'd been at getting me to spill the beans. Dad used to warn me about asking Mom for help or seeking her opinion if I didn't have the time to be schooled in her wisdom.

Yeah, I'm your son from the future. Whattaya think about that? "No. I just finally realized my feelings for Coop are no longer brotherly or just best friends," I began, suddenly registering that I was having a very unusual discussion with my mother about a boy. "This is weird, Mom."

"What? Admitting that you discovered your true feelings for Cooper? Or telling your mother about it?"

"Both. I think I messed up with him because earlier I told him I loved him as more than a friend," I confessed. "He looked crushed, Mom. You know how he gets."

"I do know how Cooper gets. He's sensitive, Michael. He looks to you to lead and he needs to feel safe. You've managed that since you were toddlers."

"Any suggestions on how to fix it?"

"You know what I'm going to say," she reminded me. I did, but she still went ahead. "You start with two words and you follow those up with three of the most important words. Remember?"

"I'm sorry and I love you," I said quietly.

"Start there, honey. This is Cooper we're talking about."

I stood in front of her and extended my hands which she accepted so I could pull her from the floor and into a hug. "I'm sorry, Mom, and I love you."

"I love you too, and tell him just like that, son."

I watched as she made her way to the door. My mother was a special person, here or there, and in any universe.

CHAPTER THIRTY-NINE: Cooper

"Do you need extra money this weekend?" my mother asked after my father left for work. My father wasn't big on extending advances on my allowance even though neither of them wanted me working until I got through college. "I know Saturday is prom and you'll ha . . ." she began, stopping mid-sentence. "How does it work when it's two boys? Do you both pay? Who asked who? Does he pay? Did you ask Michael Hastings or did he ask you?"

"Take a breath, Mother. I'm not going," I said.

"But, Cooper, honey, you've always wanted to go to a formal dance with a date. Michael seems like such a nice boy too."

"He asked me, but I think I changed my mind."

My mother pulled a chair from under the table and sat next to me. "Prom is less than a week away, son. Canceling seems a bit unkind this close to the dance, don't you think?"

"I'm not sure Hastings is even gay," I said. "I'd hoped to be going with a boy that liked me that way."

She reached for the salt shaker in the middle of the table and rolled it around in her hands before speaking. "He knows you're gay though, correct?" she asked. "And it was him that asked you, so why would you think he doesn't assume it's a date?"

"He talks about girls and flirts with them," I admitted. "And right in front of me too."

"Hmmmm," she mulled. "Sounds immature to me. And Michael is what, seventeen?"

"He's eighteen," I announced.

"Oh, well okay, an adult for sure. Sounds like a boy that might be confused about things, wouldn't you agree?" she asked. "I mean seventeen or even eighteen, plus you add being in high school. Hmmmm?"

I frowned at her. "I hear what you're saying," I said. "But I know I'm gay. And I know for sure. Like forever even."

"But honey, you're mature for your age. Perhaps you've had more time to be comfortable in your skin?" she counseled. "And Michael Hastings has been here what, a year? You don't know who he was before starting school here."

"I think he has the hots for Jennifer James and hangs around me because of Mikey and her."

"What does Mike think about him if that's the case?" she asked.

"He doesn't see it," I said. "Maybe he doesn't care. I don't know."

"Is this about Mike Hill or Michael Hastings, honey?"

My mother knew exactly how I felt about Mikey Hill. She'd witnessed a million tears over the years. "I just wish . . ." My voice broke and I stopped speaking before I added another gallon to the tear well.

"I know what you wish for, Cooper. But I also know that Mike loves you more than anyone could love you. Maybe more than me and your father do if that is possible. Wouldn't you agree?" She grabbed my hand and leaned into me. "You know he does."

"Just not the way I want him to," I replied, deciding to keep what happened that afternoon to myself.

"I suspect that you know he'll never feel that particular way, but in some ways what you have is better, honey."

"Do you think people can change?" I asked. "Maybe they wake up one day and decide they see you like you see them?"

"Maybe," she said, shrugging her shoulders. "But I don't want you setting your heart on something that is kind of unlikely, honey. Mike is such a wonderful young man and you share a very unique closeness with him. I recommend you count that as a wonderful gift."

"So you don't think he could decide he's gay one day?"

191

I saw the heartbreak on her face. She didn't want to deliver bad news or destroy her only child's dream, but she also didn't want me to waste my life waiting for an improbability. "Not usually. I guess it's not impossible, honey, but it is unlikely."

"You're probably right," I said.

"If it helps, you have Mike as your best friend and I think that's a lifetime thing you can always count on."

I bit the inside of my mouth and stared at the clock on the wall. Mikey hadn't texted or called the night before and that wasn't like him. "Yeah," I whispered. "He is that."

"And your father and I love you very much, so you have us too," she said. "And of course you have Kathleen."

"I guess I'll need some money then," I said.

"So, you're going to go to prom?"

"I think it's the right thing to do."

"I think so too, honey." She hugged me and kissed my head a couple of times. "I'll sneak some cash into your sock drawer, okay?"

"Thanks," I said. "And, Mother?"

She smiled and waited for me to speak.

"I still wish things were different with Mikey and me."

"I know you do."

I made my way upstairs to get ready for school. She was probably right. I figured gay people must always know they're gay early in life because I had. As much as I wished Mikey loved me that way, I'd rather we remain best friends than lose him. After all I'd been through with longing for him my whole life, finding out later that he wasn't gay would probably kill me. Besides, Hastings was handsome and he'd asked me to prom. That was something, wasn't it?

I went to my closet and dug my journal out from under a Nike shoe box where I kept it hidden. Walking back to my desk, I turned to last night's entry.

Mikey kissed me today. A real kiss. Tongue and everything. Not like our joke kisses or goodbye smacks on the lips like we've done forever. He says he loves me like I love him. ~~I hope I didn't imagine this.~~ *No, I believe him.*

He said he was finally giving in to me. ~~Liar. I should have known it wasn't for real.~~ *Maybe he's confused because I have a date with Hastings. I bet that's it.*

He did kiss me though and the kiss was magical. Way better than any I've imagined. He's acting weird though. Something isn't right with him. Maybe that's why he told me he wanted to be with me like boyfriends. ~~This can't be real.~~ *Yes, it can.*

"No, it can't," I muttered, slamming the journal shut, just in time to see Jennifer pull in front of his house and honk. Mikey and I didn't have cars so Jen usually picked us up. Mikey hadn't texted so I didn't bother to text Jen for a ride to school. She wouldn't know we'd had a disagreement the night before so I kept quiet about a ride.

I waited, watching his front door and wondering if he'd look up to my window when he came out of his house. A minute went by. I looked at his bedroom window but he'd closed the wooden shutters, something he never did. Another minute went by and nothing. Jen honked again, this time annoyingly longer than the first. Her royal highness did not like being kept waiting. She had a school to rule over, another title to win, and votes were happening for prom queen.

Mrs. H. opened the front door and motioned for Jen to roll her car window down. I saw her mouth moving but couldn't hear what she said. A moment later Jennifer pulled away without Mikey. Was he sick? Was he avoiding me after his big news yesterday because he couldn't face me? I bet he'd changed his mind when reality set in.

I'd always dreaded that if things didn't work out if we crossed a line, that it would be bad. I would be embarrassed for going there. Mikey would be ashamed. We both would be weirded out and try to act like nothing happened. We would avoid each other as time went by and our friendship would eventually end. How could it not? He would be humiliated by participating in a gay act and we'd stop talking. I'd be psychologically destroyed.

The end was nearing.

CHAPTER FORTY: Mike

J en honked twice, the last peace-breaker was long and obnoxious, revealing she was pissed that I was keeping her waiting. Prom voting was that day and she'd called me late last night telling me what to wear and how to act at school. She had decided that she was going to be the first to win both the homecoming queen title as well as wear the prom queen's crown. And with that revelation, she decided I'd be the first double-crown-winning boy by her side.

"I'm not going to school today, Mom," I said after she knocked on my door after honk number one.

"You're telling or asking?" she asked through the closed door.

Forgetting she was the boss and I was the child, I changed my tune. "Not feeling well."

"I'll be right back," she said. I heard Jen's car pull away, followed by Mom's steps on the stairs. Mom had specific protocols when either Dad or I weren't well. Her cure could be lengthy and full of special potions after she determined the illness. I'd better keep my faux diagnosis simple for my own good.

"It's unlocked," I said, after Mom knocked. I liked the fact that both of my parents had made my bedroom my personal space as soon as I proved I could act responsibly. Neither of them ever barged in without knocking.

I was still in bed, having barely slept the night before. I tossed and turned, wrote letters to Cooper, tore letters up, rewrote them, paced, laid down, almost called him, and almost went over to his place. I did pretty much everything but speak to him.

"Okay, what's wrong?" Mom asked, grabbing my wrist to check my pulse while simultaneously holding her palm to my forehead. "Throat? Tummy?"

"I'm fine, Mom. Well, physically."

Her eyes narrowed and she came closer to my face, carefully studying me. "You stuffed all that anger down yesterday didn't you?" she asked. "I can see it behind your eyes."

"No, you can't," I said. "And I didn't do any stuffing either," I quipped.

Mom swiped at my nose then pulled my top sheet down to my waist before running her hands across my warm chest. "Blotchy," she announced. "I knew it."

"Mom," I whined, looking at my bare chest and not seeing what she saw.

"You cannot go to bed when you're angry or stressed, Michael. I've told you that a million times." She had. I remembered. "Your body responds to outside negativity and then it manifests into an overall malaise," she began, tugging on my earlobes for some strange reason. "Stress is a slow killer. Sneaks up on you."

"I'm seventeen, Mom," I argued.

"Open up." She forced my mouth open and peeked inside. "Is your tongue dry?"

I swatted her hand from my chin. "It will be if you keep prying my mouth open," I said. "I'm tired, is all, and I didn't sleep well last night. Besides, there's nothing happening at school with less than a week to go. I won't miss anything important."

"After all that negativity, of course, you didn't sleep well," she accused. "You are too young for all these worries, son." If she only knew. Even at twenty-seven I'd felt the battle deep inside my bones. I wondered if my body knew I was in my late twenties now. My brain sure as hell did.

"I just need to lay around today," I said. "Plus, I have work tomorrow."

"Of course, honey, but you're drinking one of my elixirs."

I'd forgotten Mom used that word for the major battles. When the illness or the negative event required average ammunition, she used her potions, but *elixirs* meant busting out the big guns.

"No marigolds," I stated.

She looked at me oddly, her lips drawn into a frown. "Now why would I use marigold?" she asked. "We aren't summoning the dead, for gosh sakes."

I was tempted to ask additional questions about *summoning* the dead, but my three days back in my childhood home circa 2013 had taught me a valuable lesson. Less talk. More listen.

"Lay still and be peaceful. I'll be right back," she ordered.

Once Mom was downstairs I went to the window, opened the shutters, and looked across the street. Coop and his mother were heading to Charla's car. Cooper didn't look toward my bedroom window when he slid inside the car. I watched as they backed out and drove toward school, wondering what he was thinking when I hadn't gone with Jennifer. Maybe he hadn't noticed, but I knew her honking would've alerted him.

I heard Mom coming up the stairs so I dove back into bed.

"Here you go," she said, handing me a plate with what looked like a piece of black licorice, a wedge of lemon, and a mug of warm cloudy liquid. I brought the mug to my nose and sniffed before making a face. It smelled horrible.

"Garlic and warm soda water," she announced. "Drink up."

"Gross, Mom," I stated, my upper lip curling in disgust. "What is this concoction?"

"I just told you. Now squeeze the lemon into your mouth and then drink all of that in one swig. Once you drink every drop, then chew on the licorice."

A decade ago in my other life I would have fought her over it, but now I had insight that my mother had certain unearthly gifts. Plus, why not go along with her? I knew healing others pleased her and if the stinky elixir worked that was an added bonus. Even if there was nothing but confusion and worry causing my made-up troubles, garlic, lemon and licorice wouldn't kill me.

I did as she said and drank the liquid then ate the licorice to kill the taste of the raw garlic. "Where do you get these cures or whatever you call them?" I asked.

"My books. Sometimes my Facebook groups," she stated, taking the mug from me then checking my forehead again. "Some I make up after researching ancient indigenous medicine men or Chinese herbalist cures. You know, all the experts."

"How about a *real* doctor's advice?" I teased.

"When needed I suppose, but why poison ourselves when there are natural ways to fight illnesses and pain," she advised. "Western medicine is amazing too but I prefer my alternative approaches."

"Yeah, I know," I said. "Thanks, Mom. I'll rest a bit." A horrible taste built in my mouth as I continued chewing on the black licorice. I spat the dissolving piece onto my hand. "Yuk. What kind of candy is this?" I asked, still trying to push tiny pieces of the nasty licorice out of my mouth.

"I never said it was candy," she said, grinning. "Now put that back in your mouth and swallow."

I looked at my hand and then back at her, suspicious that she was trying to poison me.

"It's all natural. I wouldn't give you something that you couldn't handle," she insisted.

Really? Like a potion that transported me through parallel universes? "This stuff tastes horrible," I said.

She shifted my hand to my mouth. "Eat it," she ordered. "I'm going to the library again today." She reached into her apron pocket and pulled out a cell phone. "Here, you can have this back."

I turned the Apple iPhone around, squinting at the backside to make out the model. The phone was a 3GS from 2009 or earlier. It was a relic for sure. "Thanks."

"We'll have some organic soup when I get back. Loads of root veggies," she said, moving to the door. "Relax and think positive thoughts while I'm gone."

"I will. Thanks again for the phone."

Mom smiled and hurried down the stairs. She was on a mission. Sick child alert. Call out the big guns.

"You are really something," I mumbled, laughing to myself.

After turning the phone on, I noticed dozens of texts; some were several days old, even before my arrival from the other world. Today's messages were all from Jennifer.

OMG! You're not coming today?!?! This is only THE most important day of high school, Michael!

That one arrived three minutes after Mom told her I wasn't feeling well. Jennifer didn't mention anything about me being sick or offering to help.

I can totally work the votes for me because I'm here. I can't do the same 4 u 2! Gawd! I'm so pissed, Michael!!!!

Four exclamation marks. She *was* pissed.

When I get crowned without you . . . OMG! I can't EVEN imagine, and if Hastings or Mark Nelson is standing by me, I WILL NEVER FORGIVE U! EVER!

So, there had been evidence of a future Jennifer in this younger version.

I scrolled through a dozen more rants from my girlfriend and then went to Cooper's. Not much from the last couple of days. He'd sent one Sunday that said I seemed odd that morning. He'd sent another after we'd spoken about how I'd hurt his feelings in front of Hastings, but that he still loved me and forgave me. Nothing before the kiss or after the curbside disagreement. Silence from the only person that mattered. The text history could come in handy as I tried to piece some current information together. I scrolled back a few weeks.

Coop: *He asked me to prom.*

Me: *That's great, buddy.*

Coop: *I don't know tho. Should I say yes?*

Me: *Do you like him that way?*

I noticed a time gap after the last text I'd sent. About three minutes passed before he responded to the question. Why was Coop hesitating?

Coop: *Maybe. He's nice enough. Cute too I guess.*

Me: *We could have a double date.*

Coop: *Yeah, maybe.*

Me: *I say you tell him yes. It'll be fun.*

Coop: *I suppose. Maybe.*

After that day's messages, Cooper's texts were shorter in length and he shifted the conversation to us not spending as much time together lately. *"He missed me,"* he'd said. It was clear that Cooper hadn't wanted to go to the dance with Hastings even back then. Perhaps I was reading into things, but from the gist of his texts he was either seeking my permission or wanted me to talk him out of it.

I distinctly remembered that time during our senior year. I hadn't liked Hastings back then. I'd listened to Coop as he'd told me about how Hastings wasn't gay but still wanted down-low head and I'd found him to be a creepy fucker. But in this version of history, Hastings was gay and seemed like a typical teenaged boy who was genuinely pursuing Coop.

"You're interfering, Mike," I whispered.

Reality dawned on me in an instant. Even in this universe I couldn't expect Cooper to be on the same agenda as me. I shouldn't have rushed to announce that I was in love with him either. The timing was too soon and had not been set up properly. I shouldn't have kissed him before understanding what was happening in this version of our lives. I was twenty-seven, he was only seventeen. Even though we were both seventeen in this universe, it felt odd. As much as I wanted Cooper, wouldn't I be influencing his choices based on my past with him? What if we weren't meant to be together?

Unfortunately, he hadn't lived an additional decade, or even another few months to make a choice about us. But I'd known how he actually felt about me because of the letter he'd left on my desk the day he died. No confessions have been written in this universe yet because I jumped ahead. Perhaps there never will be. My arrival felt completely unfair.

Suddenly I was unsure of the correct course to take. Future Mom had said I should prevent Cooper's drowning in this parallel universe, thus changing the trajectory of our future and giving me a chance to tell him how I felt. Declaring my love right away should alter things, shouldn't it? I was learning that the reality of this world was *almost* the same, proving that unfolding events that appeared *parallel* were not necessarily *identical*.

I had a major decision to make. I understood that my approach had to be different. How was I supposed to rectify what I've done? How could I win Coop's love and not use knowledge for advantage? And truthfully, did

I have an advantage or were we on equal footing because I was emotionally immature where he was concerned?

This wouldn't be easy. But was anything worth having ever easy?

CHAPTER FORTY-ONE: Cooper

I remained in the car after my mother pulled into the parking lot of the grocery store where Mikey worked. I immediately noticed him running groceries to a customer's car. He hadn't spotted me.

"Didn't Mike miss school today?" Mom asked when she recognized him pushing an empty cart back to the store.

"Yeah, he did," I mumbled, scooting lower in my seat. I hated feeling so anxious seeing him. This was how it would go from now on. He hadn't called or texted and I hadn't either, which has never happened between us.

"Coming in?" she asked.

"I'd rather not."

"What's going on? Do we need to talk about the two of you?" Mom asked, sniffing out drama better than a hound chasing a coon ever could. "Does this have something to do with this morning's chat?"

"I'd rather not do that either, Mom, if that's okay?"

"What did you say to Mike?" she asked.

"God, Mom! Why do you assume it's me?" I asked, resenting that she always took Mikey's side.

"Because Mike is much more laid back than you, Cooper. And you were acting funny this morning," she stated. "Are you pressuring him, honey?"

"Pressuring him to do what?"

"You seemed confused about whether you were or weren't going to prom, and then asked me about people changing their minds and other things," she began. "Did you overstep boundaries with Mike?"

"Oh, I see," I said, raising my voice in anger. "I overstepped. It'd have to be me because Mikey would never do such a thing."

"Well?"

"For your information, Mom. Mikey overstepped. How about that?" I asked, looking away and chewing on my lower lip as I stared out the window. I never raised my voice at my parents and I was immediately disappointed by my behavior. "I'm sorry for raising my voice," I offered. "But Mikey did something this time, Mom, not me."

"And what would that be?" she asked, still suspicious I'd over thought something.

"He told me he's gay and he wants to be with me."

She stared at me in disbelief.

"Don't look so shocked. I'm serious, he did."

"What about . . .?" she began. "And . . ." She couldn't gather her train of thoughts.

"I know, Mom," I soothed. "I know."

"What are you going . . .?" She stopped speaking.

I assumed she was going to ask what I was going to do. "I don't know, Mom," I cut in after her thoughts got derailed again. "We had a disagreement afterwards, so we aren't speaking," I updated her.

"Does Kathleen know?" she asked, searching for some kind of solid footing, something a mother could grasp ahold of after hearing the stunning news. "I mean, does she even know?"

"I'm going to assume she does. Mikey and her talk about everything. You know how Mrs. H. is. She's into expression and truth. Nothing bothers her."

"I'm not bothered," she argued.

"I know that, Mom. That's not what I meant," I responded. "Can we calm down for a second? I'm the one that should be freaking out."

We watched from a distance while Mikey exited the store with another customer. He was with our neighbor, Mr. Peterson. This time Mikey noticed us in Mom's car. He tilted his head toward us and waved.

"Should we go home?" Mom asked.

"That'd be weird, Mom. Can you please just go in? I'll talk with him."

"Will you be okay, honey?"

"It's Mikey, Mom."

"Of course it is," she agreed, patting my leg. "Talk later?"

"Talk later," I agreed. "Go ahead and go in please," I added while Mikey assisted Mr. Peterson.

Mom hurried into the store, nervously glancing over her shoulder three separate times. *Good job, Mom. Act normal.*

I hopped out of the car and waited for Mikey while he held a conversation with Mr. Peterson. The usual ache that often set up shop in my heart was back. There are things in life that people covet or desire so strongly that a physical response to loss is not uncommon. I was in that category. In my inexperienced mind, Mike Hill was everything that I wanted in a lifetime mate. I think I figured that out when I was about twelve which was when I saw him as someone other than a friend.

The longing and love I felt was overwhelming from that day on. I'm not embarrassed to say that he was my breath, my life, the one thing I thought about nonstop. I couldn't imagine my life without Mikey. So far, I'd been able to suppress my desire in exchange for what he *could* give. After knowing that there was a possibility that he felt the same way, our friendship would be different, maybe impossible for me now.

Mikey strode over in that masculine dude-walk sorta way that drove me wild. He was such a guy and I guess that was a whole heap of my attraction to him. His appeal was his walk, his demeanor, that had recently been hitting me in areas I'd never recognized. He was handsome in khakis and a short sleeve button-down with the top unbuttoned at the collar and a loose tie reaching toward his belt. He was boyish and he took my breath away. A fresh stab hit me square in the heart.

"Hi," I said, when he walked up smiling. "How's work today?"

"It's okay." He had trouble making eye contact. This was it. The beginning of the end.

"Jennifer said you were sick," I said.

"Yeah. I had Mom tell her that," he answered, raising his eyes from the pavement and watching me carefully, testing my mood I suppose. "I'm not though."

"That's good," I said. "I was worried."

"You were," he asked, lighting up and jamming his hands into his pockets. "Thanks," he added. "I was worried too."

"About?" I inquired.

"You. Us," he began. "Yeah, maybe more about us, I guess."

We stood two feet apart yet the distance felt like miles. "You were?"

"Mmmm-hmm," he mumbled, fidgeting uncomfortably. "I'm sorry, Coop." Mikey's eyes filled and he hiccuped.

"I'm not mad anymore, Mikey. I know you were just confused about what you said and all."

"You do?" he asked. "Not my finest hour, huh?"

"Or mine," I agreed.

"You want to talk about it?" he asked, looking toward the market, checking to see if his boss was watching. "We can if you want to."

"How about we don't," I said, smiling and hoping we could go back to us. "I'm okay if you are."

"Sure. Yeah. That'd be okay too."

"Okay. Good then," I said, wishing my mother would hurry up and save me from this agonizing moment. "See you at school tomorrow?"

He appeared saddened by my question. "I could come over tonight after work. I'm off at eight," he quickly suggested.

"That's okay," I answered.

"Or you could come over to my house if you prefer?" he asked. "I bet Mom would like to see you," he added.

"Maybe another night?"

"Sure. Yeah, another night, buddy," he agreed. And just like that, we were back to buddies.

Neither of us moved. I was just trying not to run into his arms and cry. He seemed sad. Mikey looked away and wiped at his eyes. The movement caused a release from mine and my throat clenched shut like it was prone to do when I couldn't express my emotions.

"Okay then," I whispered. I turned back to Mom's car.

"Cooper?"

I quickly turned back.

"I . . . I . . ." He couldn't finish.

I nodded slowly after he got bogged down with whatever he wanted to say and turned back to the car before he saw my tears. I opened the door but waited to see if he finished his thought. He couldn't so I got in and closed the door. I didn't dare look at him as he lingered for a moment near the car. He finally walked away.

The degree of pain I felt was beyond words. I was literally ripped open, exposed, and left completely alone. A lifetime of love and friendship yanked out from under me because I'd believed he wanted me the way I wanted him. At the first sign of interest, I'd jumped at the chance without asking more questions, subsequently losing the only thing that mattered to me, him.

Tomorrow was a new day. I hoped we'd find our way back to our friendship.

CHAPTER FORTY-TWO: Mike

I t was ironic how I'd describe my current state of being. When I was a *real* teenager, I would go through short periods of time where I wanted little interaction with others. My isolation wasn't often and I rarely excluded Coop. I can't remember exactly why, but at the time I was questioning my place in the world. I had hair on my balls and jerked off three times a day. All that frustrated release didn't solve the unknown desire I felt inside. My life was confusing.

Mom would call me Mopey. She'd announce to Dad, *"Hey, Mopey's back"* or *"Mike is moping around again. Hope this time it's a shorter visit from Mr. Mopey."*

Being thirteen and fourteen, I'd roll my eyes and say something dumb in response, but now that I've recognized I'm feeling exactly the same way as I did back then, I had to laugh about it. I suppose if I were really seventeen I wouldn't care, but acting mopey in my early teens hadn't been successful, and this time wouldn't be either. I had to come up with a better solution to my predicament.

The parking lot interaction hadn't gone well. I'd tried to say *I'm sorry* a second time, while taking Mom's advice and adding that I loved him, but my throat shut down. I'd hit a roadblock on how to overcome my stupidity at being too forceful and too abrupt regarding my change of sexuality. And it sure as hell hadn't helped that I said I *finally* gave into him. Perhaps if I hadn't said those words, none of our current problems would've happened. I might have had more time to ease us into the change.

* * *

School on Wednesday was a blur. Keeping a low profile didn't help either. Jennifer was still pissed about my absence on Tuesday, so she was punishing me with the silent treatment. Honestly, I appreciated the break.

At lunch I was about to enter the cafeteria alone because apparently Hastings was Team Jennifer and he had immediately launched from our class at the bell, ignoring me. When I walked in I saw the usual group at our table: Jen, Coop, Hastings, and Meg with her on-again-off-again boyfriend, Greg. Hastings was seated beside Jen so she obviously did not save my space. High school drama was still the same and I felt like I just couldn't bear trying to overcome any shortfalls that I'm sure were being debated amongst my peers.

Coop wouldn't be participating, I knew that for sure. He knew what it felt like to be judged and he would have nothing to do with talking smack about someone who wasn't there to defend themselves. And despite our troubles, I felt fairly confident that he would still defend me if my name came up, and I was certain it would.

Prom was in three days and I wasn't sure about my date status. Jennifer would need her chosen king beside her, so she most likely wouldn't bail on short notice. If she'd had an extra month or so, she could've crafted a new scenario to create a new king from the many suitors waiting in the wings. I wasn't dumb, I knew what Jennifer represented in the eyes of the other males in my school. She was entrance into rarified air, plus she was too hot for any boy who encountered her charms to say no to her. So perhaps prom was still a go for us.

I backed out of the cafeteria and decided to hang out on the bleachers after seeing the assembled clique. I was sitting in the top row by myself for five minutes when I heard voices below me. I listened carefully to see if I recognized them. Barely a second went by when I heard a voice I knew, one unlike any other I've ever heard. Cooper's. The grating voice was Hastings'. They must've arrived shortly after me.

Slowly lifting my feet from the aluminum stands, I lay on my side on the bench seating so as not to be seen and to attempt to catch the conversation below me. Cooper seemed to be defending his position on our double date for prom.

"I don't think we should," he began. "Mikey and I need time to fix our friendship. Not to mention all of us being together in Jen's car would be difficult because we're fighting."

I hadn't heard he was backing out of the double date since we hadn't been communicating either.

"No, it won't be," Hastings argued. "Talk to Hill and tell him to get over whatever's up his skirt. I want to go with them."

"I don't know, Michael. Mikey and I never fight and this time it's pretty serious," he said. "And I'm not even sure he wants us to go with them anymore."

"So I have to miss out because you pissed him off?"

"You could go alone," Coop suggested. "I'm *completely* fine with that."

"But I wanna be the guy that takes you to your first formal dance, Cooper," Hastings said when he switched gears. "Because going is important to you, it's important to me." He was shrewder than I imagined.

I suppressed an instant desire to puke. There was something about Hastings' whether it was his tone of voice or his clever way of speaking, I'm sure he wasn't presenting an authentic package. At least I knew Cooper wouldn't fall for a line that lame.

"Really?" Coop responded. "That is so thoughtful. Thank you, Michael."

I was wrong.

"Totally, babe. I'm thinking about *you* here," Hastings continued, slime oozing from his voice.

Calling Coop *babe* had certainly taken me aback. I didn't like the endearment one bit.

"You deserve to enjoy your senior year."

"Well, I suppose we could go," Coop agreed.

"Great," Hastings said. "I'll talk with Hill and smooth stuff out. If Mike acts all tough and shit at the dance, I'll look out for you too, babe," he added, sounding like a bad imitation of a school thug.

"Mikey wouldn't do that though," Coop said, defending others as usual. "Well just in case then. So, yeah, I'll hit him up later about it," he said. "Cool. Good, we're going then, right?"

"I guess we are," Coop responded.

"I'd give ya a kiss, but you know, school and all," Hastings said. "I'm gonna head back and let Jen know we're still on if she hasn't dumped Hill by now."

And with that, Hastings jogged off, leaving Cooper below me. I wanted to clear my throat to let him know I was there but he looked completely dejected. Cooper stood silently and watched Hastings disappear into the cafeteria. He appeared defeated and small from my vantage. I wanted to jump down and comfort him, beg him to believe what I had admitted to him, but I was frozen in place. Getting tangled in high school romance drama would continue to be a huge mistake. I had to find a way back to him that didn't involve me behaving like a seventeen year old kid.

Since Cooper had accused me of acting more mature, I should do just that. I could admit he was correct. I'd let him know I was feeling more like a man, maybe add in that since Dad had died I was trying harder to behave more like an adult. That was what he was sensing about me so why not cash in on the allegation? I'd mention that I was almost eighteen and had decided to act like a man which included wanting to be true to myself about my feelings for him.

There were two issues troubling me. First off, how do you act like you're trying to be a man at seventeen when you're really twenty-seven trying to act seventeen? Secondly, what to do once I confessed my love for him a second time? Prove it?

We were both seventeen for a couple more weeks, but I felt slightly bothered about knowing I was actually an adult in my head and he wasn't yet. The facts were the facts though. We were both biologically seventeen in this universe. No laws would be broken and I shouldn't freak myself out about it. And the Coop I knew was inexperienced, so I imagined he'd be afraid of jumping right into a physical relationship which would provide me the cover to not feel like a creep.

CHAPTER FORTY-THREE: Cooper

"Mikey isn't going to be happy, Mrs. H.," I said, sitting in her kitchen and waiting for him to arrive home from work.

"Trust me, he will," she insisted. "Even if I have to make him be."

"It was just a misunderstanding," I said, trying my best to warn her away from bringing my last conversation with Mikey up again. "You know how we fight once and a while."

"This isn't that, young man," she said, setting a plate in front of me as she set up three place settings.

Mikey's Mom had texted me Thursday after school and requested that I share dinner with her and Mikey when he got off of work. We hadn't hung out since Monday and she didn't need to be a rocket scientist to know that wasn't the norm. I skipped dinner at my place, telling my mother that Mrs. H. asked me for dinner and asked whether I should pass or not.

"You absolutely should go," she said. *"I agree with Kathleen one thousand percent. You boys need to clear the air,"* she added. *"I suggest you two talk this through and then get right with each other again. Kathleen is right. This has gone on long enough."*

"It's barely been three days," I'd responded.

"Which is a lifetime for you two," she argued. *"You're going."*

So here I was, in a home I'd practically lived in my entire life, afraid of what would happen when Mikey got home. The tradeoff was the lasagna I smelled and the giant loaf of garlic bread Mrs. H. had on the counter waiting to be toasted.

Kids always think the food at other kids' houses is better than at home because it's not their own parents' cooking, but in my case, it definitely was. My mother couldn't cook. Neither could my father. So Mrs. H. was a five-star chef in my opinion.

We ate a lot of prepared frozen food and take-out at my house. Maybe that's why I hung out at Mikey's more than he did at our place. I didn't blame my parents because they worked; certainly not my mother because she had an important job with long hours. One of the worst things about growing up in a house with no cooks was that I wouldn't learn how to cook either. I could microwave like a Martha Stewart Wizard though.

I heard the front door and looked at Mrs. H. in panic.

"You'll do fine, kiddo," she assured me, wiping her hands on a dish towel. "Just be you, okay?"

I nodded.

"In here, honey," she hollered to get Mikey's attention.

Mikey's dress shoes were loud on the hardwood floors when he clomped to the kitchen. "Smells so frikkin good, Mom. I'm star . . ." He stopped, surprised to see me, but his face didn't sour or anything. "Coop," he said before turning to look at his mother.

"I invited Cooper to join us, honey," she stated, stepping forward and untying his tie and smoothing the front of his shirt. "Take this and go change into something comfier," she added, handing him his tie. "Garlic bread going in now so no dilly-dallying."

"Cool word, Mom. Very hip." Mikey turned his attention to me. "Thanks for coming over, Coop. I'll be right down." He hurried around the corner and up the stairs.

"See?" Mrs. H. asked. "He's happy you're here. I knew he would be. What do you say we get things back on track tonight?"

"What do you know exactly?" I whispered, cupping my hand in case Mikey could hear. There'd be a slim chance since I heard his footsteps above us in his bedroom.

"Everything," she said. "Mikey told me."

"He told you . . . e-ver-y-thing?" I asked, dramatically pronouncing each syllable.

"Yep," she casually responded. "He sure did. And guess what?" she asked, grinning like a Cheshire cat.

I let out a long sigh full of anxiety and shook my head.

"We are going to talk about it. Isn't that wonderful?"

"We can't," I insisted, standing and moving toward her. "No, Mrs. H.. We can't talk about that," I repeated, tugging on her arm. "He'll die of embarrassment, and then so will I. He'll never talk to me again. Please don't?" I begged, appealing to her senses and to the woman who'd always listened to reason.

"This will be fine. I already told you that he told me everything. I know about the off-handed comment," she remarked. "And I know he told you he is gay. I know it all, so we are going to clear some air so that the two of you can get back to being close."

"Oh my God, oh my God," I said, covering my face with my hands. "He'll hate me."

She pulled my hands away from my face. "He won't. He loves you, Cooper, and we are going to discuss precisely that," she declared. "I don't usually get caught up in your boys' lives but this is a biggie. Do you understand me? A biggie. Huge," she added, spreading her hands apart. "Best to nip this in the bud right now."

"Nip what in the bud?" Mikey asked, jumping to the floor from four steps up and smiling at me once again. This was the old Mikey. He didn't seem angry or sad, or any of a dozen things I imagined he'd be. He was my typical happy-go-lucky Mikey.

Mrs. H. pointed to the table. "Sit. We'll eat first."

Mikey saluted his mother and slid toward the table with a burst of energy. Sliding past his chair and he grabbed on to me. "Thank you, kind sir," he quipped when he saluted me too. "It seems our mother is planning something big, Coop. For it would appear she's made her famous lasagna," he announced in a British accent. "Shall we eat her food and then bail?"

I was confused. Seriously confused. Mikey was acting like nothing had happened. "Sure," I answered, wanting to also act normal. "There's garlic bread too," I pointed out.

"Then eat we shall," he joked. "We'll double team her later. Demand she stay out of our affairs."

I wished.

* * *

Mikey and I rinsed the dishes and filled the dishwasher. My plastic margarine container full of leftovers sat at the end of the kitchen island. I desperately wanted to thank Mrs. H. for the meal and head home immediately before she fulfilled her intervention.

"You boys full?" she inquired.

"Sure am," Mikey concurred. "How 'bout you, Coop?"

I nodded.

"We are, mother dearest, so what's up?"

"Sit," she began. "I'd like the two of you to clear the air," she added, folding her hands on the table top. She turned to Mikey and waited for him to sit and give her his full attention. "I told Cooper earlier that we spoke about the unwise comment you made and the news about your sexuality."

"I see," he calmly replied. He turned to me next. "Sorry about that, Coop. And I'm incredibly sorry I said that to you, but I'm mostly sorry about her," he said, tilting his head toward his mother. "She seems to think that our personal life is hers to interfere with."

"I forgive you," I whispered. I *really, really, really,* didn't want to have this discussion in front of Mrs. H.. "And I'm sorry too. I was partially to blame. I'm dumb, is all it was. I probably misunderstood you and then blew it up in my head. You know how I am, Mikey."

Mikey's Mom's eyes moved from me to him, like an umpire at a tennis match watching and judging, but staying out of the actual match.

Mikey rolled his eyes and placed his hand on hers. "Mom is right. I was wrong for what I said and I regret it," he started. "I could never be talked into being gay if I wasn't actually gay, and I did not mean to imply that I thought you had done that. I care about you. You're my best friend and I would never do anything to jeopardize our love for one another. I owe you a big apology, Coop. Please forgive me?"

Man, he could talk grown-up. His voice and words were exactly what I had pointed out to him before when I'd noticed the change in him. Mikey sounded like an adult, and I found myself staring at his mouth as he spoke. Oh yeah, it was Mikey all right, and I was seriously turned on by the change which only added confusion to what he was saying.

"That was nice, Michael. Well said and heartfelt. I appreciate those carefully chosen words," Mrs. H. said. She focused on me next. *Uh-oh.* "Cooper? How do you feel, son?"

"I feel . . . I feel good," I stammered. "Really good actually. And happier too."

My answer was true, but I was still trying to figure out what Mikey was expressing. Was he gay? Not gay? Did he love me like I loved him? Were his words to help me move past everything? I was more confused now than when I'd arrived.

"Still love me?" Mikey asked.

"I do," I responded.

"Am I forgiven?"

"You are."

"Wanna go up to my room and hang out?" he asked. "Maybe get away from the Spanish inquisition here?"

I turned to Mrs. H.. "Thank you for dinner, Mrs. H., but I have to go home and do homework," I said, standing from the table. "See you tomorrow?" I asked, looking at Mikey.

His face fell but he quickly reset and smiled. "Yeah, sure, Coop. Want me to walk out with you?"

He pushed back from the table but I held up my hand. "It's okay," I answered softly before grabbing my backpack and heading for the door.

"Cooper?" Mrs. H. asked when I got to the front door. I turned back toward her and Mikey. "You okay? Are we good here?"

"Yes, ma'am."

"Okay, honey. Glad you came over. Tell your mother hello, will you?"

I nodded and stepped outside, closing the door quietly. What just happened?

CHAPTER FORTY-FOUR: Mike

M om thought Thursday night's dinner had gone swimmingly. I wasn't convinced.

"You were well spoken, honey," she'd said. *"Surprisingly articulate as well."*

"Uh, thanks, I think?" I questioned.

"No, I just mean you sounded so mature, Michael. That was precisely what Cooper needed to hear."

"He walked out, Mom. I don't think it went as well as you think it did," I'd challenged.

She waved me off. *"You'll see. I still say bravo to you."*

Mom was wrong. Cooper avoided me like I had COVID all day Friday. *Holy fuck, they don't know about COVID.* At any rate, nothing had changed between us and I didn't like it much.

He all but completely ignored me in second period and we sat next to each other for fuck's sake. I grabbed his sleeve when students funneled out the door into the hallway after the bell rang, pulling him back into the empty classroom. Mr. Hicks had already left for his hallway monitor duties in between classes.

"Hey, are we good?" I asked, trying to act calm and cool.

"Yeah, I think so," he answered.

"You only think so?" I asked, concerned I'd been correct and Mom had misread the mood. "Then how about you help me understand what's happening, Coop?"

"I heard you loud and clear at dinner, Mikey. I get it now," he began, nervously watching the open door and the crowded hallway. "I just need more time, is all."

"What part did you get?" I pushed, being careful to not appear threatening or upset.

"You weren't forced to give in to me, and you *may* or *may not* be gay," he began. "I think I heard what I needed to hear."

Cooper was distant and cold, and it broke my heart. I felt alone in my attempt to get us back on track and wasn't sure what to say or how to act. And in that moment I didn't know how to fucking breath when I looked into his empty eyes. I'd hurt him somewhere deep and I needed to know how to undo what I'd done. I was suddenly fearful that I wasn't in his heart anymore. His eyes proved that much.

I backed away. "You don't feel the same about me, do you?" I whispered, loosening my grip on his wrist. "I've destroyed what we had."

He couldn't look at me, a tell-tell sign that he'd checked out and possibly moved on. I'd seen Coop quit on people who had hurt him before, and I knew it took a lot to lose him. Had I done that?

He removed my hand from his wrist. "You took something that I believed in, our friendship to be exact, and you changed it," he started, choking up. "I trusted in what we had. I've never told you this, but I built walls around my heart to protect me from how I felt about you, Mikey."

"But . . ."

He checked the door again. "I'm not done," he stated, sounding unlike himself. "And then you *out of the blue* tell me what you told me?"

"I meant the part about being gay," I interjected. "This is me, Coop. Why would I lie about something like this?"

"I don't know. You tell me," he said. "I see you standing here, and I know you look like you and all, but you *are not* you. You're . . . you're . . . different, Mikey. Something is not right."

"Because *I am* different," I protested. "I'm growing up. I'm almost eighteen. Besides, why would I lie about wanting to be with you that way? I wouldn't do that to you, Coop. I just wouldn't."

He sighed and shrugged his shoulders, probably frustrated by my words.

"What happened last Sunday?" he demanded. "If you want my trust then tell me what happened."

"Nothing happened," I lied. There was no way I could tell him that I'd suddenly zapped into a parallel dimension. If he was confused now, that news would put him in the loony bin.

"I don't believe you."

"Coop, listen to me," I began.

He pushed me away and stepped around me. "No thanks, Mikey. You either admit that something has changed with you or I don't want to be around you anymore."

"Jesus, Coop," I hissed. "Maybe it's you that's changed."

He was almost out the door but suddenly stopped, spinning around quickly. "Maybe I have," he stated dismissively. "Maybe I *actually* want to be what you said I was to you. How about that? But you aren't gay and you know it. What you are though, is mean, Mikey. That joke you pulled was mean."

And with that, he left me standing there with my mouth hanging wide open. Cooper had also changed, but this was his world, not mine.

I walked directly out of school after my interaction with Coop. It was Friday and the last day for senior's, but I didn't give a fuck by that point.

My cell phone began blowing up about five minutes after I didn't show up for my class with Jen. I was halfway home by then. After reading a ton of her questions about where I was, why I'd ditched school, and how I could miss her final cheerleading assembly performance, I switched my phone off.

I walked through my front door, tossed my backpack on the floor, and shuffled to the kitchen for a Coke. I was surprised to see Mom had company. A woman I'd never seen before in either universe sat at the kitchen table with Mom. Trust me, I'd have remembered this woman if we had met.

"Hi, honey," Mom said, twisting her wrist and checking her watch before raising an eyebrow. "Early dismissal on your last day?"

"For me it was," I said, being careful to tone down the smart-assed comment I had dialed up. "Hello," I said, to the woman that resembled my mother in the style department but had kicked it up fifty notches.

Mom's guest wore a ton more jewelry than I thought was appropriate for a human with any sense of style. She had one or more rings per finger and at least thirty bangle-type bracelets per wrist. But it was her headdress or whatever the fuck she had wrapped around her skull, that made me look away before I stared too long and said something outrageous.

I restrained a need to laugh out loud before returning my attention to her. A brightly colored scarf with images of neon moons, stars, and galaxies was covering her head and was tied into a knot directly above her forehead. Pinned below the knot was a ceramic brooch of an eye that was about the size of a saucer. The eye itself had the illusion of rays of sunshine or bursts of cosmic light coming out of the iris.

Her eyes were outlined in black eyeliner with exaggerated curved lines drawn up and away from the corners of each eye, while her lips were a vibrant orange in hue. I'd never laid eyes on a more unusual looking person in my life. She reminded me of an actress that was on a Nick at Night rerun of a nineteen-sixties comedy who played the mother of a witch. Mom often watched the show because she absolutely loved the mother's character.

"Michael, meet Druzella."

CHAPTER FORTY-FIVE: Cooper

"Don't know. Don't care," I stated, answering Jen's question and shoving another tater tot into my mouth. I was definitely not going to miss cafeteria food. Even the cafeteria pizza was getting boring and that was everyone's favorite.

"He hasn't returned a single one of my texts. Not one," Jennifer bitched. She bothered me. How Mikey put up with a complainer like her was beyond me. Maybe that's what drove him to say he was gay? I sat staring at Jennifer and wanted to poke her eyes out with my last tater tot. God, I'd tried to like her, but as I sat listening to her go on and on and on about Mikey being a disappointment, I resented sitting with her. Now I was pissed that I wasted the past four years of high school praying she liked me enough. *Well, fuck that.*

"You look angry, Cooper," she said, moving her mirror and presenting the phoniest face I've ever witnessed. That was a lie. I've witnessed this face a million times. *Where's my tot?*

My internal dialogue was still cussing, something I never did out loud, but she was on my very last nerve. My very last and tiny, tiny, tiny, *darn* nerve. *Calm down.*

"Nervous I guess," I said. "You know, about prom, graduation, stuff like that."

"It'll all be great after we graduate, you'll see," she declared, checking her makeup for the tenth time. "All of us in Seattle at UW. Just imagine the freedom."

I added another item to my *Mad at Mikey* list. He hadn't told her he was going to Washington State in Pullman yet, not UW. What was wrong with him? But then again, maybe I wasn't going to college with him anymore either.

"That's not it," I said, locating the tot and holstering it up in my hand.

"Oohhh," she giggled. "Is Hastings pressuring you to give it up?"

My eyes doubled their normal size.

She leaned closer. "I bet you're gonna do it on prom night."

"Uh, I doubt that."

She quickly looked around at who might be in ear shot. Hastings hadn't come to lunch and Meg was fighting with Greg at another table. "Hastings told me his folks will be gone this weekend and he wants us to come to his house after the dance," she said, wiggling her eyebrows and making the letter O with her mouth like something naughty might happen. "I think he's planning his move, Coopie," she squealed.

"Are you and Mikey going?" I asked. "Does he know about Hastings' folks being gone?"

"Hmmm, probably," she murmured. "Don't know actually, but I'm not putting out even if we do."

I knew her and Mikey weren't doing it. He'd have told me if they were. I had wondered why they hadn't yet but he always blamed her. *"She won't even rub my dick,"* he'd said, while we were showering. I certainly would've if he'd asked me back then.

Jennifer leaned even closer. Another six inches and she'd have been across the table and sitting on my lap. "Are you going to . . .?" she paused and looked around us again. "You know," she asked, winking and making a strange face.

"No. I don't think I do know," I said.

She moved her finger to her lips and pushed back and forth, an extremely poor attempt at imitating a blow job. She pointed at me and then back to her mouth, this time opening her lips a bit. "To Hastings if he wants you to?"

I knew what she was asking but this was far too much fun to stop messing with her. "Kiss him?" I asked.

She shook her head, pursing her lips. "No. The other thing," she whispered, turning a wonderful shade of red. This was fun.

"French kiss him?" I asked.

Her shoulders fell and she huffed out a breath. "Stop acting like you don't know what I'm talking about, Cooper. It's the one thing all of you boys want." This time she pushed her finger further into her mouth and pulled it back out, repeating the movement a few times.

I saw Hastings walking up behind her so I gave him a look that said, *hold on, check this out.*

"Oh, that?" I asked, pretending I was shocked. "Not me."

Hastings leaned around her. "What are you doing, Miss Perfect?" he asked, leering at her. "Apparently I've been missing out." He looked across at me. "You taking lessons?"

"Gross," Jen shrieked. "I'd never. Oh my God. No way."

He laid a hand on her shoulder. "Calm down. We hear ya, cheer queen. You'd never. How about you, Cooper?"

I wanted to say *not with you, perv,* but my options were getting even more limited.

"Just kidding," he added, swiping my tot and plunking it in his mouth. *You're kinda gross.*

"I'm saving myself," Jennifer stated.

"Even if Hill moves on?" he questioned. "Because I doubt he'll wait, Mother Mary."

"Have you *even* seen me?" she asked, adjusting her top and dragging her fingers across her breasts. She dragged them up her neck to her chin, then placed her thumb and middle finger along the edges of her mouth lustfully. "Trust me, he'll wait."

"Damn, girl," he declared. "Holy fuuuccckkk. *I'll* wait."

It was at that moment that I began to see Michael Hastings as something he claimed he wasn't. Straight. And not only that. He wanted to be the new Mr. Jennifer James.

"Where's your other boyfriend?" Hastings asked, gesturing to me. "Heard he skipped school," he added.

"Don't know," I muttered.

"You hear that, Jennifer? Cooper doesn't know where Mike Hill is. Guess I don't have to be jealous anymore."

After the morning I had, I'd reached my limit of BS. "You know something, Hastings," I began. "You can F off."

He covered his mouth and fake gasped. "No fucking way," he said. He walked around the table and leaned over me, placing his palm to my forehead. "You okay, rebel?"

I pushed his hand away and gave him a nasty look. "Why are you such a dick?"

"Cooper!" Jennifer gasped. "You cussed. You don't *ever* say naughty words."

"Well, fuck that," I stated, sliding off of the bench seat. "And fuck you, Hastings."

I took three steps away and stopped, then walked back and got in his face. "Besides, I want a meal, not a snack," I hissed. "And I wouldn't suck your needle dick if you were the last guy on this planet. And don't pick me up for prom either."

"But, Cooper," Jennifer begged. "You gotta go. We're double dating and we all match."

"Wake up, Jennifer," I stated, gesturing toward Hastings. "He's practically crawling up your ass. Go with him."

"Wha . . . what . . . Well, I've never," she blubbered.

I grinned maniacally at her and then at Hastings. "Maybe that's the problem."

I walked out of school. I was ashamed of my outburst. I didn't swear. I wasn't cruel or someone who made fun of people. I was Mr. Nice Guy to all I met and had been since kindergarten. What exactly had that gotten me? Nothing. Zip. Zero.

I was going to change.

My house was empty when I got home. I still felt awful about dumping my anger on Jennifer and Hastings but couldn't change anything now. At half past twelve, my parents were both working so I trudged up to my room.

The reality of what I'd said to two of the most popular kids at school finally settled in. I didn't know where the rage came from but I would have to apologize or beg for forgiveness if I wanted to be included ever again.

I stared across the street at Mikey's house. A purple VW Beetle decorated with giant flower stickers was parked in the driveway. I hadn't noticed the car until then and it stood out like a clown car. The glare from the sun hid whether Mikey was in his bedroom or not. It probably didn't matter anyway. I'd pushed him away and to add frosting onto the proverbial cake, I'd just insulted the other two stars of high school.

I pulled the bottom drawer out from my desk and rifled under old school work, doodles, and other junk, including a Reese's candy bar I had forgotten about until my fingers felt the glossy picture that I sought. The photo was of Mikey and me at Campbell lake last summer. Jennifer had snapped the picture on her cell phone and then made two copies and gave them to Mikey and me for our birthdays last year.

We were both bare chested with our arms around each other. Mikey was giving me rabbit ears and the two of us were grinning like fools. I leaned into him while he held me close. I'd cut the picture into a heart shape and hidden it from him because I thought he'd think my act too much for guy friends. Sun lit our faces, our white teeth even brighter due to our tans. Several people said we could have been brothers because of how similar we looked at times. We were very close, but I'd never wanted that comparison to be true.

I brought the photo closer, noticing for the first time the weird rings of light around our heads. Blinking my eyes, I squinted and tilted the photo towards my window to make sure the circles weren't a weird reflection. At that moment I had one of those déjà vu feelings pass over me as if I'd visited the lake recently, which I knew I hadn't.

I flipped the photo over, carefully reading the date. July 2012. "It *was* last year," I whispered, running my hand over the date. I nearly fell off my wooden chair when dried ink from a year-old photo smeared onto my finger.

224

CHAPTER FORTY-SIX: Mike

"Nice to meet you, Druzella," I said, extending my hand as I made my way to her. I wanted a closer examination of the woman who'd been involved in turning my life literally upside down and inside out. I wasn't sure how to describe moving between cosmoses.

She rested her hand gently in my open palm. Her grip tightened as she gazed into my eyes. If you had asked me a month ago if we exchanged something unspoken during the handshake, I'd have laughed at the absurdity, but now?

"You're an intuitive soul, young man," she said, looking at Mom and nodding to confirm her assertion. Her free hand moved across my inner arm when she squeezed harder with the one holding my hand. "Very strong impulses," she added.

"Strong willed," Mom interjected. "Like his father."

"Oh, yes," Druzella agreed. "Your late husband's spirit is inside this creature." I gently tugged my hand back but she held tighter and wouldn't release me. "You Cancer's are a willful bunch, aren't you?"

"I never mentioned that Michael was born under Cancer," Mom said, looking from her mystical friend to me.

"You didn't have to, Kathleen," she purred. "I can spot someone born under the fourth sign immediately. He's just like his mother." She turned to Mom, not letting go of me. "Your son is sensitive and protective."

"I'm not sure I believe in those things," I admitted. "I get that Mom likes this stuff, but I'm harder to convince."

As soon as I spoke I had an electrical sensation flow through me. Mom

225

picked up on it too and grabbed Druzella's arm, linking all three of us.

"That's not true, child," she stated, surprising me when she called me out so easily. "You and your mother share a powerful astrological sign for sure, but I'm sensing a trinity." Her eyes closed suddenly.

I quickly looked at Mom and made a face that said *what the fuck is this?*

"Druzella?" Mom whispered.

Druzella's eyes popped open. "But your departed husband is not Cancer, Kathleen." Mom shook her head, confirming Dad wasn't. "But there exists a trinity? There is a bond within this trinity that involves some kind of jewels," Druzella murmured.

What the . . . ? She knew about the ring and the three rubies in the setting.

And then as if she'd been jolted by an unseen power, she jumped back and released my hand. Her eyes widened while she studied me closely, her eyes darting between Mom and me.

"Are you okay, Madame Druzella," I asked, fearing her head was about to spin three hundred and sixty degrees.

All color faded from her face in an instant. "Where did you hear that name?" she asked.

Mom turned her attention to me. "Michael?"

"I'm not sure," I lied. "I just said it." Apparently neither of them were aware that Mom referred to her as Madame in the future. Maybe she'd earned a certificate? How the hell would I know?

"Who are the three Cancers in this household?" Druzella demanded. "And I need to see the cat?"

"We don't have a cat," Mom clarified slowly. "And it's just Michael and I that live here, Druzella. What's wrong?"

"That cannot be so," she said, eerily looking around the space and clutching a necklace I hadn't noticed until it was in her hand being handled like a rosary. The piece she held was a circle with a sun in the center with the astrological signs going around the circle's edges like a clock.

"His name is Cooper," I said. "He doesn't live here but he comes over often."

She turned to Mom. "Like a son to you." And then toward me "Like a brother to you," she stated calmly. "But not quite," she added, slightly grinning.

"Do you sense danger?" Mom asked.

"Not at all, dear, but there is a force at work in this house," she announced.

Now normally I would chalk this up to crazy talk. Mom and Druzella, Mom's potions and her books, their shared spiritual interests and stuff, but I had a different point of view now. I was smack in the middle of crazy. In fact, I was the duly elected mayor of Crazy Town.

"Have I spoken to you about the transitory aspect?" Druzella asked Mom.

I became interested in what Mom's friend asked and slid into a chair, waiting for Mom to answer the question.

"Is that when a planet moves into position with the location that another planet had on the day you were born?" Mom asked.

Druzella snapped her fingers. "Precisely," she stated. "The locations of the planets at the moment of your birth are recorded and calculated as part of your astrology chart."

"Cooper and I share a birth date," I contributed. "Mom, him and I are all Cancers." I had a gazillion questions and figured I should tamp down my sudden interest in what this unusual woman was speaking about. "You know, if it matters."

Her face changed and the alteration was hard to describe. Fearful, grave, dread. Those were words that came to mind.

"There is another commonality," she began, setting her gaze on me. "But the shared event isn't about birth."

"What is it?" Mom piped up, her voice laced with fear.

Druzella grabbed both of our hands. "This Cooper, where does he live?" she asked.

Mom and I simultaneously pointed at the picture window and toward Cooper's house.

She focused her attention on me, her eyes rolling into her head. "You and Cooper were born on the same day," she began, turning to Mom, her eyes popping open. "And you and Cooper share . . ." She let go of our hands suddenly and pulled back from us.

A death date. She knew.

I had to change the conversation before things got weirder. "Can I ask you about parallel universes?" I asked.

Mom, who had been entranced with her friend's words, spoke up. "You're still interested in that, Michael? I'm sorry, honey, but I keep forgetting to bring home the books from the library."

"Do you know anything about parallel universes?" I asked Druzella. "How they work, are they connected with astrology or birthdays? Stuff like that?"

"Umm, not really my area of expertise, young man," she stated.

"Really?" I asked. "You seem like you'd know about that stuff. I mean, you're so interested in those types of things. Right, Mom?"

"Well, honey, Druzella is experienced in many things but perhaps that subject is not an area she delves into seriously," Mom said. "I'll get you some books."

The discussion got quiet as we looked from one another, checking on whether anyone had another topic. Druzella was gathering her things and pushing her chair away from the table. A minute before there had been tarot cards, a star map, and some small metallic pieces depicting stars and moons arranged on the table. What I needed was a fucking map home before I blew my cover.

"I think I should leave," Druzella said. She checked her wrist for the watch that was buried between twenty bracelets. "Yes, it is getting late," she added. "Thank you, Kathleen.. We'll finish your reading another time."

I wasn't prepared to give up so easily. This exotic woman knew things I needed to know and I wanted answers. But how to get them?

"Don't go so soon, Druzella," Mom said. "How about staying for dinner?"

By then Druzella was standing and slinging her bag of goodies over shoulder.

"Great idea, Mom," I encouraged.

Druzella was already heading for the living room, steps from the front door. "No thanks," she said, scurrying away in a hurry.

"Wait up," I said, rushing to get the door for her. I turned to Mom. "I'll walk your friend to her car, Mom. Be right back."

I followed Druzella down the sidewalk, struggling to keep pace with her. "Are you coming back soon?" I asked. "I'd really like to talk to you about parallel universes."

She stopped abruptly and turned around so fast that I nearly bumped into her. She grabbed my hand and stared into my eyes for what seemed an eternity. I was uncomfortable and felt a chilling sensation come over her. Her hands were ice cold even though it was eighty degrees outside in late June and she was covered in layers of colorful clothes.

"How long have you been here?"

Her question floored me and I felt the rush of fire burning across my face. But how to answer her question was my biggest concern. Currently, nothing was normal in my life, so why should this exchange be any different?

"My whole life?" I answered in the form of a question in case she hadn't noticed me following her out the door.

"How long *this* time?" she asked, reframing her question.

I froze. How should I answer? Did she actually know?

"I'm . . . well, I'm not quite sure what you mean," I stammered.

"I think you do," she stated.

Oh, I did alright, but I wouldn't admit to something this insane to a person I'd just met, even if it was the illustrious Madame Druzella from 2023.

"You're what, seventeen or eighteen?" she asked, studying me.

I nodded.

"But not actually, am I correct?"

I didn't respond.

"You're going to make me say it?"

I nodded again. Better her than me. I no longer thought she was nuts, but she didn't know that.

"I cannot pinpoint your precise age, young man, but you're no teenage boy. Your aura is far too mature to fool me. Is your mother buying this version so far?"

What do I say?

"So," I began, revealing nothing. "Do you know anything about parallel universes?"

She stepped closer so that her face was inches from mine, glancing toward the front window in case Mom was watching. "I know you don't fuck around in them. How about that?"

"Helpful. Direct," I stated.

"You seem like a wise man, Michael," she said. "So listen closely."

I held my breath out of fear that I may have already *fucked around* in this dimension.

"Do what you came to do and then stop tinkering; or better yet, leave."

"That's where you come in, *Madame Druzella*," I asserted. "I don't know how to go back."

"You're barking up the wrong tree, my celestial friend."

"But I'm not," I stated. "You're the one that sent me here."

CHAPTER FORTY-SEVEN: Cooper

T he rented tux hung on the back of my bedroom door, still in the zip-up bag. I'd really wanted to wear the formal suit, especially after Mikey said I looked better than a model during our fitting on Monday afternoon. Hastings joked that I was too short to be a real model. I didn't think five-eleven was particularly short, but maybe in comparison to him and Mikey who were both two inches over six feet, I was short.

Hastings hadn't texted or called after my outburst, so I figured my prom date had canceled on me. Without Mikey, Hastings, or even Jennifer texting me my cell was dead quiet which was an accurate exhibit of my future. No more Mikey, no more high school, no more popularity. My summer was stacking up to be the most boring summer of my life.

I heard a car door slam across the street so I sat up in bed to see if someone was at my house. Jen's bright-red BMW was parked along the curb in front of Mikey's but she wasn't getting out of the car. I got out of bed and sat at my desk and waited for Mikey to come out. Maybe they had a date before the dance or errands to run. I no longer knew anything about Mikey's plans, which left me feeling even lonelier.

My anger was subsiding, nevertheless. Now I was afraid with a pain too difficult to describe setting up residency in the pit of my stomach. I was nothing, and I had nothing without Mikey. The reality of life without him was unimaginable to me. He was everything to me and I'd been an asshole to him. In a matter of twenty-four hours I'd gone from *I'm finished with him* to *how do I live without him?*

This had never happened before. Sure, we had fights and disagreements.

Boys argued like everyone else until they settled their dominance standing or accepted roles within their friendship. And Mikey and I had done all of that. Several times, in fact, but those separations were always brief and we mended our friendship because we knew we needed each other.

I've never had a romantic relationship, so I can't be sure, but I likened our disagreement to when a couple fights and then makes up. Once back together they're mushier, maybe they even have make-up sex, profess their love over and over. Mikey and I weren't dissimilar. We'd settle things eventually and then we'd find every reason to touch each other, hug more, grab and wrestle one another. In a sense, the renewed connection was our sexual dance. Perhaps Mikey grew out of it. I never had.

He was growing out of many things and I think I was paying attention. What if I'd missed his growth because I felt the same blind love and devotion for him regardless of our ages? We were born on the same day, making us the exact same age. But Mikey had always acted older. He'd been my leader and I was okay with that. I still was if I were honest.

Mikey stepped outside in gray gym shorts and nothing else. I swallowed hard when the pain in my heart suffocated me at the sight of him. He was simply the hottest guy I had ever seen. He walked like a total dude and didn't even realize he did. His stride was confident, but not arrogant; his chest was out with his head held high, yet he seemed welcoming and kind. I knew he was all of those things. I admired him so much.

He crossed his arms and waited for Jennifer to meet him halfway. Why had he stopped before reaching her car? I felt like I was invading their privacy but I couldn't stop watching, so I adjusted my blinds to conceal my presence. Just in time too because Mikey glanced up at my window.

Mikey waited for about a minute before he turned and headed back inside. But then Jen stepped out of her car and made her way up the sidewalk, her hands animatedly gesturing. I knew her well. She was articulating her displeasure at not being catered to. A queen likes to be worshiped at all times. She was no different.

They didn't hug. Mikey appeared unhappy based on his posture and facial expressions. I wished I could read lips. Of course, it would have only been a one-sided conversation because Mikey was the only one facing me. They talked for several minutes before Mikey began walking in a circle, pointing at her occasionally, and then stopping to listen.

Jennifer raised her arms and then let them fall to her sides a couple of times in what could only be described as frustration. Then it was Mikey's turn. Eventually Jennifer stepped forward and tried to hug him but Mikey resisted, pushing her arms away from him. The slap came out of nowhere.

I shrunk lower in my chair, barely able to watch because I was ashamed I was witnessing their argument. But the scene was like a car accident on a freeway and I couldn't look away.

Mikey rubbed his cheek, dumbfounded that she'd actually slapped him. I was shocked and wanted to yell for her to back off or even run downstairs and protect him. Instead I held my breath and continued to watch. Shaking his head, Mikey went inside his house.

Alone on the Hill's front lawn, Jennifer crossed her arms and turned toward my house. She stared at my window, looking upset when she did something I could've never imagined Jennifer James doing. She flipped me the bird. Not once, but twice when she waved both her hands at my window with surprising ferocity.

She only stopped when Mikey reappeared. He was carrying a medium sized cardboard box. I recognized the teddy bear in a cowboy hat that Jennifer had gifted him that was peeking out of the top of the box. Picture frames and assorted artwork she'd made for him were also in the box. Was Mikey breaking up with her?

Jennifer pointed her key at her car and the trunk popped open. Mikey walked down the sidewalk to the curb and placed the box inside. Leaving the trunk open, he retreated when she came closer to him. Perhaps a second slap didn't appeal to him. He yanked his arm away from her when she attempted to touch him again, so she walked to the trunk, removed a framed picture and threw it on the street. The glass shattered everywhere and the frame broke. Then Jennifer threw another, and another, and another.

Holy shit.

After flashing another middle finger at Mikey and then her other middle finger at my house while giving us both the bird at the same time. Mikey glanced over to see if I saw her before he glared at her, saying something that elicited both middle fingers to swing in his direction. She slammed the trunk shut and got in her car, peeling away from the curb with a final finger waving in the wind.

Mikey watched her car disappear down the street before looking my way. I squatted and waited. After a minute, I peeked out. Mikey was still staring at my window, arms crossed, pain etched on his face. I recognized this face. This was his mouth tightly closed, quivering lips, try-not-to-cry look, and it broke my heart.

I lifted my blinds, revealing myself to him and admitting that I just witnessed everything. He touched his heart and then pointed toward me, asking if he could come over. Tears fell from my eyes when a familiar emotion awoke in my heart.

Mikey needed me.

I nodded and waited.

CHAPTER FORTY-EIGHT: Mike

I sat on the edge of Cooper's bed. He was still seated at his desk but had turned the chair around to face me. He was quiet. I was hunched over, staring at my feet, trying to overcome the inability to speak without crying.

"You okay?" he whispered.

I couldn't answer. I could barely nod let alone hold a conversation. Perhaps I should have waited before rushing over and unloading my emotions on Cooper.

The previous night had been a roller coaster of concerns. I was haunted by decisions I needed to make, regrets, and genuine fear. The advice delivered by Druzella had helped me make a decision about my current situation. I decided that I could no longer sit back and try to blend in or act like I was an actual teenager. I had choices to make and they needed to be made quickly. Of course, Coop wouldn't believe me, but I didn't have to convince him that I was a visitor here. There were some secrets I knew I could never reveal and Druzella had confirmed that.

"Do what you came to do and then stop tinkering; or better yet, leave," she'd insisted. *"Don't fuck around."*

I didn't know how to leave or if I was even able to. What I could do was convince Coop that I loved him, wanted to be with him, and wanted to begin a life with him right here, right now. I'd figure the other parts out later. I was there to do one thing, save his life. Let the universe work out the rest after August 30th.

Coop stood and came to my side, sitting beside me on his bed. Even

235

though we were in the same room the silence spoke volumes. He slid his hand into mine and squeezed. The kind gesture released my tears and I sobbed into my hands, while he rubbed my back gently without asking questions, just being there.

After several minutes ticked by with neither of us sure what came next, he said, "That didn't look good from up here. I'm sorry if you two are fighting."

There were several things I wanted to say but no sounds came out when I tried speaking.

Coop sensed I needed time. "That was a crazy car parked at your house last night," he offered, trying to find a path to dialogue. "A purple VW bug with yellow daisies?" he asked sarcastically. "Doesn't work in my opinion, but then again, I don't even have a car."

"Because our folks are conspiring," I whispered, testing my voice.

"You knew?" he asked, laughing at the badly kept secret.

"I figured as much," I said, turning toward him and feeling the rush his beautiful face and shaggy, unkempt, morning hair had on my heart. I'd probably seen him like this a million times in our short lives, but today I was observing with fresh eyes. "Mom says we can't afford it so I guessed that your folks don't want you havin' something I don't have."

"I wouldn't want that either."

I sat up and faced him. A couple of small tears squeezed out of my eyes despite my best effort. He repositioned himself, removing his hand from mine and stared into my eyes as we danced around the questions I assumed we both had. I knew Coop still loved me. He had to in my opinion. His love was the one thing I'd be counting on from now on.

"We broke up," I said. "I'm not being fair to Jen."

"I'd wondered," he replied. "I saw the box of stuff and the broken frames." His hands were in a wrestling match with one another in his lap. "Why?" he whispered, diverting his eyes. Maybe he was afraid of the answer, the consequences of my action.

"She deserves better than a lie," I began. "I don't love her the way I should and leading her on is a shitty thing to do."

"I take it that something's changed?" he asked.

"You could say that," I agreed. "Mostly, I've changed. I tried to tell you that the other day but kinda screwed up."

"And I reacted badly, Mikey. I wasn't thinking clearly," he said. "The kiss, your news . . . well, that was a lot to process."

"How about now, Coop? What's going through your head now?"

"Did you break up with Jen because of me?" he asked.

He'd asked a good question. One I should be careful answering. "Yes and no. Yes because I know how I feel about you and like I said, having those feelings for you wasn't fair to Jen," I stated. "And no, because even if you don't want to give me a shot, I'm still going to be gay. That won't change, but I really want you to give me a chance, Coop. I've set my heart on it."

"I think you know my answer to that."

"Yeah?"

I leaned closer and placed my lips on his, but held still so he could make the decision to kiss me. The kiss wouldn't be confused with our usual smack on the lips because I was very much aware of my feelings. In the past, perhaps he was testing me to see what a silly kiss meant to me or he just went along because that was the nature of our friendship, while I wondered what was appropriate for two guys to share. No, this time he'd know this was different.

Coop held my hand and allowed me to linger on his lips, delicately moving his lips across mine like butterflies dancing on a bloom. We didn't rush or even open our mouths, but we connected.

I pulled back a little. Our noses were still close and we kept our eyes locked, neither one sure of what came next. "I love you," I said. "I think I always have," I added.

He didn't speak. I think he wanted to hear what I had to say. He needed to know he was safe with me and could trust my words as well. He brought his hand up to my bare chest and covered my heart. A shiver coursed through me when he let out a held breath. I moved forward, connecting in the only way either of us knew how. I, of course, could visualize other ways. I hadn't done them, but I imagined I was likely to be light years ahead of Coop. I'd have to lead us and hopefully he'd trust my direction.

This time Coop leaned against me, opening his mouth and allowing me to truly feel his acquiescence. Our mouths gnashed together as our hunger overtook our inexperience. He suddenly lay back, pulling me onto him. He wore only boxers to my *going commando* under gym shorts. Once our chests collided, my flesh ignited as our hands traveled over each other with passion but lost without a map of what to do or where to go.

"I . . . I . . . want to . . ." Coop whispered, our mouths fighting to fulfill a need neither of us understood how to quell.

He lifted his butt off the bed, inviting me to pull his boxers down. I did as he wanted while he struggled to pull my shorts off. Once we were both free of the barriers, our cocks crashed together and we ground into each other; sliding, pressing, and gyrating in every possible way to achieve something significant.

I held the back of Coop's head when we kissed. His fingers dug into my ass cheeks when his hands pulled me closer to grind himself into me. We used the corners of our mouths to breathe because our tongues clashed and searched. His body writhed below mine as we naturally fell into the roles I'd always assumed we would. He'd be an involved and willing lover, but he wanted me to take control. Just the idea of being with him like this drove me insane with passion.

We violently slammed our bodies together, our mouths never detached while our hands felt, searched, explored the other's body. We'd seen each other naked a thousand times, but to experience this was on another level. Neither of us reached for the other's cock, but our swords were in a battle of their own as they slid across each other, the sweat mixing with precum.

I pushed his legs apart with my muscular thighs and settled between them, grinding my cock on his as we continued kissing. I couldn't get close enough without being inside of him but knew that today wouldn't be that day. I fantasized about how Cooper would feel for years. I had completely undersold the experience.

He gasped before he moaned into my mouth, humming and mumbling as he felt the fire building. "I think I'm gonna come," he said, his eyes wide when we gazed into each other's eyes. I licked the sensitive skin on his neck before I sucked gently while flicking my tongue against his pulse and roughly burrowed my face against him. His legs fought with mine when he stiffened underneath me. "Ohhh," he cried. "Ohhh . . . ohhh . . . I can't . . . ohhh . . . . can't stop . . . it."

Coop bucked uncontrollably under me when he released. My load shot out almost immediately after his cries of pleasure. We pumped against each other, breathing and grunting as our cock's erupted with pleasure. We held on tight until both of our quivering and breathless panting subsided. Our next kiss was gentle like the ending of a sweet lullaby bringing both of us down from the heavens.

As I had hoped, we were a good fit; natural lovers who'd finally shared the kind of love we'd longed for. I couldn't speak for Coop, but I only saw our physical love getting better. Much better.

Now could be the strange part. We'd crossed a line. Our friendship had irretrievably changed from that moment forward.

He nuzzled my neck and held on tighter, his way of asking me to help him feel safe.

I did a push-up and hovered above him, smiling down at him, sweat dripping on his face from mine, neither of us thinking it was gross. "Are you okay?" I whispered. He nodded and returned my smile. "And you'd tell me if you weren't?" I pushed.

"Yeah, I would."

I couldn't take my eyes off of him. His hair was splayed over the pillow and some curly locks were soaked with perspiration and stuck to his forehead. His sky-blue eyes sparkled as the morning sun came through his eastern-facing window. He was stunning.

A mental alarm bell went off and I checked whether the door was closed to his bedroom. I collapsed onto him, moving my mouth to his ear. "Your parents," I whispered urgently.

He let out a typically cute Cooper laugh, digging a finger into my side to get me to roll over. When I did, he crawled on top of me, switching our positions. "At the gym. They do yoga on Saturdays, remember?" he asked. "For another hour or so," he added, wiggling his eyebrows and looking where our hips connected.

"What?" I asked, making biting motions at him when he tried to hold my arms to my sides.

"This time I'm on top."

CHAPTER FORTY-NINE: Cooper

"Well, this is different," Mikey said, holding me tightly as we faced each other and the warm shower spray splashing against my back.

"Only in reality as far as I'm concerned," I teased. "I've played this over in my mind countless times."

"You did, huh?"

"You have no idea," I confessed. "Over and over and over and over."

Mikey placed a hand over my mouth. "I heard you."

I wriggled free. "I must say this is even better though."

"Turn around, you goofball," he said. "Lemme get your hair and back."

"Umm, can I share something?" I asked. "Not to be too, well . . . *forward* for a newbie."

"Am I the newbie or are you the newbie in this scenario?"

I laughed out loud, turning my back to him so I'd have the courage to admit something dirty to him. "I've always been the gay one in this friendship, so you're the newbie."

"Friendship, huh? Is that what we're calling it?"

"Stop," I said. "You know what I mean."

"Whatever. Go ahead," he said.

"What you're about to do," I began. "You know, like we've done this like, so many times, right?" I continued, probably sounding like a sorority girl with my overuse of the word *like*. "You always start by washing my hair and then you scrub my back, but only to my waist."

Mikey brought his hands around my waist and pulled my ass against his

241

cock, then snuggled his cheek into my neck. My entire body tingled with electricity. My knees were weak from his cock pressing against my butt cheeks, making me putty in his hands. He was very strong and good at manipulating my somewhat smaller body.

"But I never washed your butt, is that what you were going to say?" he snarled, repositioning his hands to my erect cock and sudsing it with soap. "I guess that was a line I was afraid to cross, Coop."

"Yeah?" I asked, moving my butt cheeks in a circular motion over his cock. "What about now? Do you think you could manage?" I moaned, reaching behind my back and grabbing his dick.

Mikey had a thick dick with a huge mushroom head that was often visible through his gym shorts or tight jeans. I'd tried my best to avoid staring at his bulge when he wasn't paying attention because I didn't want to freak him out. The things I fantasized about doing to him would play in my spank bank for days. I'd seen his dick tons of times but never had him pushing his boner against my butt before.

"You're nastier than I thought," he whispered in my ear while sliding his open hand up and down my cock while his free hand squeezed my balls gently. "I like that, pretty boy."

"I'm not wasting my chance," I stated. "Trust me, I have a million things I want to do with you."

"Fuck," he groaned. "You're dirty as fuck."

"Well?" I asked, turning my head to the side and glancing at my ass. "It ain't gonna wash itself."

Mikey pushed my head forward until I was bent over at the waist with my palms resting against the cool wet tile so he had access to my firm, round cheeks.

He moved his hands to my ass, palming my never-been-touched-before flesh in his large hands. He squeezed and lifted each one before letting the mounds drop. "You have the best ass I've ever seen," he began. "I used to spin you around and wash your back so I could look at it," he admitted. "I was afraid of the feelings I had then."

"That's kinda hot," I said. "I wish I'd known. Knowing would have helped the jack off sessions."

"No way," Mikey stated.

"Trust me. Way."

"Lemme see what I was missing."

As Mikey played with my ass cheeks, soaping and sudsing them heavily, he trailed a finger down my sensitive ass crack, stopping just before my hole, and then caressed up to the small of my back.

"Tease," I complained, arching my back to reposition my hole because I longed for his touch.

"How about this?" Mikey gripped my waist with one hand and slid a soapy finger across my asshole, stroking my button repeatedly. Each time he rubbed against my hole, my legs felt like they'd give out on me.

"That feels amazing," I moaned. "Stroke my dick," I begged.

"Listen to you, you nasty little man," he hissed, his finger swirling against my asshole. "Who'd a fucking known?"

"Don't blame me, stud. You're the one that's kept me waiting," I reminded him. "Kept me frustrated my entire fucking life."

"And your language? Who the fuck are you, Coop?"

"Shut it and stick your dick between my legs," I demanded. "Pretend you're fucking me while you jack me off."

"Jesus, dude," he growled. "Keep talking that trash."

"You still yakking back there?"

Mikey grabbed the back of my hair and yanked my head back, until his lips were pressed against my ear. "You like this, pretty boy?" He twisted my long hair in his fingers. "Because I've got plenty of my own built-up shit for you."

"Then fucking show me," I hissed. "Prove it."

He placed his hard cock between my legs and grabbed my hips to force my legs together so he could have friction for his dick as he pumped into my ass crack. I reached over my shoulder and put my hand behind his neck, pulling him closer and asking him to bite at my neck.

Mikey kept one hand on my hip while the other stroked my dick nice and slow, his cock sliding across my taint and hitting the back of my balls. I reached my free hand between us, wanting to feel his dick pump back and forth. I was no where near ready to be penetrated but I wanted the fantasy of being fucked while he jerked me off. I'd watched a shit load of gay porn and always imagined that the guy getting pounded in his ass would be me. Of course, I wanted Mikey to be the guy in charge.

He moved the hand from my hip and brushed one of my nipples, causing me to feel an entirely new sensation pulse into my needy cock. I literally convulsed at the touch which steered him in a new direction. He began to twist and squeeze my nipple making my insides feel like they would explode with agonizing painful pleasure.

"Fuck yeah. Do not stop that," I ordered. Extreme pleasure that my virgin body had never experienced before, jolted through me with so much power that I couldn't tell if it was too much or not enough of a good thing. "Harder," I pleaded. "Harder."

I grabbed the hand Mikey was using to jack me off and brought it to my other nipple. The new sexual awareness was too good and I wanted to double the pleasure.

"You like that?" he asked, gripping my other nipple while I stroked my hard cock.

"Un-huh," I panted. "I wanna shoot. Please don't stop," I begged.

Mikey had each of my nipples between a thumb and a finger, twisting and squeezing as I jacked my cock. The head was purple and angry. Playing with my meat a third time in less than an hour was a lot for me.

"Go ahead and shoot," he hissed through clenched teeth. "I'm so fuckin' close too."

With my eyes closed and I rested my head against his shoulder. Between him gnawing on my neck, twisting my nipples, and me jacking my dick, my brain's pleasure center was nearing a nuclear meltdown.

"Mmmm," I hummed, pulling on my nut sack while I jerked off. "Fuck yes, stud. Ohhh, fuuucckkk."

My third load blasted out and sprayed the shower wall when my hand shot out to brace myself against the cool tiles to prevent myself from collapsing into a pile of overstimulated flesh. Mikey's hands left my nipples and he wrapped his arms around my waist and slammed into me, pumping over and over as he attempted to reach the same point.

"Jesus H. Christ, Coop!" he yelled. "Fuck, your ass is so fuckin' hot."

"Come on, stud. Give it to me. Fuck your boy," I moaned, gripping his arms as they held me closely

By then Mikey had lifted me from the shower floor with his brute strength and pounded away between my legs. I'd known he was strong before, but the excitement that flooded my filthy mind as he held me up like a sack of potatoes was exhilarating.

"Fuuuccckkk," he gasped, a growl erupting from him. He panted like a wild animal when he released his load. "Oh fuck. Oh fuck. Ugghhhh," he groaned.

He set me down, his forehead resting against my shoulder as he inhaled and then exhaled like he'd just ran a marathon. It took him a minute to catch his breath. I could feel his heartbeat against my back.

I turned around and wrapped my arms around his waist, he leaned down and put his head back on my shoulder, still catching his breath.

I was suddenly embarrassed by my behavior. I'd never acted so naughty in front of anyone before. "Um," I began, my face flushing deeper than the hot red after that session. "I guess I was a bit . . . um . . . sorry, Mikey."

He lifted his head from my shoulder to face me. "Whatever the fuck that was, Coop. I mean, whoever, whatever, bring it on."

"You sure?"

"I'm totally sure," he stated. "That was fucking hot," he added.

"What are we gonna do now," I asked, hoping for a fourth time as soon as we could both pop another boner. I knew I was good to go with little trouble.

"Wanna go to prom?" he asked, grinning like the cat that ate the canary.

"For real?"

"Why not? You've always wanted to go."

"You'd seriously do that?" I asked. I reached for his hand. "You'd actually go to the dance? With me?"

"On one condition," he said.

Here we go. My heart sank. I was afraid this was too good to be true. "Okay."

"I'll only go if you'll be my official date."

"You sure?"

"I've seen you in your tux, Coop. I'm dead serious."

"I'm nervous," I admitted.

"Well, we can hide or we can rip the Band-Aid off and admit to the world what we are to each other."

"What are we, Mikey," I asked, needing to hear him say it out loud.

"I'm hoping we're a couple. I'd like that to be the case."

"Me too," I acknowledged.

Mikey touched his lips. "Seal it with a kiss?"

I'm glad my eyes were closed. I wanted to cry.

CHAPTER FIFTY: Mike

"Mike," Coop's mother whispered while curling her finger to gesture for me to get closer. Mom, Coop, and his dad were in my kitchen.

"What's going on, Charla?"

"Can I just get a word real quick?" she asked when she adjusted my bow tie before smoothing my tux's lapel.

"Sure thing."

"Well, son. I just hate getting involved in things that perhaps a mother should keep her nose out of."

"Okay," I interrupted. "What can I do to make you feel better, Charla?"

She gazed at me for an extra moment before continuing, "Gosh, Mike. You do seem so grown up lately, honey. Cooper was right."

"He told you I was acting more like an adult?"

She nodded, studying me closely.

"I'll admit I've been trying. You know, since Dad died and everything."

"Well, truthfully, Mike." She paused, searching for her words.

"You're worried," I interrupted. "About Coop, right?"

"Well, I guess I am," she admitted. "I know I'm sticking my nose where it doesn't belong, but you know us mothers."

"I love him, Charla."

"You do," she verified but needed more evidence. "And you love him like he loves you?"

"I do. I get it, trust me," I said. "This may seem out of the blue and all so I understand what your concerns are, but I am *in love* with Coop."

"Oh, honey. I just worry so much about you boys," she said. "And you know my son. Cooper is sensitive and I worry about that."

"Please listen to me," I began, hoping I could help her feel better about our relationship. "I love you and Roger like my own folks and I promise you, Charla, that my heart is in the right place. I know I'm young, but I realized that I have always loved Coop. I guess it just took me longer to figure out."

Her eyes welled up after I finished and she reached for my hands. "Roger said the exact same thing," she said. "He said it probably took you longer than Cooper, and he told me to trust you because you're a wonderful boy who we've known for your whole life, Mike. I'm sorry I stuck my foot in my mouth."

"I'll do my very best. I promise," I said. "I appreciate you speaking with me and hope you're there for both of us if we need you in the future."

"See? Right there," she remarked, stepping back and appearing mystified. "Cooper was right. You seem so . . . so . . . grown up. Kathleen must be so proud of you, honey."

"I'm trying." I leaned in and hugged her then held at arm's length when I stepped back. "I love him. I always have."

"I believe you."

"Shall we go see what they're up to?" I asked, gesturing toward the kitchen.

"Don't say anything to Cooper, okay?"

I mimicked zipping my lips closed. "Not a chance."

We walked into the kitchen and found Mom and Roger fawning over Coop while fumbling over his tie, so I motioned them out of the way. I unraveled their messy attempt and then made a perfect bow tie.

My mother looked perplexed. "How'd you do that?" she asked. "You've never worn a bow tie, Michael."

"I've worn one several times," I countered.

"When?" she insisted.

Oh fuck.

I tried to play it cool and adjusted mine to sell my made-up story. "In my dreams when I was thinking about this day," I quipped, feeling pretty smooth.

Mom's eyes narrowed when she stared at me. I smiled and she averted her eyes for a moment before looking at me a second time. Something in her expression said she wasn't convinced by my explanation.

"Pictures," Roger said. "Lots and lots of pictures."

"Daaaaaad," Coop whined, looking at me and mouthing the word *sorry*.

"I agree," I hollered over the racket our date had caused with our folks. "Let's get a ton of 'em."

* * *

"We're just gonna walk straight in and act normal?" Coop asked. "Like nothing's going on?"

"Exactly," I answered, feeling the butterflies. "We're just another couple going to our high school prom."

"Except you're a four-year starting quarterback who's cheerleader girl-friend is in there," he argued.

"Ex-girlfriend," I corrected.

"Even worse."

We arrived thirty minutes past the prom start time and stood quietly in the full parking lot looking around at all the cars. The gymnasium lights were low for a romantic ambience, and the sound of dance music vibrated through the brick walls. I noticed Jennifer's car parked in the front row closest to the front entrance. Where else would she have parked?

"Let's do this," I said, grabbing Coop's hand and heading for the door. "We'll go in, people will be shocked, and then we'll just go about our business."

"You don't have to do this for me, Mikey," Coop said, slowing down the closer we got to the main entrance. Two classmates were at a table outside the door collecting tickets. They were the first to notice us holding hands. One of the girls covered her mouth and leaned toward the other.

"Hey, Tina," I said, waving as I pulled Coop behind me. "Just two guys holding hands here."

"Yeah, only the two hottest guys in school," the other senior classmate,

Sara, quipped before running to the door.

"You hear that, Coop? The *two* hottest guys in school. Hastings isn't gonna like that news," I joked, squeezing his hand.

Coop stopped before we went inside. "I can't do this?"

"You can," I encouraged. "I've got you."

"They're gonna hate us," he said. "It'll ruin you, Mikey."

I pulled him away from the door and behind a huge column supporting the gym's overhang above the sidewalk. The entrance door opened and four students peered out, I assumed to see what the hell Sara was talking about.

"I'll leave if you want, Coop," I began. "But this won't be the only time folks will stare at us or make nasty comments. You get that, right?"

"I know," he spoke softly. "But your reputation at school."

"If my rep is as great as you say, then they'll be open to us. We live in Idaho Falls, Coop. Being gay and a couple is never gonna be easy."

"How come you're so cool with this?" he asked. "I should be the one waving flags, not you."

"You're not the parade type and you know it," I teased. "It's just a bunch of kids."

He paused and looked at me in a strange way which made me think he was questioning my word choice or delivery. *"Yeah . . .* just like us," he stated.

"That's what I meant," I corrected. "Just two kids going to the prom that happen to be gay. Hell, I bet we aren't even the only gay couple here."

"Shelly and Kim don't count," he said. "They've been together and out as lesbians since eighth grade."

I kissed his nose. "And we'll be two more of the *out* kids in exactly two minutes if you go in there with me."

Coop chewed on his lower lip, looking from me to the door that was now wide open and filled with prom attendees. "Everyone's coming outside," he whispered, motioning to the forming crowd.

"See? We're already out."

Coop tilted his head toward our classmates. "Well, okay then. You lead

250

the way. I'll watch our backsides," he joked.

I leaned closer to him so I could whisper in his ear. "And remember, in a few months, none of these people will matter. This is just high school."

"You're acting weird again," he accused.

"But you love me, right?"

"Shut up and lead the way."

We both inhaled deeply and turned to face the music, literally.

CHAPTER FIFTY-ONE: Cooper

The crowd blocking the doors parted when Mikey walked into the gym with me in tow. I was gripping his hand tightly and staying as close to him as I could.

Sophomore and back-up quarterback, Mark Hanson, stood with his mouth wide open. I imagined he thought his hero, Mike Hill, was pulling the best prank ever. He shoved the guy next to him to make sure he was seeing what he was seeing.

We walked straight in and waited for the students on the dance floor to catch up with the developing news. It took less than a minute. It was like watching a group of deer after the first one sees the wolf at the edge of the herd. One notices and then all heads turn, row after row after row.

Even Todd Sidwell, a senior classmate who was the night's DJ, forgot to queue the next song so the one playing ended while everyone stared at us which replaced the music with a low buzz that vibrated through the huge room like a swarm of bees.

And out of that swarm came the queen bee herself with Hastings in tow. The crowd parted for her royal highness like it did anytime she moved through a space. Her influence was incredible to witness from this side. My new side, the banished, the voted off the island, the excommunicated.

"Fuck," I said, grabbing Mikey's hand with my other hand.

"Well looky here, Michael," she said, referring to Hastings with a name she vowed was reserved for Mikey. "I should have known he was gay. I mean, what normal guy would break up with me?"

"Play fair, Jen," Mikey said. "We can all have a nice time here tonight."

"You'd like that wouldn't you?" she stated, stepping to her left and zeroing in on me. "Why are you hiding, Cooper? Mike forced you to come?"

"Leave him alone," Mikey said. "It's not Coop's fault."

"Then who's is it?" she demanded. "You're replacing me with him. Of course it's his fault."

Hastings stepped forward and grabbed for Jennifer's hand which she yanked away from him. "Calm the fuck down," he said.

"Do not speak to me like that," she hissed, pushing his shoulder and glaring at him. Jennifer turned to refocus her anger on us. "You two were probably sneaking around behind my back the entire time, weren't you?

"I wouldn't do that to you, Jen, and you know it," Mikey defended. "I'm gay and that's all there is to it." The crowd gasped at the announcement, pushing closer while they watched fireworks.

"You aren't gay," she said. "He forced you."

I stepped from behind Mikey. "Do I look like I could force him?" I asked incredulously. "Seriously? And besides, nobody forces someone to be gay."

"Then you tricked him," she said.

Hastings abandoned her and stood beside Mikey and me. "Shut the fuck up, Jennifer. Jesus Christ! You are not *that* stupid," he railed.

"What the . . . ?" she asked, huffing and puffing like someone had knocked the wind out of her. "You can't talk to me like that, Hastings."

"The fuck I can't. You need a person that will call you out on your shit," he countered before spinning in a circle and gesturing to the assembled crowd. "We get it, Jennifer. You're fucking hot and we all know you're on the top of the food chain, but for fuck's sake, girl, they just want to be in love. Let 'em be."

"How can . . .?" she started, looking at everyone frantically. "But, why can . . .?"

Hastings stepped up to her. "Because being gay is okay, Jennifer." He turned to Mikey and held out his hand. "I give mad props to Hill for showing up here with Cooper. Mad fucking props."

Jennifer's face fell in defeat. "But . . . but . . .."

Hastings yanked her toward him and planted his lips on hers. At first, she struggled to fight him off. Was his move bold? Did it border on violating her rights? Of course it did, but Jennifer began to relax and let Hastings continue to jam his tongue into her mouth. The crowd began hollering and wolf-whistling at the pair until they eventually parted.

Jennifer looked shellshocked.

"I've always wanted to do that," Hastings declared, pulling her to his side and claiming her like a caveman would do.

A flummoxed Jennifer went along with it.

"Lead the way, boys," he said to Mikey and me. "We have some shit to celebrate tonight."

Mikey led me to the dance floor when the music came back on. Teacher chaperones had watched the entire thing unfold and were impressed with how it went down, backing away after Hastings defused the argument. I'd been right. Hastings had the hots for Jennifer the whole time.

Mikey pulled me close and whispered in my ear. "Now *that* was weird," he exclaimed. "And you think I'm the one acting strange in this town?"

And just like that we were officially a couple. Summer here we come.

CHAPTER FIFTY-TWO: Mike

O ur eighteenth birthdays were here before we knew it. Coop was excited because he said he felt like a legal adult and everything. I felt old. This was my eighteenth *and* my twenty-eighth. *How to broach that subject?*

"You fucking look amazing, Hill," I joked, studying my reflection in the mirror. Still not a single wrinkle. I noticed facial hair for the first time. Officially the second time, but I couldn't remember the first.

A knock startled me and I jumped away from my bedroom door.

"Michael, are you up, honey?"

I pulled the door open. "Hello, Mom," I said, bowing and motioning for her to come in.

She rolled her eyes at me good humoredly. "I'm glad someone's happy," she said before scowling at the dirty clothes thrown about my room. "You're eighteen, honey. Could you please pick up after yourself?" I had bad news for her. I was a decade older than that. Still hadn't learned. Doubt I ever would.

I pulled her in for a hug. "What has you all up in arms so early?"

Mom had gotten used to and seemed to love how affectionate I'd become. I was her son. I loved her and I wanted to show her. "I have a mile-long list of things that I have to do before the party," she said. "I'm falling behind and Druzella just called."

"What did *Madame* Druzella want?" I asked, speaking eerily and haunting.

"Why do you insist on calling her that?" she asked, fussing a hand at me.

I wanted to remind her that she had spoken of Druzella long before I'd met her. Or was that long after now? But of course I couldn't mention that.

"She seems like a madame to me. Very mystical woman, Mom."

"She's wise, Michael. Trust me, she knows stuff that hasn't even happened."

"I bet she does," I agreed. *Boy did she.*

"Honestly, I don't know why I waste my breath with you." She began gathering the armful of dirty clothes and ceremoniously dumping them into the hamper in my bathroom. "You're just like your father. You both think I'm crazy."

"Aww, come on, Mom. I don't think you're crazy. I *know* you're crazy."

She ignored me and pointed at the bathroom. "And clean that bathroom."

"Why you bustin' my balls today?"

"And enough with your language," she snapped, looking around the room. "Now why did I come up here?"

"You're unhappy. You came up to spread good cheer," I quipped. "Mission accomplished."

"Oh yeah," she began. "Charla and I are going to Hennessy's bakery in Shelley."

"You're going that far for a cake?"

"It's only 10 miles and they have your boys' favorite cake. Then we're going grocery shopping afterward."

"I'm hearing that you need something from me," I said. "I'm off today so I won't be going into the store."

"Druzella is stopping by at one for a reading. I might be late."

Yikes. That wasn't what I'd expected. "Can't you be back by one?" I asked. "No offense, Mom, but she kinda creeps me out."

"Just be here," she stated. "And answer the door, Michael. No loud music either."

"*Moooommmm,*" I complained, getting pretty good at remembering what a brat I used to be and scarily slipping right back into my teenage self.

Mom walked out of my room and headed down the stairs. "I mean it, young man!" she yelled.

Perhaps Druzella's visit wasn't so bad after all. I had more questions and she'd been *full* of advice when I last saw her. Even if some of it was delivered with a warning.

* * *

I'd forgotten Druzella was coming until I heard the doorbell ring. I tugged on a tank top and flew down the stairs, answering the door just as it rang a second time.

"Hello," Druzella said, standing on our front porch in an outfit that could best be described as circus big-tent-esque attire. She wore a tunic in loud colors with a horizontal striped pattern from neck to knees. Bright orange leggings were visible from the knees down matched the gumball sized earrings that almost touched her shoulders.

"Mom's not home yet," I immediately reported, hoping she understood the underlying suggestion to stay in her purple clown car.

"Good," she stated before walking past me like she owned the joint. "We need to talk and I'll need you to get me my green tea first," she added, walking toward the kitchen. "Oh, never mind. I'll get the tea," she said over her shoulder. "I know where Kathleen keeps it."

"Help yourself."

"Any idea when your mother will be back?" she asked.

"Nope. She's been gone about ninety minutes, so maybe another thirty or so," I explained.

"I'll microwave the water to save time," she said, then pointed at the table. "Sit. I have many questions."

Druzella somehow knew where the mugs, the tea, and the sugar were located. She hastily moved around the kitchen like she'd been here many times before. Strange thing was that I didn't recall meeting her before last week.

"I'm not into Mom's sort of stuff," I said. "You know, the astronomy stuff."

"Astrology," she corrected. "So time travel, parallel universes, and rips in time *stuff*, those are more your thing?"

"Hardly," I replied, leaning against the island while I watched her. "Don't blame me for Mom and your handiwork."

"Not me," she argued, tossing a tea bag into her nuked water. "That was all Kathleen."

She pointed toward the table again. "Hurry and sit."

I begrudgingly sat across from her and watched her pull out spirit toys or whatever one called the baubles and cards. She looked up after arranging her tools of the trade between us, a serious look on her face. "So, when exactly did you arrive?"

"That's a tough one if you're talking about what I think you're talking about."

"Cut the shit, kid."

"Jesus, lady," I huffed. "You're the so-called expert ain't ya?"

"Like I told you, I didn't do whatever this is," she replied, waving her hands around while gesturing toward me. "Dates," she insisted. "Give me dates."

"So, you're buying my story?" I asked. "No questions asked?"

"Trust me, I've got questions, but I don't need convincing that you're a visitor to this realm. I knew that the moment I held your hand last week."

I stood and crossed the open space to the front window to check if Mom was home. "You didn't hear this from me," I began before returning to the table. I leaned forward and lowered my voice hoping the crazy I was about to drop on her wouldn't get me committed. "I left this same house on September 7, 2023, and woke up in my bedroom upstairs on June 13, 2013, three and half weeks ago."

"No shit?" she asked. Not the reply I'd expected. "How'd she do it?"

"With your help I was told."

Druzella leaned back in her chair and stared into space for what seemed an hour but was maybe three minutes tops. "Was September an important date?"

"No, August 30th was the important date for Mom, but the ritual or whatever, had to take place seven days after according to both you and Mom," I explained. "You know," I whispered. "Mom and her illness."

Druzella went white and clutched at her odd necklace that she was wearing the first night I met her. "No . . . oh no, no, no, no, no," she moaned in shock. "I can't believe this and I haven't seen any signs of her illness in my visions. And of course you're sure because you were there."

I nodded.

"So she sent you back to warn her? Try to save her life?"

"Not exactly," I said.

Druzella let go of her necklace and spread her tarot cards out, breathing loudly and wincing when she touched a card.

I watched intently as she mumbled and reacted to certain cards until she held one up for me to see.

"Who else died on August 30th? Your father? A relative? There's a third loved one coming through," she began before dropping the black card suddenly and lowering her voice to a tone that seemed otherworldly, which honesty was how she seemed to me from the jump. "The trinity is dead," she stated. "And what about the jewels I keep visualizing?"

"Dad died but not in August. The other person . . . well . . . he's not dead . . . yet," I said. She looked at me like I was a ghost. "And I came through holding the ring that you keep seeing."

"The three Cancers," she mumbled. "You, Kathleen, and who else," she asked.

I pointed across the street.

"The boy," she stated.

I nodded. "He's eighteen today, like me."

"So, both of you were born on the same day," she mused, speaking to herself and staring at Coop's house. She reached for the dark and foreboding card she'd earlier dropped. "Let me guess," she began, rubbing the card between her palms. "Kathleen and the boy?" she asked without saying the word *died*. "On August 30th?"

"That is correct," I said.

"And the jewels?" she asked.

"A ring that Cooper and I gave to Mom after Dad died," I explained. "All three stones are ruby. Our shared birthstone."

"Of course they are. There's the trinity," she whispered. "Of course that is it."

"What is?" I asked, but then I heard a car door. "What is what?" I insisted, realizing Mom was probably home.

"I'm not exactly sure."

"Are you kidding me?" I raged.

She shoved a card at me that had her contact information on it. "Take that. Hide it. Call me tomorrow and I'll have more," she stated.

I heard the key in the door. Mom was home.

"And, Michael. Be careful what you affect by being here," Druzella advised.

"What the fuck? Tell me now," I demanded.

Druzella held up a hand and brought a finger to her mouth, shaking her head no just as Mom walked through the door.

CHAPTER FIFTY-THREE: Cooper

I watched as my mother, Kathleen, and the goofy looking lady with the purple VW stood chatting in front of Mikey's house. The strange woman had arrived about thirty minutes before our mom's had returned from errands. After texting Mikey to ask what she was doing there, I went back to cleaning my room while I waited for his response.

I was making a birthday card for Mikey and was trying not to be too mushy. After years of imagining him as my boyfriend, I had a million things I wanted to express, but fear of pushing him away was still haunting me. I hoped beyond hope that I was truly what he wanted. I'd decided to trust him because I loved him, but I was only human. I was worried.

I glanced at Mikey's bedroom window which was above where the ladies were visiting. He was standing in his room and watching me too. I held my phone to my ear, suggesting he either call me or asking if I could call him. My cell rang instantly.

"Hey, handsome," he said when I answered. "Miss me?"

"Sure do," I replied. I checked on the women just below his window. "What are they talking about over there?"

"Who knows? You know my mom," he said. "Could be just about anything."

"Who is that lady?" I asked, having noticed her last week. "She sure dresses unusual."

"She's some madame who sees shit," Mikey said. "I don't know exactly what she's called, but she talks to Mom about the stars and the future I think."

"That's what I figured," I stated. "I should show her something weird that I noticed."

"Oh, hell no," Mikey replied. "Please don't do that."

I was about to drop the topic but my curiosity got the better of me. "Do you remember the pictures that Jen gave us last year?" I asked. "The one of us swimming in Campbell Lake?"

Mikey was silent.

"Hello?"

"Yeah, I remember, why?"

"Do you still have yours?"

"Mom stuck mine in a photo album, why?" he asked.

"I'd rather show you," I said. "Could you grab yours and come over?"

We'd been watching each other as we spoke and I saw him duck out of view and then pop back up in the window. He held up a dark colored photo album in the window. "Got it. Hang on a sec," he said. I could hear the pages flipping, him laughing occasionally. "God, we can be weird. Some of these pics are stupid," he commented. I heard the static sound of stuck plastic pages crackling as he sifted through the album. "You're talking about the one in the water, right? Arms around each other with me making bunny ears?"

"That's the one. Bring it over here, 'kay?"

"Why? What's wrong, Coop?"

His remark caught me off guard. "I didn't say anything was wrong. I just want to compare them," I said.

"So, there *is* something wrong with your pic?"

"I didn't say that, Mikey," I sighed. "Can you just please come over?"

"Are we gonna shower?" he asked, lowering his voice to a growl. "I'm feeling dirty," he added.

"About that," I started.

"What?"

"Just bring the picture over and then we can talk about the other topic."

"Does it involve sex?" he asked. I laughed at him, watching as he lifted his tank top and tweaked his nipples. "Because if it does. I can move faster."

"It could involve your dick in my mouth," I stated.

The call ended and he disappeared from his window, a minute later he came flying out of his house and sprinted across the street, barely checking either direction when he crossed.

The ladies in the front yard stared after him when he threw open my front door.

I heard him running up the stairs seconds before he burst through my bedroom door, breathing hard.

"You . . . you . . . put my what, where?" he questioned, huffing and puffing with his hands on his knees. "Did you say *in your mouth?*"

"That's all you heard?" I quipped, laughing at him. "You have that picture?"

He waved the photo up above his head, still bent over while he caught his breath; but he managed to look up at me, grinning like a fool. "Right here," he said, panting like a dog in heat.

"I wanna show you something first," I said, turning to my desk.

Like a leopard waiting to pounce, he was on me the next second, tightly embracing me from behind and rubbing my ass with his erection that had popped up in his favorite gray gym shorts. I would bet money he was commando.

"Let's shower first. Please, please, please?" he begged. "Your mom is across the street and your dad's car is gone. Come on, Coop. I'm *so fucking horny.*"

"Because of what I said?" I teased.

"Well, duh." He spun me around and our lips almost touched. "Were you serious?" he whispered, grabbing my hand and shoving it down the front of his shorts. Yup, commando just like I thought.

I decided Mikey needed to get a little more worked up because I was enjoying his behavior. "I've been watching porn," I announced.

"You have?" he asked. His eyes widened when my hand grabbed his enormous cock. "What was . . . what hap . . .?"

I loved when he was mesmerized by my every word when I was being a tease. I had been more proactive when we explored each other's bodies these past couple of weeks. I figured he'd imagined he'd have to coax me along or perhaps convince me to try new things, but he'd been very wrong about my perceived shyness. I was crazy in love with Mikey and I was also crazy for his body which made me just plain crazy.

"You wanna know what happened in the videos I watched?" I asked. "Is that your question?" I added, aggressively stroking his dick that was still in his gym shorts.

His cock flexed in my hand. The head of his cock was engorged and swelling. I lifted the bottom edge of his tank top, hinting for him to get naked.

"Yeah. Tell me everything you saw," he said, his breath elevated because I continued to tug on his cock. "What happened in the porno? Was it on your iPad so the video would be bigger? What were they doing? Why didn't you watch it with me?" He rapidly fired his questions.

I removed my hand from his shorts which caused him to frown. "Calm down, boy," I soothed, pulling my T-shirt over my head and sliding my boxers lower on my hips but keeping them on; my throbbing cock making my own tent. "Help me out of these and then kiss me really good. Then maybe I'll show you what I learned. How 'bout that?"

Mikey could barely speak, he was so excited when he nodded before tugging down my boxers. After I kicked them to the side, he pulled his shorts down; his upright dick reaching above his belly button. I swallowed hard at the visual. Perhaps my video studies hadn't taken into consideration his significant asset.

The way Mikey stared at my nakedness with raw desire sparked my sexually awakening mind. The past couple of weeks had turned me into a walking sex machine. Whenever. Wherever.

Stepping forward, he wrapped me in his arms, smothering me in his strength and planted his mouth on mine. He took his time, simultaneously grinding his cock into mine and kissing me gently as he began to explore my mouth with his tongue. I went limp in his strength so he held us both upright. Mikey had serious power and the way his masculinity fed my desire to be manhandled was doing a number on my will power. I could've shot my load just from the kiss and his hold on me.

My hands rubbed around his lean waist and then moved to his solid ass cheeks where I pulled him as close as possible. Mikey had muscular, round, cheeks that were bigger than mine with an athletic dimple on each one. He was smooth all over except a dusty blond trail of pubic hair that led to the prize I was going to experience in my mouth for the first time.

For the past week after many sessions of humping and rubbing on each other, I was ready to go to the next level. Over the past couple of years Mikey had often mentioned how much he'd wished he could get blown but I had been helpless since that hadn't been part of my job description as his best friend. But now that I was his *boyfriend*, I wanted to fulfill his wish. For him of course, but also for my desires as well.

I'd spent countless hours at night viewing porn on my cell phone. I wanted to learn the techniques that would get him off and figured porn videos would be able to offer master classes on the subject. Of course, after watching several dozen videos, it doesn't take long before you're down a rabbit hole of interesting things to discover. I'd viewed many positions that I wanted to put to practice, but I decided to start with giving him mind-blowing head before asking him to fuck me.

"Shower time, stud," I said, detangling myself from his arms. "I have a surprise for you."

"Oh my God. Fuck yes," he moaned. "I fucking love this Cooper. So hot."

Normally he'd adjust the water temp for me and wait for me to get in the walk-in shower first, but he ran in first and began rinsing off, his boner still at full mast.

"Someone looks happy," I teased, grabbing the bar of soap and lathering my hands. "How does this feel, big boy?" I asked, stroking his shaft and massaging his balls.

Mikey put his head back and leaned against the tiles, his hands by his side while I moved my sudsy hands over his slick cock. "Easy, Coop. I could blast off so easily."

"We wouldn't want that, would we?" I teased before I stepped closer and kissed his chest. "How about you turn around so I can rinse the soap off that cock of yours?"

"Anything you say," he said, turning toward the spray.

I came up behind him and wrapped my arms around his waist before I pushed his hands away so I could move mine back to his dick. I rubbed and rinsed his throbbing tool while he moaned in agony from my touch.

"I could fucking come," he moaned. "Fuuuccckkk. Just let me come, Coop."

"What fun would that be?" I teased. "One more second, stud," I said, before lifting his nut sack so the warm water ran over his privates. "There we go. Now how about you turn back around and face me?"

Mikey spun around and I slowly knelt down in front of him.

I looked up to his wide-eyed face and grinned.

"No fucking way," he growled before reaching for the back of my head.

I quickly brushed his hand away. "Easy, boy. Keep your hands to yourself for a minute. Can you do that?" I asked.

He nodded eagerly as his cock flexed against his abs. I placed my mouth on his balls and slowly licked them, just like I'd learned from the guys in the pornos. I noticed they started there before any cock action. I didn't touch his dick. I just licked then sucked a ball into my mouth, rolling my tongue over his sensitive skin.

Mikey's legs trembled as he let out a sound similar to a wounded animal. "Holy . . . fuuuccckkk," he said, his knees buckling before he locked his legs so he wouldn't fall. I ran my hands over his thighs that had bulged with muscle. "Are you gonna suck my dick, Coop?"

I ignored him and kept slobbering all over his balls, avoiding his dick entirely. The key thing I'd taken from porn was to take my time and build the desire by teasing the guy until he practically begged you to take his cock in your mouth.

"Mmmm," I moaned. "So fucking nice, Mikey," I said, knowing my nasty language would get him hotter. "I can't wait to taste your dick," I added.

He grabbed his cock and moved it toward my mouth. "Suck it," he begged. "Just the tip, Coop. Come on already," he cried.

"Not yet," I insisted, swatting his hands away from his cock. "I'm not done with your huge balls yet. They're so full of come for me, big boy."

266

Just the sound of my voice, perhaps the dirty words I spoke, caused his knees to weaken and his body shook with anticipation of greedy lips. He placed a hand on the top of my head and smashed me against him, grinding and moaning from the agonizing pain of needing release.

"Jesus, Coop," he growled through gritted teeth. "I . . . I . . .."

He fell silent from the shock because I pulled his erection to my open mouth and inserted the tip; swirling my tongue and suctioning his throbbing head slowly. His knees locked again and he grabbed the sides of my head, trying to get his dick all the way into my mouth, but I pulled back so I could keep him right where I wanted him; several inches from my throat. I was in no hurry.

"Oh, fuck. Oh fuck," he hissed. "So fucking good."

I kept him pinned against the shower wall with my arm while I continued working his dick head.

He'd push forward.

I'd push him back.

I pulled off of him and gazed up while waiting for his reaction to me stopping.

"Had enough?" I asked. "Maybe practice is done for the day?"

Mikey grabbed me under my armpits and lifted me to my feet before pulling me closer and smothering my mouth with his. He invaded my mouth with his tongue, breathing heavily and gripping my ass. After a minute of passionate kissing he pulled away. "Now on your knees, boy, and suck my dick. No more fucking around either."

His hands went to my shoulders and he forced me back to my knees. A rush of adrenaline flooded my brain because he took control, demanding I suck him off. His commanding voice was exactly what I'd needed.

I stared at him with my lips parted to encourage him to guide his dick into my waiting mouth. "Make me," I whispered.

Mikey grabbed my hair and yanked my head back before feeding his cock to me. "Nice and easy," he growled. "All of it."

My cock sprang to life instantly. This was what I craved from Mikey. He was the natural leader and I needed him to be that man for me. I actually felt powerful in my role as his sexual partner. I wanted to service him, his cock, and his desires.

The tip of his cock moved across my lips. This time he was the tease, taking his time when he moved his dick further in before pulling back. His hands moved to the sides of my face as he guided his meat into my hungry mouth. He'd push a couple of inches in and then hold me there until he extracted his cock again, waiting to repeat the motion. Now it was me feeling impatient because I wanted as much of him in my mouth as I could take. I wanted to test my oral skills on his huge cock.

"Yes, Mikey," I moaned after he pulled his dick out and before he shut me up again with another mouthful.

"You're a good cocksucker, boy," he growled, his voice deep and manly. "You gonna swallow my come?"

"Mmmm hmmm," I mumbled, four inches of cock knocking on the back of my throat.

He pulled out again.

"Test my limits," I dared.

"So you wanna test your gag reflex, do ya?" he asked, yanking on my hair.

I nodded enthusiastically.

"Okay then. You asked for it." He held the back of my head and slowly pulled me onto his dick inch by inch until he hit the back of my throat.

I gagged and coughed but that didn't stop him.

"Come on, boy. You can do better than that," he hissed. "You little cock tease."

He stared down at me with a dirty gleam in his eyes, firmly holding my head and pushing ever so slowly until I took another inch by relaxing my throat. After a second of him in my throat I pulled away quickly, gagging and sputtering while he watched me, grinning like a possessed man.

"That's as much . . ." I began before he guided me back to his waiting dick.

"Come on, boy. You started this."

I opened up so he could slide his dick as far as he could again.

He held the back of my head, forcing me to take him. "There you go.

That's my boy," he encouraged.

His praise caused my cock to jump again so I began stroking my dick while he pumped my mouth, keeping his grip on the back of my head. I brought my free hand to his dick and began to swirl it up and down in sync to his pumping by stroking, twisting, and pulling to build friction on his dick.

His knees slightly buckled and he adjusted his grip on my head, the other hand supporting him against the shower tiles as he leaned back. His breathing became elevated as I jacked and sucked him off. The force of his hand on the back of my head became stronger. He was close.

"Fuck yes. Just like that, Coop," he instructed. "Just . . . like . . . that. Don't fucking stop."

Mikey pumped into me faster and I kept my grip on his cock while I jacked my dick. The thrill I felt from giving him such pleasure surged through my body. He was hot. The act of blowing him was hot. I was beyond excited from servicing my boyfriend and felt like I had all the power while working him over.

"I'm gonna shoot," he cried, placing his other hand behind my head and holding me in place. "Fuuuccckkkk," he roared when he released into my mouth.

His warmth flooded my mouth. I wondered how this would feel. How he would taste. Would I freak out or what? I felt satisfaction from giving him his orgasm. He'd given into my power, my mouth, my actions, and he'd enjoyed it. That was what I felt.

I focused on the pulsating dick in my mouth and his grip on me as he continued unloading. My own release was seconds from erupting. I kept his cock in my mouth and jacked my dick furiously. The idea that I had successfully sucked him off was what triggered my explosive orgasm. I deep throated him as I released, focusing on his dick in my mouth. My mind exploded with my release, overloading my senses with complete satisfaction.

My eyes popped open and I gazed up at Mikey. He was wiped out and grinning when he reached for my hand and helped me to my feet. Our mouths met and he forced his tongue past my lips, tasting himself on me.

Once we'd come down from the high of such an amazing act, he shook his head. "Wow," he said. "Just fucking wow."

"You just wait until I tell you about the other videos," I said. "That was just the introduction."

His eyes widened. "Next time, I'm watching with you, wise ass."

CHAPTER FIFTY-FOUR: Mike

"We better get up," I said, stretching my naked body while Coop remained tucked under my arm. "I heard your mom come in. Unless it was your dad," I corrected.

"Dad won't be home until five," he said.

"But still, there's the party," I said. "Mom told me six-thirty at our place," I added.

"Well, at least they said we'd have the rest of the night to do what we want," Coop said. "And I have just the idea."

I moved a hand to the top of his head. "Why wait? I've got three minutes," I quipped, wondering if I came too soon when I received my official first blowjob. "I didn't last long, did I?" I asked, unsure about BJ protocol.

Coop moved my hand from his head, laughing at my comment. "No worries, big guy. Must've been my skills."

"That's for damn sure," I agreed, groaning when I stretched. "We'd better get a move on."

Cooper bounced out of bed and headed for his desk. "But not before I show you something super weird," he announced.

"Oh, yeah. The picture," I replied, leaning over the edge of the bed and checking the floor for my copy. "Grab that," I said, pointing at the photo sticking out from under my tank top next to his desk.

"You grab it," he replied. "And hurry up. I need you to check mine out over here under the light."

Coop held what appeared to be his copy even though it was a different shape. I got off the bed and bent over to pick up my copy then walked across the room to him while studying my picture and noticing nothing different. I'd recently gone through the photo albums Mom made for me hoping they could refresh my memories. I'd paid a lot of attention to this particular photo. This image was taken nearly a year before Coop had drowned at that same lake. I'd fucking hated the picture ever since.

We stood bare naked near his window but quickly ducked out of the way when Mom glanced out the front window of our house. "Sun glare," I said, both of us chuckling. "She can't see in here."

Coop held out his copy of the picture for me to see. "Speaking of glare," he began, using his finger to draw a circle around our heads in the lake photo. "I never saw that before."

I smiled and kissed him on the cheek. "Aww, did you cut this into a heart shape because of me?" I teased. "You were crushing on me back then too?"

"I've been crushing on you for eighteen years, Bozo, and you know it, so buzz off."

I took the heart-shaped picture and tilted it toward the sun shining through the window. "What?" I asked. "I don't see anything. What are you talking about, Coop?" I'd voiced my question prematurely. *There it was.* A chill of recognition inched down my spine. "When did you notice this?" I questioned too aggressively which caused Coop to step away from me, his eyes questioning my reaction. "Sorry," I muttered.

"So, you see it too?" he asked.

I nodded.

"I've never noticed the rings before. That's why I asked you to bring yours over so we could compare."

I didn't need to look at my copy. Mine hadn't changed but I pretended to go along and rechecked. "Mine doesn't have the rings of light," I said nervously, my stomach clenching with anxiety. "Where do you normally keep this?"

He pulled out the bottom drawer of his desk. "In here."

"So never in the sun?" I asked, wondering if exposure to the sun could've created the effect. Who was I kidding? I immediately thought of Mom and Dad's picture from the Oregon Coast. Same damn thing. Same summer in fact. The year Dad died. The year before Coop drowned. This was no coincidence.

"Weird, huh?" Coop asked. "And flip it over. Check that out."

I turned the picture over and noticed the smeared handwriting. "You didn't let it dry?" I asked, handing it back to him.

"But I did, Mikey. More than a year ago," he explained. "This happened the other day when I was looking at it."

"No fucking way," I disagreed. "You sure?"

"Totally," he replied. "And I've held this photo tons of times and this didn't happen until recently. Swear."

"You're right," I said, hoping a simple acknowledgement would do. "Strange as fuck."

He shoved the photo in my face. "Look at the light around our heads, Mikey," he insisted. "Strange isn't the word. Don't they look like halos to you? Because it sure does to me." He snatched my copy from the desk. "See any halos in this one?" he asked, his voice raising an octave. "This is freaking the shit outta me," he added.

"I'll admit, it does seem odd," I said, still staying the course with my casual dismissal even though my mind was rolling around with crazy theories like marbles in a small sack. I walked to his bed and sat down then placed my elbows on my knees, chin resting in my palms. "It'll all be good, Coop," I insisted after noting his worried expression.

"You don't get it, Mikey," he began, his hands gesturing wildly. "I was just sitting here at my desk looking at the picture when those damn halo thingies appeared out of nowhere. Out of thin air, and I'm not joking."

"Come on now, Coop," I said. "You just *think* you saw something."

His posture changed. He was seriously troubled by the image. "Listen to me, Mikey. Those . . . those . . . rings. They just happened." He made his way to my side and gripped my shoulder.

I turned to face him.

He actually appeared terrified and the more he shared with me, the more upset he became. "And the . . . the . . . ink," he started again. "It smeared just after," he explained, his face turning paler by the second. "It never smeared before, Mikey. I'm telling you the truth here. I was sca . . . I *am* scared."

I stood and faced him, taking his hands in mine. "I'm not gonna let anything happen to you, Coop."

"It gave me the heebie-jeebies," he said. "That shit ain't normal."

He was right about that. Halos appearing in photos wasn't normal by a long shot. I know because the same fucking thing happened to me in the house across the street. Heebie-jeebies or not, this was strange and I had a sinking feeling this was related to me and parallel universes. How do I explain something like that to my boyfriend and keep myself out of the nut house?

"I'll protect you," I stated, hugging him tightly and kissing the top of his head. "Don't I always?"

"But from what?" he whispered, shivering in my arms even though it was hot for July in Idaho. "I don't like it."

"I know, Coop. How about I take the picture home and keep it over there for now? Think that would help?"

"Better yet," he began. "Let's go show your mom right now."

Not a fucking chance. I had to act fast with an excuse. "Maybe not," I said, making a sad face. "Mom has been kinda low because of the anniversary and everything. You know, Dad's death."

"Oh, okay then," he answered, disappointment lacing his voice because he didn't have a solution to his issue. "How about the VW lady? You said she was like your mom with her spirit world stuff. Looking into the future and all that. I bet she'd know."

"Maybe," I said, figuring the same damn thing. "I'll take the pic home and hang onto it until we decide what's best. That way you'll feel better and I'll know you're not freaking out."

"Sure thing," he agreed. "Gives me the creeps, Mikey, and I loved that picture of us. I love Campbell Lake too."

I certainly didn't need to hear the comment about liking Campbell Lake. My mind was reeling as I tried to keep calm during the conversation. Of course the image was tied to everything. But the halos again? This time on mine and Coop's head, not Mom and Dad's?

Jesus H. Christ!

Mom and Dad both died.

"Let's keep this between us, Coop. Okay?"

"Yeah, I understand," he muttered, still fixated on the photo in his hand. "Here. Take this."

He handed me the photograph and as soon as I touched it, the halos disappeared. I damn near shit myself and almost threw the fucker to the floor. My heart was racing when I quickly grabbed my shorts and buried the picture in the pocket.

Madame Druzella had a shit-ton of explaining to do.

CHAPTER FIFTY-FIVE: Cooper

Summer after graduation, like most of my previous summer breaks, flew by. The difference this year was that Mikey and I wouldn't be returning to high school in the fall. We were already in mid-to-late August and planning for our move for college. After Jennifer and Mikey split up, he finally told her that he intended to go to Washington State University with me.

My desire to attend WSU was due to their veterinary school and the reputation of the program. There were five vet schools in Idaho but only the one in Washington State. Applying to an in-state program would have been cheaper for me, but after I visited WSU and knew I just had to study there. I liked the professors and the small town vibe of Pullman. The university was just far enough away from home to feel like I was on my own so I could experience being an adult. Sharing an apartment with Mikey or pledging to the same frat house was our goal.

Even though Mikey and I had enjoyed a fair amount of freedom as teenagers, our parents loosened the strings even more after our eighteenth birthdays. Not much changed considering I lived on a small allowance and Mikey bagged groceries for nine bucks an hour, but we enjoyed hanging out at each other's houses. Kathleen, his mother, was super cool and loved having the both of us there. My folks felt the same way about Mikey, so we came and went as we pleased; eating far too much, working out, and having a lot of sex.

We wondered if our parents felt any different about our frequent sleepovers now that we were officially a couple. If they had, nothing was mentioned so we kept up the same routine as usual with me staying mostly at Mikey's almost every night.

Mikey seemed more like himself after we graduated. He remained slightly more serious than I'd remembered after that Sunday when I'd found him in his room acting odd. He explained he was trying to be mature and act more like a man, so I let up on him since he had been doing precisely that. He seemed to have grown up overnight and sometimes I felt like I was lagging behind.

He wasn't a braggart about grades and scholarships, but Mikey was a star pupil in high school. Besides being a stud athlete, he always made the honor roll as well. He graduated second in our class and was given some odd title that he couldn't have cared less about. I didn't tease him because I couldn't even pronounce the name of the title. I believed he made sure his GPA ended up just a hair under Keith Gillie's so he wouldn't have to give the Valedictorian address. He denies it of course.

I brought up the change in him several times, even trying to say it in a complimentary way so as to not be accusatory, but he'd simply shrug and say he was growing up. I pushed harder one night because I was tired of his simple answer so he finally did expand on why. Of course, what he'd said that one time was all I'd needed to hear.

"I want to be the best for us, Coop," he'd stated. "I need to act like a man to be a man so I can take care of us."

"I'm going to be a vet, Mikey," I'd argued. "I'll make plenty of money for us."

"Not that kind of take care of you. I want to protect you and always be there for you," he'd stated. "I need to be a man to do that."

I stared at him after his declaration. He was serious, and the tenderness in his voice was so sincere and incredible that I burst into tears. I think it was that precise moment and those tender words that proved to me how much he'd matured and that he did truly love me. I never questioned him again.

My cell buzzed and it was him texting to let me know he was off to work and would either see me at my house or his after nine PM. I watched for him from my window until he came out of his house and waved. He hated wearing his khaki slacks, a shirt, and tie. I insisted he looked handsome. He said he looked like a Mormon missionary, to which I replied, *even hotter.*

I let him know I was meeting Hastings at McDonalds to catch up and say hi, and that Jen would probably be there. *Suit yourself* was his response. I loved that about Mikey. He just wasn't jealous and never held grudges.

* * *

"Where's the ball and chain," Hastings asked when I joined them at a table in the back. Jennifer had her head resting on Hastings' shoulder. Apparently she'd landed on her feet just fine after the blowup at prom.

"Work," I said. "Till nine again."

"Jesus, dude. Your summer's ruined because Mikey works so much," Hastings said.

"He did the same last summer," Jen added, dipping a fry into a chocolate shake. Mikey jokingly mentioned her French fry dipping trick to me in the past. I watched as she slowly slid it across her lips as she gazed at Hastings, before moving it back and forth into her mouth. Poor, poor, Hastings. From what I've been told, he'd better plan on having blue balls. *Should have stuck with me.*

"We're going out to Campbell Lake later, " Hastings said. "Why don't you come along? Megan, Greg, and a few others will be there."

There was nothing more I'd like to do than go swimming. The temperature was higher than ninety degrees and I wanted out of cleaning the garage but knew my dad would be pissed if I didn't.

"Can't," I stated, trying out Jen's fry to shake method. "Not bad," I said, winking at Hastings.

"I fuckin' wish," he complained.

"I promised I'd clean out the garage for my dad," I said, getting back to the reason I'd have to miss hanging out with the old group, a gang to which I was thrilled I still belonged to. I wasn't a great swimmer but I would've loved the cool lake and the company.

"Next week then," Hastings said.

"Must be nice being loaded, and not having to work," I added, motioning toward Jen's BMW. "We don't even have a car," I bitched.

"We?" Jen asked. "As in you and Michael Hill?"

"Yes, that'd be us," I said, hoping that Jen had let stuff go by now. Prom night had done major damage to her reputation and thankfully she was heading to Seattle and a new school to stab her way back to the top.

"So," she began, turning to Hastings. "You were right, Michael Hastings." It annoyed me the way she insisted on using full names. "How's that?" I asked, stupidly taking the bait.

"This Michael said the two of you would be together forever," she explained. "He says you guys are the marrying type and that you'd probably had your hearts set on one another since like, forever or something."

"That I did," Hastings confirmed. "And I'm pretty sure I'm right."

Surprisingly, Jennifer wasn't awful. "Maybe it's kinda romantic. Yeah, maybe, actually," she said, batting her eyelashes at me. "Michael Hill does seem the type," she threw in for good measure.

"Let's hope so," I concurred, smiling back at her. "Gotta run, kiddos."

"I'll text you next week when we go out to Campbell again, buddy," Hastings said. I guessed we were destined to be buddies from then on seeing he'd landed the real queen.

"Tell Michael Hill I said hi," Jen chimed in, twirling her hair and tilting her head to the side. I swear she resembled a Bratz Doll.

I got in my mother's car and watched through the window as Jennnifer put on a show for me and kissed Hastings with two fingers holding her gum in the air. She was gorgeous to look at, that was an undisputed fact. Thankfully for my fragile mind, Mikey made me feel wanted because there was no way I could compete with her.

I stopped by Mikey's work and sat in the parking lot until I saw him come out. After he assisted Mrs. Johnson to her car, I honked twice. He noticed me and jogged over.

I remained in the car and rolled the window down. He looked in all directions and then leaned closer for a quick kiss. "I miss you, Coop."

"Miss you too," I returned, rubbing my cock through my mesh basketball shorts and raising my brows.

Mikey reached in and grabbed my boner. "Fuck me," he whispered. "Leave that alone until I get home, you nasty little boy."

"Maybe," I teased.

"I mean it, mister."

I shifted gears deciding to save the sex talk for later. There was zero chance we'd get it on in the parking lot. "I met up with Hastings and Jen."

"Yeah. You mentioned you were going to hang out. How's life with those two?"

"I think they're an item."

"Good for them," Mikey said, not giving a shit and reaching back into the car, trying to get his hand inside my shorts. "Damn, boy. You come all up in my work with that thing in your shorts."

"Hurry home," I advised. "Maybe I've watched another video or ten?"

"You wise ass," he said, kissing me quickly and standing up outside my door. "What were they up to today?" he asked.

I assumed he was referring to Hastings and Jennifer. "Going out to Campbell," I answered. "They invited me but I gotta clean the garage. I told them I'd go next week. Maybe you can come if you're off?"

Mikey appeared alarmed. I knew he wasn't jealous because that wasn't his style. He squatted down and positioned his hand on the door's edge near my elbow. "Please don't go out to Campbell Lake without me?" he asked softly. "I'd worry, Coop."

"Okay," I said. "But what's the big deal? I'm getting better at swimming but if you don't want me to, I can pass."

"I don't wanna be a nag but I'd just worry about you too much."

"Okay," I repeated. "Are you okay?"

"Yeah, I'm good. Just promise me, okay?" he asked.

"Yeah, I promise."

"Love you," he said, squeezing my hand. "See you a bit after nine."

I nodded and gazed into his eyes. I wasn't sure why he was afraid or worried.

"And you're sure you're okay?" I asked, needing some kind of assurance.

"Perfect now that I've seen you."

I watched Mikey walk back to the store, turning twice to check on me. I was madly in love and hoped he would never change. I felt safe.

CHAPTER FIFTY-SIX: Mike

"We've got a problem," I hissed, lowering my voice because Mom was downstairs and might overhear my phone call.

"*We?*" Druzella asked. "I have nothing to do with your dilemma."

"The hell you don't."

"Does your mother know you talk to adults like this?" she asked.

"I *am* a freakin' adult, remember?" I reminded her. "Mom gets the eighteen year old I am in this dimension, but you get the ten years older version. The version you created."

I shouldn't speak to her this way but I was getting more alarmed by the day. My problem was that the anniversary of Coop's death was a mere ten days away and I had no clue what I should do. Her and Mom had supplied the way here but we'd never actually spoken about what happened after.

"Listen to me carefully, Michael. I cannot possibly know how you got here. I only have your limited details of how the event took place and the evidence there is scant at best."

Figuring she was my best hope for advice, I toned down the forceful edge to my voice. "I really need your help. I don't know what to do next."

Druzella was silent for a moment before responding. "We need to involve your mother," she declared, surprising me.

My calm approach lasted three seconds. "Not a chance," I argued. "How do we explain that? *Gee, Mom, I'm your future son and I'm back to blow up the course of history.*"

"You have to admit, it's usually the direct approach that works best," she replied.

Her idea made sense, but how to begin that conversation? "To use your exact words against you, *don't fuck around and get out.* Remember that advice?"

"And I stick by those words," she stated. "You need to involve as few people as possible, Michael. The more people who know, the crazier the impact could be on their future lives, not to mention everyone around them."

"Two of these people die," I reminded her. "One is here and the other from where I came from."

"Actually, they're both here," she corrected. "And neither one of them knows."

"I only came here to try to stop Cooper from going swimming. Now the subject of swimming has come up. I'm terrified that I won't be able to control the outcome," I said. "Mom, you, somebody, hell, probably me for agreeing to do this, didn't think this through. I need to prevent his death."

"Okay. And what about your mother's?" she inquired.

Her question hurt my heart. Mom and I had discussed this before she died. We'd argued for days after I asked her why not have me warn her of her illness far in advance. Mom had said that she wanted to be with Dad, and that she wasn't concerned about her fate because she believed we had many lives that we experienced in infinite universes. Of course, I'd argued she was crazy to reject help, but now look where I was. She'd actually been able to get me here.

"She didn't want me to tell her," I choked out. "I'm struggling with that, Druzella."

"Then don't," she stated rather bluntly.

"Just like that?" I asked. "Do you agree with her?"

"I don't know anything about parallel universes, Michael. I've told you that several times now, but if Kathleen asked you not to tell her about her death, then she's made your decision for you. Do you understand?"

"I guess," I mumbled. "I want to tell her so bad."

"I know your mother quite well, son. She is a kind and caring woman, but she is strong-willed as well," she began. "But more importantly, your mother fervently believes that outside forces impact our lives. Convincing her to believe you regarding this spectacular event you've experienced, will not take much effort on your part."

"Can you be there with me?" I asked. "Mom trusts your insight."

"Yes," she agreed. "I'm seeing her the day after tomorrow. How about we do it then?"

"Thank you," I said. "I have something that might provide the proof she'll need."

"Terrific. Do me a favor though," she began. "Don't tell me yet. Provide it to me at the same time as your mother. If we concocted this plan in the future, I want to keep myself as unprepared as possible so as not to affect my own future."

"Okay," I replied. "The proof is stunning, Druzella."

"Of course it is."

We hung up and I replayed our conversation in my head. Druzella was right. I had to involve as few people as possible. Even without outright dropping the news on anyone, I'd already changed the course of my future with Jennifer and her course with whomever. The question now was do I get a couple of months to love Coop or a lifetime?

One of the biggest worries was staying here in this realm and having to relive ten years of my life. Would it be possible to make changes or choices that didn't affect those around me? I've already changed too much.

A more serious concern was could I keep my sanity while pretending I didn't know more than I should? How could I repeat college and not be bored out of my mind? I hadn't been happy in tech and wished I'd done what I truly wanted to do, teach. Perhaps that was the answer.

Remaining in this universe meant having opportunities to make changes in my life, but I was scared shitless wondering what would happen in my original universe. What changes here had dramatic effects on Mike Hill there? My options were unlimited knowing what I knew about the future. I could change majors. I could create new challenges, correct mistakes so I could learn more and worry less. *Shit!* I could predict the stock market. There were a shit-load of advantages, but what were the perils?

I'd been miserable for more than a decade while I mourned Cooper. Now that I had the advantage of being back, I realized that I'd been in a decade-long funk. I loved Coop in a way that I hadn't understood until I had ten years to suffer, wondering why my life felt empty even though I had plenty. Every bad choice and every mistake happened because I didn't know I was allowing his loss to affect my life and my choices. I had simply gone along, gave up my power, and trudged through ten years of my life.

Perhaps that was the lesson here, the gift actually. Now I had the opportunity to be present in my life. I had agreed to Mom's hair-brained scheme because I desperately wanted to be with Coop again. I still did, so why not make the best of a second chance?

Going back might be impossible now but wasn't the tradeoff of repeating the next ten years far better than living a single minute more without the love of my life. Mom had given me the greatest gift a parent could give. Love.

I owed the people I'd hurt the same fair chance. Even Jennifer deserved to marry her soulmate, so perhaps by me coming back to save Coop I could help others.

CHAPTER FIFTY-SEVEN: Cooper

I gazed dreamily at Mikey while he slept, the rays of morning sunshine filtering through the blinds. The weather was warm so a thin top sheet was all we needed with a fan at the foot of the bed. He liked the white noise. I liked the breeze. He liked to spoon only until we began to fall asleep. I could have spooned all night long.

So many things about us were compatible. The similarities had always been that way. Born on the same day and growing up together was bound to cause parallels in our likes and dislikes. Trust me, we had many disagreements, but the likes that we shared outweighed the dislikes, and perhaps that's what connected us to each other.

Sometimes I needed to pinch myself because we were a couple. I'd stopped asking why and had decided to live fully in the *why not*. I'd loved him my whole life, truly understanding the type of love I had for him the past four to five years. The change in our relationship came with its fair share of worry as well. I'd wanted this my entire life, thinking that he would never reciprocate my love in the fashion that I desired. But he had and here we were. My guess was that Mikey hadn't put it together until recently. That didn't make his love any less than mine in my selfish opinion.

Not even his partially opened mouth, his unruly hair, or the tiny bit of dried saliva on the corners of his lips could change my mind about him. He was my everything and I'd spent the past month thanking any and every one for the gift.

* * *

"Of all the Gods in here, which one do I need to thank for Mikey's love?" I'd asked Mrs. H. one evening while Mikey was at work. We were hanging out in their living room. I was holding a statue of a woman with eight arms.

Mikey's mom smiled and studied me carefully, moving her eyes around the room in thought. *"Thank yourself, Cooper,"* she'd finally said. *"Michael loves you because of you, not one of my deity's."*

"You advised me to give him time. Do you remember saying that?"

"I do," she'd confirmed. *"But even I hadn't held out much hope for this sort of change, son."*

I wondered what she meant by her words. Did Mrs. H. like that Mikey was gay? Was she disappointed about grandkids? I wanted to assure her that kids were still on the table.

"Are you disappointed by his choice?"

"Oh, honey. Of course not," she'd declared. *"How could I be? Michael is so fortunate to have someone who loves him the way I know you do; I couldn't be happier about that. And, I'm proud of both of you."*

I took the opportunity and asked her a question I'd been hanging on to for far too long. *"Why do you think he finally realized he has feelings for me?"* I'd asked, afraid I could jinx my good fortune.

"He simply grew up, Cooper," she'd said. *"I don't mean that he was immature or anything like that, but I suppose that after his father died, he understood what he truly wanted in a partner. He just didn't know that the person had been right by his side the whole time. I'm happy he noticed."*

"You've noticed the difference in him too?" I'd asked, wondering if it wasn't just my observation.

"Absolutely I have. And I love it," she'd declared. *"He's growing up, Cooper. Actually, he grew up, and you're what he wants. I'm quite pleased with his choice, son."*

* * *

Mikey rolled over to face me, grumbling and stretching. I held my breath, hoping to not wake him because it was Sunday morning and he was off of work. He needed the rest.

His eyes popped open. "What?" he asked, smiling at me. "You're staring at me again, Coop."

"Can't help it," I admitted, moving under his arm when he invited me closer. "You're so darn cute."

"It's Sunday," I said. "You know how I am about Sundays."

"Yeah, I know. *Every day* is like Sunday to you, Coop," he stated before yawning and stretching again.

I sat up and yanked the covers off of him, exposing his golden skin and perfect body. He worked hard as well as *worked out* hard. His body was the evidence.

"I'm hungry," I said, licking my lips.

His eyes were closed so he didn't see me staring at his morning wood. "It's Sunday, pretty boy. I'm sure Mom is making breakfast," he groaned, his eyes still closed when he flexed his legs which caused his dick to bounce off of his stomach.

I slid down the bed until my face was near his erection. "I prefer a bigger sausage."

I glanced up at him but he either fell back to sleep or was pretending to be so I lifted my head from the mattress, rested my cheek on his stomach, and sucked the tip of his dick into my mouth. His hand immediately came to the back of my head. He *had* been paying attention.

Mikey let me tease the tip for a few moments before he pushed me off of him and rolled to his side so that his cock moved deeper into my mouth. While gripping the sides of my face, he pumped his hips, moaning softly. I let him use my warm mouth and kept my hands off of his cock as he manipulated my head to his liking.

He liked being aggressive. I liked him being aggressive. Part of my attraction to him was his power and the way he made me feel when he controlled me. There was the gentle power he wielded in everyday life. How he walked and carried himself so confidently was a turn on for me. I was turned on by the way he looked out for me, protecting me when he probably didn't notice he was doing it.

But Mikey wielded his power sexually as well, and that's what turned me on the most. I went crazy when he used my mouth or held me down and wrestled me while we were naked and grinding our cocks into each other. His moves and strength overpowered me, and I couldn't help myself. I wanted to be the one he manhandled and I sensed he was very aware of my desires.

"I'm gonna come," he moaned, after a minute.

Getting his cock first thing in the morning always had him coming fast. Most guys were like that. Most of us woke up with wood. Sometimes because we had to piss, but even that didn't prevent a quick orgasm. And typically, Mikey was ready to go five minutes later if need be.

I grabbed his balls with one hand and squeezed, tightening my mouth around his dick. We were only one minute in but my reward was seconds away. I'd become the master at reading Mikey's body language and cock signals. Sometimes I enjoyed edging and teasing him, but today I knew he wanted a release so I let him pump until he cried out in sweet agony.

"Fuuuccckkkk," he moaned, holding me against his pubes and unloading.

I never complained about him coming in my mouth. Of course, he'd never asked either. We both swallowed. I guess that's what we thought a person did according to the porn we watched.

"Good morning, sleepy head," I said, sliding up to join him on his pillow.

"You're so good at that, stud. I should probably tell you I like that a lot," he said, rolling on top of me and then pushing up, grinning at me. "Want one?"

"I mean, if you insist," I replied. I glanced at the alarm clock on his nightstand. "You just sucked me off less than seven hours ago," I teased.

"And I'm very sorry it's taken this long to get back to you."

We could have sex all day long. We were both eighteen and constantly horny so why not?

"It ain't gonna suck itself," I stated, pushing the top of his head toward my needy cock.

"You're a nasty little fucker," he whispered on his way down. "And I like that too."

I didn't manage to last much longer than Mikey, and within minutes his mother was yelling up the stairs that breakfast was ready.

"See?" Mikey teased. "Every Sunday. Just like clockwork."

We jumped out of bed and headed for the bathroom, both of us needing to clean up from our morning session.

"I hope we have bacon," I quipped, following closely behind him. "I don't think I can handle more sausage after the meal I just had."

Mikey stopped and turned around, briefly eyeing me and shaking his head in amusement. "Boy oh boy, was I wrong about you, Coop."

"How's that?" I asked, bumping into him on purpose.

"I had you pegged as a bit of prude about sex and talking smack," he explained.

"I wasn't having sex, so I guess you were wrong."

He laughed out loud. "Good point. I guess you weren't," he agreed. "I sorta wished I'd known though. Think of the blue balls I coulda saved myself from."

"How about I prevent you from suffering such a horrible plight in the future?" I teased.

Mikey pulled me into his arms and held me tight. "I love you so much, Coop. I hope you know that."

"I'm beginning to," I whispered, his hug straining my ability to breathe. "Unless of course you smother me to death."

He released me and held me back, his hands on my biceps, studying me as his eyes welled up. "I need you to believe me," he said. "I'm sorry I took so long."

"I believe you," I whispered, struggling not to burst into tears. His words of affirmation were exactly what I craved every single day since he told me he wanted to be with me. "Doesn't mean that I'm not afraid sometimes though," I confessed.

He lifted my chin so he could look into my eyes. "I'm afraid too, Coop."

"You are?" I asked, wondering how that could be possible. "But you know I've been crazy about you our whole lives, Mikey. I've always wanted to be with you."

He grabbed my hand and led me to the bathroom, positioning me in front of him and in front of the mirror above the sink. "See that?" he asked.

I nodded, holding his hands that were locked around my waist.

"I want this forever, Coop. I can't lose you."

We locked eyes in the mirror and I felt something significant in his words. Mikey was intense and purposeful in his words. "I can do that," I stated.

"And you're sure?"

"As sure as I possibly can be," I answered. "I've loved you all of my life. How could I stop now?"

Mikey smiled and rested his chin on my shoulder, gazing at my reflection. "There are so many things I want for us, Coop, and I don't want to waste a single day."

I spun around and met his gaze. "I don't want to beat a dead horse here, Mikey, but you are so different lately."

The corner of his mouth turned down.

"Hold on. Hear me out," I advised. "I was going to tell you that I like the change. I like the confidence that you have in us too. You make me feel that even though we're still young that we can do anything as a couple."

"Because we can, Coop, and I want to experience everything with you by my side," he said. "I'll never be able to explain to you what you mean to me, but I plan on spending my entire life trying to prove it to you."

"You just did," I said, kissing him on the cheek and stepping around him then heading toward his dresser.

"Boys?" Kathleen yelled from downstairs. "Breakfast is getting cold."

"I'm digging Sundays," Mikey said, following right behind me. "I'm beginning to see why you like 'em so much."

"Just you wait," I stated, flinging a pair of clean boxers at him and helping myself to one of his pairs. "You'll see. Every day is like Sunday."

"I'm counting on it," he said while adjusting the waistband of my boxers. "You are so fucking sexy."

I held my hand up to his face. "Don't start," I warned, already feeling my boxers expanding. "I mean it," I added as I squirmed away, fighting off his advance and running for the door.

He grabbed me and spun me around, smothering my mouth with his. He kissed me with such longing that I swear I felt it in my toes. "Hang onto that until after breakfast," he said.

"Boys. Breakf . . ." Kathleen began.

"Coming!" we yelled in unison, cutting her off.

We hurried down the stairs to breakfast, like so many times before over our lifetime of friendship. A friendship that had evolved into a dream come true for me. I couldn't remember ever being happier.

CHAPTER FIFTY-EIGHT: Mike

Druzella's car door shut, alerting me that she had arrived for her weekly session with Mom. A minute later the doorbell rang. I waited until they'd exchanged greetings and moved to the kitchen table where they always held their meetings.

The plan was for me to casually show up and feign interest in what they were talking about. Sometime during our conversation I was supposed to tell Mom my big news. Druzella and I hadn't quite figured out how that was to happen. How was a person to announce they'd recently arrived from the future and another universe?

"Hey, Mom," I said, turning toward Druzella. "Hello again," I added, feeling nauseated at the prospect of defending the type of story I planned to tell. "What are you two up to?" I asked. "Casting spells? Poking voodoo dolls of the neighbors?" I teased.

"Mapping the charts, honey," Mom said. "Nothing your skeptical mind would care about."

I pulled out the chair near Mom. "That's not true," I said, sitting down. "You never know."

"Speaking of that," Mom began, sliding out of her chair.. "Hang on, Druzella. I got Michael something from the library yesterday that I want to give him."

Mom headed to the living room and I looked at Druzella. "Do you want me to bring up parallel universes or are you going to?" I whispered. "Maybe it'd seem more natural if you did," I added.

Mom was back in an instant.

I nervously tried to act normal even though I'm sure I failed.

She handed me a book. "Parallel Universes," she proudly stated, tapping on the cover of a book that had a photo of deep space on it. "Just like you've been talking about."

I flipped the book over to the picture of the author on the back. He appeared to be a science type nerd. "Thanks," I mumbled before handing it to Druzella.

"I thumbed through it," Mom said. "Too much science for me but it does offer some unique perspectives."

Druzella opened the book and leafed through a couple of pages before speaking up. "Anything astrological or spiritual with regards to these universes?" she asked, sliding the book across the table to me. Apparently we were playing a game of Hot Potato.

"Not really," Mom stated. "Mostly scientific theory and what-ifs."

"Kinda weird huh, Mom?" I inserted, thinking now was as good as any to dive in. "Could you imagine?"

"Ever since you brought it up to me, son, I've been thinking about parallel universes," she began. "I've read that déjà vu might be related to them."

"That sounds plausible," Druzella inserted. "I certainly believe in infinite possibilities in our world, so why not?"

"Could you imagine multiples of us?" Mom asked, directing her gaze to Druzella. "That would really be something, wouldn't it?"

"Absolutely," she agreed. "There are still so many unsolved realities to our known world. Ripples in time or even time travel," she added. "We might have many parallels to our lives. I think the concept is fascinating."

Mom looked at me. "I wonder if a person would know?" she questioned, and then answered her own question. "Probably not. I mean, I don't sense anything about another me out there somewhere."

"But what if you could?" I blurted out.

Mom puckered her lips, placing an index finger to her bunched up lips as she gave serious thought to my question. I sensed Druzella inhale as we both anticipated her reply.

"Nope, not for me," Mom answered. "I don't think I'd want to know."

"Well that's interesting, Kathleen," Druzella observed. "You've always seemed to be a woman interested in discovery."

"Good point," Mom agreed. "But *discovering* on my own terms."

"Valid point," Druzella concurred. "I imagine that our stars and their alignment might be involved in these parallels," she added. "Opening doors to them perhaps?"

I saw an opening that Druzella had just skillfully delivered. "You like that, right, Mom? The stars and stuff?" I asked, perhaps too eagerly.

"I do, yes, but we're talking about multiples of ourselves. This is where I'm unsure," she pondered. "I wonder if you'd know?" she repeated, seemingly stuck on that part of the crazy theory. "Because I've experienced déjà vu but just not to the point that I've seen myself in another dimension."

Mom was so involved with the topic that I struggled to know how I should proceed with telling her my truth. I kept looking at Druzella but all she did was make a barely perceptible nod with her head to encourage me to keep talking.

"Here's a wild idea, Mom," I interrupted.

She smiled and directed her attention to me, seeming to be happy that I'd shown interest in the book she'd brought home for me.

"Let's say that in this parallel universe that you could have a second chance because you knew you were there before?"

"Oh yes, that's interesting. Now that does require more thought," she said. "So, in your scenario I'd be aware. Is that what you're asking?"

"Yes," I murmured, feeling like my stomach could empty their contents. "Something like that."

Mom's face softened, reaching for my hand. "Oh, honey. You're wondering if I'd try to save your father, aren't you?"

"Well maybe," I acknowledged. "I mean if he was in that universe."

"I'm sorry, Michael, but I'm not sure," she stated without hesitation. I sensed Druzella watching me from the corner of my eye. Mom's answer was unexpected. "I love the idea of parallel universes though. It gives me comfort to think that I'd get the chance to live many lives. I'd love to trust in that theory because it aligns with my belief that there is something more and that we get many lives. Reincarnation is a cornerstone of Buddhism, so I like the idea of continuing on. Possibly over and over."

"So, you're open to it?" I pushed, waiting to make a decision about whether to tell her. "Even if reincarnation wasn't actually part of the plan?"

"Sure. I'm open to ideas that I don't understand. But maybe the knowing part wouldn't work for me?" she said. "I prefer the surprises of life because I like to think I'll get to experience many more lives so I won't stress on tragedy so much while living this one."

I simply couldn't take the back and forth any longer. After all of our debating I wasn't sure Mom was for or against the possibilities. This mother was different from the one I'd experienced in my latter teens and early twenties of the new millennium. This inquisitive version was at the beginning of her spiritual search which caused me to hesitate.

"Would it freak you out if I told you I knew stuff about parallel universes?" I asked, pushing the book she'd borrowed out of my. "I think I have more, shall we say, concrete information?"

Druzella turned to me and smiled, encouraging me to move forward. "I'm certainly open to your perspective, Mike," Druzella stated.

"Michael?" Mom asked. "Do you have something you want to share?"

"Do you trust me, Mom?" I asked. Her eyes narrowed and she leaned back, crossing her arms. I pulled her hand closer so I could hold it. "And I mean *truly* trust me? In a way that would upend everything that you know to be true? You'd be required to open your mind like never before."

"Well, honey, you're scaring me now."

"Please just listen, Kathleen," Druzella said. "With an open mind if you can."

Mom was surprised to hear Druzella's input, turning to her she asked, "You know what Michael has to say?"

"I do," she confessed. "He has consulted me."

"Then it must be serious," Mom said, tugging on the edges of her long sleeves and looking around nervously. "I have to admit I'm a bit surprised, maybe even hurt that you didn't involve me, Michael."

"Mom, please hear me out. I didn't purposefully go behind your back. In fact, Druzella sorta knew something was up when we first met," I admitted.

"And what exactly did she know?"

Druzella and I exchanged glances and she nodded encouragingly, silently telling me it was go-time.

"That I'm from another universe."

How to describe Mom's reaction? Was it a snort and a laugh? Was it an uncomfortable laugh that sounded like a snort of disbelief? Whatever the reaction, she definitely appeared flummoxed.

"You are from another universe?" she asked, raising an eyebrow and then smiling like she was in on a joke; or better yet, the victim of one.

"Yes," I said.

Her smile faded. "You're serious?"

I nodded. Druzella nodded.

We both waited.

At that exact moment, the front door burst open. "Hello?" Coop hollered. "I'm here and I'm hungry. Anybody home?"

CHAPTER FIFTY-NINE: Cooper

"There you are," he said, rounding the corner into the kitchen. He abruptly sucked air in when he saw Druzella. "Oopsie," he said. "I didn't mean to interrupt."

For some reason Mom slid the library book under an oversized notepad she used when Druzella visited. The three of us stared at one another while Cooper's eyes bounced between us.

"Hi," I said, standing and pulling him in for a hug. "I was just yakking with Mom and her friend."

"Should I come back later?" he asked. "We actually do have food at our house, but it's just not as good as your guys' though."

"Leftover meatloaf is in the fridge, Cooper," Mom said. "Make yourself a sandwich."

I had a better idea to get Coop out of the house. "You know what?" I asked, tweaking his arm. "I'm craving McDonalds fries. How about we go get some and a burger?"

"Excellent choice," Coop pointed out. "No slamming your meatloaf, Mrs. H.," he wisely added.

I grabbed Mom's keys from the decorative bowl on the kitchen counter where she dumped them in and dangled them in the air to get her permission to use her car. Mom nodded and reached for her purse that was hanging on her chair.

"I'm set with money, Mom, but thanks. Let's go, Coop."

"Did I interrupt something?" Coop inquired again. "Because I feel like I did."

I yanked on his arm so we could leave. "Just a bunch of Mom's mumbo-jumbo stuff, Coop. If anything, you saved me."

Both her and Druzella gave me the stink eye.

"I only have an hour," Coop stated, as we headed out. "I promised Dad I'd go to the lumber yard with him later."

I gave the ladies a quick glance and handed Coop the car keys. "Can you go start the car and start the AC? I'll grab a clean T-shirt and be right out."

I waited until I heard the door shut behind him. "Do *not* go anywhere, you two," I said. "We need to finish this when I get back."

"Is this a joke, Michael?" Mom asked. "I have time for you but if this is a silly prank or something like that, I'd rather not."

"I know you're totally thinking that, Mom, but I'm serious about what I said. I can't just ask Coop to leave and not have him freak out that something is wrong. Especially since a lot of what I want to discuss is about him."

Druzella waved me off. "Go," she shooed. "I'll catch your mom up the best I can."

Coop was sitting in the car jamming to "Same Love" by Macklemore and Ryan Lewis when I hopped into the driver's seat. "I love this song so frikkin much," he announced. "The lyrics are about same-sex love, and I for one think it's amazing for a rapper to sing about that."

"Yeah, I agree," I said. "The chick who wrote the chorus is from Seattle. I believe her name is Mary Lambert. Did I ever tell you I saw her at a poetry slam once?"

"You did? When was that?" he asked. "I think I'd remember something like that."

I'd just royally fucked up. Cooper had died before that happened which caused me to attend the University of Washington instead of WSU with him. I'd seen Mary Lambert on Capitol Hill in Seattle with Jennifer after we began freshman year.

I had what I thought was a perfect cover for my mistake and I doubted he'd verify the timing. "Jennifer made me go listen with her. Remember when I toured UW with her to get her off my back about not at least giving her choice of college a chance?"

"Oh, yeah," he replied. "But wasn't that before this huge hit?"

I didn't know that answer. "Yeah. I'm sure it was. Doesn't matter, Coop," I said. "But I do love the song. Crank it up." He did as I asked and I let out my breath, hoping I hadn't sounded confused about dates and shit. "What does your dad need at the lumber yard?" I asked, hollering over the music and swiftly changing the topic.

Coop lowered the volume. "He wants to price lumber for a new deck."

"Why do you need to go if he's just pricing the shit?" I asked.

"You know my dad. If he likes the prices he'll buy today and he needs the cheap labor to load up the truck," he explained. "Oh my God!" he exclaimed. "I love this part." Up went the volume as Coop sang along.

I breathed a sigh of relief and drove us to McDonalds.

When we pulled into the parking lot I spotted Jen's car. Her and Hastings, along with Megan and Greg were outside sitting on one of the bright yellow picnic tables scarfing down combos, Jennifer's ever-present chocolate shake sitting in front of her.

"She's got her milkshake, Mikey," Coop quipped.

"Should I tell her I get my dick sucked whenever I want now?"

"Yeah, right," he scolded. "Only if you want the last time to be *the* last time."

"Aye, aye, Cap'n."

I parked next to Jennifer's car and we hopped out, heading toward their table. Hastings and Jen were wrapped up in each other like two pretzels. I was actually happy for them. Hastings had been good for Jen and didn't take any of her shit. Jen would never admit it, but I think she secretly liked not being the boss and controlling everything.

"You go ahead and grab a seat, Coop. I'll grab our fries and a coupla McChickens," I said, "Hey, I see they're buy one get one. Want two each?"

"Does a bear shit in the woods?" he asked.

"Not if the bear's in a zoo," I replied, dusting off an oldie but a goodie.

I stood in line, got our food, and headed back outside. While I'd been inside, Cammie Swenson and her girlfriend Josie had shown up and were sitting at the table with the group. I'm positive I turned as white as a sheet at a Klan rally when I noticed her. Cammie was the classmate that had egged Cooper on the day he died. Other kids had said she'd teased him so much he'd finally given in and attempted to cross the lake, thus drowning because he was a weak swimmer.

There was no way in this parallel universe that Cammie could possibly know that I hated her fucking guts. In fact before Coop had drowned, I'd liked her and her bold choice to live out and proud as a lesbian in Idaho. Particularly because she was as feminine as they came and could've hidden the fact had she wanted to. With that said though, she also spoke like a goddamn trucker.

After the funeral I got in her face and said some horrible things to her. Most of our classmates had witnessed us and things went south for her after that. In fact, Cammie never returned from college. I hadn't seen her in more than a decade, and here she was sitting right in front of me with no clue about what had happened. Hell, for that matter none of them did. I paused and took a deep breath. *She doesn't know, Mike. She doesn't know. Nothing has happened. Calm the fuck down.*

"Hey, Mike," she said, patting the space beside her. "You *have* to join us tomorrow, dude."

"For?" I asked, ice running through my veins.

She didn't need to tell me. I'd already been expecting this.

My pulse quickened as dread filled my body to the point where I could have puked. Today's date was August 29th. Tomorrow was the 30th. The *day* and the *reason* I was here in their universe.

"We're all heading out to Campbell Lake and Coop said he's in so I figured you'd be coming along," Cammie said, updating me. "Unless you're a chicken shit," she added. She was pretty but she was a piece of work.

"Yeah, hardly," I stated. "I'm working. Coop and I can't go."

"When did you become his boss?" she asked, turning to Jennifer. "Jeez, girl. You dodged a bullet with this chauvinist pig."

Jennifer laughed out loud, pumping her fist in the air.

Yeah, I still hated Cammie. "He won't go without me," I casually said. "We like hanging out together as much as we can. Sorry though."

"You hear that, Cooper? Daddy says you can't go," she said so everyone could hear. Cammie loved to stir the shit. Funny how I'd forgotten that fact. "Sounds to me like someone's been neutered."

I'd heard enough. "Do me a favor, Cammie, and fuck off. How about that?"

"Ouch," she half-seriously spoke. "That hurts, Mike," she added, making a pouty face and touching her chest.

"Doesn't matter because I'm actually going," Coop stated. "With or without you."

"I don't think so," I corrected. "Maybe another time."

By then Hastings and Greg decided to share their two cents worth. "Jesus, Hill. Lighten the fuck up," Greg said, high fiving Cammie.

"Fuck Hill, Cooper," Hastings interjected. "I mean, I assume you are fuckin' him and shit, but you can ride with me and Jen. I gotcha, bruh."

I'm sure I had to be red with rage by then but had no reasonable way to explain my behavior. I was tempted to pop some heads then grab Coop and go the fuck home.

"We aren't going," I stated emphatically. "Zero chance. Nada. None."

"But I want to go," Coop said.

"You can do what you want, Coopie," Cammie egged him on, glaring at me. "Big bad Mike Hill will just have to deal with it. Right, guys?" she asked, glancing around and rallying the troops.

Everyone agreed with her and kept razzing me. I was as angry as a murder hornet getting its nest busted apart but had to try and mask my reaction. I was supposedly a teenager as well, and they were right, I did sound like Coop's father. I was fucked three ways to Sunday no matter what I said or did.

I tucked my tail between my legs and glanced at Coop. "I'd better get you back home now," I spoke softly, turning to leave.

"I'll see you guys tomorrow," Coop said. "Text me when you're heading over."

They all cheered while I unlocked the car door, sliding in and pounding my hands against the steering wheel. Coop got in and stared at me like I'd lost my mind.

We were halfway home before either of us spoke. He was stubborn as fuck so I broke the ice. "You're not going."

"Yes, I am," he declared. "What's up with you? Of course I want you to go, but there's no reason I can't go just because you're working, is there?"

"I just don't want you to." I had no ground to stand on but I'd beg if I had to. "Please just don't go. I . . . I . . . can't explain why but I need you to stay home, Coop."

"You're serious, aren't you?" he asked, sliding his hand into mine after hearing my quivering voice.

My eyes had welled up when I turned to him. "I'm afraid, Coop. I know I'm acting crazy here, but I'm totally anxious about something right now."

"Okay, Mikey. I won't go then."

His announcement surprised me. "You promise?"

"I promise. You know my word is my word."

"And you swear? On us?" I asked.

"What is going on? You're freaking me out, Mikey."

"I just feel like something bad is going to happen," I answered. "I know. I know. My *whatever* feeling probably sounds crazy. I get that, but I'm really scared, Coop."

"Then I won't go. Simple as that," he said, squeezing my hand. His brow furrowed and he looked at me. "Your hand is sweaty, baby."

Cooper had never called me baby or any nickname except for Mikey. If I'd been in near panic and about to have a full-on anxiety attack before, his endearment crushed my heart. I was so in love with him and what I feared was about to happen. This was *the* event and I was freaking the fuck out.

"I can't lose you, Coop. I just can't, and now I'm embarrassed about what just happened in front of our friends."

"Pull over," he said, motioning to the road.

I pulled onto the shoulder and shifted the car into park. Cooper leaned over the console and laid his face in the crook of my neck. His free hand ran up and down my arm.

"You are all that matters to me," he whispered against my skin, his kind voice pulling on my heartstrings. "You asked me not to go so I'm not going. Do you honestly think I'd ever put our friends before you?" he asked.

I mumbled what I hoped sounded like no.

"I wouldn't, Mikey. Not today. Not tomorrow. Not ever," he vowed.

"I'm not going to work tomorrow," I said quietly.

His brow twisted again but he quickly relaxed after noting I hadn't calmed down. "Because of this feeling you have?"

"Yep," I stated. "Don't trust it."

"Would you like to spend the entire day together tomorrow then?" he asked.

"If you can, I'd like that a lot," I admitted. "Can you stay overnight at my house tonight?"

"I sure can."

I felt the fear subside a bit. I wasn't sure how this August 30th was going to play out. Not to mention I'd realized this universe wasn't exactly like the one I remembered. "Thank you, Coop. And thank you for calling me baby. I kinda liked that a whole bunch."

"You caught that, huh?"

I grinned at his sweet face, overcome with how handsome he was. "I love you."

"I know you do, Mikey. Trust me, I know."

CHAPTER SIXTY: Mike

Coop's dad was waiting in the driveway at their house when we got home so Coop hurried across the street after a quick kiss. Old man Holder, who lived next door to the Mathews' household, was talking with Coop's dad, Roger, and did a double take when he witnessed the kiss. Both of us let out a laugh at how shocked he looked.

I was nervous and unsure of what waited for me on the other side of the front door at my house. Due to Coop's arrival, I'd rushed out an hour ago when Mom had seemed confused after my announcement that I was from a parallel universe. But then again, why wouldn't she be?

I walked into a hushed kitchen. Druzella was consulting her tarot cards while Mom was looking through the library book. Neither were in a rush to speak.

"Find anything yet?" Druzella asked Mom. "Even a minor detail could be important."

"From what I can tell this book is mostly about physics. A bit on black holes and how they may warp time," Mom spoke, her finger scanning paragraphs of highly technical gobble-de-goop.

"Might warp time, huh?" Druzella mused, finally acknowledging me. "Sit," she ordered.

"Seems impossible a black hole would be involved if what Michael says is true about parallels. Don't black holes swallow everything? But then again what do I know?" Mom added, smiling at me.

The room felt like an episode of the *Twilight Zone*. Neither of them were sitting there bawling their eyes out or banging their skulls against the wall after my newsflash.

"What are you two doing?" I asked.

Druzella pointed at Mom and explained, "She's the one who figured out how to do the time travel trick, so I guess we're trying to figure out how she brought you here?"

I was in total disbelief. Mom hadn't said anything about where I'd come from, who I might be, how the switch was possible, or even that I must be entirely out of my mind.

I turned to Mom. "So, you just believe my story?"

She nodded and smiled, getting back to her book.

"I tell you I'm from the future and you're just like . . . like . . . shit, I don't even know what you're like right now."

"I'm *like* your mother first off, and secondly, you don't cuss in my house, young man. I don't care how old or young you are. You are still my son. And of course I believe you," she said.

"Just like that?"

"Just like that, Michael. Why would you lie to me?"

"Did you two want some sorta proof?" I asked.

"I know you're not eighteen, Mike," Druzella stated. "I sensed it the second I met you, but sure, why not show your mother what you have. I can't lie, I'm as curious as a cat too." Druzella glanced around the room, mostly the floor area. "And you're sure you don't have a cat?"

Mom hadn't looked up from her book but still managed to follow the conversation. "Michael's father was allergic to cats," she said. "But I think he just despised the clever animals to tell you the truth."

"I sense a cat," Druzella said. "Here. In this very room."

Mom looked up. "Nope."

Druzella gathered her cards and then folded her hands on the table top. "Okay. What ya got?" she asked.

Mom closed the book and both of them leveled their gazes on me. After ten seconds someone finally spoke. "Well?" Mom asked. "Let's get this show on the road, son."

I pointed upstairs. "In my bedroom. Follow me," I said, pushing away from the table and heading upstairs. The three of us marched single file up the stairs, me leading the way. I paused at my bedroom door until we were all in the hall. "Like so much other shi . . . stuff," I quickly corrected. "What I'm about to show you is strange."

I opened the door and gestured for them to step inside. I made my way to my desk and pulled a drawer out, retrieving a file folder I'd buried under a bunch of crap I'd collected as a teenager when I first lived here. I opened the accordion style folder and reached inside, pulling out a necklace with a ring dangling from it.

"Recognize this?" I asked.

Mom gasped. "Where did you find that, Michael, and why is there a chain on my Mother's ring?"

I smiled at Mom, preparing for something of which I wasn't quite sure of. I figured we'd start here before I dropped the big bomb and blew their minds. Since securing the contents of the folder, I'd run through this situation a million times in my head. How would Mom react? Would she be afraid, sad, or even think I was a demon or some shit?

"You *always* misplaced this ring," I began. "Whether at the kitchen sink, your bathroom, or the garden. You'd take it off and think you'd lost it. Three years ago I was visiting from Seattle and you dropped the ring down the drain," I continued, watching Mom's eyes filling. "I removed it from the drain and then bought you this necklace at Kelso's jewelry for your birthday."

"And you did this in the future?" she asked. "I haven't even told you I lost it again," she added.

"I know, Mom, but you will tell me. We'll find it when we dig Christmas stuff out of the closet this year. You just don't know that yet," I said. "You lose the ring several more times. But then you started wearing it around your neck, kissing it whenever one of us reminisced about Coop in some crazy story."

Her eyes widened.

Druzella understood immediately and reached for her hand.

"No," Mom whispered. "No, please, Michael," she pleaded, realizing what

I meant.

I reached for her hand to calm her down. "You told me about this shortly before August 30th of 2023. You explained to me that I had to have the ring in my hand or around my neck before I followed your other instructions to get here."

A tear trailed down Mom's face when the reason I was there became clear. "Cooper died?"

"Tomorrow, Mom," I whispered.

"You have to do something, Michael," she urged, panicking and turning to Druzella. "We . . . we . . . have to help him."

"That is precisely what Mike is trying to accomplish," Druzella said.

"Can you sit down in my chair?" I asked. "I need to show you the final proof, Mom."

"Is it bad? Do you know our future, Michael?" she gasped.

Druzella interrupted. "Him being here alters the future now, Kathleen. We cannot be sure how it will change from here on out."

Mom appeared frantic. Staring at me and then at Druzella while scratching at her arms in despair. "I don't want to know things," she insisted, her voice rising. "I *cannot* know anything about myself, Michael. Promise me you won't . . . please, son?" she cried, grabbing my arm.

"I won't," I promised. "The thing is, Mom, you sent me here because you wanted me to find happiness with Cooper again. My life was going, well . . . . I was unhappy. You somehow had this connection to Coop. Apparently, you spoke to him. Druzella and you discovered or invented something, hell, I don't know how you pulled it off, but I woke up here on June 13th of 2013. More than ten years earlier than where we were. Even Druzella was there but I didn't meet her until I came here."

"You can't live without Cooper, honey," she declared, still stuck on the horrifying news. "How'd you survive his death?"

"I'm not sure I did, Mom. You obviously don't know but I was married and was about to . . ."

She held up her hand, shaking her head forcefully. "Nope. Zip it."

She didn't even want minor details of our lives in the future. "You must've known I was dying inside without Coop," I stated. "You knew I needed another chance."

Mom turned to Druzella. "That explains the insanity of whatever we did, Druzella. Michael could never exist without Cooper. They were matched from birth," she explained.

Druzella's eyes expanded. "Of course," she whispered, placing a hand to her cheek. "I get it now. I knew that but how did I miss the chart match? Michael and Cooper share the same chart," she added, seeming to still be analyzing the situation. "But the August 30th connection? Mike mentioned that date to me. So very specific for you, Kathleen. I don't get that angle."

I caught Druzella's attention from behind Mom and slowly shook my head. *Don't do it lady. Do not go there.*

Thankfully she caught herself. "Probably not as important as the dual birthdates," she added, adjusting her inquiry.

Mom became excited when she'd understood Druzella's idea. "And the ring with the three identical stones," she began. "Of course. Me, Michael and Cooper. Three birth months and three ruby stones in a golden circle. We completed the circle of life," she said.

Druzella gestured to the folder. "What else?" she asked.

"I've seen enough," Mom replied.

"Whatever he has could be important, Kathleen. Let's have a look, Mike," Druzella insisted.

"Please sit, Mom," I urged, reaching into the folder. Mom sat down while Druzella moved to her other side. "I won't bore you with the technicalities, but I managed to do something that at the time seemed impossible," I began. "I emailed myself from the future, backdating the email so I could send evidence in case I forgot what happened to me, and apparently it worked. I pulled the printed copy of a photo from the folder, staring at myself as a man, and then slowly turned the paper around to face them both.

Mom reached for the picture and gazed at it for at least a minute and a half. She began to softly weep and dab at her eyes as she studied the details of my face. When done, she lifted her eyes to mine. "It's you, Michael," she whispered.

"You recognize me, Mom?" I asked.

"You're my son. Of course I recognize my own son," she stated. "Honey, you are so handsome," she said, running a finger across my image. "So grown up too, but there's such sadness in your eyes. What happened?"

"Cooper died, Mom. And to a certain extent, so did I."

Mom held the page closer, examining the image before handing it to Druzella. "Look at the date on the newspaper," Mom urged. "August 30th, 2023." Druzella handed the page back and Mom spent more time looking at the photo. "We put French doors in the kitchen?" she asked. "I love them."

"We did that in 2021 or 22, I think. You wanted to open the kitchen to the back yard," I explained.

"Where is the Michael that lived here on June 12th?" Mom suddenly asked. "The Michael from before you got here?"

"What do you mean, Kathleen?" Druzella asked.

Mom looked confused or distressed. Maybe both. "The boy who went to bed on the twelfth right here," she explained, touching the edge of my bed from her position on the chair. "What about you, Michael? Did you switch places?"

"I'm not sure, Mom," I responded. "I know less than you do."

"Who will be here if you leave? Are you leaving?" she asked, the reality of my disclosure finally hitting her. "Is he leaving, Druzella? Who's left when he does?"

"We have no way of knowing that answer," Druzella answered. "I'm not sure if Mike *can* leave to be honest."

"Michael?" Mom asked. "But you're really twenty-eight, correct?"

I nodded a confirmation.

"Do you want to live here in this house as a twenty-eight year old?"

"I'm not sure I have that choice, Mom."

Mom looked past me, staring at something only she could see in her mind. The woman I knew as rock solid, the epitome of optimism and positivity, was completely perplexed.

"I've lost ten years with my only child," she said. She returned her gaze to me. "And you've gained ten years."

"You haven't lost ten years, Kathleen," Druzella reassured. "Mike has ten years of experience that you aren't aware of, but you'll still have the years ahead with him."

"I don't want you to be stuck here, honey," she stated, reaching for my hand. "That wouldn't be fair."

"I made my decision, Mom. I wanted to see Cooper again. I wanted to spend more time with him and with you."

Watching her face as understanding of what I said dawned on her, was gut wrenching.

"Oh my God!" she exclaimed, studying my face. "I died too, didn't I?"

"Mom?" I whispered, choking up. "You said no information about you."

"Why else would I have done this?" she asked, making more of a statement than asking a question. "You were about to tell me you divorced. Knowing me I waited until your marriage ended, didn't I?" Mom looked at Druzella before placing her hands over her face and leaning forward to let out a devastating sigh. "You were without him. All those years without your Cooper. Of course, I wanted you to be happy. Why else would I have done this?" she repeated, her voice muffled due to her hands over her mouth.

I bent over, touched her arm and encouraged her to look at me. "You gave me a wonderful gift, Mom. A gift I will forever be grateful for. Thank you for this."

"But you're stuck here, honey," she whispered, lifting her head, her face wracked in pain.

"Yeah, maybe I am, but I'm stuck here with the two most important people in my life," I said. "Trust me, I can easily repeat ten years with the two of you."

The three of us spent another hour talking about what had happened. We went over the repercussions of my choice and what that could mean for all involved, but ultimately Mom and I agreed we were fortunate. I assumed Mom would have a million questions. I figured she'd want to know all about my life, her life, her friends, maybe even the world, but she didn't want to know a single thing. We agreed that no matter what, we'd never speak of what was to come.

Druzella agreed with the decision. Her reasoning made sense as well. She figured that my arrival could change our paths from then on so why not plan on being open to new possibilities rather than try to have me keep track of what comes next from my list of memories.

"I'll never know why this happened or how I did it," Mom told me. "But we certainly live in a wonderful world, don't we?"

Druzella and I nodded.

Her words were never truer than then. "How about we make the best of it, Michael?"

"How about we do exactly that?" I concurred. "I love you, Mom."

"I love you too, honey," she said, smiling through happy tears, her stunning green eyes sparkling. "How about we start today? Is Cooper coming over for dinner?" she asked.

"As always," I said.

Mom stood up and grabbed the necklace from the table and placed it around my neck. "I think I'd like it if you'd wear this for us, son," she said. "And how about we add a stone for your father too?"

"What stone is for April?" I asked, liking her idea immensely.

"Diamond," Mom said proudly. "Like a diamond in the sky. That was your father."

I squeezed the ring tightly in my hand causing the necklace to tighten around my neck, a reminder of all that matters in our lives. The love for family and the families our love creates.

CHAPTER SIXTY-ONE: Cooper

"You're smiling at me again, Mrs. H.."

She blinked and shook her head after my observation. "Oh, am I?" she replied. "I'm sorry, Cooper. I guess I'm happy you joined us for dinner."

"I always eat here, Mrs. H.," I stated. "Figured you might be sick of me by now."

Mikey's mom rested her chin in her hands, gazing at me and smiling again. "Can you do me a favor, Cooper?" she asked.

"Will you stop staring at me if I do?" I asked.

Mikey grabbed my arm. "Be nice, Coop. Mom's been swooning nonstop all day."

"Okay, Mrs. H., lay it on me."

"Could you call me mom?" she asked. "Like Michael does."

That wasn't the favor I'd imagined. "Really?" I asked, looking from her to a grinning Mikey. "Just Mom? Just like Mikey does?"

"I'd like that, son," she said, reaching for my hand. "I think of you like another son already."

Of course, I cried over her request. Why wouldn't I? I had the best boyfriend in the world now and an extra mom to boot.

"Okay, you two balls of mush," Mikey said. "Enough of this gooey stuff."

"Why now? I asked. "Is it because Mikey and I are a couple?"

"Something like that, kiddo," she answered. "That and I just love you so much."

"Gee, Mrs. . . . Mom," I corrected. "I feel so special right now."

"That's because you are and I haven't told you that enough."

"Is someone dying?" I asked jokingly.

Both Mikey and his mom sat up straight in their chairs.

"God no," Mrs. H. said, covering her mouth and turning white.

"Thank God," I stated. "I just got a new boyfriend and another mom. I'm set for life," I added.

"That you are," Mikey agreed. "Let's help *our* Mom clean up. Tomorrow is the first of September and we have to start packing for college."

"Where'd the summer go," I asked. "Maybe we can catch a swim before we leave town?"

"How about we have you take some swim lessons first?" Mikey suggested. "I'd like to brush up too."

"Good idea, boys," Mrs. H. said.

"That's why I have you, Mikey," I stated. "You said you'd protect me, remember?"

He stood up and grabbed my plate. "That I did, Coop. That I did."

* * *

"Your mom was so sweet tonight," I said while undressing. "She really was nice to me."

"Like she said, she loves you, Coop. And so do I."

"I think she's just happy we're a couple. My mom and dad have been acting all goofy as well," I said. "I bet they'd hoped for this to happen for years."

Mikey pulled his T-shirt over his head. "I think so too."

I moved closer to him after noticing a necklace around his neck. "Why are you wearing this?" I asked, lifting the ring from his bare chest. "Shouldn't Mom be wearing her Mother's ring?"

"She asked me to wear it," he said. "She wants to add Dad's stone to the ring too."

I rolled the ring around in my fingers, wondering why she'd ask him to wear it, while also trying to not go all molesty on his chest. "Looks good on you. Maybe I can wear the necklace sometimes?"

Mikey pulled me closer and kissed the top of my head. "I bet Mom would like that?" he whispered into my hair. "She loves you," he added.

"I gathered," I quipped. "She seemed different tonight."

Mikey nudged my stomach with his elbow. "Don't start that, mister."

I jumped back, tugging him toward the bed. "Well she did," I defended. "In fact, both of you did."

Mikey turned the light off on the nightstand and elbowed me to my side of the bed, facing me. "We both love you, Coop. Especially me."

I snuggled closer and kissed him. "Wanna have sex or snuggle?" I asked, feeling warm and sort of tired.

"How about we snuggle? And I won't let go of you all night, promise," he whispered before kissing me lightly.

I lifted the necklace from his skin and held it against my cheek. "A stone for your dad will be nice," I said. "I bet you miss him."

"More than I thought possible, Coop, but I'm happy I have Mom and you."

"You'll have me for as long as you want, Mikey. I hope you know how much I love you."

"Is your love enough for a lifetime?" he asked, kissing my eyelids?

"That, plus one thousand years," I answered.

"I'll take it, my love."

"*My love?*" I teased. "That's a first, Mr. Hill."

"But not the last. I have a lot of time to make up for the years I missed, Coop."

"That's okay, Mikey. Eighteen years wasn't that long."

He pulled away and the light from the street lamp revealed his wet eyes. "You're right. How about we take it a day at a time and make sure we count the days slowly?"

"I like that," I said. "Can I hold this in my hand while we snuggle?" I asked, tugging on the necklace.

"As long as you hold me tight too."

"Deal."

I don't remember falling asleep that night. I guess it didn't really matter because my life felt brand new for some reason.

EPILOGUE: Mike

Ten Years Later. Again.

T he noise from a lawn mower woke me from a fitful sleep. I'd tossed and turned all night, having the oddest dream. There was no need to feel the other side of the bed before I opened my eyes because I knew who was mowing our lawn this early in the morning. I just hoped the new neighbors didn't complain.

The bedroom was dim since Cooper hadn't opened the blinds like he usually did to annoy me on weekends. I scrunched up our pillows, his familiar smell invading my senses, before I propped myself up to admire our recent handiwork. The bedroom remodel looked amazing. Gone was Mom's gaudy wall paper print of huge green banana leaves, with the matching valance over the window. We'd replaced it with sensible beige paint to match the overall contemporary look of the remodeled house. Mom would've hated the monotone design.

I ran my hands over my abs, admiring what the new home gym had allowed me to accomplish over the summer. Summer meant no school for me. I missed the kids I taught, but I loved being at home with my garden and Mom's goddamned marigolds.

I hadn't been able to stop planting the stinky flowers each spring because I knew Mom had been obsessed with their beauty and the mystical powers she swore they possessed. Marigolds were commonly offered as sacrifices to the gods in many religions and embodied the power of resurrection. Mom was big on resurrection, swearing I'd know one day if we ever crossed paths again. I never understood her affinity for the flower, but I liked having them near me nowadays. Like my mother, I began to see them as the connection between life and death. I found comfort in having them around the home I'd lived in my entire life.

The mower cut off and three minutes later the bedroom door burst open. "Darn," Coop huffed. "I wanted to wake you up."

"You did, you goofball," I corrected, gesturing toward the front yard. "Your frikkin mower had the pleasure."

Cooper stood shirtless in the doorway, looking better than a thirty year old should ever look. He was ripped and almost as big and muscular as I was, except his height. I had him there by three inches. We both had changed our hairstyle from floppy blond bangs, and over-the-ear styles, to neatly trimmed haircuts that fit our status as new thirty somethings.

"I love when our birthdays fall on a Sunday," he stated, walking to the window and pulling the blinds up. "And look outside," he suggested. "Absolutely stunning, don't ya think? And why is that?" he added.

I rolled out of bed and walked over to him, kissing him on the cheek and sliding my arm around his waist. *"Because everyday is like Sunday?"* I mocked in a teasing voice.

"You best shut it, mister or I'll tell your mother," he threatened.

I tweaked his rock solid ass. "Go ahead. She's under the garden," I quipped. "Tell her enough with the weeds already while you're out there yakking with her."

"I like talking with your mom," he insisted, his pouty face reflecting back to me in the window. "I miss her."

I pulled him into my arms. "I know you do, baby boy. I do too."

"Mom and Dad are coming over for the barbeque later as well," he said. "I know you wanted a low key thirtieth with the twins, but they want to see our godsons too."

"What time will Hastings and Jennifer be here?" I asked. "And of course Mom and Dad are welcome," I added, loving Roger and Charla like my own parents.

"Jen said after their naps," Coop said. "You know how grumpy they can get without their naps."

"But today is their birthday too," I complained. "I love Jen like a sister but lighten up lady."

"That's why she's the mom and you're not," he scolded. "Now get dressed. I need help edging the driveway and then we have the backyard to mow, so hurry up, hubby of mine."

"You're killing me, smalls," I bitched.

"Hush," Coop ordered, squeezing the arm that was still around him. "I really like this room," he said. "The color is relaxing," he added, picking up the framed photo of my parents from the dresser. "I love this picture of them. They look so happy, don't ya think?" he asked, laying his head on my shoulder.

"They do," I agreed, drawing a circle around Mom's head as if she had a halo there. She didn't but she deserved one, nonetheless.

Coop gave me a quick kiss. "I love you, Michael Hill," he said, looking me directly in the eye. I adored it when he called me Michael. I thought of Mom when he did since she was the only person I liked calling me by my formal name besides him.

"I'll be right out after my coffee."

"Your mug is already on the counter," Coop said, turning and heading back outside.

I walked to the kitchen, most of it completely gutted and redone since Mom ruled the room. The French doors remained though because just like her, I liked having easy access to the garden, where her marigolds brightened the flower beds around the deck.

I poured coffee into my oversized ceramic mug which used to be Mom's. The words on it read: *I'm not from this universe but I'm friendly.*

I let out a laugh like I did most times when I thought of how silly the saying was, but also knowing it fit her to a tee.

Cooper wasn't in the driveway when I stepped out the front door. I checked across the street and saw him and his dad rummaging through the garage looking for something Coop probably wanted to borrow. The sun felt nice on my bare chest as I meandered around the yard, making my way to the driveway edge that needed my attention.

"Hello, young man," a voice said from beside me. I jumped slightly, not expecting anyone next door since the house had recently sold. "I'm your new neighbor," a pleasant woman stated, extending her hand for me to shake. "Katie," she introduced.

"Mike," I acknowledged. "Welcome to the neighborhood."

She was a pleasant looking woman, maybe in her fifties. Her eyes unnerved me with their color. I'd only seen that color of green on one other person.

"I'm sorry if I startled you," she apologized.

"No problem," I said. "It's just been awhile since we've had neighbors next door. My husband is over there," I said pointing across the street, not sure why I needed the new neighbor to know I had a husband.

"Yes, I've met Cooper," she said, smiling. "Him and I were talking about your flowers over there near the walkway. My cat was laying in the middle of them earlier."

"So you have a cat?" I asked. "Cooper is a veterinarian," I added.

"Yes, he told me that when he picked Sunday out of your flower beds. She seemed to take to him right away."

"Your cat's name is Sunday?" I asked. "That's kind of an unusual name for a cat."

As soon as my words left my mouth, a black cat came out of her open garage door and headed straight for me and encircled my legs.

"She likes you, Mike," she said. "Sunday doesn't normally like anyone but me."

I bent over to pet the affectionate cat. I'd never had a cat as a child because my father was allergic to them. I could take or leave them but this cat was friendly. I stood up and watched as the cat headed for the flower beds again.

"Anyone else live with you," I asked, hoping I wasn't being too forward, but I wanted to like our new neighbor since we'd been very close to the old neighbors.

"Nope. Just me," she answered, seeming nonplussed by my question.

I couldn't help myself. "Kind of a large house for one person."

"That's what the realtor said," she replied. "But I guess the house just spoke to me."

She was warm and her personality was refreshing. I felt compelled to know this woman after three short minutes. "Where'd you move from?" I asked.

"Seattle," she offered. "I lost my husband a few years ago and wanted to find a smaller town to live in so I have the opportunity to bond with more folks. Seattle can be a little uptight and I like people," she added.

"I've heard about the Seattle chill. I almost attended college there but landed at Washington State instead," I said.

"Yes, Cooper told me you both graduated from WSU."

I'd apparently missed the initial *get-acquainted* meeting. "Him much later than I did of course. You know, vet school and all."

"I understand," she said, staring at my necklace. "May I?" she asked.

"Sure," I replied, letting her hold the ring attached.

"Birthstones?"

Her eyes were disarming. "Yes. Mine, Cooper's, and my folks'," I answered. "I like to keep them close," I added, not in the least bit uncomfortable that she remained so close to me examining the ring.

"How long since they passed?"

"How'd you know they passed?" I asked.

"A mother knows these things, son."

"So you have children?" I asked.

"Nope. Never had the privilege."

Her response caught me off guard. She wasn't a mother but inferred that she was. And I'd only known one other mature adult that used the word *nope*. My mother. The same green-eyed person who I missed terribly.

"I'm sorry to hear that," I said.

"That's quite alright, son," she said. "I've managed to make friends. Some young like you and Cooper even."

Katie let go of the necklace and took a step back. "Three of you are Cancers I see. Who was Aries?"

"My mother, Cooper, and I are Cancers. Dad was an Aries but he didn't believe in all that sorta stuff," I admitted. "Mom sure did though," I added, laughing at the memory.

"Sounds like a wise woman, your mother."

"Today is all of our birthdays," I said. "Well, Coop and I, that is. And this probably sounds impossible, but our twin godsons also share our birthday. They're coming over later actually."

Katie grinned and nodded like she had a secret. "Want to hear something that you might think is even more impossible?" she asked.

"Go ahead," I encouraged. "I learned to believe in the impossible because of my mother."

"Today is also my birthday."

We stood in silence while I processed her words. I was speechless and wondered if Coop had discovered all the fascinating similarities we had with our new neighbor.

"No way."

"Way," she joked.

"Well then, Katie. Happy birthday to you. Maybe you'd like to join us later? Meet the whole gang?"

"I've met Cooper's parents already. I feel like I've known them for years. They're quite proud of you two boys," she said.

"Look at me," I said. "I guess I was late to the meet and greet."

"It seems I've saved the best for last, Michael," she said, giggling a girly laugh and filling my heart with a beautiful memory. "May I call you Michael?"

"I think I'd like that."

The two of us stood staring at one another. There was something there but I couldn't quite put a finger on what that something was.

"I feel like I know you, Michael."

"You read my mind," I stated.

"Well okay then," she said.

I wondered if we were done talking. I didn't want to be done just yet. I reached for her hand. "Lemme show you my marigolds in the backyard. You're going to love them."

THE END

About the Author

Michael Robert is an author residing in Seattle, Washington. The Crow Flies Free is his debut novel. Michael enjoys traveling and he aspires to visit the locations of his upcoming novels so as to provide vivid and accurate descriptions of them. He enjoys tennis, road trips and fast cars. Please look for his future projects, the next story coming soon.

Also by Michael Robert

The Crow Flies Free

The anniversary edition includes the original full-length novel with an extended epilogue, and four all-new chapters. The story continues with an update on Joey and Caleb, as well as the return of Landon Alexander.

Joey Crow and Caleb Hollings first see each other across the rural Oregon country road that separates the farms they live on. The two seven-year-old boys make an instant connection that spans the following eleven years.

Joey, an orphaned Native American boy, has come to live with his grandparents on their farm after the mysterious disappearance of his parents from the local reservation.

Caleb is the only son of devoutly Christian parents. He is raised in a strict, conservative, and church-going family, where modern technology is forbidden.

The Crow Flies Free follows the two young men in the summer of their eighteenth birthdays. As they begin to recognize their loving friendship has grown into a deeper kind of love. Follow Joey and Caleb as they start a journey that answers the question of Joey's parents' disappearance and their coming-of-age love story.

Letters: Book One

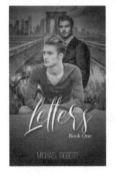

New York City financier, thirty-nine-year-old Perry Jackson, discovers a letter from his deceased husband, Jack. Jack's recent death leaves Perry reeling and alone. After eighteen years together, Perry has no idea how he can move forward.

Lucas Jenson, a nineteen-year-old residing in Beaufort, South Carolina, has lost both his mother and the man he dreamed of sharing his life with. Lucas discovers a letter from his mother that directs him to a safe deposit box at the local bank. The box contains two letters that reveal life-altering revelations.

Join Perry as he takes his dead husband's advice and begins a journey of discovery and love. Perry's journey begins with the meeting of a mysterious boy. Will this boy provide the answers to the future, or will he only be the first stop that leads Perry to a destiny with Lucas?

Book one of Letters is a story about how we pick up the pieces of our lives and make the choice to live again. Are Perry and Lucas destined for love? Does the ethereal boy from Virginia still figure into the journey of the two men with letters?

Letters: Book Two

In Letters Book Two, we find New York City financier, forty-year-old Perry Jackson, broken-hearted and heading home to the Hamptons. After four months of a promised one-year journey, Perry concedes that his destiny with Lucas has failed. In yet another serendipitous moment, Perry once again encounters the ethereal young man, Chad.

Perry and Chad met in the beginning of Perry's journey while he searched for love and a new life without his deceased husband, Jack. Chad, sensing he was not the one, encouraged Perry to continue his search for love and the two parted ways. Does another chance meeting add up to love for Perry and Chad?

Lucas Jenson, a twenty-year-old residing in Beaufort, South Carolina, hung his heart on the chance for love with Perry. The young man from the wrong side of the tracks found it difficult to imagine a life with the multi-millionaire. The differences in their lives seemed too great to overcome. With a heavy heart, Lucas gave up on love. Love had never been something he could count on. Afraid he would be left first, he told Perry he will not join him in New York.

Nothing about Perry and Lucas's journey has been easy, but now they both have choices to make. Does Perry consider that Chad is the man he should have chosen? Does Lucas regret letting Perry go? What about Clint? Is Clint in love with Lucas? What circumstances ultimately put Clint's life at risk over his devotion to Lucas?

And finally, what about Jack? Do dead men really tell no tales? Not exactly. Jack cannot speak, but he still has plenty to say as the story comes to the ultimate conclusion.

The Bird Catcher

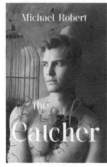

Happily married, Seattle furniture designer, Ben, comes home early from work on his thirtieth birthday. After finding his husband of twelve years already celebrating in the shower with the party planner, Ben decides he needs a fresh start.

Logan, a twenty-five-year-old residing in Idaho, is trying to escape from an emotionally abusive relationship. Can Logan break the bonds that keep him tethered to his abuser or will Coach fulfill his threats to never let Logan go?

Seabrook is a quaint, idyllic beach-front town on the coast of Washington state with less than three hundred full-time residents. The tiny dot on the map seems like the perfect place to escape the pain by offering a fresh start.

Yet as the saying goes, we can run, but we can't escape our past. What awaits the two men as they begin their separate journeys?

Join Ben and Logan when they both choose Seabrook as their hideaway destination only to discover new challenges. With fate playing with their lives, they struggle against the loss of love. Yet, in Seabrook, their chance to find real love might be possible if they can outrun their past.

The Ranch

Josh West left the family ranch at eighteen, swearing to never return to Cody, Wyoming again. After the untimely death of his parents ten years later, he leaves the mess of his soon-to-be-ex behind in Seattle and returns to the ranch as the now fourth-generation owner to handle the sale of the land.

Connor Price, fresh out of foster care at the age of eighteen, arrived on West ranch as a new ranch hand two weeks before Josh left for Seattle and college. Their brief two-week-long encounter has been on Connor's mind and in his heart ever since.

Seth Gering, the only child of neighboring ranchers, grew up the best of friends with Josh until their boyhood friendship evolved into a different kind of love. Much has changed in the ten years since Josh left and their years-long relationship ended, including inheriting his own family's ranch.

What happens on West ranch when the prodigal son returns? Will Connor finally share his decade-long feelings with Josh? Does Seth still love Josh, or is it that Josh has something he desires more than love? Will Josh rekindle things with either man? Can he find true love with boys that are now men?

Join this cast of characters looking to get down and dirty as Josh navigates his past and attempts to decide the direction of his future.

Landon Alexander

Eight years ago, Landon Alexander's father was imprisoned for committing an unspeakable crime, and Landon is still picking up the pieces of his shattered life. With his mother a shell of her previous self and the family business in peril, Landon's in over his head as he attempts to restore the legacy he was born into. He needs a qualified construction manager to handle that side of the business while he concentrates on saving it.

Owen Reed suffers a devastating loss at the sudden death of his husband. To add to his pain, his adoptive father picks blood over skill and chooses his unfit brother to run the family empire. Owen makes a move away from Montana to Portland, Oregon, to interview for a construction manager position and to begin anew. A chance encounter the night before his interview has Owen questioning his vow to never fall in love again. But when he shows up for the job interview he discovers the person from the one-night stand is also the owner of the company he hopes to work for.

The two men find themselves at a crossroads.

Landon the playboy has never been in love. Owen believes he's already had his great love. Can these two men find their way to each other? Or is their love affair doomed from the start?

Suddenly, Last Summer

I professed my love for Jordy when I was seventeen. He was leaving for his last year of medical school after working another summer at my family's Banks Lake resort in the Pacific Northwest.

Desperate for him to know how I felt even though he was my older brother's best friend, and fearing that he wouldn't return after that summer, I decided to take the plunge and admit my feelings while I had the chance.

As the adult in the situation, Jordy wisely chose to discount my confession as simply a teenage crush. But my last spoken words to him were that I'd wait patiently for him.

And I always kept my promises.

JORDY HALL

I'd been away from my small hometown for nearly five years. Life and a stressful medical residency had kept me busy, but I finally returned to fulfill my best-man duties for my best friend's upcoming wedding.

His younger brother, Trey, was a sweet, sensitive kid when I left years ago. The shy, lean teenager who'd tearfully professed his love for me my last summer there had grown into a sexy, confident man. I was intrigued by what I saw, though I probably should have walked away again.

Had he actually waited for me to return? Did I hope he had? He was nine years my junior and my best friend's little brother. But he could be so much more.

After five long years, it was suddenly last summer.

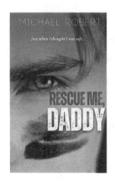

Rescue Me, Daddy
TIM MILLER

My life in Valentine, Nebraska, wasn't easy. At just nineteen, I found myself homeless and jobless with no prospects on the horizon. A life of abuse crushed people, but I still h
ad space in my heart for love. With the support and guidance of an elderly widower, my life finally began to turn around.

Being young and gay in a small town brought challenges but I had goals for my life, one of which was to be loved. The arrival of a world famous author to our small community turned my world upside down. What did I have to offer a man like Davis? I have nothing but my heart. I hope it's enough.

DAVIS HILL

After the end of my five-year relationship in Malibu, I was desperate for change. Even though my career was successful, I could still use an infusion of ideas for my next book. So I did the unthinkable and decided to randomly stick a pin in a map and relocate. My friends may have labeled me insane, but I couldn't resist the temptation. A fresh start in a new town offered the chance to distract myself while I heal from the pain of a failed relationship.

Coming to the rescue of Tim on the very first day we met, was the beginning of one story I hadn't expected. I had relocated to find a great story, but hadn't expected to discover my own love story. Could a small town in the middle of nowhere offer a new beginning for both my heart and my career? Little did I know that small towns could have dark secrets that could threaten to shatter my heart.

Take Me With You

The tropical storms that roll into The Low Country of South Carolina are fierce. High destructive winds pummel the coastlines and rivers along the Atlantic, blowing debris and wreaking havoc. Storm surges crash up the river, depositing all sorts of rubble along the river's shores.

The morning after one such storm, Bo Dawson, a 20 year old born on the wrong side of the tracks, discovers that a body has washed up on the shore in front of his fishing shack. With the area suffering from the devastation of the tropical storm, Bo is forced to care for the unconscious stranger. The stranger who doesn't remember who he is or where he's from.

For five weeks these two navigate the turbulent surprises delivered by life and brewing storms. But what happens when Hayes starts to regain his memory? What happens when he doesn't want to go back to his other life?

The Butler

A twenty-one year old college student has the rug pulled out from under him when his professor boyfriend abruptly ends their relationship, replacing him with an even younger teacher's assistant.

A year after his heartbreak, Deklyn Dalton is still at a loss as to how he can move forward when an unusual job offer, one he's not qualified to perform, comes his way due to the connections of a friend.

Thirty-nine year old billionaire, Lincoln Carrington, fresh off of losing the love of his life to a best friend and employee, is headed to his mega yacht to heal from the devastation brought on by the betrayal he recently suffered.

One man is a desperate college graduate who happens to land a two week job as a butler in a world of wealth and opulence. The man he is to serve is surrounded by the successes of his wealth but lacks the one thing he desires the most: true love.

The butler and the billionaire are on a collision course in this tale from the high seas. Can two broken men from different stations in life find their way to love or are some arrangements doomed to fail before they even begin?

The Butler originally appeared as a novella in the anthology, Cruising, released in 2022. This update is the full length novel with twice the content and an epilogue conclusion not to be missed.

Made in United States
Troutdale, OR
04/28/2025